"Feeding time for the pigs!"

Suddenly, his hand shot out and grabbed her by the throat. Where he summoned the strength from, she didn't know. The bowl of soup crashed to the ground. Wildly she tugged at the arm while gasping for air. His fingers squeezed her throat so hard, she gasped for breath. She wasn't a weak woman, yet even by using all her strength she couldn't remove his hand. Not a sound came from her lips except some gurgling. Somehow he had loosened the strap on one wrist and undone the other and the one around his forehead.

She must have caught him in the act because his feet were still bound to the chair. They crashed to the ground, the chair prohibiting him from moving further. Her heels dug into the ground trying to find foothold to get away from him, but his hands pinned her. He breathed heavy into her face, his eyes resembling a rabid animal, foam bubbling from his lips. Her nails raked his neck, the side of his face. Droplets of blood dripped slowly onto her face. It all seemed to happen in slow motion and she couldn't scream, couldn't call for help as the breath was slowly squeezed out of her, and she felt herself falling, her surroundings fading...

This book is a work of fiction. Names, characters, places, and incidents either are products of the author's imagination or are used fictitiously. Any resemblance to actual events or locales or persons, living or dead, is entirely coincidental.

Blueprint for Revenge
Copyright 2007 by Martine Jardin
ISBN: 978-1-55487-095-0
Cover art and design by Martine Jardin

Published by Devine Destinies
An eXtasy Books imprint
www.devinedestinies.com

Library and Archives Canada Cataloguing in Publication

Jardin, Martine
Blueprint for revenge / Martine Jardin.

ISBN 978-1-55487-095-0

I. Title.

PS8569.A589B58 2008 C813'.54 C2008-904171-2

BLUEPRINT FOR REVENGE

MARTINE JARDIN

To my daughter and her friends.

May their friendship continue throughout their lives.

PROLOGUE

SHE GAZED OUT OF THE WINDOW. TRISTAN HAD LOVED THE WAY her eyes changed color with the tide of her emotions, reflecting the depths of an inky sea or the sunlight on shimmering smooth blue water. Like the eyes of a mannequin, they watched vacantly, devoid of life and recognition. Her irises remained fixed, the eyelids motionless. At least, he thought she did not see anything. At times he could have sworn he glimpsed a flicker of life, but it was merely his imagination—his silent wish that Johanna would return to the real world.

Tristan wheeled the chair closer to the window and knelt beside it. He frowned worriedly as he carefully watched her face, her eyes, for any sign of life.

Nothing.

Not a flutter of her eyelids or a tremor of her full lips. His hand trembled as he stroked her cheek. Then he laid it on her hands resting so still on her lap, folded—as if she were in prayer. But she wasn't. It was just how the nurse had placed her hands and they remained that way unless someone moved them.

"Johanna, I wonder if you can hear me," he murmured softly. "I love you so much. Where are you, my darling? Why are you hiding from me and all the people that love you?"

Her small heart-shaped face remained quiet, beautiful and serene. He wondered if she even had feelings. She'd tripped several times during her daily outings and hurt herself, but there was no change, no outcry of pain, not a twinge that she even knew what had happened.

With a sigh Tristan stood up, brushed her forehead with his lips and reached for the hairbrush. Gently he brushed the long blonde locks, holding and brushing each strand as if it were made of spun gold.

A nurse entered the room with Johanna's lunch tray. "No change in her, Mr. MacDonald?" she said, sending him a smile while she put the tray on a small table next to the wheelchair. "Would you like to feed her?"

Tristan did not return the smile. His heart was bleeding for the girl he loved and his mood was dark. It was almost six months now since the accident. "Yes, of course."

"You spend so much time with her. It must be wonderful to have a man in your life who loves you so much. I'll take her to the bathroom first. Come, Johanna. Time to let Mother Nature do its job." The nurse gently took Johanna's elbow and tugged her arm to suggest that she wanted her to stand up.

It was strange how she responded to a gentle prod, to the touch of a spoon on her lips, would open her mouth for food, could walk to the bathroom—yet was lifeless as a doll.

Like an automaton Johanna stood and slowly allowed herself to be led to the bathroom by the nurse.

Tristan pulled up a chair. He ran his fingers through his black hair turning it into a tangled mess, while he watched his beloved walk to the bathroom like a zombie. He sank down onto the chair to wait for her.

Zombie...

The word echoed through his mind. Suddenly his sharp reporter's mind took over. Somewhere he'd read something about catatonic states induced by some drug. It was in a foreign country. The natives would administer the drug and then the victim would behave like the living dead—*like a zombie.* Why hadn't he thought of this before? That bastard husband of hers was capable of anything, who says he couldn't have gotten hold of such a drug?

Alert now, he sat up and waited for the nurse to lead Johanna back to the wheelchair. After the nurse left the room he fed Johanna the soup. When the spoon touched her lips she automatically opened her mouth and swallowed.

Excited and anxious to go home to his computer, his usual patience now on edge, he tried to feed her as quickly as possible. His mind roiled while he spooned the food into her mouth.

The specialists who had studied Johanna's case had diagnosed her with catatonia, but she did not have the regular symptoms preceding such a case. They were baffled.

As they all were.

Usually catatonia was diagnosed in patients with severe mental illnesses. But Johanna was a normal, bright young woman before her marriage. The specialists had ruled out schizophrenia or manic depression. There was just no explanation.

Until now—maybe...

Could it be? Voodoo? If only he could find Paul Blake—he'd be the one with the answers and if need be he'd beat it out of the man.

The specialists had tried several sedative drugs, and Johanna had not responded to any of them—but she should have. There was one treatment that she had not received—electroconvulsive therapy. John and Leslie Von Hertzenberg, her parents, refused to sign the permission forms for the treatment. They still hoped for a miracle.

They took turns. Johanna's father usually visited early in the morning and fed her breakfast. Her mother visited at dinnertime. In between, her three best friends, Jennifer, Shawna and Paula visited and chatted up a storm about their respective love lives and parties, but nothing stirred Johanna.

Tristan spent as much time as he could with her. Sometimes, if he didn't have a story to work on, he'd stay with her till late at night until the nurse put her to bed and she lay staring up at the ceiling. Her eyes never closed. The pupils didn't waver and remained fixed.

He scraped the bottom of the bowl and fed her the last spoon of pudding. The sound snapped Tristan out of his speculation and he quickly put the bowl on the tray, then wiped her lips and chin. "Honey, I think I'm onto something that could help you. I'm not sure, but maybe it's the answer to your condition that we've been searching for," he said softly then stood and bent down to kiss her on the lips. "I have to go home now, Johanna, to do some research. I'll be back soon."

His hand rested on her forehead for just a moment then softly stroked her hair. It was always hard to tear himself away from her, but this time he left the room with a sprinkle of hope in his heart.

I CAN HEAR YOU, Tristan—sometimes I can see you—feel your arms around me—your lips on mine—Tristan—don't leave me—please...

Johanna sat immobile. The outside world was still very real to her, but she couldn't move voluntarily. She couldn't speak or even utter the slightest sound.

The door clicked softly when Tristan left the room and she screamed silently, *Tristan—don't go—please don't go...*

But he was gone and her call for help went unheard.

If only I could talk, a sound—anything to let him know, or someone else, that I'm aware of them. Paul must have put something in the wine each night that made me so tired all the time. And then that last night I felt so utterly exhausted I could barely get my ski clothes on and I finally knew. I realized what Paul had done to me and I was powerless—I couldn't speak anymore. Tristan, I wanted to stop you from leaving the castle, but I could hardly move, couldn't talk. And then Paul took me skiing. He took me to the slope that's closed down and pushed me. I saw the broken trees and branches and I didn't want to go down, but I was powerless to resist. He tried to kill me. Tristan—where are you—come back...

Each day and night that passed became a continuous nightmare. The only way she could determine the passage of time was by the darkness that enveloped the room after the nurse turned off the lights. It was like her body didn't belong to her anymore, that her mind and limbs were severed from each other. Even when she had to go to therapy, the therapist would guide her onto the treadmill and place her hands on the handles. Her legs would move automatically but her mind was usually somewhere else. She didn't mind the therapy and exercises, the massages. They kept her muscles from degenerating. Mostly, she enjoyed her time outside in the gardens, when her parents, one of her friends, Tristan or a nurse would take her out in the wheelchair. But once outside, they'd guide her out of the chair and holding her arm they'd walk her around the grounds for a while. More than ever she appreciated nature, because that's all her mind and eyes could focus on when outdoors. At times she was reminded of a wind-up doll that was one of her favorite toys when she was little. She'd wind the doll and it would walk stiffly toward her.

When she was alone her mind dwelled on how it had all started and slowly the pieces fit together. She went over it countless times, but she couldn't show anyone the almost completed puzzle. It was locked in her mind. Her hand rested quietly on the locket. She could feel it beneath her fingers, but even though she used all her willpower to close her hand around the brooch, she couldn't. Her heart cried out. The unshed tears that burned behind her eyes seemed to flow into her body directly to her heart and they scalded the bleeding wound left there by her experience.

I was so stupid—I should have listened to Jennifer. She never liked Paul, thought there was something strange about him from the very first time she met him, and Mom and Dad tried to convince me that it was too soon to get married, that I should get to know him first. Why didn't I listen to them? Why didn't I answer the call of my heart? I'm so damn impulsive, pig-headed. I should have known that it was Tristan I loved, not Paul with his devious charming ways. Oh, Gran, I'm so glad you're not here to witness this.

At the thought of her sweet grandmother, stabs of pain shot through her heart. *Gran, if only you hadn't died—or if you'd at least willed the castle and the money to Mom and Dad then none of this would have happened—I never even got to see what was in the little carved box you left me—Gran...*

Day after day she fought to break the bonds that bound her and caused her to be a helpless vegetable. In her mind she had relived her ill-fated honeymoon so many times she could almost recite it off by heart. Angry bitter thoughts consumed her. The only time she felt at peace was when Tristan was with her. Sweet loving Tristan. She had felt attracted to him from the moment their gazes locked, but she'd already met Paul and accepted his proposal. The date for the wedding was set, the announcements in the papers.

Johanna tried to break free of her thoughts and concentrated on her hands. The thought that Tristan could be in terrible danger devastated her and she focused all her willpower on her fingers to try and make them move.

Nothing happened.

Sheer willpower couldn't break the spell and inwardly she cried though not a tear left her eyes. *Oh, to sing, to love, to laugh again, to be happy without limits, to do whatever I'm inspired to do, without restriction. To wander, to walk unhindered through fields of wild flowers, to listen to the first birds' songs as each dawn begins to announce another day of creativity. To walk on a trail, to gaze at the stars or run with my feet never touching the ground and feel the warm perfumed wind flowing past my face whispering stories and tales of unending adventure...*

The pounding of her heart resumed its normal steady beat and slowly she allowed her mind to wander back to the last evening she spent with her grandmother and the six months that followed...

CHAPTER ONE

"GRAN, I GUARANTEE YOU'RE GOING TO LIVE TO A HUNDRED!" Johanna closed the photo album that she'd been looking at with her grandmother and planted a firm kiss on the old woman's cheek.

"Easy now. My poor old bones are becoming frail. You almost squeezed me to death, child."

Johanna carefully put the album back into the drawer and then sat at her grandmother's feet in front of the fire she'd just built.

Juliana gazed for a moment at her only grandchild. She'd so hoped that John and Leslie would have more children, but it never happened. Neither did her son want the inheritance that was hers to give away now. When her parents both passed away years ago they left it all to their only daughter. At the time she was already in her sixties herself and felt too old to have an interest in the castle she'd not known about and never seen.

Canada was her country. It was the land where she was born and raised and met her husband who turned out to be a distant relative and to her father's delight carried the same last name. So she had always stayed a Von Hertzenberg. Her son had told her to sell the castle and the land, but somewhere deep down she felt it should stay in the family. The castle, the place where her mother had been born and raised, was their heritage. And the castle and the mystery it held had remained a secret shared only with her only child, John. The mystery, she thought, maybe Johanna will finally solve it. She's enterprising enough and filled with dreams and thoughts of adventure.

Her granddaughter had always shown an interest in old things, historical books, and often asked about the great-grandparents she'd hardly known. If only she had a husband to lead and guide her…

"Gran, you're very quiet," Johanna looked around at her grandmother. "I'm sorry. Were you dozing?"

Juliana smiled. "No, I was just thinking about the past."

"Good or bad thoughts?"

"Good thoughts, Hannah. I look forward to joining your grandfather one day soon."

"You loved him very much, didn't you, Gran?"

"Yes, I did. William was a good man and I've missed him these past fifteen years."

"I remember him. I was nine when he died."

"Johanna, you're twenty-four now. No plans for the future yet?"

Johanna knew what her grandmother was referring to. "No, Gran. I haven't found the right man. I'm waiting for a love just as great as yours and that of your parents. It's so romantic the way they eloped and got married in Canada. I wish I knew the story behind it all and why her husband took the Von Hertzenberg name."

"I hope you don't wait as long as I did to get married. As for the reason behind their elopement, all they ever told me was that my mother's parents were against their decision to move to Canada. Mother was very reluctant to talk about it all. Yet she was very proud of the Von Hertzenberg name and her ancestry. The name goes back hundreds of years. I never did understand why she was so secretive about it. People in the olden days didn't talk much about their personal feelings. They were very private."

"It's still romantic, almost like a romance book. Gran, I'll wait forever for the right man if I have to."

Juliana took her glasses off and polished them. "You'll have need of a man soon."

This statement brought Johanna to her knees. She stopped poking the fire and turned to face her grandmother. "What is that supposed to mean, Gran?"

"Oh—nothing. Just remember my words. And now I'd like you to fetch my jewelry box from the bedroom. There is something I want to give you now while I can do it personally."

"You're awfully morbid tonight. Can't we do this some other time? I have to run home soon and get to bed. I have day shift tomorrow."

Juliana shook her head. "No, I want to do it now. Please go and get it for me?"

To avoid upsetting her grandmother Johanna fetched the large ornately carved wooden jewelry box from her grandmother's dressing table. "There you are, Gran. Happy now?" she said with a smile.

She watched her grandmother open the box using the small key she always carried on a chain around her neck. As a small girl the box had fascinated her because Gran always managed to produce a little trinket from it. At times she'd managed to glimpse inside the box and seen lots of sparkling goodies. Gran was very secretive about the box and would never let anyone see what it held. Now, the fascination was gone. Johanna presumed that the box just held old memories and the sparkling trinkets were probably magnified in her eyes when she was small.

While her grandmother's small, dainty hands, the blue veins protruding sharply through the parchment skin, rummaged through the box, she waited patiently.

"Here it is," Juliana said and pulled a small brooch from the box. She held it up for a moment and the light of the dancing flames caught the sparkle of blue sapphires and diamonds. A small locket dangled from a dainty bow of gold set with precious stones.

"Grandma, it's so pretty," Johanna said as she gazed at the small brooch.

"Yes, so it is." Juliana opened the locket and stared at it for a moment before she handed it to her granddaughter. "It's yours now. The pictures inside it are of your great-grandparents when they were young and in love. You look like your great-grandmother and you were named after her as you know."

Johanna examined the pictures closer to the light and saw that she indeed resembled her great-grandmother a great deal. It was hard to tell the coloring because the black and white pictures had faded into pale sepia, but she noticed that her great-grandmother had very blond hair like her and the eyes most probably were blue. One day she was determined to have them reproduced and framed. "Are there no other pictures of them, Gran?"

"Not when they were so young. Later, years after they settled in Canada, they took more pictures, but that's when I was already in my teens. Johanna, this is also for you—to wear at your wedding." Juliana handed her granddaughter a blue velvet box.

"Gran, I don't want this now. You can give it to me the day I get married," Johanna said and tried to give the box back to her grandmother.

"I don't think I'll be at your wedding, poppet," Juliana said softly. Tears filled her faded blue eyes as she gazed at her only grandchild.

"Gran, I don't want to hear such talk. You're perfectly healthy, and..."

"Johanna, I have a feeling that I'll join your grandfather very soon. I want you to have it now. You'll have most of it after I'm gone, except this property. This house and land will belong to your parents. Now I want you to listen carefully. The old desk in my bedroom has a secret panel. After I'm gone, pull out the three drawers then run your fingers along the edge and you'll feel a small piece of wood. Turn it and the panel will open. Whatever you find there is yours too. The rest will become clear to you when my will is read. Now open the box and see what's inside. They are for you to wear on that very special day. I wanted to experience the joy of giving them to you in person."

Johanna noticed the lonely tear that hovered on her grandmother's cheek and saw the slight trembling of her hands so she opened the box and gasped. Facing her was a beautiful diamond and sapphire necklace with matching earrings, bracelet and a ring. "Gran, I don't know what to say. I never knew you owned such jewelry. Are they real?"

"Very real, poppet. They match your pretty eyes. My mother told me to pass the jewelry on to the daughters. Of course I had a son, but then he presented me with a lovely granddaughter, and so now they're yours, as will most of my jewelry be when I'm gone."

The use of the old pet name for her had not escaped Johanna. She swallowed hard to hide the emotions that cropped up. Desperately she tried to squash the thought that her grandmother would soon be gone and tried to make light of it. "Gran, it's so beautiful. It's scary to have something so valuable in the house. Maybe you should hang on to it for me until I get married."

"No, I want you to have it now. You never know what the future will bring. I hope to grow old gracefully and die a peaceful death, but at my age you never can tell. I could be in the hospital when you marry, or in an old age home. You can get a safety deposit box at the bank and keep them there."

Johanna carefully closed the velvet box. She pinned the brooch to her sweater then put the box in her pocket and placed her arms around her grandmother. Silently she held her for moments while she fought the tears that threatened to spill. "Thank you so much, Gran. I'll treasure this moment forever," she said softly. She stepped away and grinned to hide her emotions. "As for an old age home, you can forget that. I'm a nurse, remember, and I'll look after you if that need should arise. I really have to go home now, Gran. I'll never get up in the morning and tomorrow afternoon I plan to go Christmas shopping, so I have a busy day ahead of me."

"Off you go, child. I'll have your cup of tea ready in the morning," Juliana said with a loving smile.

Johanna kissed her grandmother on the forehead and quickly left the cottage. Her father had cleared the snow off the path to the main house. Slowly she sauntered back home, her thoughts troubled.

The house was already in darkness. Her father usually got up at the crack of dawn. Even though he didn't need to work so hard since he had staff to do the work for him, he preferred it that way. His trees and plants were his charges and he tended them tenderly from early morning till evening.

Softly she entered the house and tiptoed up the stairs to her bedroom. Before she hid the velvet box in a drawer under some sweaters she looked at the contents one more time. A tender smile formed on her lips only to disappear quickly when she thought about the reason she had received this gift so early.

Before she drew the drapes, she gazed at the cottage for a moment and noticed the lights still on. "Gran, why haven't you gone to bed yet? Are you reminiscing about the past?" She pictured her grandmother with the still open box on her lap and smiled. Sleep did not come easy to the elderly.

But neither did sleep come easy for her that night.

THE NEXT MORNING, JOHANNA almost slept through the alarm. After she showered and got ready for work she hurried to the cottage to have her regular morning cup of tea with her grandmother. Her parents were already in the greenhouses. She could see them through the fogged glass. She hollered loud enough for them to hear, "Bye Mom, bye Dad," and continued on to the cottage.

It made a cozy picture amidst the evergreens that were laden with snow, their branches almost touching the ground. It was the original cottage that her great-grandparents built when they first bought the property so many years ago. Then when their only child got married they built the main house for Juliana as a wedding gift and they lived out their life in their small home. When John and Leslie got married, her grandparents lived in the main house, but after Juliana's parents died they too moved into the cottage to give John and Leslie their privacy.

The cottage had always been Johanna's haven. Whenever she was upset, she sought refuge with her beloved grandparents and to this day she had a daily cup of tea with Juliana, whether it was six in the morning or after an afternoon shift, her grandmother always had the tea ready.

Rubbing her cold hands for a moment she glanced up at the gray-blanketed sky. The forecast was for more snow. She turned the brass knob. The door was never locked.

"Gran, how come you don't have the fireplace lit?" she said as she walked into the living room, but she stopped dead in her tracks.

Her grandmother sat exactly as she'd left her last night. The box still rested on her knees, the lid open and her hands inside it. Her silver head tilted slightly to one side, but the faded blue eyes now stared sightlessly. They held no greeting—or life...

Johanna shook her head. She took a step toward the still figure, then another... "Gran?" she said in a trembling voice. "Grandma?" as if she couldn't believe what her eyes told her.

Then, her throat constricted and tears flowing down her cheeks, she spun around, ran out of the cottage toward the greenhouses. "Mom, Dad, come quickly—it's Grandma!" she shouted.

John and Leslie ran to meet her. "What's wrong, honey?" her father asked, a worried frown on his still handsome, fair face.

"It's Gran—she's gone," Johanna sobbed.

"You mean..."

"She told me last night and—and—she—she's really gone," Johanna stood very still, and through her tears watched her parents run to the open door of the cottage.

"No smoke from the chimney—I should have known," she murmured softly. "Goodbye, Gran..."

CHAPTER TWO

"He leadeth me beside quiet waters, He restoreth my soul. He guideth me in paths of righteousness..." the minister's voice droned on, the words of her grandmother's favorite psalm hardly registering in Johanna's mind.

Slowly the casket disappeared from sight. Johanna swallowed hard. Her eyes pooled with tears. They ran down her cold cheeks and dripped onto the fresh snow that settled at her feet. Through the blur her gaze was fixed on the mound of dirt that looked black, stark and forbidding against the pristine snow. Soon that dirt would descend on the mahogany coffin. The thought of her grandmother in that box, deep in the ground, caused an attack of panic. She broke loose from her trance-like state and ran to the grave.

"You can't do this. Dad, we can't just bury her in the ground like this—do something—Dad..." she yelled while kneeling beside the grave. Her hand reached in as if to pull out the coffin.

John ran to join his daughter. He placed his hands under her armpits and gently forced her away.

Sobbing, she flung her arms around her father. "Dad—I'll miss her so—why didn't she... why didn't she tell me—she must have felt something—chest pains—I could have taken her to the hospital, and..."

John held his daughter tight, his own emotions held in check as he tried to calm her. "Honey, Mother lived a full life. She reached an old age and always remained healthy. I suppose it was just her time to go and join your grandfather."

"Dad, she knew—the way she talked last night—she must have felt ill—why didn't she say something—I should have known—it's my fault..."

"It's not your fault." He brushed Johanna's damp hair away from her eyes. "Even if Mother knew she wasn't well, I think she was tired. She's waited a long time to join Father and now she has her wish. We need to feel happy for her now that she's finally with her beloved husband."

"But I'm a nurse, and..."

"And nothing. Stop blaming yourself, because there is nothing you could have done. Remember how much she loved and cherished you and be grateful for the years you were allowed to know her. Honey, we didn't bury your grandmother. That coffin only holds the shell that housed her soul. Grandma has moved on to higher realms now. Her spirit lives. She'll always be part of us and her love will remain with us forever. She wouldn't want us to grieve, but rather rejoice. She was tired. Come now, dry your tears." Inwardly, his heart shed tears, but for his daughter's sake he remained calm.

Johanna's sobs slowly subsided. After she stepped away from her father and had wiped the tears off her face with an already soaked tissue they slowly walked back to the group of mourners.

Leslie grabbed her daughter's hand and squeezed it hard. "Are you okay, pet?"

"Yes, Mom. I'll be okay," Johanna murmured, though deep down she wasn't so sure if she'd be all right. It would take a long time before she would get used to Gran not being there for her.

After the ceremony, several people expressed their condolences and regrets that they could not attend the wake. Johanna hardly cared. She didn't look forward to the wake and the large crowd her parents expected.

Paula, Jen and Shawna, her three best friends, hugged her. They didn't say anything. The three girls had never lost a dear one and so did not know how to express their sorrow at Johanna's loss. They stood close by her and waited until the last of the mourners left for their cars.

John placed an arm around Leslie's shoulders and bent to whisper something in her ear. Leslie nodded then turned to Johanna. "Pet, it's not necessary for you to attend the wake. Why don't you go with the girls and Dad will give you money to go eat out somewhere."

Johanna hesitated. "Mom, don't you need my help? People will find it weird if I'm not there."

"People will hardly notice and the caterers will take care of everything else. It's better for you not to be constantly reminded or asked questions."

"Yes, Jojo, come with us," Jenny said. "We'll go to my place and order pizza or something."

Paula, vivid, outspoken and exuberant, supported the suggestion. "I agree. I think wakes are stupid anyway. People need to mourn the loss of a loved one and not be surrounded by a greedy bunch of pigs that only come there to stuff their faces and drink free booze."

Leslie smiled. She'd known the girls so long and knew them well. "Grandma was held with high respect by many Langley residents, Paula. Some people are genuinely mourning her."

"I'm sorry, Mom, I didn't mean..." Paula stammered.

Leslie gave Paula a brief hug. The girls often called her Mom. Especially if they had done something wrong. "It's all right, Paula. I knew what you meant." She turned back to Johanna. "Well, pet? What do you think?"

"If you and Dad don't mind?"

"Dad suggested it, Johanna. Off you go with your friends."

Johanna hugged her parents then followed the three girls to Jenny's car.

Leslie grabbed her husband's hand and they started for the black car that awaited them. "She'll be all right, John. Johanna is a strong girl. Once she's over the initial shock, she'll get on with life."

"Yes, she's strong. She'll need to be when she hears my mother's last will and testament."

"I've never asked you, John, but now that Mother is gone—what's in that will?"

"Mother made me promise not to disclose it. Not even to you, even though that went against my grain. I'll have to respect her last wishes. You'll have to wait until tomorrow when Mr. Douglas reads the will."

"Mother already turned over the deeds of the nursery and property to you. She wasn't a rich lady—surely the will can't be that bad. What is so mysterious about it?"

John waited for his wife to get into the limousine. "You'll see, dear." He answered as he joined her.

"NO, I CAN'T STAY, JEN. Dad said I had to be there for the reading of the will. Mr. Douglas will come to the house in an hour."

"Are you in the will, Johanna?" Jen asked while she pulled her dark blond hair into a ponytail.

"I doubt it. Unless Gran left me some of her trinkets."

"Then why is it so important that you're there?"

Johanna sighed. "I don't know. I guess it's a family thing. By the way, I'm going back to work tomorrow."

Paula's head surfaced out of the sleeping bag. She stretched. "What time is it? Why would you go back to work already, Jo? You've got a week's leave of absence."

"I'd just mope around the house. When I'm at work my mind will be on other things. Jen, can I borrow a pair of sweats and a top? I never want to see those funeral clothes again. You can chuck them in the garbage."

Paula was ready with a witty remark, but Jen jumped out of bed and yanked Paula's long black curls. "Get up lazybones. We have to get ready for work. Shawna, wake up!" she yelled and tugged at the other sleeping bag.

"Ouch! What did you do that for?" Paula yelled and promptly lunged for Jen's leg, which caused her to fall on top of Shawna. Within seconds the three girls were wrestling on the floor and Johanna jumped out of the way of the tumbling bodies.

After she had donned sweat pants and shirt she escaped to the kitchen and phoned for a taxi. "Don't these girls ever go shopping?" she muttered while she gazed into the empty fridge. For lack of anything else to drink she quickly gulped down a glass of water and then returned to the bedroom.

"The taxi will be here in ten minutes. I'll go wait downstairs in the lobby," she yelled to make herself heard above the din.

Jen scrambled up from the floor. "Why did you do that? I'll drive you home."

"It's okay. You have to go to work this afternoon. I don't. Thanks for being there for me last night, friends. Call me after work, okay?"

They'd stayed the night at Shawna's apartment. She was the only one of the four musketeers, as they called themselves, who had left her parents' home and moved into her own place.

When Johanna reached the lobby the taxi had just pulled up. Quickly she got into it and gave the driver the address. She huddled in the corner of the back seat—the familiar landscape flying by like white strips of linen hardly registering in her mind. As they neared the tree farm Johanna's mood darkened. Her three friends had managed to lift her spirits last night, but now the realization of her grandmother's death returned in full force.

After she paid the cab driver she walked with leaden feet toward the back door. She tried hard not to look in the direction of the cottage but she couldn't help herself. For moments she stood and gazed at it, but as tears threatened again she quickly slipped into the house.

It was unusual to find her parents in the living room dressed in their Sunday best in the middle of the week. She kissed them and sank down to the floor in front of the fireplace.

Leslie noticed the dark rings under her daughter's eyes. "Did you sleep last night, Johanna? Have you eaten?"

Johanna managed a wan smile. "No, to the first question and no to the second. I'm not hungry. Do you have coffee on, Mom?"

"Yes, I'll get you a cup," Leslie was already on her way to the kitchen.

"Do I really have to be present for the reading of the will?" Johanna asked her father with a frown.

"Since your name is in it, yes you do," John answered.

"I don't know why it would be. I didn't have a chance to tell you because you were already in bed when I came home that night, but the evening before, Gran gave..." her voice broke and she had to swallow to continue. "The evening before, Gran gave me a valuable gift that she wants me to wear at my wedding."

"The diamond and sapphire necklace that she wore at her own wedding. I knew she was keeping it for you," John smiled. "There is more. Mother cherished her jewelry because Father bought it for her and some she inherited from your great-grandmother."

"There's more? I never knew Gran had such valuables," Johanna sighed. "It's a beautiful set, Dad. I'll have to get a safety deposit box."

Leslie returned with the coffee. The doorbell chimed through the house at the same time and she quickly handed the cup of coffee to Johanna. "It's Mr. Douglas. He's right on time." She walked to the entrance hall to open the door.

Johanna sipped the hot liquid and watched her mother return with a short, stout, balding man. She'd heard Mr. Douglas's name mentioned as he was their family lawyer, but she'd never met him.

Mr. Douglas declined the offer of coffee and got right down to business. Johanna listened, but without interest. Her grandmother's testament sounded straightforward and rather boring, so at times her thoughts wandered off to the past, to her grandmother, and sadness drowned out the monotonous reading of the will.

"I leave and bequeath my entire estate in Switzerland and the deeds to Hertzenberg castle to my only granddaughter, Johanna Von Hertzenberg, to be held in trust until the day she weds." Mr. Douglas stopped for a moment to glance at Johanna, but she gazed into space. She'd not heard his words.

John cleared his throat. "Johanna, are you listening?"

Leslie's face was one big question. "A castle? John, you never mentioned a word."

"Remember, Mother made me swear not to tell a soul. I don't know why she wanted it kept secret although she gave me her reasons, but I kept my word. Johanna, are you with us now?"

"Mm? A castle? What are you talking about?"

"It seems your grandmother has left you a castle, honey," Leslie said softly.

The statement caused a giggle to break through her sadness. "Don't be silly. What would Gran be doing with a castle? Surely we'd have known about it?"

"I knew," John sipped his coffee before he continued. "The castle has been in the family for many generations. Mother didn't want anyone to know about it."

Mr. Douglas flipped through the remaining pages impatiently indicating that he wanted to get on with the reading. "May I continue? Would you like me to read that last paragraph again?"

"Yes, if you don't mind? I don't think my daughter heard it," John replied.

Mr. Douglas repeated the last paragraph. He ignored Johanna's gasp of astonishment and continued to read. "I leave and bequeath my desk and its contents to Johanna Von Hertzenberg. I leave my jewelry to Johanna except for the Cameo necklace, earrings, brooch and bracelet. I leave those to my daughter-in-law, Leslie. To my dear friend, Patsy Williams, I leave and..."

Johanna waited impatiently for the man to finish reading the last paragraphs. Her sadness was now replaced with wonder and the questions in her mind smarted impatiently to be spoken out loud.

Mr. Douglas put the will back in its large envelope and took a manila envelope out of his briefcase. "Your grandmother left this letter for you, Ms. Von Hertzenberg."

With shaking fingers Johanna took the thick envelope and gazed at her grandmother's familiar neat handwriting. She pressed the envelope against her chest as if to cherish this last thought her grandmother had left her.

"I suppose this is all for now," Mr. Douglas handed John copies of the will. "This is for you and your wife and a copy for your daughter. Does anyone have any questions?"

John shook his head. "No, thanks, Douglas. Mother and I discussed her will intensively not too long before she died. If Johanna has any questions I'll answer them, but I'm sure my mother's letter will explain much."

"Good. I'll be in touch then."

Leslie saw Mr. Douglas to the door. Johanna was very quiet until she heard the door close. "Dad, now that that horrible little man has gone, what gives? Is this all for real? Gran really owned a castle?"

John smiled. "Yes, honey. Your grandmother was a baroness. Now that she's gone I suppose I've got the title, but I don't want it. One day you'll inherit it."

Johanna shook her head in disbelief. "You're now a Baron? I don't believe any of this. It's a huge joke."

"It's true, Missy. Your great-grandmother, Johanna, was the eldest and only surviving daughter of Baron and Baroness Von Hertzenberg. Your great-grandmother apparently fell in love with a man her parents didn't approve of so she eloped with her lover to Canada, but when her parents passed on she inherited the castle and the title. From what Mother told me, your great-grandmother wanted nothing to do with the castle or its history. Mother and Father were happily married and comfortable with their way of life. The castle seemed like a faraway dream and Mother wanted it left that way. Her reason for keeping it a secret was that she didn't want the media's attention. I wasn't even allowed to tell your mother because your grandmother feared that she'd let it slip and within a short time reporters would have hounded her."

"That's rather silly. Mom is not a gossip."

John nodded. "I thought so, but I respected her wishes."

Leslie had returned to the living room and listened to John's explanation. "To be honest, I don't know if I could have kept it entirely to myself. Grandma was right. It would have been so easy to make a slip in conversation. Is the castle still intact? It must be very old, John."

"Yes, I believe it's still in pretty good shape. Along with the legacy comes a considerable amount of money that my grandmother kept in a Swiss bank. As far as I know my grandparents never touched a penny of that money. They arranged for a caretaker and for a lawyer to take care of the necessary expenses and upkeep of the castle, and Mother left it that way."

Johanna's knuckles showed white as she clutched the envelope to her chest. "It's all too weird and unbelievable. Do you mind if I go read Gran's letter in my room? I'll share it with you later."

"Go ahead, hon, we know you're anxious to read it," Leslie said while she gathered the coffee cups. "It's a private letter from your grandmother to you. You don't have to share it with us if you don't want to."

Johanna skipped up the stairs to her room, closed the door softly behind her and leaned against it for a moment. "Gran, are you for real? A castle? I still can't believe it," she said softly. While she walked to her bed, she carefully tore open the envelope and took out the letter.

Slowly, she sank down onto the bed and started to read...

CHAPTER THREE

My sweet poppet,

Johanna's eyes brimmed over when she read the familiar endearment and quickly wiped her eyes with the back of her hand.

When you read this letter, I'll be gone from the world as we know it and will have moved on to another world. I'll be with my beloved William. But, don't fret, child. I'll be watching over you and I'm sure William will be by my side. I don't want you to grieve over me, because I did not die. Only my earthly body, the container that held my spirit, was put in the ground, but my soul lives on. I know you'll miss me, but just pretend that I've gone on a long journey and one day we'll be together again in this much better world where I am now.

Douglas must have read my will to all of you by now and your mind will be spinning. I know mine was when my parents died and I learned about my title and the castle. They, too, kept the secret until their death.

The idea of a title and owning a castle fascinated me, I must admit. But, poppet, by the time my parents passed on I was too old for adventure. And believe me, the inheritance entails adventure. At least if you want to make it so. It'll be entirely up to you.

I would like you to keep the castle in the family. What you further do with it is up to you. Perhaps you'd like to turn it into a museum. There are all kinds of possibilities and there is plenty of money in the bank. Its interest alone will take care of the upkeep of the castle. The only thing I ask of you is that you do not sell it or turn it over to the government.

So many years have passed now. Perhaps it's time the secret of Hertzenberg castle is uncovered. You're so young. While I'm writing this letter you're only eighteen, but I've not felt well lately and I know my years of separation from William are slowly coming to an end. When you receive this letter you'll still be young and full of energy.

I hope you'll be energetic enough to travel to Switzerland and eager to unravel the mystery the castle holds. I have a gut feeling the answers are there.

I have also left you my desk and all its contents. Behind the three small drawers is a secret panel. Pull the drawers out and then feel along the side for a small piece of wood. Turn it and the panel will slide down. In the secret compartment behind the panel is a carved wooden box. It is the same as my jewelry box, except smaller. The contents should fascinate you as they did me.

I've made up my will in such a manner that you cannot claim your inheritance until_you're married. I feel you need a man beside you before you set out on such a big adventure. I, therefore, sincerely hope you'll soon meet the man of your dreams and that he'll help you in your quest for the truth.

In my desk you'll also find some sketches of the castle.

Poppet, I love you so much. We have always been very close and you were like my very own daughter. As I'm writing this letter it breaks my heart when I think about leaving you. But, all things pass and my life is almost over and yours is just beginning. I've lived a full and happy life and I wish the same for you. Take care, sweet Johanna. Trust in God and all will go well for you. Don't be too impulsive as I know you can be at times. Think carefully before you make decisions and then, follow your dream.

Your loving grandmother,
Juliana Von Hertzenberg

The letter slowly sank down to her knees. Tears now ran down her cheeks in a steady stream, until with an angry swipe of her hand she wiped them away. Carefully she folded the two sheets of paper and put them back into the envelope.

"So it's true then. Gran, you've been holding out on us. A castle? It seems so unreal, but I guess it's true," she whispered softly. Then, as the reality of it finally settled in her mind excitement suddenly coursed through her veins and set her heart beating faster.

"A castle! I really own a castle—I've got to tell Jen!" She quickly picked up the phone to call her friends.

"Jen, guess what my grandmother left me?"

"I don't know. You just caught me in time. What did she leave you?"

Johanna giggled. "Take a wild guess."

"I wouldn't have a clue, Johanna. Your grandmother wasn't rich, as in rich, so what was there to leave? Her Bible or something?"

"You wouldn't guess in a million years. My grandmother was rich and no one knew. She left me a castle."

Silence at the other end.

"Jen, did you hear what I said?"

"Jo, I'm tired and trying to get ready for work. I'm not in the mood for silly jokes."

"Jen, it's not a joke. I'm dead serious. Gran left me a castle and money too. But I won't get any of it until I get married."

"You've got to be kidding. Shawna, Paula, go get on the phone. Quickly!"

Johanna heard Jen tell Shawna and Paula the exciting news, and within seconds the two girls rushed to extension phones. Her three friends bombarded her with questions, but she couldn't answer any of them except that the castle was located in Switzerland.

Her friends had to go to work, so the conversation wasn't long. Disappointed that she couldn't air the rest of her excitement and talk to her friends for a while, Johanna put the phone down and curled up on the bed, the letter held tight against her chest. "Gran, I wish I could talk to you," she whispered softly. "I'm so excited I could burst. You were probably wise to keep the secret though. Imagine all the fortune hunters that would have come after you when Grandpa died."

A sad smile played on her full lips when she imagined her grandmother being hounded by the press and courted by countless money hungry men.

Suddenly she bolted upright. "Oh, nooo," she groaned. "I forgot to tell the girls not to breathe a word about this to anyone." She glanced at her watch and felt her stomach sink when she noticed that it was past 3 p.m. They'd already started their afternoon shift.

It was too late. By now the hospital staff would be buzzing with the news. Johanna could hear her friends' excited voices in her mind. "You know what? Johanna inherited a castle and a fortune from her grandmother. It's true! She phoned and told us..."

Some of the excitement quickly died down as she realized her mistake, but she soon saw the brighter side. "Well, even though I've inherited a castle, it doesn't mean I'm rich. Mr. Douglas said there was money for the upkeep of the castle, but he never mentioned any figures. It's no big deal. It'll be the main topic in the hospital for a few days, until some other juicy gossip overpowers it. Not to worry," she tried to tell herself, but deep down she was troubled.

An hour later, she phoned the administrator and canceled her leave of absence. She wanted to return to work the next day.

By the time she got hold of Jen, her worst fears were confirmed. The news was out and the hospital staff was buzzing with excitement to have a real heiress on their staff.

It started that evening. A Vancouver Sun reporter phoned to ask for an exclusive interview. Johanna declined. But the phone never stopped ringing.

Her father, exasperated, finally pulled the plug and silently walked through the house to unplug each extension. When he returned to the living room, he grumbled, "Johanna, it wasn't very smart of you to tell your friends about your inheritance. Reporters and fortune hunters will hound you."

"I know, Dad. I'm well aware that I was stupid," she snapped. Then, "I'm sorry. I realized my mistake after it was too late. If only I'd told the girls not to tell anyone..."

"You'll have to deal with the consequences, young lady. I can't advise you what to do, but you'll have to come up with something to get the hound dogs away from our house. I won't put up with it."

"I'm sorry, Dad. Maybe if I grant one reporter an interview, then the rest will leave us alone."

"I hope you're right," he replied in a disgruntled tone. "I see now how wise your grandmother was to keep her inheritance a secret. Well, your mother has already gone to bed, and I'm tired too. Morning comes early. Goodnight, Missy."

"I'm going back to work tomorrow, too, Dad. I already called them to cancel my leave of absence. Goodnight," she said and headed up the stairs to her bedroom.

Excitement and wonder of the unknown overrode her sadness and caused her a restless night until she fell into an exhausted sleep plagued by dreams of castles and reporters hounding her.

THE NEXT MORNING SHE woke up to the sound of cars, voices and the doorbell. "What's going on?" she muttered as she got out of bed and put on her sweats.

She glanced at the clock and knew that her parents were already hard at work in the greenhouse getting a shipment of Christmas plants ready.

The doorbell rang consistently. Johanna, still half-asleep and feeling rather groggy due to the restless night, skipped down the stairs to the front door.

When she opened it she faced a crowd of anxious reporters. Instantly she was wide-awake, suddenly feeling as if she were the prey of a howling pack of wolves.

"Johanna, how did you feel when you heard the news?"

"Johanna, did you know about the castle and your grandmother's fortune?"

"Johanna, what are your plans for the future?"

"Johanna, is there a man in your life?"

They hurled the questions at her until her mind swam. "Go away," she said in a shaky voice. "Please, my grandmother just passed on. Leave us alone!"

But her voice was lost in the din. Desperately she tried to close the door, but one reporter boldly put his full weight against it. Cameras clicked. Feeling overwhelmed, she backed away toward the stairs, and was grateful when her father entered the house from the back entrance and ran toward the front door.

John grabbed the bold reporter by the shirt and shoved him out of the door. "Get out! All of you, leave this property now!" he shouted. "Have some respect for the deceased and the people who mourn her. Go away or I'll call the cops!"

He slammed the door and bolted it, then walked to Johanna who sat on the stairs shaking her head. "Are you all right, Missy?"

"I'm sorry, Dad. It's all my fault," she whispered softly. Her romantic inheritance suddenly didn't seem so exciting anymore. Unshed tears burned to spill, but she fought to control them.

John stroked his daughter's tangled hair. "The damage is done, poppet. It's too late now, but we'll keep the hound dogs away from you. Never fear."

At the familiar endearment, it was almost as if her grandmother had spoken to her and the dam burst loose. The pent-up emotions and tears spilled. Sobbing, she fell into her father's arms.

He waited patiently until she calmed. Then he led her to the kitchen and poured her a cup of coffee. "There, that will ease the nerves," he said while he handed it to her.

"I'm so sorry, Dad. In Gran's letter, she warned me not to be too impulsive. I shouldn't have called Jen right away."

"Honey, it's only natural you'd want to share this exciting news. Jen, Paula and Shawna have been your best friends for a long time. Don't worry. We'll get through this."

When the reporters kept bothering them that morning, John closed the large gates and hung up a sign for his customers to call ahead for appointments so someone could open the gates for them. Fortunately, most of his orders came via the business phone or fax.

Johanna plugged her phone back in to call her friends, but as soon as the plug made contact, the phone rang. She stared at it and contemplated pulling the plug again, but she wanted to call her friends.

Carefully she picked up the receiver. "Hello?"

"Miss Von Hertzenberg?"

"Yes. Who is this please?"

"My name is Tristan. I'm a reporter for the Langley Advance and I just want to extend my sympathy at your loss."

"A reporter?" she replied in a sarcastic tone.

"I'm sorry. I wasn't going to lie to you. I'm interested in your story, but I know you're still grieving and don't want to hound you."

"You've certainly got a different approach," she snapped. Then in a lighter tone, "At least you've got manners. Perhaps I *will* give you an exclusive. Call me back in a few days?"

"Thank you. I'll do that. Again, I'm sorry. From what I've heard, you were very close to your grandmother. I've dug up some old archives and Juliana Von Hertzenberg was a respected citizen of Langley for many years."

Johanna listened to the deep, warm, vibrant voice and felt drawn to this unknown man. "She was. Gran was a wonderful lady. Please call me on Saturday? Eh—I'm sorry, I didn't catch your last name."

"Tristan. Tristan MacDonald."

"I'll talk to you on Saturday, Tristan MacDonald." After she hung up she could still feel warm vibrations quiver through her body. Somehow his voice had instilled a calm within her, touched a cord deep within that echoed in her heart. Before the phone had a chance to ring again she quickly picked it up to dial Jen's number.

"Jen? I'm going back to work this afternoon. I've already called in that I'm available for full duty again. I'll pick you up as usual."

"Already? Why don't you take it easy for a few days? Isn't that kind of soon after..."

"Yes. I'll be much happier keeping myself busy."

"Excuse me for trying. I've never met anyone so obstinate. Once you make up your mind, there's no way you'll let anything or anyone change it, no matter what the consequences. Jojo, did you see this morning's paper?"

"No. Which one?"

"The Vancouver Sun."

"We don't get that."

"I'll bring ours. You can read it when we get to work. You've made the front page."

Johanna answered in a bitter tone. "I'm not surprised. If you'd have seen the reporters in front of our door this morning, you'd have flipped."

"Really? Johanna, I didn't breathe a word to anyone. I swear."

"No? One of you did. How else would the news have gotten out so quickly?"

"Maybe Shawna or Paula? I didn't see them after work last night. They were gone before I left."

"It doesn't matter now. It's my own fault. I should have warned you guys not to tell anyone. I'll see you later?"

That afternoon, the four girls met in the cafeteria. They were lucky to all have the same shift these last weeks. Sometimes, each had a different shift and getting together was difficult.

The main topic, half-hour before they had to report for duty, was of course Johanna's castle. Then, as they rode the elevator up to the second floor, Paula turned to Jen and said, "Jen, did you tell Johanna about the hunk we have on our floor?"

Jen shook her head. "In all the excitement about the castle I forgot."

Paula's rolled her black eyes and batted her eyelashes. "Jo, he's just gorgeous. He could have stepped straight off the cover of Playgirl."

Johanna grimaced. "I'm hardly in the mood for romance right now, Paula."

"Just wait and see. He's one of your patients. His name is Paul

Blake."

Shawna sighed in an exaggerated manner and ran her fingers through her tawny hair. "She gets all the breaks. Jo, why didn't you stay home? They had me working your patients while you were gone."

"What's wrong with him?"

"He was admitted with abdominal pains last night. They're running him through a battery of tests."

"Well, I'll check him out. Your idea of a hunk is not necessarily mine. What color hair does he have?"

"Sort of sandy blond."

"There you go. I don't fall for blond guys. I like the dark, broody type."

"I don't like him. He's too pretty for a guy," Jen said.

Paula moaned. "Shut up, Jen. Just wait till you see him, Jojo. He radiates such animal magnetism it sends shivers all down your spine, and..." The elevator stopped. "Oh well, you'll see. Ciao!"

AFTER LISTENING TO THE dayshift's report, Johanna did her rounds. Though she pretended to have no interest in the new patient, the girls had stirred her curiosity. But to her disappointment he was not in his bed. She'd have to wait until evening meds.

When it was time to hand out medication Paul Blake seemed fast asleep. Only part of his hair showed above the blankets. Gently Johanna tapped the hump that looked to be his shoulder. "Mr. Blake, I have your pain pill for you," she said softly. Paul Blake moved a little, a soft groan issued from his throat, but he didn't wake up.

Johanna put the small cup that contained his pain medication back on the cart and moved on to the next patient. If Paul Blake needed something for pain, she was sure he'd buzz.

Much to her disappointment, the patients were all quiet that evening. She'd returned to work to take her mind off her grandmother's death and the strange inheritance. A very busy evening would have been preferable. To keep herself occupied she set about tidying up the linen room.

Every now and then she glanced around the corner to make sure no lights were lit above the rooms, but apparently all patients slept soundly. With a sigh she lifted the pile of sheets she'd just folded and climbed the short stepladder. Even so, she had to reach to put them on the top shelf.

"That's the shapeliest pair of legs I've seen in a long time," a male voice spoke behind her. It startled her so much that she dropped the sheets and almost fell off the ladder.

After she regained her balance she turned to look at the speaker and felt blood flood her cheeks. Facing her was the handsomest man she'd ever seen. He was almost too perfect. His blond hair was combed neatly back from a high forehead. He had finely chiseled features, creamy smooth skin and a small, well-shaped mouth that seemed more suited for a woman than a man. His eyes were very light blue. They appraised her openly. Johanna knew then that she'd met Paul Blake.

"Mr. Blake, what are you doing out of bed? You're supposed to be asleep."

"I can't sleep."

"Would you like something to help you sleep? Perhaps you'd like something for pain? I'll go and..." Johanna started to climb off the ladder, but his next words interrupted her and made her stop in her tracks.

"No thank you. I'd much prefer if you read to me for a while. You have a lovely melodious voice."

"Mr. Blake, it's not part of my duty to read to you. Tomorrow I'll send you one of our candy stripers."

"I don't want some silly young school girl. I want you to read to me," he asked softly.

Johanna hesitated. His request sounded endearing. Almost like a little boy's. For moments he gazed into her eyes, but then turned swiftly. Too swift for a man with severe abdominal pain. Johanna watched the open backed hospital gown flap around his legs. He wore no pajama pants that were usually given to male patients. His naked buttocks were lean. She watched muscles ripple on his thighs and his tanned body was a startling contrast against the white of the gown as if he'd just returned from a tropical holiday or used tanning beds daily. Her gaze was riveted on his firm buttocks until he disappeared from sight. A lock had escaped from her tightly drawn back hair. She wiped it away with a clammy hand. "Phew—Paula wasn't joking," she murmured and tried to concentrate on the task she'd allotted herself.

After she finished tidying the linen room, she returned to the nurses' station. Jennifer and Shawna joined her. Quietly they checked charts and made the necessary notes, until Jenny swung her chair toward Johanna.

"So, did you check him out, Jojo?" Jen asked.

Johanna could not hide her blush when she answered. "I caught a brief glimpse of Mr. Blake when he approached me in the linen room. He wants me to read to him."

"You're kidding. You call that a brief glimpse? So why don't you go and read to him? The floor is quiet, so there's no reason why you can't."

"He's not in dire agony, Jen. Now if he were dying..."

"That's morbid," Shawna said. "Now if he would have asked me..." Her eyes rolled in exaggerated adoration.

"I've got no interest in the man. Yes, he's handsome. That doesn't mean a thing."

She'd no sooner spoken, or a light started flashing on the board. Johanna checked the number of the room and with sinking heart noticed it was Paul Blake's bed.

"I'll be back in a sec, Jen," she said and swiftly walked to the room.

Paul shared the room with three other patients. Johanna shone her flashlight briefly at the other beds and saw the other three men were fast asleep. Quickly she turned his emergency light off and approached his bed. "What can I do for you, Mr. Blake?" she asked softly.

"I've been waiting for you," he whispered. "Why didn't you come?"

Johanna thought fast. "I can't read to you in a whisper, and even then it would disturb the other patients. Try to sleep, Mr. Blake."

"I can't sleep. Especially now that I've met you. Your name is

Johanna. It's a beautiful name and becomes you."

Unconsciously Johanna fingered the nametag pinned to her pink uniform. "It was my great-grandmother's name."

"It's uncommon. You're very pretty. Matter of fact, you're beautiful. I love your striking blonde hair. Are you Scandinavian?"

"My ancestors were from Switzerland."

"I wish you weren't on the night shift. I'd like to get to know you better."

"Hospitals are hardly the place to get to know someone," Johanna's whisper was almost a hiss. "And I don't fraternize with my patients. Goodnight, Mr. Blake. Try to get some sleep."

She started to walk away from his bed, when he said softly, "But I feel so much better. After I'm discharged, may I call you?"

"Goodnight, Mr. Blake," she said again in a firmer tone while she proceeded to the door.

"I won't stop buzzing you, until you agree," he whispered loud enough for her to hear.

The rubber soles of her white nursing shoes squeaked as she swiveled on her heels. "Mr. Blake, really!"

"I mean it." His hand reached for the buzzer.

"All right. Now please try to get some rest?"

CHAPTER FOUR

SLOWLY THE THRONG OF REPORTERS GAVE UP. THEY HAD EVEN bothered her at the hospital, until security put a stop to it. Peace and quiet returned to the Von Hertzenberg residence and nursery, and life was again back to normal.

Except for the silent cottage and the empty space in her heart.

No one could ever fill that space again. It was reserved for her Gran and the love she bore for her.

"Johanna, you put in a twelve hour shift last night. Are you sure you're not overdoing it?" Her mother startled Johanna out of her thoughts.

She nibbled at the stew. It smelled delicious, but her appetite had not returned since her grandmother's death. "Mom, work is the best medicine."

John dished up another helping of stew and glanced at his daughter. "You look mighty pale, Johanna. When are you off again?"

"In two days. I start graveyard next week Thursday. I'll have four days off after this stretch."

"Good. Maybe we can get some of your grandmother's things sorted out and the desk moved into your room. Unless of course you'd like to move into the cottage? You'd have your own little place, and..."

"No, Dad. Maybe in the future, but not yet. And I don't want to see that desk for now. Please leave things the way they are for a while?"

Leslie sent her husband a warning glance. "It won't hurt to leave the cottage as it is for a bit. We'll keep the fireplace going so the pipes don't freeze. I have taken your grandmother's jewelry box and put it in your room, Johanna. I don't like the idea of it sitting there on her dressing table. It's almost an open invitation for a thief."

THAT AFTERNOON, JOHANNA STARTED her daily walk to the cottage, only to stop halfway. Just for a few moments she'd forgotten that her grandmother was no longer in the small house. She watched the smoke spiral from the red brick chimney. "Oh, Gran, I miss you so," she whispered as she spun around and headed back to the main house.

The jewelry box sat on top of her dressing table. Her gaze kept wandering to it while she braided her hair, but she wasn't ready to open it. The box reminded her too much of that last evening with her grandmother. Resolutely, she finally grabbed it and put it away in the closet.

While she drove to Jennifer's house, her thoughts were concentrated on Paul Blake and his pursuit of her. Unsure of her feelings and undecided, she spoke softly, "Gran, if I could only talk to you now. I know you wanted me to find a good man and marry, but is this the guy? I'm not sure, Gran. Where are you now that I need your advice? I feel attracted to him, but I'm not sure if it's love. Should I go out with him when he's discharged?"

Her mind dwelt on her grandparents and how they'd met. She'd heard the story so many times. How they'd looked into each other's eyes and their souls had touched. "Gran, how do you know if you touch a man's soul? How does it feel? You never explained that part to me properly."

She felt so troubled that she almost drove by Jen's house. When she applied the brakes, the car skidded on the icy shoulder. Her heart thudded for a moment as she fought to gain control over the car, but then it slid to a halt just near the driveway.

Jen got into the car and shook her head. "What were you trying to do, Johanna?"

"I hit the brakes too hard."

"I noticed. So have you made up your mind? Are you going to go out with him?"

"I don't know if I should. I hardly know the man."

"Well, the only way to get to know him is to go on a couple of dates with him. If it were me, I wouldn't."

"Why? I never hear you gushing over him like Paula and Shawna. Since you don't know him at all, you must have a reason."

"It's weird. I know I've barely seen the man, but the glimpses I've caught of him caused me to have the chills. Call it a premonition, foreboding, whatever. So, what's it to be? I know I wouldn't if I were in your place."

"Maybe I will go out with him. I don't know yet."

"You're unbelievably stubborn and naive. What's with no tunes?" The sudden blast of the radio stopped any further conversation, but Johanna didn't mind. All three of her friends ached to go out with Paul Blake and couldn't understand her hesitation.

Listening to the day's reports, she found out that Paul Blake was discharged that morning. A twang of disappointment shot through her heart. It's fate, she thought. I'm not supposed to go out with him.

With extra vigor she tackled her duties that evening and was almost happy when several serious cases were admitted to her ward.

Just before she was ready to hand over her shift a phone call came through for her. She recognized his voice immediately. He had a soft-spoken voice for a man. If he hadn't pursued her so ardently, she would have almost thought him gay.

"Johanna? This is Paul."

"Hi, Paul. You were discharged this morning. I'm not supposed to receive personal calls at work," she replied, then chided herself for the stupid answer. It was obvious that he was discharged.

"Yes. Everything checked out okay. Can I have my answer now? Will you go out with me tomorrow night? I checked with the day nurse. It seems you're off for the next four days."

Johanna let the phone sink for a moment. "You've done your homework," she whispered softly and put the horn back to her ear. "Yes, I'd like that."

"Good. I'll take you out to dinner. How does Heidi's sound to you? I'm not all that familiar in Langley as yet."

"Heidi's sounds good, Paul."

"I'll pick you up at 7 p.m. Can I have your address and phone number now?"

She gave him her address and phone number. "We're close to the border, Paul. Just drive all the way down Two-hundredth Street, then turn left just before you get to 0 Ave. You'll see the big sign out front. It's called Von Hertzenberg Nurseries."

"I'll find it. I look forward to seeing you in a pretty dress instead of that starchy uniform."

"Starchy?" Johanna had always thought her pink uniform quite fashionable.

"Well, you know what I mean. I like to see a woman in a pretty long dress."

She quickly visualized her wardrobe in her mind. She'd never been one for wearing dresses. Jeans and T-shirts was her main attire. "I'll see you tomorrow night, Paul," she said and put the horn down "Jen, I'll have to rob your wardrobe," she muttered while she walked to the locker room to fetch her coat and purse.

THE NEXT DAY, SHE RIFLED through Jenny's wardrobe and tried on a dozen or more dresses. Her three friends lounged on Jen's bed and watched her with interest.

"You don't seem the least bit excited, Johanna," Paula sighed. "If Paul had asked me out, I'd be going out to buy a new dress. You're so lucky!"

You've got no idea that my stomach is tied in knots and butterflies are creeping up to my throat, Paula, Johanna thought. Aloud she said, "Why spend money on clothes I may never wear again? It's just a first date, Paula. It could also be a last date."

"Oooh, I don't believe you. I'd have swooned if he'd asked me out," Paula exaggerated and rolled her black eyes.

"Paula, don't be silly. He's just another man," Johanna struggled into a mini skirt then did a pirouette before the tall mirror on the wall. "Too short. It shows my fat legs too much."

Shawna shook her mane of tawny hair. "Honestly, Jojo, you've gone through just about all of Jen's clothes. You don't fit into any of mine, or Paula's. Why don't you spend some money on a new dress?"

Jen jumped off the bed and pulled a box from underneath it. "I just bought this one to wear for Christmas. The price was too tempting to let it go. I haven't even worn it myself, but I guess I'd let you wear it if it looks good on you. Try it on, Johanna." She pulled out a shimmering full-length blue gown and handed it to Johanna.

Johanna held it up by the shoestring shoulder straps. "Jen, it's so pretty, but I don't want to wear your new dress before you've had a chance to wear it. Don't you think it's too fancy for Heidi's?"

"Hey, you're an aristocrat now. You should wear beautiful gowns and expensive jewelry," Shawna said.

"Heidi's is not such a fancy restaurant, but I'll try it on." Quickly Johanna pulled the gown over her head and let the silky material slide down her body.

"It shows half my bra," she grumbled.

"You don't wear a bra with it, silly," Paula said. "You're so lucky, you don't need one. Take it off."

Johanna took off the offending item then stood before the mirror to inspect the dress. It's low neckline scooped down in gentle folds. It molded to her body as if it were made for her. A long slit on the side showed her shapely leg. The sapphire blue material sparkled as she spun around to face the girls. "Don't you think it's a little risqué?"

"No. You're so conservative, Jojo. It doesn't hurt to show a little cleavage. You look stunning," Paula sighed.

"You can have the dress, Johanna," Jen said wistfully. "It's too long for me anyway."

"I can't accept it, Jen. You just bought it."

"Yeah, but it's too long and it looks better on you."

"Are you sure? I'll pay you for it then."

"Yes, I'm sure, and you can pay me whenever. I got it on sale so it's not that expensive."

Shawna jumped off the bed to finger the material. "I'd take it if it fit me. Johanna, Paul will fall head over heels in love with you when he sees you in this. Pin up your hair, wear the necklace and earrings your grandmother gave you, and you'll look every inch a titled lady."

"As if I'm in the mood to fall in love with anyone or have anyone fall in love with me. You three are making too much of this inheritance and of my date. The castle is probably unlivable and my father has inherited the title. He's now Baron Von Hertzenberg."

"And one day you'll be a Baroness. I'm green with envy," Paula sighed.

"The title doesn't mean a thing to me, and I want a guy to fall in love with me, not with my exterior or my title," Johanna retorted. "I'll have to buy shoes to match the dress. How much do I owe you, Jen?"

"You can pay me later. If you want to buy shoes, you'd better get going. And watch yourself with that man."

"Why? I thought the three of you wanted to go out with him so badly."

"Three? I don't recall mentioning that I wanted to go out with him. Paula and Shawna did. He's good looking enough, but there's just something about him, a weird feeling I've got."

"Oh, you and your weird feelings. For goodness sake, lighten up, Jen. Johanna hasn't been out with anyone in ages. You're just jealous," Paula said.

"Why would I be jealous? I've got a boyfriend."

"You don't have to rub it in," Paula pouted.

"If you didn't try so hard, stopped rubbing your boobs in guys' faces, maybe you'd luck out too, Paula!" Shawna said.

"Okay, that's enough. I'll phone you later to tell you all about my evening, okay?"

AFTER HURRYING TO LANGLEY mall as fast as the snow would allow her, she had trouble finding just the right shoes and a purse to match. High heels would make her too tall. Paul wasn't a tall man. She guessed him to be about five feet ten inches. Finally she chose a pair of dressy black flatties and a small black evening purse and hurried home.

Johanna dumped her parcels on the kitchen table, then grabbed the milk out of the fridge and put the bottle to her mouth.

"Hi, pet. What did you buy? Johanna, don't drink from the bottle. It's unhygienic," Leslie gently scolded her daughter while she pounded beef into a loaf pan.

"Mom, don't count on me for dinner tonight. I'm going out."

"Oh? Where are you going?"

"I've met this guy and he asked me out for dinner."

"You haven't talked about any new young men in your life. Isn't this rather sudden?"

"I know," she sighed. "But, Mom, he's gorgeous. Just wait till you see him."

"Be careful, honey. Looks aren't everything. What do you know about him? Is he from Langley?"

"Mom, you're so old fashioned. I don't know where he lives or where he's from. He mentioned he didn't know Langley that well. We haven't talked that much yet."

"I hope you know what you're doing. Where did you meet him?"

Johanna grinned. "His name is Paul Blake and he was a patient in the hospital for a few days."

"Well, it's good to see you in such a happy mood. You need something like this—to take your mind off everything that has happened."

A shadow crossed Johanna's face. "I guess I'll go to my room now to get ready," she said softly. Her mother's words had brought back the memory of their recent loss.

Johanna struggled with her silky hair. Finally, she gave up trying to pin it up and allowed it to fall free over her shoulders and down her back. She'd applied just the barest of make up. Her cheeks were naturally pink, caused by the excitement that surged within her. The dress clung to her body accentuating her small waist and rounded hips. She groaned. "Why can't I be slim and trim like Shawna," she muttered. "I'm really too fat for this dress. Too late now. I don't have anything else to wear."

Last of all, she put on the sapphire and diamond necklace, earrings and bracelet, and then inspected herself in the mirror. "You're just a tad overdressed, milady," she grinned at the image.

After she transferred her driver's license, lipstick and some money into the small purse, she ventured down the stairs into the living room. Her mother sat by the fireplace absorbed in a book, and her father was buried behind the newspaper. She cleared her throat.

John lowered the paper to glance over it at his daughter. Leslie's book slid slowly from her lap and fell to the floor with a thump. They stared at their only child. Just hours ago, she'd still been a tomboy. Now, before them, stood a lady of quality.

"What's wrong, you two? I'll go and take it off if it's that bad and I'll just wear my dress jeans."

John shook his head. "No, pet. I guess you've just surprised us. We're struck with awe. You look absolutely stunning." He turned to Leslie. "Doesn't she?"

Leslie nodded her agreement. "Hardly the tomboy we raised. Honey, you look like a movie star. I'm anxious to meet the young man who caused this transformation."

Johanna glanced at the clock just as the hands clicked to seven p.m. "He should be here any moment, but I doubt if he'll come in."

John grunted. "A gentleman should always come and fetch his date at the door. This modern business of honking the horn is very uncouth."

"We're living in the twenty-first century, Dad." She'd no sooner spoken the words when the doorbell sounded through the house. Her heart sped up a beat as she walked to the entrance hall and opened the door. She tried to suppress a gasp and secretly was glad she'd worn the dress. Paul wore slim black dress pants and a white dinner jacket. Rather than a shirt, he had on a black turtleneck. He looked strikingly handsome. “Paul, you’re right on time. Would you like to meet my parents?” She tried to sound confident and hoped he wouldn’t pick up on her insecurity as she stepped aside to let him into the house.

“Mom, Dad, I’d like you to meet Paul Blake,” she said softly.

Paul walked toward her father with his hand held out. “Mr. Von Hertzenberg, I’m so pleased to meet you.”

After he’d shaken John’s hand, he gallantly bent over Leslie’s hand and kissed it. “Now I see where Johanna got her beauty. Mrs. Von Hertzenberg, you two are like sisters rather than mother and daughter.”

He parents glanced at each other then made polite conversation with Paul. Johanna picked up on their aloofness and didn’t understand.

“Paul, did you make reservations?” she asked hesitantly trying to break the tenseness that had suddenly come over her parents.

“Yes, I did. Mr. and Mrs. Von Hertzenberg, it was so nice to meet you. I’ll take good care of your daughter.” He shook John’s hand again, and brushed Leslie’s hand with a gallant kiss, then joined Johanna in the entrance hall. He helped her into her raincoat. “Johanna, I haven’t told you yet, but you took my breath away when I first saw you. This coat hardly becomes your attire. We’ll have to change that soon.”

Johanna felt heat rush to her cheeks and hated her tell tale red cheeks. “Thank you, Paul. You look very handsome this evening yourself,” she said lamely.

JOHN AND LESLIE WAITED for the door to close before they spoke. “What do you think, Leslie?” John asked while he folded the paper. He stood up and paced the floor and without realizing it, started rubbing his chin, a sign that he was concerned.

“He’s too slimy to my liking. It’s almost as if he’s putting on a big act. I don’t like his eyes, John. They have no expression in them.”

“My sentiments exactly. Although he scored a few points when he came to the door rather than wait for Missy to come out. At least he has manners. I’ll say that much for him. I just hope Johanna sees him with wide open eyes, and not through rose colored glasses.”

"So do I, though she has a level head on her shoulders and we have to trust she'll use commonsense."

John stopped short in his tracks. "Commonsense? What if she falls in love with the man? Where does commonsense come into such a situation? She has a level head, yes, but she could easily lose her head over that guy and throw all commonsense into the wind."

"Maybe we're overreacting because she's our only child."

"Perhaps. It could just stay with one date. We'll just wait and see."

"At least she's getting out of the house instead of sitting around moping."

"True, but I'd much rather have seen her go out with her friends than this loser."

"Just watch. It'll just be this one date and that will be the end of it."

CHAPTER FIVE

THE HOSTESS LED THEM TO THEIR TABLE. VERY MUCH AWARE OF the stares and whispers that followed them, Johanna felt embarrassed. "I feel overdressed," she whispered to Paul.

"Don't be silly. They're just jealous. Johanna, you look like a movie star tonight"

Gallantly he pulled the chair out for her and waited till she was seated.

"Would you care for wine before dinner, Sir?" the hostess asked while she handed him a menu.

Paul glanced through the list of wines and decided on the house wine.

It didn't take Johanna long to make up her mind. She'd had dinner at Heidi's many times and loved their Wiener Schnitzel with red cabbage, apple sauce and baby baked potatoes.

Paul folded his menu, then picked up his glass and held it out to her. "A toast to the loveliest lady I've ever met. May she fall in love with me, just like I've fallen in love with her," he said softly.

Hesitantly, Johanna touched his glass with hers. "Paul, I hardly know you." She sipped the white wine.

"I feel as if I've known you forever, Johanna. I've already decided that you're the woman with whom I want to spend the rest of my life."

Her face felt so hot, she was sure her cheeks were scarlet. To hide her awkwardness, she sipped the wine a little too fast. Soon, because she hardly ever drank alcohol, her head felt light. The whispers didn't bother her anymore. She glanced around the restaurant she knew so well. Suddenly, the paintings on the walls held more meaning than they ever had in the past. They were murals that depicted the Swiss Alps and typical scenes of small towns. One mural showed a castle situated in the mountains. She stared at it for quite a while and tried to imagine her own castle.

"Johanna? You're miles away. I've been talking up a storm and you haven't heard a word I said," Paul spoke in a louder tone.

"I'm sorry. I was lost in a dream."

"May I share that dream?" he asked with a slight smile.

She hesitated, but then decided that since everyone knew about it anyway she might as well tell him. "My grandmother passed away very recently. She left me a castle in Switzerland."

"Surely you're joking. A real castle?"

"Yes. The murals reminded me of it. It still seems so unreal."

"Are you going to Switzerland, Johanna?"

"Eh, no. Not just yet. Perhaps one day. Tell me about yourself, Paul? What kind of work do you do and where do you come from? I detect some American twang in the way you talk."

"I'm from the States. I was born in Tennessee and raised in an orphanage. The last ten years, I've traveled a lot. I'm an investor. That's how I make my money. Right now I'm trying to close a deal right here in Langley."

"I'm afraid that's a subject I'm not very knowledgeable about. Soon I may need your expertise advice though. Paul, how old are you?"

"You mean how young am I?"

He sent her a disarming smile that sent shivers down her spine.

"I'm thirty-four."

"Ten years older than me," Johanna commented. "It's sad to have no family. Have you ever tried to trace your roots, your birth parents?"

"No. They wanted to get rid of me when I was born so I have no interest to find those people," he answered in a bitter tone.

"I'm sorry."

The engaging smile formed on his lips again. "That's all right. I've learned to live with it."

"How long do you plan to stay in Langley?"

"Now that I've met you, I hope forever. Johanna, since you agreed to go out with me, I suppose there is no man in your life?"

"No, not anymore," she answered in a crisp tone. "I was badly hurt by a man about three years ago, and since then I haven't dated much."

"I'm sorry to hear that. That man needs to get his head examined."

"There were ethnic problems, Paul. His family opposed our relationship. We could never have married."

"Would you like to get married, Johanna?"

"Yes, to the right man."

"And do you think you've met that man?"

Goosebumps puckered her arms and she felt strange sensations flow slowly through her body as his gaze openly raked her. It made her feel almost naked. Unconsciously she placed a hand over her chest to hide the exposed cleavage. "Paul, I don't know. It's too soon. I've just met you, and..."

"Allow your feelings to run wild, Johanna. Let yourself go."

The waitress interrupted them. Johanna was glad their dinners were ready because she felt unsure and his persistence made her uncomfortable.

They ate their dinner in silence. His gaze was on her constantly. It made her feel clumsy and self-conscious and the schnitzel didn't taste half as good as it normally did. While she toyed with her red cabbage, he suddenly interrupted her thoughts. It was almost as if he could read them.

"I'm sorry, Johanna, if I make you feel uncomfortable. Will you forgive a fool in love?"

That made her smile. "Is falling in love being a fool, Paul? I'm sorry I can't return the sentiment. I'm too down to earth to believe in love at first sight. I must admit though that I do feel attracted to you."

Her hand rested on the table. He reached across the table and took it in his and squeezed her fingers gently. "It's a start. May I see you again tomorrow? I thought we'd take a drive up to Whistler. Do you ski, Johanna?"

"Yes, I do, but..."

"Good. I'll pick you up early. Does eight in the morning sound all right?"

"My grandmother has just passed away, Paul. I don't think it's appropriate for me to go out and have a good time. A quiet dinner is all right, but to go out and have fun doesn't sit well with me just yet."

"I'm sure your grandmother wouldn't want you to sit home and mope. It will be better for you to be out and about to get your mind off your grief."

"I suppose you're right. Gran wouldn't want me to brood about her death."

Paul saw her to the front door. "Thank you for a lovely evening, Johanna. I'll see you in the morning then?"

She made up her mind to go skiing. Paul was right. It would help take her mind off everything. "Yes, I'll be ready. I'm sorry if I wasn't the greatest company this evening. I hope you understand."

"Of course I understand. You've just lost someone very dear to you. I enjoyed your company, Johanna." He took her in his arms and kissed her on the lips.

Johanna allowed the kiss. She waited for those special feelings she always read about in books, but she felt virtually nothing. The kiss was gentle, sweet, almost as if he'd kissed a sister. It's me, she thought. I'm just not ready for a relationship. Maybe it's because my mind is still so much on Gran.

Her parents had already gone to bed and she closed the door softly behind her and leaned against it for a moment. "He's a really nice guy, Johanna. What's wrong with you? Isn't this what Gran wants for you? I should respect her last wishes and settle down."

Deep in thought she walked slowly up the stairs and to her room. After she'd undressed and crawled into bed, she continued to talk softly to her grandmother. "Gran, if you can hear me up there, what should I do? Is Paul the man I'm meant to be with? Is it coincidence that he entered my life just now? Did you send him my way? Gran, I wish you could answer me..." Her voice broke and she cried into her pillow until sleep finally overtook her.

"WHERE ARE YOU OFF to so early, Johanna?" Lesley poured coffee for her daughter and placed a plate of muffins on the table.

"Paul asked me to go skiing with him. We're going to Whistler."

"Oh? Aren't you moving a little fast?"

"He's really nice, Mom, and Gran did so want me to settle down."

"You need to settle down because you want it and because you love a man, not because your grandmother wanted it for you. Be careful, Johanna."

"I will be, Mom. Paul is very pleasant company. I'm sure you and Dad will get to like him once you know him better."

Lesley frowned. "And how well do you know him?"

Johanna grinned at that. "You're right. I've just met him and only been out with him once. He seems like a good guy."

"Don't rush into anything. Marriage is a lifetime proposition and not to be taken lightly. Your father wondered if you'd like to live in the cottage now that your grandmother is gone. What do you think? You could redecorate it, and..." Leslie said, trying to interest her daughter in something else and get her thoughts off Paul.

"Mom, please stop it? Can't you just leave the cottage the way it is for now? No, I don't want to live in it or even see it for a while. It holds too many memories."

"I'm sorry. I guess that was insensitive of me. How about the desk? Would you like Dad to put it in your room?"

"No, not even the desk. Just leave it where it is."

"Aren't you the least bit curious what is behind the secret panel?"

"In a way. But right now I don't want to deal with it."

"Okay, I'll tell your father to leave it there for the time being. What about the mystery of the castle your grandmother wrote about in her letter?"

"I'm sure it's nothing. Gran had a vivid imagination." The doorbell chimed. "Oh, there's Paul. I'd better get my gear ready," she said and jumped quickly off the chair to run to the front door.

"Paul, you're early. I'm not ready yet. Would you like some coffee while you wait for me?"

"No thanks, Johanna. I've had my share of coffee for the day. Will you be long?"

"No, I'll be down in a few minutes. Make yourself comfortable," she said as she started up the stairs.

CHAPTER SIX

JOHANNA STOOD FOR A MOMENT AT THE TOP OF THE SLOPE AND watched Paul as he soared down gracefully. She breathed in deeply from the fresh, tangy air and could almost smell the snow. Down below, Whistler Village looked like a picturesque Christmas card. Langley's air wasn't bad, but here it felt like she was breathing the air God originally created, enjoying nature and the mountains and their majestic beauty. For a moment she allowed the awe to overwhelm her, to dream of Switzerland and its beauty, her castle. Gazing down at the village below, for a second it was replaced by the vision of a fairytale castle and she sighed deeply. Her breath left her lips in small puffs of white mist as if she were smoking a pipe and drifted before the vision.

Snapping out of her dreams, she readied herself and started down the slope. In a few moments she gathered speed and as always, felt the exhilarating thrill of the fast descent, the feeling of freedom, of having gained wings and flying like a bird toward the man she knew had more than a friendly interest in her. All thoughts and worries left her mind as she absorbed the moments of freedom, of a bird in flight swooping down toward its prey, of power.

After skiing till closing time she was exhausted. Paul had been right. The day had taken her mind off her bereavement. Skis slung over their shoulders, they walked back through Whistler Village to where Paul had parked the car. Johanna stopped for a moment to look around the Village. It had been so long since she'd been there last and the little shopping center had changed. Her gaze dwelt on the Swiss or Austrian style architecture then on the mountains that flanked the village. In her mind she pictured her castle against the snowy mountain, surrounded by tall firs. I wish I could stay longer, she thought. I wonder if Switzerland looks like this. Maybe it's even prettier. Paul interrupted her thoughts. It was uncanny how he guessed her thoughts.

"Johanna, why don't we stay the night? We can ski again tomorrow. You're a very good skier."

"Paul, I really don't think..."

He stopped her before she could continue. "Separate rooms of course. How about it? We could have dinner at the Chalet, then crash for the night in a motel."

"I didn't really come prepared to spend the night. I'd have to call my parents or they'll worry." She thought about it for a moment and made up her mind. "Okay, I'm all for it. I'd like to get some more skiing in while the powder is good."

Paul sent her a disarming smile. "Great. Why don't we go book the rooms then and you can dump your stuff there, shower and get ready to go for dinner, and call your parents."

THEY SPENT HER FOUR days off in Whistler. At times Johanna wondered if he could afford so much free time away from his work, but she didn't pose the question.

On the last day, she told Paul they had to leave around noon.

"Why so early, Johanna?"

"I start graveyard shift tonight. I need to get a few hours of sleep before I go to work."

"I have a better idea. Why don't you crash at the motel for a few hours? We'll have dinner here in Whistler and I'll have you home in time for work. I promise."

She still felt hesitant. The thought of her only one clean uniform played through her mind. "I don't know. I have to wash..."

He wouldn't take no for an answer. "Whatever it is you're going to tell me, I won't accept as an excuse. Please, Johanna? I want to ask you something very important."

"Okay. But we have to leave right after dinner. It's a two-hour drive and I have to get ready for work. Can we eat early?"

"How early?"

"Around five? If we leave at six, it will still give me enough time to do some washing when I get home."

Though she tried, Johanna could not sleep. Her body ached from the four days of continuous exercise. But that's not what stopped her from sleeping. Questions tumbled through her mind. Thoughts about Paul and the castle she could not claim until she was a married woman. Do I love Paul? Are my feelings for him just lust or is this finally real love? I've never really known love. What I felt for Darren was sheer infatuation. My friends all had boyfriends and so I convinced myself that I was in love with him. Admittedly it hurt when he dumped me, but that was my pride hurting. Paul is a good man. He's a real gentleman and though I don't experience stars and fireworks when he kisses me, that can come later when I get to know him better. Isn't it better to be good friends and allow that friendship to develop into a real love?

WHEN PAUL KNOCKED ON the door, she had barely woken up. The unusual exercise and emotional exhaustion had taken its toll. Quickly, she jumped off the bed and rushed to open the door for him. "I'm sorry. I slept longer than I planned," she said,

"It's okay, honey. You needed the rest. I'll wait for you while you freshen up and change."

"I won't be long." She quickly ran to the bathroom.

She gazed at her reflection in the mirror for a few moments. "So, are you going to do it?" she asked the reflection. More than ever, she wished she could talk to her grandmother, ask her advice. Uncertainties plagued her but she couldn't quite put her finger on the reason for them.

After changing into a pair of dress jeans and a sweater, she brushed her hair and applied some lipstick. Taking a deep breath, she opened the door to join Paul.

"We really need to start for home, Paul," she said, feeling rather awkward now. "I can't be late for work."

"Didn't I promise I'd have you home on time? Don't worry about it."

Quickly, she packed her things and set everything ready on the bed so they could grab it right away after dinner.

THE MEAL WAS DELICIOUS and by the time the waitress served desert, Paul still hadn't asked her the important question. She glanced at her watch and frowned. "Paul, it's getting late."

"I know. We're almost done and then we'll get our stuff and head straight for Langley."

"What did you want to ask me? Or was it just an excuse to stay a while longer?"

"You're spoiling the romantic moment, but here it is. Will you marry me?" he asked, and took a small velvet box out of his pocket. "They found this ring on a chain around my neck when I was abandoned at the orphanage. I've always kept it for the woman I'd one day marry." He took the ring out of the box and took her hand. "So, my darling, will you?"

The gesture of the ring softened her, especially since it had to mean so much to him. "Paul, we've just met. I hardly know you, and..."

"What better way to get to know each other than to get married? Your mind is still overwhelmed with grief at the moment. You've admitted your attraction for me, so surely that will change to love once your sorrow subsides? I've been alone all my life and I long for nothing more than someone to care for, someone to love and protect. I want a family, Johanna, a real family. Someone to share my wealth with, my life and that someone is you. Finally, I've found the woman of my dreams, my one true love. Don't be cruel? Don't make me wait for an answer?"

He was right. He had to be right. She gazed into his eyes. Normally, she could read a person's eyes easily. Paul's eyes rarely changed. Right now they had changed—they were hypnotic, mesmerizing her. She made up her mind then and smiled. "Thank you. The ring is lovely. Yes, I'll marry you, Paul." She held her hand up to look at the tiny ring. It was just a plain silver band set with tiny blue stones. It wasn't anything elaborate, not the diamond ring she'd dreamed about, but it was the thought that counted. This was his only heritage, something he treasured, and as such, she'd treasure it, too. After all, she had her grandmother's lovely jewelry...

Without realizing it, she was unconsciously making excuses for the tiny ring. "And now can we go home?"

"Not until I kiss you." He stood up and walked around the table.

In full view of the other customers he pulled her into his arms and kissed her on the lips. "Now it's sealed," he whispered against her lips. "How about a Christmas wedding?"

She pulled away and grabbed her purse. As they left the restaurant, she turned to him. "Paul, Christmas is only weeks away, and I don't think it's appropriate for me to get married so soon. Gran is barely in her grave, and..."

"And would wish nothing but happiness for you, I'm sure. I don't want to wait, Johanna. Please?"

"A Christmas wedding is rather romantic."

"Okay. It's set then. We'll start making the preparations first thing in the morning."

"You seem to forget that I have a job. I'll be dog tired in the morning."

"I want you to quit your job. After all, it's not necessary for you to work anymore. I'll support you."

"But I like my work," she protested.

"Well, then how about you take leave of absence? We'll have our Christmas wedding and go to Switzerland for an extended honeymoon. I'm sure you'd like to see your castle."

While she waited for him to fetch their stuff from the motel rooms, she mused about that thought. "I am curious about the castle," she told herself aloud. "It's not such a bad idea. That's if they'll agree to let me have leave of absence for that long. I'll think about it."

"Honey, I can't wait to be with you. Will you make up your mind soon? Please?"

"I told you, I'll think about it. It's a life decision, not one to be made in haste."

"But you said you'd marry me."

"Yes, I did, but I didn't count on getting married tomorrow!"

"I love you, honey, more than you can imagine. Please consider a Christmas wedding? I want to be with you so much."

"I want to prepare my parents and Christmas is far too soon to get everything ready. Mom's always dreamed of a large wedding for me. I'll not deny her that pleasure."

"But you're so capable. I'm sure you can put everything together in time."

"Okay, but I don't know how my parents are going to react to this," she finally agreed.

After he said goodbye to her before she got out of the car, he said, "I'll see you tomorrow then. What time will you be up?"

"I never sleep that long. I'll see you tomorrow night."

"How about in the morning, before you go to bed?"

"Paul, I go to bed as soon as I get home. And when I get up, I have things to do." An overwhelming sense of irritation at his pushiness suddenly shadowed her happiness.

"Afternoon then?"

"No! If we're going to get married at Christmas, I have to get busy. I'm sure you'll want to contact your friends too, and invite them to the wedding."

"I've lost contact with all my friends because of my travels."

"I'm sorry. But you do have to understand that I'll be busy arranging everything."

"I can help you with most of it, but I do have to go away for a week on a business trip. While I'm gone you can do all the girlish things, like your wedding shower, your dress, bridesmaid dresses and all that."

"Oh? Where?"

"Europe," he answered vaguely. "Before I leave I'll help you with whatever I can. Just give me a list."

"With some things, yes." She leaned over to kiss him. "I really have to run now."

"I don't see why we just can't elope and marry quietly. I'm so eager to be with you always."

Her heart softening, feeling sorry for him that he had no family, no friends, she stroked his cheek. "We soon will be. Goodnight, Paul."

CHAPTER SEVEN

JOHANNA, THAT'S FAR TOO SOON," LESLIE GRUMBLED WHILE looking at the ring on her daughter's finger. "You hardly know the man. At least just be engaged for a year or more so you can get to know each other."

"Mom, I wish you'd stop it. Paul is a good man. He'll make me very happy. I'll not change my mind now about having a Christmas wedding. I've promised Paul..."

"And you're already sure that he'll make you happy? You're so darned stubborn. When you get something in your head you become absolutely foolhardy."

"Is anything ever sure in marriage? Look at the divorce rate. I think it's better to start out with friendship and allow that friendship to grow into a solid relationship and love."

"I don't agree with that."

"Well, it's my life. Just be happy for me, Mom. Please?"

Begrudgingly, Leslie nodded and briefly hugged her daughter. "Well, I guess I can't change your mind. Sure hope you know what you're doing."

"Come on, Mother. Cheer up. Who knows, you might have that grandchild you wish for so much sooner than you think."

"You didn't..."

"No, I haven't slept with him yet. Paul's a gentleman. He wants to wait until our wedding night. Rather old-fashioned, but quaint at the same time."

"Well, at least that's one good point I can appreciate."

"You'll learn to appreciate other good points in him. He's a perfect gentleman and so thoughtful. I've never met anyone like him." The doorbell rang, interrupting their conversation. "I'll open the door. I wonder who it is," Johanna said while hurrying from the kitchen to the front entrance.

She opened the door to face a tall man, camera in his hand. Suddenly she remembered the appointment she'd made with Tristan MacDonald. "Mr. MacDonald. Come in," she said opening the door wider.

"You had forgotten our appointment," he said in an almost accusatory tone.

"I'm sorry. I did," she admitted, again the strong timbre of his voice sending shivers down her spine even more so than it had done over the phone.

"That's understandable. After the bereavement of a close one, your mind would hardly be on talking to inquisitive reporters."

"Please, sit down. Would you like a cup of coffee?"

"Thanks, that would be nice."

"Cream and sugar?"

"Please." He set his camera on the coffee table.

Johanna hurried back to the kitchen. "Mom, it's that reporter I told you about, the one I granted an interview to."

"I'm going back to the greenhouse to help your father. Or would you prefer I stay?"

"No, I can handle it." She quickly poured a cup of coffee, grabbed the forever plate of cookies off the kitchen table and hurried back to the living room to join Tristan.

After setting the coffee and cookies on the coffee table, she sat across from him and for the first time studied the man behind the voice. Tristan had taken off his leather jacket. He wore a turtleneck black sweater and blue jeans. He had a pleasant face. Not overly handsome, but strong and masculine, the exact opposite of Paul's almost feminine good looks. His eyes were brown with twinkling golden flecks and seemed to sparkle with amusement as they regarded her. Dark brown hair curled haphazardly, almost as if he constantly ran his fingers through it. She'd already noticed that he was much taller than her, and now she studied him, she noticed his broad shoulders and strong biceps.

"Do I pass inspection?" he asked while he sipped his coffee. "Mm, this tastes good. It's cold out."

Embarrassed, she averted her glance but not before she noticed his eyes on the ring on her finger.

"Johanna—may I call you that?"

"Yes, of course."

"And please, call me Tristan."

It was almost as if his voice caressed her the way he said her name, causing even more discomfort than she already felt in his presence.

"Johanna, I don't want to fire questions at you. Why don't you tell me about your inheritance in your own words."

She watched him cross his legs and relax, a small recorder in his hand. He set it on the coffee table and grabbed a cookie. "Ready?"

"I suppose. Where do I start?"

"Why don't you tell me about your grandmother first. I've dug up quite a bit of information already, but I'd like to get to know her, if you know what I mean."

She swallowed hard. Talking about her grandmother would not come easy, but soon, she found the words flowing easily, the interest in his brown eyes encouraging her. Several times she got up and walked around the room while talking, all the while feeling his gaze on her.

When she was finally finished, she sat down and faced him again. "Was that what you wanted, Tristan?"

"Yes, that was great. Now how about yourself? What are your plans for the future?"

"I've recently become engaged and my fiancé and I are getting married Christmas."

"I'd hoped that the ring..."

"Yes?"

"Never mind. When did this happen? The last I heard, you weren't involved with anyone."

"That's hardly any of your business," she snapped.

"I'm sorry. It just seems rather sudden."

"Love is something that happens suddenly. Isn't it?"

"Yes, that it is. If I may give you some advice though..."

"You may not." She'd had enough advice already from her parents. Listening to advice from a total stranger was hardly what she wanted.

"I'm sorry. I'm overstepping my boundaries. May I ask the lucky man's name?"

"Paul Blake."

"Is he a Langley resident?"

"He's from the States."

"And what does he do for a living?"

"He's an investor and financial advisor."

Tristan frowned. "I see. May I ask how you met?"

"He was a patient in the hospital."

"That will add a romantic touch to my story," he said, his voice gruff.

For some reason, she felt reluctant to answer questions about Paul. Instead, she wanted to know more about Tristan, about this man who caused such electric tremors through her system. "Where do you live, Tristan?"

"Right here in Langley. I have for years."

"And before that?"

"Before that, I lived in Vancouver."

"Do you have children?"

He laughed, a deep throaty laugh that made her blood curdle. "So now you're interviewing me. No, I don't have children. Neither do I have a wife."

"Oh, I'm sorry. I'm just naturally inquisitive."

"That's okay. I was married once. No children. It didn't work out."

Another divorce, she thought, the words she'd just said to her mother fresh in her mind. "Again, I'm sorry. I shouldn't probe."

"And again, it's okay. We were friends and thought marriage was a good idea. Turned out that it wasn't. She met the love of her life and that was it. We weren't married for very long."

His statement caused a knot of fear to form in her stomach. "But doesn't friendship often turn into a long lasting love relationship?"

"I've heard of it in some instances. With us, it didn't. So, you met this Paul Blake when he was a patient. Sounds rather romantic, almost like a romance novel. You've known him for some time then?"

"Eh, no, we actually just met after my grandmother died."

"Love at first sight."

"I suppose."

"Suppose? You're not sure?"

"Mr. MacDonald, I've taken up quite a bit of your time. Surely you have enough information for your story now?" she told him, though deep down she wanted him to stay.

Almost reluctantly he stood up and grabbed his jacket. "Yes, you've given me more than I'd hoped for." And not enough, he thought while locking gazes with her. "Thank you so much, Johanna. Before I leave, I'd like to take a picture of you. May I?"

"I'm hardly dressed for pictures."

"You look fine. If you could stand by the fireplace? Yes, right there, near your grandmother's photograph."

The camera clicked several times. He took a picture of her sitting by the fireplace too, and one gazing out the kitchen window at her grandmother's cottage. Finally, almost too fast to her regret, he put the camera in his pocket.

"Thanks again. I hope we meet again soon."

"You're welcome," she said while she followed him to the door. As she watched him stride toward his car, she thought about Paul. Twinges of regret at her impulsive decision to marry him gnawed at her heart. She felt attracted to Tristan MacDonald, more than she cared to admit. Something had happened when they had eye contact, something she couldn't quite give a place in her thoughts.

TRISTAN DROVE AWAY FROM the Von Hertzenberg nursery. Carefully avoiding icy patches, he thought about the interview and Johanna's announcement of her engagement to Paul. "Who the hell is this guy anyway?" he muttered. "I'm almost positive there was no one in her life before her grandmother died. Damn, I should have been more insistent and interviewed her sooner." Deep down, he was aware that he'd met the woman he wanted to marry, his soul mate. When their gazes locked, he'd felt it so strongly, such as he never experienced before with any woman. For a moment he sensed their souls touching as if a golden cord had suddenly formed between them to bind them forever, until she averted her eyes and broke the magic moment. It was as if he'd met her before, perhaps another time, another place, but Johanna Von Hertzenberg was lost to him forever now. Unless something happened to stop the wedding...

The car skidded and hit the shoulder of the road, startling him back to reality. "Wishful thinking, Tristan," he said aloud as he maneuvered the car back onto the road. "She's taken. You're too late."

CHAPTER EIGHT

TIME FLEW BY FOR JOHANNA. WITH JUST WEEKS TO PREPARE for the wedding, she had quit work early. They had agreed to give her six months leave of absence, of which she was glad. For now, she had no plans to start a family and stay home to be a dutiful wife and mother. That was not in her makeup—yet. Her career was important to her. The money she'd inherit after her marriage was meant for the upkeep of the castle, though Paul kept harping about it and that she wouldn't have to work anymore. Constantly, she told him she had no idea how much there was in the Swiss bank account and at times she even felt suspicious of his constant questions. But he'd smooth things over with her and in his boyish way would worm his way back into her heart.

She was just checking off her 'to do' list, when the phone rang. When she answered, the operator asked if she'd accept a collect call. She knew it was Paul. Each time he called he reversed the charges.

"Hi, sweetness. How are things going?"

"Everything is going according to schedule, but, Paul, it would really help if you came home and helped. Trying to put a wedding together in such a short time is no mean feat."

"You're very capable. I'm sure you're handling it just fine with the help of your parents and your friends."

"That's not the point. You're the groom. You should be at my side choosing menus and all that stuff."

"I'm sorry, hon. I really have to finish this business deal, but I'll be home sooner than you expect. Have you been in contact with the Swiss lawyer yet?"

"Whatever for?"

"I've told you so many times. You need to know what you're looking at, what your total worth is."

"Paul, I don't really give a shit right now. It's the farthest from my mind. Why do you keep harping at me about it?"

"Sorry. I'm a business man, I guess."

"Then you attend to your business, and I'll attend to mine," she snapped, instantly regretting her catty words.

"You're stressed, honey. I'll be home soon to help you. Meanwhile, why don't you make that call?"

She softened her tone a little. "Paul, whatever money there is, can't be that much. What was considered a fortune years ago isn't much in today's standards. Soon as we arrive in Switzerland, I'll go and see the lawyer. Let's drop the subject for now. I've got other things on my mind. Before you left, did you look after renting your tuxedo?"

"Hon, I'm so sorry. I didn't have time. Could you at least phone and reserve one for me? My waist size is..."

"I know your waist size, dammit. Paul, just get yourself back here. You insisted on this rushed wedding, so it's only fair if you're here to participate. What about a best man and groomsmen? Did you at least look after that?"

"You know I've got no friends or family."

She could have bitten off her tongue at her insensitivity. "I'm sorry. I forgot for a moment. Is it okay if I ask a couple of my friends to stand up for you?"

"Sure. I don't really care. If it would have been left up to me, we would have been on our way to Vegas by now. It would have saved a lot of money and hassle."

"Money! Is that all you ever think about?"

"Well, I've always been thrifty and this extravagance bothers me."

"It's my parents' and my extravagance. Paul, let's stop this bickering?"

"I'm sorry, honey. I miss you so much."

I haven't had time, she was about to say, but clamped her teeth together. "Hurry home, Paul, there's still tons left to do."

"I love you, my darling. Hang in there."

She hung up, a sudden feeling of melancholy attacking her. Their conversation had disturbed her, his absence a thorn in her heart. Chewing on the end of the pencil, she thought about the phone call for a few moments. When she thought about a best man and groomsman, her heart softened. After all, he was a lonely, lost soul, with no one in the world but her. She startled when her mother spoke suddenly. She'd not heard her enter the room.

"Who were you talking to?"

"Paul, Mom."

"What I'd like to know," Leslie's voice was sharp, "is where he is right now? Shouldn't he be helping with the..."

In her heart, Johanna agreed, but she cut her mother off with an angry "Oh Mom! Must you criticize him all the time? He has his business to conduct. I've told you so many times!"

"All right, all right love, no need to shout. But I wish..."

"Wish what? Come on, out with it!"

"Never mind. The caterers called. They'd like to talk to you about the menu."

"I'll call them soon as I'm finished with this," Johanna retorted sharply, annoyed at her mother's constant criticism and interference. As soon as her mother had left the room, she regretted her harsh tone of voice, her snappy remarks. For a moment she felt like running to her mother, telling her she was sorry and crawling onto her lap to hide against the safety of her bosom. Resolutely, she pushed the thought aside. Saying sorry to her mother was like admitting a mistake and her proposed marriage to Paul was not a mistake, even though her parents and Jennifer thought so.

Are you sure, Johanna? A nagging little voice spoke from the deepest recesses of her mind. Don't you think your parents and your friend are just a little bit right? "Shut up," she muttered aloud." Can Paul help it that he has to finalize his business matters?"

JUST SIX DAYS BEFORE the big day, she had to go to the dressmaker for a final fitting of her wedding gown. Mrs. Hobson didn't live far from Langley mall, so after the final tucks and pinning, and a promise from the dressmaker that she could pick up the gown the next day she headed for the mall. It wasn't that she needed anything, she just wanted to relax for a while, to be away from the constant hustle and bustle around the house, her parents' nagging about the rushed marriage and Jen's constant harping that she didn't trust Paul.

A mannequin in the window of a sports store caught her eye. She loved the ski outfit, the color especially. It was a deep blue, the hood trimmed with white fur, the jacket embroidered in a lighter blue with shiny satin thread. She stood before the window for a while, mentally calculating her bank balance. There was no price tag, but she knew the outfit would be expensive. "What the hell," she muttered. "Why not?"

"Yes, why not?" a deep voice beside her said.

Startled, she turned to face Tristan. Her heart rate sped up, the telltale blood rushing to her cheeks. "Tristan, how nice to see you," she said lamely, though her heart was singing at the sight of his kind eyes, his reassuring smile.

"That outfit was made for you, Johanna. Allow me?"

"Allow you?" she asked, feeling stupid because she knew what he meant.

"Let me buy you a wedding present."

"A wedding gift should be for both of us, not just for me."

"I already have a gift for both of you. This is a gift just for you. Why don't you go inside and try it on?"

"I was planning to. Matter of fact, if they have my size, I've already decided to buy it."

"Would you like to go for a coffee after you're finished?"

Her first instinct was to say no, but she couldn't help herself. She felt so at ease with this man, as if she'd known him all her life. It wouldn't be cheating on Paul just to have a coffee with a friend. "I'd like that if you don't mind waiting for me."

"No, I don't mind at all. You can come and model the outfit for me."

Hurriedly, she took off her clothes and tried on the ski pants and jacket. They fitted her to perfection. Outside the changing cubicle she could hear Tristan's voice talking to the sales girl. Should she open the door and show him what the outfit looked like on her? She decided not to and quickly changed back into her own clothes.

As she approached the counter and deposited the ski suit on it, she noticed Tristan waiting for her just outside the door. "I'll take this, please," she told the sales girl.

The girl folded the pants and jacket nicely and put them in a box, then in a shopping bag. "Will there be anything else?"

"How much does it come to?" Johanna asked.

"It's already been paid for by your husband." The girl pointed at Tristan.

"My—eh—oh, I see. Thank you," Johanna said, feeling quite awkward and determined to pay Tristan back.

She left the store and joined him. "Tristan, I want to go to a bank machine first."

"To take out money to pay me back? It's a gift just for you, bought with much admiration. I'm just sorry you didn't show me when you had it on. Now I might never get to see you wearing it."

"I can't accept it, Tristan. I'm sorry, even though it was a lovely gesture." His words tugged at her heartstrings. With much admiration, he said, "If you won't let me pay you back, I'll take the outfit back to the store and you can collect your money from them."

"Without the receipt you can't take it back and that's tucked away safely in my wallet. Now how about that coffee?"

The chemistry between them caused a laden silence, the air charged around them, the hustle of the mall fading into the background as they sat and sipped their cappuccino.

Tristan finally broke the spell. "So what brought you to the mall today? Last minute shopping for your trousseau?"

"No. I had to go for a last fitting of my wedding gown and just wanted to relax for a bit, to get away from the hectic pace at home."

"I can understand that. You look tired, Johanna. Are you okay?"

"I'm fine. It's just been such a big rush and I haven't been sleeping well."

"Nerves?"

"I rarely get nervous. No, there's too much going on at once, too many things to remember."

"Isn't Paul helping you with everything? His family?"

"He has no family, and Paul had to go away for a week on business."

"You told me he's a financial advisor and has his own business. He has clients all over the country, I presume."

"All over the world, from what he's told me. Right now business is slow, so this trip was important."

"I see. What's the name of his business?"

He caught her off guard. She really hadn't asked Paul too much about his work. Each time she tried, he dismissed the conversation with a casual answer as if he wanted to keep his work separate from his private life. "You know, I haven't asked him."

"Johanna, it sounds like there isn't a whole lot you know about your fiancé. Wouldn't it be better if you postponed your wedding plans?"

"Dammit, why is everyone on my back about this? I've made up my mind, made a commitment and I never back out."

"Never?"

"Look, in a matter of weeks my life has completely changed. I need a husband beside me now."

"And you've convinced yourself of that, or has he?"

"I think I'd better leave," she retorted though she made no attempt to leave. The conversation was annoying her, as it annoyed her when her parents were on her back, Jennifer. They were all desperately trying to get her to postpone, but the harder they tried, the more stubbornly she resisted.

"Please don't leave?" Tristan asked. He placed his hand over hers, stopping her fingers that steadily drummed on the table.

The contact was electric. Her hand felt on fire, the charge crawling slowly up her arm, entering her body, reaching deep within her heart.

She looked into the inky depths of his dark eyes—felt them probing her most inner thoughts, her heart, her soul. For moments she sat, allowing the moment to happen, relishing that wonderful feeling of two souls joining for eternity. It was as if his gaze stroked her body, as if the world around them had come to a standstill and only the two of them were left. He half rose from his chair, his face slowly coming toward her...

"What the hell is going on here?"

She snapped out of it and quickly drew her hand from beneath Tristan's. "Paul, I—I—thought you were still away," she stammered.

"Obviously. Who the hell is this? I walked in on cozy little scene!"

"This is Tristan MacDonald. Remember I told you about him? He's the reporter who..."

"Who is trying to hit on my woman? Get lost, buddy!"

"Paul, you're being incredibly rude. We were merely following up on..."

"I've never heard of such a thing. One interview is quite enough. Kindly leave, Mr. MacDonald."

She noticed he'd calmed down some and let her breath out. "Why don't you sit down, Paul, and have a coffee? When did you get back?"

"Why don't I leave you two alone? I've got to get back to the office," Tristan said.

Johanna took his offered hand and felt the slight squeeze as he shook hers. "I hope you'll have the pictures for me next time we meet."

"Yes, I'll call you."

"What pictures?" Paul asked suspiciously.

"The ones Tristan took when he interviewed me."

"That can wait till after we return from our honeymoon."

"I suppose it can," Tristan said. "Nice meeting you."

Johanna watched him stride away, a sudden empty feeling overwhelming her.

"What did you buy?" Paul asked fingering the bag.

"Some clothes for Switzerland," she answered, picking up the bag and putting it on her lap. Suddenly the ski suit felt precious, as if she were holding a small part of Tristan, all thoughts about paying him back forgotten. "I'm glad you're back, Paul. You have an appointment in the morning to try on your tuxedo. I was going to cancel it when I got home because I didn't hear from you at all. Why didn't you call?"

"I was too far away and busy."

"How did it go?"

"Okay. Look, I've got to run to make some phone calls. How about we meet later tonight? And please, don't be hanging around with that reporter. I don't like him."

Trying to hide her disappointment that she'd barely seen him after his absence, she smiled. "Okay, I've got a lot to do anyway. Why did you come to the mall?"

"I wanted to buy a gift for you." He stood up, took her arm and pulled her up to face him. "I've missed you so much. It really got to me when I saw you in the company of another man and holding his hand."

Leaning against him, she sighed at the memory of that moment with Tristan. "He was just wishing me well, Paul. Tristan is a nice man."

"Mm, he might be nice in your eyes, but I saw a little more in his eyes than just well wishes. Stay away from him, okay?"

His kiss was brief and he quickly turned and walked away from her. When he was out of sight, she scanned the mall for a sign of Tristan, but he was gone too. Suddenly she felt very alone. She grabbed the bag and held it tight against her chest. She'd treasure the ski suit always and remember the special moment that occurred that day.

Hurrying home to meet with the caterers, she could not get Tristan off her mind, or Paul's behavior. Tristan's words echoed through her mind—*postpone—postpone...* "No. I've committed myself to Paul and I'll not back out now!" she said aloud as she pulled into the driveway.

"Hi, sweetie, you were gone a long time. How did the fitting go?" Leslie asked as Johanna walked into the kitchen and dropped onto a chair.

"Good. The dress will be finished tomorrow. It looks lovely."

"What's wrong, Johanna?"

"What do you mean? Nothing is wrong."

"I know my daughter. You're troubled. I can read it in your eyes."

"I'm fine, Mom. For goodness sake, I walk into the kitchen and you start interrogating me!"

"Sorry, I'm concerned about you. You look tired, worn out. These past weeks have been a crazy merry-go-round. Why don't you postpone the wedding till spring?"

"Mom, for crying out loud! Stop this once and for all! The wedding is going to happen as planned! Of course I'm tired! There's been so much to do!"

"Paul should have helped. Instead he goes running off on a business trip," Leslie grumbled.

"He's back. I ran into him in the mall."

"For goodness sake! And he didn't even let you know he was back?"

"He just arrived, Mom. Stop trying to make something out of everything."

"What was his business trip for, Johanna? You never told me."

"What does it matter? You know he's a financial advisor and has clients all over the world. He had to finalize some business matters before taking off for six months."

"It's strange that such a busy man can just take six months off."

"Mom, I don't want any of this! You don't like anything about Paul. Why don't you admit it? I'm going up to my room!"

Once in her room, she fell onto the bed, the paper bag crunched beneath her body. Tears flowed, and she didn't know why. She should be happy, floating on air—instead, she felt more alone than ever. As if seeking comfort, her hands dug in the bag and tugged out the ski jacket. Holding it tightly against her face, she could almost smell Tristan's cologne—feel his breath on her face.

She lay like that for a long time, her mind blank, her heart unfulfilled, until her mother knocked on the door and announced that the caterers had arrived.

Quickly she got off the bed, stroked the jacket longingly one more time and went to the bathroom to wash her face.

AND NOW IT WAS her wedding day, and she felt terribly tense. Jen's constant chatter and Paula's bickering with Shawna didn't help matters any. Misgivings consumed her, uncertainties roiled through her mind. The lack of love in their relationship bothered her. Since he returned from his trip, she'd seen Paul every day, but to her disappointment, she could feel no more for him than fondness. On the other hand, she had seen Tristan several times and he awoke feelings within her that she didn't know existed. The first time when she ran into him in the mall and he asked her to have coffee with him and then he'd called her and asked if he could drop off the pictures. Though her mother had been present at the time, the chemistry was still there, stronger than before, the brief touch of his hand as he handed her the pictures, disturbing. And he was constantly on her mind, the face in her dreams, and the man beside her at the altar instead of Paul... He had stayed quite a while, chatting amiably with her mother and later with her father when he came in from the greenhouse for his afternoon tea. She almost resented their presence, wanted nothing more than to be alone with Tristan, to find out more about him, his past, his likes and dislikes, and she didn't know why...

"Your wedding dress is gorgeous, Jo. I'm so jealous," Paula sighed and walked away to join Shawna.

Johanna watched the girls for a moment, listened to their plans for their own weddings, and then turned away and gazed at her reflection in the full-length mirror. She was making a big mistake she knew that now. But, it was too late to back out. The church would already be filled with guests, the hall ready for the reception. If she backed out now she'd make a fool of herself and the family, and for sure, the newspapers would have sport with her. And most of all, she'd be admitting her own weaknesses, her stubbornness in seeing a commitment through. Jen would surely gloat at having been proven right, and she'd never hear the end of it from her parents, especially her mother. He'll be a good husband, she thought. I'm just experiencing pre-wedding jitters.

"Johanna, are you sure you want to go through with this?" Jen asked softly while she arranged the veil.

"Yes, of course. Don't be silly. Why the hell would you ask me a question like that on my wedding day?"

"For some reason I don't trust Paul Blake. I think you're rushing into this way too fast, as I've told you so many times."

"He's a good man."

"How do you know?"

"I've come to know him these last weeks."

"There's something about him, Jojo. I've got a creepy feeling whenever he looks at me."

"You and your intuition. Jen, don't spoil this day for me."

Shawna had been listening to the conversation. "I've also got a gut feeling that you're making a mistake. This is all far too rushed, Jo."

"I don't understand you. When you first saw him in the hospital you were dying for a date with him, and now..."

"I'm sorry. Now that I've met him a few times, I've changed my mind about him. Looks aren't everything. But you can still back out. It's not too late, and..."

"Jen! Shawna! Stop it!"

"Sorry," Jen said. "There, it's finished. Now all that's left to put on is your grandmother's jewelry."

"Mom is going to help me with that. How about if you girls wait for me downstairs? I'd like a few moments alone."

She watched her three friends leave the room. They looked beautiful in their long, burgundy velvet gowns trimmed with burgundy fur. Paula especially looked striking with her dark complexion and black curly hair. The door clicked shut behind them and she turned back to the mirror. The woman gazing back at her seemed like a stranger. Her hair was pinned up, small ringlets framing her face. Her gown of white velvet was trimmed with soft fur around the scooped neckline, wrists and the hem. It was fairly plain, princess line style, accentuating her small waist and flaring out, a longer trail draped behind her. The fur trimmings made the gown look even richer. She had chosen a short veil held in her hair with a tiara of magnolias, her grandmother's favorite flowers.

Her gaze drifted to the picture on the dressing table and she choked back the tears that threatened. Don't be too impulsive, her grandmother told her. And what was she doing? Jumping into a hasty marriage! What did she really know about Paul? She'd asked him questions about his past, but he never told her anything. His answers were evasive, always quickly changing the subject. His past was almost a complete mystery, except the fact that he was an orphan and had no friends. He asked Dale, Jen's current boyfriend to be his best man, and Shawna and Paula had asked two of their male friends if they would stand up as groomsmen. The few times she'd been with Tristan, she had learned more about him than she knew about Paul.

Tristan...

Johanna's hands went up to the veil as if to tear it off, her mind half made up to cancel the wedding, until a knock sounded on the door.

"Johanna? Are you ready?" her mother called out.

"Come in, Mom," and dejectedly she let her arms drop to her sides.

"What's the matter, honey? Are you nervous?"

"I guess so. Mom, will you help me with Gran's necklace? I've already put on the earrings, bracelet and ring."

"Of course. Sweetie, I'm going to ask you one more time. Do you really want to go through with this? It's not too late. You can go to Switzerland on your own to see the castle and your father and I will take care of everything here."

"Mother! Enough already!"

"Sorry. I'm your mother and I love you dearly. I want nothing but the best for you. You're an adult now and it's your life." Clamping her lips tightly, Leslie continued with her task.

"Gran really wanted me to be married when I go there and Paul is depending on me, Mom."

"And who are you depending on?"

It was an unexpected question. Tristan—his name was on her lips, but she didn't utter it. Why did his face suddenly float before her eyes? Forcing him to the back of her mind, she pasted a smile on her lips. "Don't act so nervous, Mom. I'm the one who's got the pre nuptial jitters. We'd better hurry. They're waiting for us."

She noticed her mother's hands trembling as she put the necklace on.

"You look beautiful, Missy. Like a real princess. I've dreamed of this day." Emotion choked her speech.

"As did Gran," Johanna said wistfully. "I wish..."

"I'm sure she's watching you right now."

"Do you believe in a life after death, Mom?"

"Yes, I would like to believe that when we pass on, our soul continues on a higher plane."

"So Gran is an angel now?"

"Definitely, and she'll be watching over you."

Leslie hugged Johanna carefully, so not to crumple the veil and gown. "I'm going down, are you coming? The limousines are waiting."

"Just a few more minutes. You go on ahead."

After her mother had left the room, she walked to the window and gazed out at the snowy landscape. "Gran, if it's true that you're an angel and are with me, can you hear me?" she asked aloud. "Am I doing the right thing? I've heard of psychic phenomena, but never quite believed it. I'd like to think it's true now, that you can communicate with me. Will you try? I so want to talk to you..."

She closed her eyes and conjured up her grandmother's image in her mind. A draft wafted around her face. Opening her eyes she looked at the window, but it was shut tight. Again, she felt the draft and shivered.

Johanna...

She shook her head. "My imagination is playing overtime. I thought I just heard Gran call my name. Come on, Jo. Smarten up. Time to get it over and done with," she said resolutely and headed for the door just as her father knocked.

"Dad, I was just coming down."

He gazed at her for a moment before taking her arm. "I'm so proud of my lovely girl." His voice trembled with emotion. "You look breathtaking."

Thankful that she didn't have to listen to another lecture, that he had enough tact to remain quiet about his misgivings, she linked her arm through his. "Thanks, Dad. Let's go, or I'll be late for my own wedding."

CHAPTER NINE

AS SHE WALKED TOWARD THE ALTAR AND SAW PAUL WAITING FOR her, the misgivings she'd felt earlier left her. Though for a moment she felt empty as her father placed her hand in Paul's and took his seat beside her mother. This was the final cut, the separation of child from parents. She'd be bound to Paul now forever.

Seeing the admiration in his eyes soothed her nerves and she faced the pastor. The nuptials floated over her head. She answered almost automatically, her voice sounding as if it came from another dimension.

"I now pronounce you man and wife. You may kiss the bride."

Paul's lips fleetingly brushed hers and he gently steered her to the table to sign the documents. She signed her name and watched Paul sign his and then Jen and Dale sign as witnesses. It was done. She was Paul's wife, though she had insisted on keeping her maiden name much to Paul's annoyance. It was their first real argument, the issue of her name, but she had remained firm. She had insisted on a clause in the prenuptial agreement, that their children would carry her name. The Von Hertzenberg name would not die with her.

The church was filled. Faces she knew and barely knew were just a haze as they walked down the isle to leave the church. Only one face stood out among the guests, that of Tristan MacDonald. She met his gaze as he jumped in front of them to take pictures and their gazes locked. He backed toward the doors, still holding her gaze and suddenly she knew. It was Tristan she loved and wanted to be with—he was the man she should have married. Not Paul Blake.

She felt like tearing her arm out of Paul's, running into Tristan's arms. It was too late. Why hadn't she realized it before?

Tearing her gaze away from Tristan's, she forced a smile for the flashing cameras. Paul was annoyed that the media had gotten wind of the wedding. He'd asked her not to place an ad in the paper, but her parents insisted. Grabbing her arm hard, hurting her, he ushered her out of he church not bothering to pose for pictures and yanked her to the waiting limos. "Let's get the hell away from this lot," he muttered, climbing into the limo after her.

"Paul, don't be so impatient."

"Sorry, but all that attention is annoying. Why do we have to have studio portraits? You know how I hate to have my photo taken."

"One only gets married once in a lifetime. I'd like to keep memories of this day," she said softly.

"Some people get married several times."

"True, but not me and I hope you feel the same. Marriage isn't a bed of roses, Paul. It has its ups and downs."

"As I'm experiencing already. If it were up to me, we'd be on our way to Switzerland now."

The gray cloud that was already present before she left her bedroom now became darker and darker, not lightening her mood. The mistake she had just made became clearer in her mind. "Paul, you were the one who wanted to get married in such a hurry. Let's make the best of it, okay?"

"I'm sorry, honey," he suddenly said in his sweetest tone. "I just don't like all this attention. A very quiet wedding with just your parents and two witnesses present would have been quite enough."

"It'll be over before you know it. Please try to enjoy it and don't spoil this day?"

He leaned over to kiss her. "Okay, but only because I love you so much."

AFTER AN HOUR AND a half at the studio they finally arrived at the reception. The hall was decorated with white and burgundy balloons matching the colors of their gowns. The sweet scent of magnolias greeted her as they walked through the bridal bower decorated with magnolias and white and burgundy ribbons. The guests clapped, cameras flashed as they walked to the bridal table and sat down.

"Smile, Johanna," a familiar voice said.

She looked up, startled, into Tristan's eyes. He grinned. "They asked me to cover the wedding and reception for the paper. The reporter who usually does it is sick."

"I'm glad it's you," she said softly.

He caught her words and studied her face. She didn't look like a happy bride. Sure, she smiled, but the smile didn't reach her eyes. He had a sudden urge to reach out and take her in his arms, but squashed the feeling. Johanna was out of reach for him now and he had to forget about her and the feelings she aroused within him.

Johanna picked at her food, the constant clinking of glasses for them to kiss starting to annoy her. The flashes of cameras were hurting her eyes—the only one she didn't mind was Tristan taking pictures. Anything to catch another glimpse of him. At times she felt like rushing to him, to tell him of the mistake she'd made, but she couldn't do that. Not now.

Not ever...

The speeches came after the cutting of the cake. They seemed endless, one after another wanting to say their piece. Her father especially had a lengthy speech. Finally, it was over and they were to lead in to the first dance, then to split and dance with the respective parents. Only, Paul didn't have parents, so it was just her father and mother joining them on the dance floor.

"Are you happy, Missy?" her father asked.

"Yes, but I'm tired. I'll be glad when it's over."

"I bet. I remember when your mother and I got married. We didn't really enjoy our wedding night until the next day," he said, and grinned down at her.

"I can well imagine."

"Well, it's time I danced with your mother. Others are waiting to dance with the bride."

She was hustled from one pair of arms to another until she thought her feet would fall off. Until she found herself in arms she'd dreamed of, a face that haunted her at night. Tristan smiled down at her and his arms tightened around her.

"Finally I have a chance to hold you for just one time." He laid his cheek against hers.

Her heart beat a staccato rhythm as his arms circled her. This felt right. These were the arms where she belonged. My God, Tristan, I love you, she thought and felt like screaming. She giggled as she pictured herself being scooped into his arms and them rushing out of the reception hall.

"What's so funny?" He steered her away from groping hands, waiting to snatch her from his arms.

"You wouldn't believe me if I told you."

"Try me."

"No, I don't think so. It's too late for that."

"You're talking in riddles."

Looking up into his eyes, she felt them probing, searching for the answer, reading it in her eyes, she was sure. He pulled her tighter against him and danced quietly for a while, his cheek against hers, and his lips close to her neck. She felt his breath, could smell the masculinity exuding from him, his familiar cologne. If this were another time, another place...

"I haven't claimed a kiss yet," he whispered in her ear. Without waiting for her to answer, he looked into her eyes and kissed her fully on the lips.

But he didn't withdraw and her lips parted under his. Time stood still, the music and voices fading into nothingness as their lips glued together, the rhythms of their hearts blending, their bodies melding as if they belonged.

"Okay, that's long enough," an angry voice sounded, tearing them apart.

Johanna's hand flew up to her lips as if to hold what she'd just experienced. Her gaze locked with Tristan's and she read love in them and regret. Without a word she allowed Paul to lead her away.

"Johanna, what's wrong with you? You've had too much champagne. You're making a fool of yourself with that reporter. What's with you and him anyway? I thought I'd told you I didn't like him!"

She didn't answer him. Paul had spoiled the moment, but that kiss she'd treasure for the rest of her life.

"It's time for us to go and get changed and head for the airport."

"Okay. I'll find Jen. I won't be long." She scanned the crowd for Tristan, but he'd gone. An empty feeling overwhelmed her. She shook it off and headed for the ladies room, on the way grabbing Jen. "Where are Shawna and Paula? We have to leave soon."

"Already? I'll go and find them."

The ladies room was empty, much to Johanna's relief. She took off the veil and the jewelry and placed them carefully in the velvet box that her parents would take home for her. Unpinning her hair, she let it tumble down her back. She kicked off the shoes feeling the fatigue even more now in her feet. She was sure they were blistered they hurt so much. Jen took her time coming back so she struggled with the zipper herself and took off the dress. She'd not realized how heavy the dress really was, until after she'd taken it off. Shivering, she quickly put on her jeans and pulled the heavy sweater over her head. Putting on her shoes was something else. Her feet were swollen.

"You're dressed already?" her mother asked, followed by Jen, Paula and Shawna.

"You guys took so long, I managed to get out of the dress myself."

Leslie was already busy carefully folding the gown and placing it in the box. When she was finished, she embraced her daughter. "Be happy, sweetie. I want nothing more than your happiness, you know that, and we're just a phone call away, remember that."

Johanna swallowed hard. She wanted nothing more than to tell her mother now how right she'd been about Paul, about her hasty marriage. "Thanks, Mom. I promise I'll phone often. The six months will be over before you know it."

"Maybe for you. Your father and I will miss you."

"I'll miss you, too, but you knew I'd leave home sooner or later."

Leslie squeezed her one more time then let go and stepped back so she could say goodbye to her friends. Jen was first. She hugged her tight and was grateful for no more lectures. "Call us soon as you arrive?" Jen asked. "I'm dying to know everything about the castle."

Shawna was next, but too emotional to say anything.

Paula embraced her friend. "I'm so jealous," she sighed and tugged at the heavy sweater. "By the way, Paul acted like a bit of a jerk tonight. He hardly portrayed the charming man you became engaged to. What was with him? What are you doing wearing this heavy thing?" She tugged at the sweater. "You're hardly dressed for Hawaii."

"I'll change on the plane," Johanna said, ignoring Paula's observation about Paul. Not even her friends knew where they were going. Paul had insisted on complete privacy, afraid that reporters would follow them to the castle. She thought it unlikely, but had agreed to not let a soul know, except her parents.

And Tristan...

CHAPTER TEN

THE LIMOUSINE DROVE THEM TO THE AIRPORT. JOHANNA WAS VERY quiet, the tearful goodbye to her parents and friends still weighing heavy on her mind. Overshadowing that was the last glimpse she caught of Tristan as he snapped a final picture of her getting into the limo.

She glanced at Paul. His eyes were closed and he snored loudly. *This is the man I have to spend the rest of my life with.* She shivered as she thought about his surliness that evening, his constant grumbling about picture taking. The way he acted when he interrupted her dancing with Tristan. Then again, he might have noticed that the kiss was more than just a congratulatory kiss...

She gazed out at the passing landscape, at the white blanket covering the ground and the snow still falling in heavy flakes from the sky. Tomorrow is Christmas. I should be spending it with my parents. This will be my first Christmas away from them. Why did I ever agree to this crazy wedding?

A tear escaped. She wiped it away angrily, mad at herself for having been so stupid, for not realizing that she had no feelings for Paul and never would have. She'd stepped blindly into a marriage for which there was no hope. If Paul's behavior of that evening was anything to go by, she could look forward to a miserable life. Divorce... The thought played through her mind. She didn't believe in divorce and she had to at least give the marriage a chance before it had even begun. Paul was stressed. Tomorrow, everything would be different.

"PAUL, AREN'T YOU OVERDOING it?" she asked when Paul ordered yet another double whiskey.

"Shut up, Johanna. You're starting to sound like a nagging wife already!"

She watched him down the drink in one gulp and sighed. "Why are you so testy, Paul? I would think you'd be happy now that the wedding is behind us and we're on our way to Switzerland."

"Happy? What's that? Can you define that word?"

"What the hell's gotten into you? You've changed overnight. I feel like I don't know you."

"I'm sorry, honey. I shouldn't snap at you like that. Blame it on the stress of the last few days." He leaned over to kiss her on the cheek.

She recoiled at his alcohol laden breath. "Please don't drink so much?"

"I always do on a plane trip. Then, if the thing falls from the sky, I won't feel a thing."

"You're afraid of flying? You never told me."

"I guess there are many things we don't know about each other yet," he slurred.

The plane trip was boring. She tried to read, but couldn't concentrate. Paul again slept so he was no company. As the announcement came they were approaching Zurich, she nudged him. "Paul, we're going to land soon. You'd better wake up."

He opened his eyes and looked at her groggily, the drinks he'd downed soon as the plane took off showing the after effects. His eyes were bloodshot and his face looked pasty.

Johanna sighed. This was hardly the wedding night she'd imagined and dreamed of. Looking at the blue skies and pretty landscape below, she tried to remain cheerful and hoped this day would be a new beginning for both of them. "Look out the window, Paul. It's beautiful!"

"Looks just like Canada from here. Not much difference. Just another bunch of snowy mountains."

"You're the one who wanted us to honeymoon in Switzerland, at the castle," she couldn't help snapping. He was starting to really irritate her with his attitude. Was he now showing his true colors?

AFTER STUDYING THE MAP the lawyer had sent, they left the airport in their rented car. It took a few wrong turns before they finally headed in the right direction.

"Are you sure we're going the right way now? I'm getting sick and tired of getting nowhere fast," Paul complained.

"We're on the freeway, or so it seems," Johanna said trying to keep her patience. Paul was quite hung over and in a rotten mood. This should have been an adventure instead of constant arguing and bickering.

"Did you see those quaint houses? It looks exactly like the pictures in Heidi's restaurant. I can't wait to go sightseeing," she said trying to lighten his mood.

"Who gives a damn about the scenery or the houses? I sure as hell don't. We're on our honeymoon. Newlyweds usually hibernate. But no, my wife wants to go sightseeing."

"It hardly feels like Christmas. It's my first time not celebrating Christmas with my family and friends," she said wistfully, his nasty remarks making her nostalgic for home, the Christmas atmosphere, her mother's eggnog...

"I've never celebrated Christmas. Don't believe in it."

"Is that why you argued about getting married in church?"

"Yes. Don't like the company of all those holier than thou people."

"I'm one of those."

"I didn't see you going to church every Sunday."

"I've always gone to church. Maybe not as regular lately as I should have, but I plan to in the future when my shifts allow it, and I want to raise my children in a Christian home."

"Children? We're barely married, Johanna, and you're already talking about kids? I don't want a family. Thought I told you that."

"Stop! We were supposed to take that last turnoff!"

"What the...! Don't yell like that. I almost went off the shoulder of the road! Stop your damn nattering at me so I can concentrate and just look at that map!"

THEY ARRIVED AT THE castle late that afternoon. Johanna hardly noticed the scenery as they continued their journey. She felt miserable, Paul's attitude and constant arguing about directions playing havoc with her already unhappy state. When they approached the castle, she finally sat up to peer out the window and take notice. "It's beautiful. Paul, look at it!" she said excitedly, finally feeling a little more cheerful and thrilled to see the castle for the first time. She hardly noticed his lack of enthusiasm because she was too absorbed in the picturesque scene.

The castle was situated against the mountains. Nestled among tall pines it looked picturesque, almost like a castle from a fairytale. Its towers gazed majestically over a snow spotted valley, the red roofs a splash of color against the wintry scene and green trees. Snow-laden mountains flanked it on both sides and at the back. The road to it was narrow, windy and slippery in places. When they cleared the forest and the castle loomed before them, she gasped. She felt awed and it didn't seem real that she was the owner of such a beautiful estate.

They entered through tall gates. Close to them was a small red cottage with smoke spiraling from its chimney indicating that someone was home. It had to be the caretaker's cottage. The castle's whitewashed walls looked maintained—its grounds were neat and tidy though the flower gardens were overgrown with weeds. The driveway changed into a circle, in its center a large fountain. Lilies drifted lazily on the stagnant water. The centerpiece comprised of two cherubs hugging each other, smiling down as if welcoming them. She could imagine it in spring and summer, water spouting up high, birds and swans lazily drifting on clean water amongst a colorful array of lilies.

Paul pulled up before the steps and entrance. "Well, this is it. It's a monster of a place."

"It's beautiful. Wonder what it looks like inside. The caretaker knew we would be arriving today and is supposed to have everything ready. I wonder if the doors are unlocked," she said.

"Only one way to find out. If not, we'll have to go knocking on the caretaker's door. I presume he lives in that small house we passed."

She was already out of the car and skipping up the steps. Massive oak doors faced her, beautiful carvings and ornate brass handles and a knocker. She tried one of the handles and pulled. The door creaked slightly as she pulled it all the way open.

Taking a deep breath she stepped into the hall. It was like stepping from one world into another, into history. It was fairly dark and her eyes had to adjust to the dim interior for a moment before she could see properly. She made a mental note to have more lighting installed as she peered around. Once her eyes were used to the dim interior, she spotted a wide staircase. The wall beside it was decorated with huge paintings, all the way to the top. She also spotted paintings upstairs, on the landing. The hall, too, was decorated with scenic paintings, antique chairs and side tables, a large grandfather clock and several suits of armor. The hardwood floor shone as if it had been polished recently. In the center lay a deep red Persian rug, hardly worn.

A musty odor reached her nostrils—it was the scent of a house that had been closed a long time.

"It stinks in here." Paul plopped down their suitcases.

"Once we open some windows and air the place out, it should be okay. Let's inspect the rest of it," she said, his comment not dampening her spirits.

Carefully, she turned the knob of one of the oak doors. Just as she was about to open it, a discreet cough sounded behind them. She swung around to see an elderly man, cap in hand, standing in the open door. His face was lined, but keen gray eyes sharply scrutinized the new lady of the castle. His silvery hair was combed neatly. He wore high rubber boots and was dressed in a heavy jacket and wore thick gloves against the frosty weather.

"You must be the caretaker," she said walking toward him with extended hand. "I'm Johanna Von Hertzenberg."

He smiled and shook her head warmly. "Jakob Stein. I work here long time. My father and mother work long time, and their father and mother. You come stay at castle is good. Ghost go now."

"Ghosts?" Paul asked in a loud voice. "Did I hear that correctly?"

"Paul, don't be silly. Old castles often invoke legends. I don't think he knows much English. Communication will be difficult."

"Well, tell the old man to find some hired help. We're going to be living here for six months. You're rich. No need for you to be slaving in the kitchen or cleaning."

They were the first kind words he'd uttered since before the wedding. She turned back to Jakob. "Can you find people in the village to work here? Cook? Cleaning?" she asked, hoping he would understand.

Though his English was sparse, he understood the meaning and nodded, his bushy silver eyebrows drawing together in a thoughtful frown. "Jawohl, Jakob do."

Jakob left, closing the door behind him. As they inspected each room, Johanna noticed that only a few had been readied for them. Many were laden with dust, cobwebs and accompanying spiders, the sheets covering the furniture and beds sparking off a cloud of dust when she removed one of them.

"For God's sake, Johanna. Leave that stuff alone. The place needs fumigating. I suggest we stay at a hotel."

"That costs a lot."

"So? You can afford it."

"Paul, you know as well as I that I haven't a clue how much there is in the Swiss bank account. Until I see the lawyer in Zurich and the bank manager, I can't even touch whatever money there is. Right now, we're living off my savings and yours."

"I'm broke," he muttered.

"Really," she said through tight lips. Nothing about Paul surprised her anymore. What her grandmother had been afraid of had come true for her. Through her stupidity, telling her friends about the inheritance and the newspapers, she had married a fortune hunter. Whatever regard or feelings she'd felt for him, were now totally gone and disgust took their place.

"So you married me because I'm an heiress."

"Honey, don't take everything so seriously. I love you," he whined. "I can't help it that the business deal I tried to make before our wedding fell through."

"Yeah, right."

"Don't let's fight on the first day of our honeymoon. How about we find the master bedroom?"

She shivered, the thought of going to bed with him nauseating now. But, he was her husband and all she could do was make the best of this shambles of a marriage. Silently, they opened doors only to close them again just as fast as dust bunnies greeted them.

Finally, they found the master bedroom. Johanna stopped and gasped in awe. A huge ornately carved canopy bed stood in its center, cherub angels flanking the bed and carved into the headboard. Matching night tables flanked each side. The room was huge, the floor highly polished. A marble fireplace was at the far end of the room, a roaring fire keeping it warm and cozy. Scatter rugs complemented the picture and beautiful paintings.

"So where's the bathroom?" Paul asked gazing around the room.

Glancing at the bowl and pitcher on one of the night tables, Johanna grimaced. "There possibly isn't one. Remember, this place has been empty for many years."

"Surely they renovated a bit? The last time someone lived here it wasn't the Middle Ages anymore. For crying out loud, next you'll tell me that we'll have to use a chamber pot."

"I don't know. My great-grandparents eloped to Canada in 1910. I have no idea when their parents died and the castle became unlived in. We'll have to look around and see if we can find at least a toilet."

Further down the hall they did discover a bathroom. It looked like it had once been a bedroom renovated and turned into a bathroom. A very old fashioned bathtub stood in a corner, the taps old and tarnished, the porcelain stained. A high toilet stood in the other corner, next to it a stained washbasin.

"First task. Installing modern bathrooms," Paul muttered. "I want you to go to Zurich today to find out about the account so that we can start renovating. I don't know why you want to hang on to this place. What's the purpose anyway? You're not going to live here all your life."

"I've got plans for it," she murmured.

"And those plans are?"

"We'll talk about it later. I'd like to rest for a while. You seem to forget, it's Christmas. We'll go to Zurich tomorrow, that's if anything is open."

"You lie down then. I'm going to investigate the rest of the castle. Maybe there's a good bottle of wine hidden away somewhere. If not, we'll have to at least go shopping in the village."

Feeling relieved that he showed no desire to go to bed with her right away, she waited for him to leave and took off her clothes, leaving just her panties and T-shirt on. She pulled back the covers and noticed the fresh, starchy sheets on the bed. Grimacing, she climbed up on it and pulled the covers up to her ears. She'd not realized how tired she really was, mentally and physically exhausted.

Within seconds her mind went blank and she felt herself drifting off only to jump upright when a ghostly voice sounded next to her ear.

Johanna...

"What? Who's that?" she muttered and wildly looked around the room. Remembering Jakob's mention of a castle ghost, she shivered and decided it was her imagination. This time she pulled the covers all the way up, covering her ears.

CHAPTER ELEVEN

COME ON, LAZYBONES, WAKE UP. YOU'VE SLEPT AROUND THE clock," Paul said and pulled the covers off his sleeping wife.

Johanna opened her eyes and blinked. "Where am I? Oh, yes, the castle. I'd forgotten for a moment." She looked at her husband standing next to the bed. "Why did you wake me up?"

"You've been asleep ever since you crawled into that gruesome bed. Honestly, it has to go."

"It's a beautiful bed. We only need to replace the mattress," she said while climbing out and stretching. "Where did you sleep last night?" she asked, noticing the still fluffed up pillow beside the one she'd used.

"Downstairs, on an uncomfortable couch in the parlor."

"Why?"

"I didn't want to disturb you. I'm starving. How about you go and have a bath in that wonderful bathroom and we'll go to the village for brunch. After that we'll drive to Zurich so you can take care of your financial affairs. While you're doing that, I'll go and talk to some antique dealers so we can get a good price for all the furniture."

"The furniture stays," she said firmly.

"Like hell it does."

"The castle is mine and I'll do what I want. It stays, Paul. I won't have any argument about it."

"Fine. We can store it in the attic. I'll find a builder then so we can have some renovations done. We also need to buy a ton of groceries and a fridge. And you might want to replace the stove, too. The kitchen is empty. Nothing there for food and there's an old woodstove."

"Nothing goes to the attic and you can take care of those things while I'm taking care of business. Did you find your bottle of wine?"

"I found a wine cellar. Thousands of aged bottles. Damn good wine."

"I'm glad you like *something* about the place. How about towels, did you find any?"

"Yes. There's a huge linen closet downstairs in what you might call a laundry room. The washing machine, if you can call it that, is nothing but a large wooden tub with a handle on the side that you have to turn manually, and there's a hand wringer on top of it. A wood stove serves to heat the water for washing and there are zinc tubs for rinsing. It's primitive. I feel as if we've gone back to the dark ages. I brought some towels up for you, too. They're in the bathroom."

She hauled one of her suitcases up on the bed and shivered. The fire had gone out and the room felt damp and cold. "Can you light a fire?"

"Do I look like your servant? Get Jakob to do it."

She shrugged and pulled clean clothes out of the suitcase. "Fine. Freeze then. I'll see you shortly."

Johanna felt gratified that at least the bathroom had a gas heater installed for hot water. Though she longed for a shower, the bath would have to do for now. Before she took off her panties and T-shirt, she turned the large key in the lock. She had no desire for Paul to see her naked.

As she relaxed in the steaming warm water, she closed her eyes and thought about her disastrous marriage. *What do I do if he doesn't smarten up? I'd be the first one in the family to get a divorce, but I can't live with a man like that. How do I stop the wedding night from happening? I've got no desire to have him make love to me...*

A loud knocking startled her out of her thoughts. She sat up and called out, "Yes? Paul?" No answer.

"Stop playing games. What do you want?"

Still no answer. Disgruntled even more with him and his childishness, she washed her hair and then her body. After she was done, she sat on her knees to rinse with clean water. Just as she turned off the taps and wrung out her long hair, she heard knocking again, but it didn't seem to come from the door. It sounded as if it came from the walls. "Must be the pipes," she mumbled and grabbed one of the towels and wrapped it round her head. The other towel she used to dry herself with but she found it raspy, like sandpaper. Mentally she added a note to buy new towels when they were in Zurich.

Paul had disappeared when she returned to the bedroom and got dressed quickly to ward off the cold. Going downstairs, she glanced at the wide, gleaming banister and was tempted to slide down it. She'd often seen it in historical movies on TV, but she decided against it. With her luck, she'd fall and break a leg.

She found Paul in the parlor, waiting for her. "Aren't you going to shave?" she asked, noticing the shadow of a beard appearing on his face.

"If I could find a plug that worked, I would."

"You didn't buy an adaptor? I've got one."

"Too late now. Let's go. I'm starving."

WHILE THEY DROVE TO the village, she tried to talk to him. "Paul, this is supposed to be our honeymoon. Why can't you enjoy the adventure of staying in an old castle? This was after all, your idea, not mine."

"Just give me time, honey. This is all so new for me."

"And it isn't for me?"

"I suppose. I guess I'm just disappointed."

"In what?"

"That you're so obstinate about modernizing the castle."

"I want most of it to stay as it is. We'll do some renovating, but only what's absolutely necessary."

"That's your decision then, but I don't have to like it."

"No, you don't, but you could lose the attitude and at least pretend that you're a happy newlywed."

"That part of it is okay. There's a restaurant. Let's go and eat."

CHAPTER TWELVE

THE RESTAURANT, CALLED EDELSITZ, WAS COZY, REMINISCENT OF Heidi's at home. It brought back the memory of that first date, when she'd felt so strongly attracted to him—what had happened to that attraction? To the attentive, charming man she had dinner with that night? She glanced at his sulky face, suddenly noticing the cruel twist of his lips, the hardness of his eyes and remembered her mother's words, seeing him through rose colored glasses...

The restaurant was empty except for one customer so they picked a table near the windows. Happy, red-checkered curtains added to the European décor. Brass ornaments sat atop the mantelshelf of a large fireplace, its flames crackled and sent a pleasant warmth throughout the room. Copper and brass hung on the walls and when Johanna looked at the paintings she saw one of Hertzenberg in its full glory. She stood up and inspected the painting closer. In her mind she could already see the castle restored to its original beauty, the gardens a picture of color.

"Are we going to order, or what?" Paul snapped. "The waitress is waiting for you."

"Sorry, I didn't see her." She quickly joined him and ordered the only thing she could read from the menu, schnitzel. Paul told the waitress he'd have whatever his wife ordered.

While they were eating Johanna suddenly thought of something. "Paul I forgot. Getting married on Christmas Eve has thrown my mental calendar out of whack, there isn't a thing we can do today. It's Boxing Day, everything will be closed, especially businesses."

"Damn, I hadn't thought of that. I wonder if there are any grocery stores open."

"I told you yesterday, remember? It seems awfully quiet out on the streets. I guess we're lucky to have found this place. Maybe they'll do a take-out for us so we'll have at least food for tonight and tomorrow morning."

"Great."

"Let's just make the best of things. Just pretend we're camping, roughing it. Hey, do you know that the village once belonged to the castle?"

"No, but thanks for telling me."

"I'll go and talk to the waitress about taking home some food. What would you like?"

"Frankly, I don't care as long as it's food."

Johanna finally managed to make the girl understand what she meant. She walked back to their table and sat down. While tackling her desert, she told Paul, "The waitress said they'll be happy to make takeout food for us. They don't often get such a request, but after I explained carefully what I meant, she understood. By the way, I was right. No use going to Zurich. Most places of business are closed today, just like back home. And she said most department stores are closed as well."

"Back home, at least department stores and grocery stores are open on Boxing Day," he grumbled.

She tried to make pleasant conversation while they waited for the takeout food by talking about the castle but that didn't go over too well.

"So what the hell do we do tonight? We don't have a TV, no stereo, do we twiddle our thumbs to make the time pass?"

"How about relaxing with a good book and a glass of wine in front of that wonderful fireplace?"

"Mm, sounds okay, that's if you can get a fire started."

"How about when we get back you go and talk to Jakob. I'm sure he can teach you how to start a fire."

"And what will you do in the meantime?"

"Investigate the rest of the castle. There are lots of rooms I haven't looked in yet."

"Okay, deal."

The waitress brought several paper bags filled with the food Johanna had ordered. She smiled and thanked the girl and after paying the bill, gave her a good tip. The girl beamed from ear to ear, clearly unused to large tips.

This time, as they drove back to the castle, Johanna took notice of her surroundings. She marveled at the beautiful countryside, reminiscent of Whistler and surroundings, but even prettier. She tried to imagine what it would look like in Spring when all the flowers were in bloom—it would indeed resemble a fairytale place.

They stopped at Jakob's cottage. She waited in the car while Paul talked to Jakob hoping that he was at least polite to the old man.

Paul soon came back with a smile on his lips. "The old man said he'd take care of lighting fires. Of course I promised him a handsome tip."

"He's quite old, Paul. He shouldn't be doing too much."

"Nonsense. He's a healthy old man and obviously loves this place. Who did all the preparation work then in the castle?"

"I believe they hired people for that. Jakob is merely here to keep an eye on the place for looters and unwelcome visitors."

"As if he could ward off anyone and by the time the cops got here, he'd be dead."

"Well, this seems like a very quiet out of the way place."

"That doesn't mean a thing."

"I suppose."

SHE LEFT PAUL TO take care of the fireplaces and after taking off her jacket and boots, went upstairs to investigate the countless rooms they hadn't looked in yet. They were all much the same, obviously meant as guestrooms, except for one. That room was tightly locked. She had to go down to the kitchen to fetch the large ring with keys that hung there in order to open it. After trying several keys, she finally found the right one and wondered why only this room was locked.

After she entered and stood in its center, she had a strong feeling she belonged there. She had no idea why, until she started removing the dust covers and uncovered what was obviously a girl's room. She waited for the clouds of dust to settle and walked to the window to open it to let fresh air in, but the window was nailed shut. Frowning, she turned to survey the room. The canopy bed had a lace canopy and matching bedspread. At the top of the bed sat a row of porcelain dolls. It was almost as if their gazes followed her as she wandered around the room. A large dresser graced the far wall, a gold brush, mirror and comb set on top of it. Small, girlish ornaments were scattered across the top, at the far end a large jewelry box similar to the one her grandmother had.

This had to be Johanna's room, her great-grandmother's. An old sepia-colored photograph hung on the wall. Interested in the girl in the picture she walked closer and drew in her breath. It was like looking at a picture of herself dressed in old-fashioned clothing. The first Johanna could have been her twin. Going back to the dressing table, she opened the drawers and found neatly stacked piles of blouses, cotton underwear, corsets and nightgowns. Carefully, she took out one of the white cotton nightgowns and noticed the fine needlework and embroidery. The gown had long sleeves and a high neck, tiny buttons down the front, but it was beautiful. When she opened the wardrobe doors, she saw a row of beautiful gowns, long skirts and more blouses and some long coats. Lace up shoes stood on the floor of the wardrobe.

Last of all she opened the jewelry box. It was filled with trinkets, none of them really valuable, but obviously a girl's keepsakes. A drawer at the bottom of the box needed a key. She rummaged around the trinkets and found the key to it. When she opened it, she saw a diary. Eagerly she took the diary from the drawer and leafed through it. The ink had faded but was still legible. It was her great grandmother's diary, given to her on her twelfth birthday.

Leafing to the last page, she looked at the date. It was July 5th, 1909. Moving closer to the window she read the spidery handwriting, but it was in German so she had difficulty understanding it. A word here and there looked familiar. She decided to have the diary translated. Perhaps it would tell her something about the mystery her grandmother talked about. The photograph she would take to a photographer and have it restored.

She sank onto the bed and lay gazing at the dolls. Their eyes looked so real. She wondered what stories these dolls could tell if they could talk. Carefully, she took one and held it up. It was hard to imagine her great-grandmother had played with these dolls.

Johanna...

Putting the doll down she sat up straight and looked around the room. This time she was sure it wasn't her imagination. The voice was soft, female, and it had called her name. Maybe the castle ghost wasn't just a legend after all... If only Jakob could speak more English.

"Johanna, where are you?" Paul's voice echoed through the halls.

Jumping up from the bed, she put the diary beneath a pillow and returned the doll to its place. Soon as she had cleaning materials, she'd start on this room. She didn't want a stranger's hands to touch the precious memories that had been locked in this room for years. She quickly left the room, locked the door and followed the sound of Paul's voice.

"Where were you? I looked all over for you."

"Just roaming around the castle. I found some interesting things." For some reason she didn't tell Paul about the room, it felt private, a place she wanted to share only with her great-grandmother's memories.

"Well, don't stay away so long. Jakob lit a fire. He showed me how to do it."

"Good. We can enjoy a cozy evening in the parlor. I brought some good books along from home. Do you want one? They're upstairs in my suitcase."

"No thanks. I'm not much of a reader. And your books are probably nonsensical romance anyway."

"Oh well, be bored then. I'm going to get one of them and sit and read for a while."

"I'll go and get a bottle of wine from the cellar. When the work crew arrives that I've asked Jakob to hire, that's one of the places that needs fumigating. You wouldn't believe the dust and cobwebs down there."

"I can well imagine."

"Jakob said they'll be here tomorrow. So will the cook, the housekeeper and a maid."

"Good. I'm glad you have things under control."

After fetching the book from her suitcase, she went down to the parlor and curled up in one of the armchairs.

PAUL CAREFULLY WALKED DOWN the creaky steps swiping at cobwebs and muttering under his breath about spiders. The light was dim in the cellar. He determined to buy a flashlight the next day when they were in Zurich. He glanced at the dozens of wine racks caked with dust. He dug in his pocket and held up a small vial filled with yellowish powder. Smiling evilly he put it back in his pocket and produced a pack of cigarettes. He lit one and thought about his plan. Obviously, the so-called honeymoon would not be a success or even any fun. The sooner he could get out of there, the better. But, if he set his plan into action now, would anyone be suspicious? "Accidents happen all the time," he muttered softly as he started to wipe dust off bottles and held up his lighter to read the labels.

He came to the end of one rack and as he turned to look at the next rack, his gaze fell on the wooden wall. Finding it strange that there would be a wooden wall there, whereas the other walls were brick, he wiped the cobwebs away and noticed a faint line running from the ceiling to the floor as if they'd run out of wood and added a different kind. He banged on the wall with his fist, coughing at the cloud of dust this action produced. It sounded hollow. Carefully he ran his fingers along the seam until he felt something protrude. Crouching down, he clicked on the lighter and held it close to the wall. A wooden carving of a wine bottle had been glued to the panel. Finding it strange, he fingered the carving then pulled at it. It moved to the side a little. Twisting it further, a loud creaking sound echoed through the cellar causing him to scramble up and jump away.

Slowly the wall opened to reveal a dark passageway. "This is interesting. Secret passages," he mumbled. He held the lighter up. Just like the cellar, the passages were gray with dust and cobwebs formed a silvery barrier. Far as he could see, the passages went both ways and one straight down. His mind started working overtime how he could use them. The metal of the lighter became burning hot and scalded his fingers. "Damn. First thing we need to buy is a flashlight," he muttered.

JOHANNA LOOKED AT HER watch and wondered why Paul took so long. She didn't really care, but for some reason she didn't like him roaming around the castle too much on his own. She couldn't put her finger on it, but there was something strange about him. Jen was right, she thought. Jen's intuitions are usually right and I should have listened to her...

Paul finally returned with a bottle of white wine and two crystal glasses already filled to the brim.

"I found these glasses in the cabinet in the dining room, a whole set of them. Beautiful crystal. Must be worth a fortune. I found a corkscrew, rather old fashioned, in the kitchen last night," he told her as he handed her a glass of wine.

"Thanks." Johanna sipped the wine savoring the smooth taste. "It's good."

"It better be. It's over one hundred years old."

She tried to concentrate on reading, but for some reason started to feel tired. She didn't know if it was the fireplace or the wine, but her eyelids felt heavy, her body ached as if she was coming down with a flu.

"I don't feel so good, Paul. I think I'll go and lie down for a bit."

"I'm sorry, sweetheart. It's probably nerves and the stress of the last few weeks. Finish your wine, it'll help you if you have a fever."

She drank the last of the wine down rather fast. Within seconds, the room spun around her and she almost fell. Vaguely, she felt Paul take her arm and lead her upstairs to the bedroom. When she lay down on the bed, she hardly felt him taking off her jeans, her socks or his hands on her body. It felt as if she was far away and whatever was happening to her was happening to someone else and she was observing. She saw his satisfied smile, as if he was happy that she felt ill. He pulled up her T-shirt and kneaded her breasts. Why was he making love to her now that she felt so sick? He pulled the shirt over her head and threw it on the floor, tugged off her panties and threw them somewhere behind him. She watched them flutter through the air resembling a bird in flight. This wasn't right. It wasn't the way it was supposed to be... Was it even real or was she dreaming?

"Paul..." her voice was barely a whisper. The room seemed misty as if she were seeing everything through a feverish haze. She watched him take off his clothes, saw him kneel between her legs, coming toward her and she was powerless to resist. Her whole body felt as if it was filled with lead. She tried to lift her arm, but couldn't. He squeezed her breasts so hard that the pain was unbearable. She tried to scream but not a sound left her throat. He pinched her nipples hard, slapped her around the head several times until her ears rang. Then he roughly spread her legs wider. Desperately, she tried to pull them together, shame at the exposure suddenly filling her. She managed a groan. It sounded strange, as if the voice belonged to someone else.

"I'm here, baby. Just be still," he said in a commanding voice.

His head dove between her legs, his teeth biting down hard. The pain was excruciating as he continued to bite. She watched him lift his face, look at her, his eyes demonic, his lips twisted into a savage snarl while his fingers spread her open, dug deep within her. He sat on his knees, he was erect and throbbing against her, his hands reaching for her breasts. Powerless, she lay there, suffering his abuse, listening to his heavy breathing.

While his hands squeezed her breasts tightly together until the nipples felt as if they would burst open, he entered her. It had been so long since she'd made love, that his slamming penetration without lubrication was further torture. She felt as if her vagina had just split in two. He fell on top of her then, his body heavy on hers, suffocating her, pushing her hard against the bed, his teeth biting her nipples, hurting... "Paul..." she tried again, but it was no use. Not a sound came from her lips.

She felt him shoving further into her, invading her privacy, grunting. It seemed to take a long time before he finally moved off her. She felt exposed, violated and there wasn't at thing she could do about it.

She saw Paul look down at her and smile with satisfaction.

"That was good and even better that you won't remember any of it. Sleep now. You'll feel better tomorrow, honey."

His voice sounded so far away. She tried to speak, but only a whisper came from her lips. "Paul, I..."

"I know, my sweetling. You've got a bad dose of the flu. Just go to sleep. That's the best medicine."

Her mind swam, the room spun. Fighting to stay awake, she tried one more time to lift her arms, but couldn't. Slowly, the room became dark, black. The last thing she heard was a female voice.

Johanna—danger...

He waited by the bed until he was sure she was asleep. "It worked again, as always," he murmured softly, "but maybe I gave her too much of the stuff to start with. I have to take it slower." After drawing the covers over her, he dressed and went downstairs to finish the bottle of wine.

CHAPTER THIRTEEN

JOHANNA STRUGGLED TO WAKE UP. HER BODY ACHED ALL OVER AND SHE felt so tired. Groggily, she tried to sit up but fell back against the pillows. "That's all I needed, the flu." Her throat felt parched, her tongue as if it were made of sandpaper. She groaned. "And I have to go to Zurich today to see the lawyer and the bank manager. How the heck can I when I feel so sick?" Her voice sounded strange, slurry. She tried to remember what she did last night, but she couldn't remember anything past Paul giving her a glass of wine.

Closing her eyes to ward off a dizzy spell, she found she could hardly think. Her brain seemed to swim, her thoughts confused.

"I see she's finally awake," Paul said while walking into the room. "How do you feel? Better?"

"Not really. I feel awful. I think I'll stay in bed for a while."

"Why don't you eat and drink something. You had too much of that wine last night."

"I don't remember drinking more than one glass. You mean I've got a hangover?"

"Obviously. You're not used to drinking so much, and that wine is quite strong. It's been sitting in the wine cellar for more than a hundred years. You kept asking me to get more from the wine cellar."

"Really? I can't imagine me doing that."

"I'll run the bath for you and when you come downstairs I'll have the food warmed up. Jakob lit the woodstove for me in the kitchen."

"That was nice of him."

"Come on, girl. We have work to do today. I'll have the bath ready for you in a few minutes." He left the room then but shook his head, angry with himself that he'd overdone it the night before. He had to be careful and take it slower or she'd become suspicious and as long as she could talk, she could give everything away. After he'd filled the tub, he went back to the bedroom to see her sitting on the side of the bed.

"Paul, can you hold my arm? I feel wobbly," she said and tried to stand.

"Sure."

"Did you undress me?" she asked while leaning heavily on his arm.

"Yes. Your clothes are in the wash. You spilled wine all over them."

She remembered just in time to take off her watch. Glancing at the time she noticed it was early yet, barely nine in the morning. Slowly, the steaming water soaked the aches from her body, though she still didn't feel right. When she got out of the tub, she managed to stand on her feet without feeling dizzy. Paul was right. The bath had made her feel better, but everything still seemed so far away, so distant. Sounds sounded hollow in her ears and she had a throbbing headache now. While drying herself, she winced. Even her private parts felt sore, her nipples ached and when she looked in the mirror, they looked red, inflamed. "I had that once before," she said softly. "When I was twelve or so I remember them becoming infected for some reason. Maybe it's the same thing. When we're in Zurich I'll go and see a doctor."

She dressed quickly and went downstairs and joined Paul in the kitchen. He had set the large wooden table and the aroma of warming food that they'd bought at the restaurant smelled appetizing. But she didn't feel that hungry.

"Eat up, Johanna. You'll feel better once you eat and drink."

The orange juice soothed her parched throat and dry tongue. She gulped it down greedily and asked for more.

"Pity the juice is warm. We need to buy a fridge today and a stove. Hopefully they'll deliver the same day."

"You didn't think of putting it outside? We'll have to find an electrician, too. I don't know if you've noticed, but there's only one plug in this kitchen. I'm also going to look into getting phone service hooked up. I feel isolated without any contact with the outside world."

"You're the one who wanted to rough it, remember?"

"Yes, but a phone would be nice. I want to call my parents."

The last thing he wanted was for her to have access to a phone. It could spoil his plans completely. "Why don't we look into buying a cellular?"

"That's a good idea. We'd better get going then. There's a lot to do in just one day. I think I'd better see a doctor, too."

"You'll be fine. Why would you see a doctor for a lousy dose of flu? We'll find a drugstore and get you some flu medication."

"Good idea."

He handed her her ski jacket and boots. "Here, sweetie, let me help you."

She pushed his hands away impatiently. "I'm not an invalid. Okay, I'm ready. Let's go before it gets too late. It's a long drive to Zurich."

CHAPTER FOURTEEN

After they arrived in Zurich, she sent Paul off to buy necessities, look for appliances and search out renovation companies and electricians. Though she still felt very tired and her headache was no better, it felt good to be by herself without his attitude to make things worse. Neither did she want him present when she dealt with the lawyer and the bank manager.

When she arrived at the lawyer's office, Herr Schneider greeted her like a long lost friend. "Miss Von Hertzenberg, it is so nice to meet you," the elderly man said while meeting her halfway in the office.

"Please sit down. I have all the paperwork ready for you to sign."

Johanna looked around the office. Furnished with antique furniture, a woodstove sending cozy heat throughout the room, it hardly looked like the modern offices she was used to back in Canada. A cuckoo clock ticked merrily, adding to the atmosphere. Herr Schneider was as wide as he was tall with a shock of iron gray hair and piercing blue eyes. They twinkled at her now, but she was sure they could turn steely if business demanded it. She waited for him to give her the papers to sign and examined the rest of the office. The floors were highly polished, a Persian rug in the center. On the walls hung diplomas and pictures of Herr Schneider in his youth and family pictures of his wife and children.

"Here you are. The papers are all in German, but I have added translated copies for you."

"Thank you so much. You're very thoughtful," she said while taking the papers and looked for the translations. "This all looks quite straight forward. You've looked after the estate all these years and I'd like to retain your services. Did you make out a paper accordingly?"

"Yes, I was hoping you would like me to continue to advise you. After I retire, which will not be for a few years, my son will take over. It's all there, in the file. I also have drawn up a will for you to sign according to your grandmother's wishes."

She leafed through the papers and looked for the will. Before she got to it, she found a copy of her grandmother's will and read it first. She'd never read it completely and now discovered the codicil. It was as if her grandmother had a premonition of events to come. The codicil stated that Johanna's husband could never touch the castle or the funds left to her. They were there for her use and her children's and their children. When she found the will Herr Schneider had drawn up for her, it overruled all previous wills leaving everything to her father first and then to her children. Thinking about the will she'd bought at an office supply store before the wedding for her and Paul, and leaving their estates respectively to each other, she sighed with relief. She felt sure now that Paul had married her because of the inheritance.

Quickly she signed all the papers. The stack seemed endless, but finally she signed the last sheet of paper and handed the file back to Herr Schneider.

"Thank you. Do I get a copy of the will?"

"Yes, of course. After I've registered it, I will send you a copy."

"Could you please send it to my Canadian address?"

"Yes, I will do that. Is there anything else you would like me to look after?"

For a moment she was tempted to ask him about the divorce laws in Switzerland, but then squashed the thought. "Perhaps later. I have plans for the castle that may need further paperwork. Thank you for all your help, Herr Schneider."

"You are welcome and it was so nice meeting you. If you have any questions, please call me?"

She accepted the business card and after listening to directions to find the bank and shaking his hand, put on her jacket, left the office and headed for the bank, now the proud legal owner of an ancient castle.

The bank wasn't hard to find using Herr Schneider's directions. Quickly she hurried inside and told the receptionist that she had an appointment with the manager.

The bank manager, a small balding man with a rosy red face, ushered her into his office and offered her a chair. The air was thick with aromatic tobacco, a burning pipe waiting in an ashtray on his desk, the smoke spiraling lazily to the ceiling. It reminded her of her grandfather. When he was still alive and she visited her grandparents in the cottage, the cozy aroma of pipe tobacco always greeted her. A grandfather clock ticked loudly, the office furnished much the same as the lawyer's, except for the desk. The manager sat in a huge leather chair facing a large mahogany desk. Its highly polished surface gleamed as if recently buffed, the pictures that sat on top reflected in the gleaming surface. The rug on the floor reminded her of the one in the parlor in the castle. In the background the soft notes of Chopin's concerto surrounded her with a sense of peace and tranquility.

"It is so nice to meet you, Ms Von Hertzenberg. And now you would like to know about the inheritance, yes?"

"Yes, if you could give me a recent statement? And I need signing authority on the account."

"I have prepared the necessary papers. Mr. Schneider already called me and informed me of your inheritance. He has faxed the necessary paperwork. We have checks all ready and prepared for you."

"Thank you. Is it possible to withdraw cash, too? The castle has not been modernized and there are some big items I need to purchase."

"Of course, of course. I will also give you a conversion chart so you can calculate the difference between the dollar and the Euro."

"Thank you so much, you're very kind."

"Here is the statement of your account."

Her eyes widened when she saw the final figure. At first she thought she was mistaken, but she wasn't. The small fortune in the bank had accumulated a lot of interest over the years and she could now consider herself multi-millionairess. "I have no idea what this is worth in dollars and how much to withdraw. I need money for daily living as we'll be spending at least six months at the castle, and I'd like to buy appliances, modern bathroom accessories and other things. I presume I can pay contractors by check?"

"Of course. I will withdraw an amount suitable for your present needs and if you require more, you can withdraw from any bank machine with your visa card. Approximately in American dollars, your fortune amounts to sixteen million dollars."

She gasped, a feeling of unreality overwhelming her, as if this were nothing but a nice dream. At the same time, apprehension filled her heart at the thought of being so rich. After digesting this piece of information for a moment, she said, "Good Lord, I'll never spend that much money in sixteen million years." She took the visa card he handed her. "Can you also advise me the best stores to shop at?"

The meeting with the bank manager took longer than she expected because she asked so many questions and he was eager to help. He provided her with a map of the city, wrote down names of stores and advised her the best dealer to buy a car from. She didn't want to rent a car for six months. Though she was now rich, she had no intentions to just squander the money. Neither did she want to buy a brand new car, not just for six months' use.

Half an hour later she drove around in a Volkswagen beetle bug. It was old, but completely restored and repainted. The dealer specialized in restoring beetle bugs, he told her. It was a hobby. She'd also bought one for Paul so she wouldn't be dependent on him to take her places. Quickly, she drove back to the lawyer's office to find Paul already waiting impatiently.

"Where have you been? If we're going to buy things for the castle, I need you with me."

"I bought a car for both of us. You can take the rental back to the airport. I'll follow you and then I'll drive you to the dealer to pick up yours."

He glanced at the beetle bug and smirked. "You bought that piece of shit? I hope you bought something nicer for me, like a sports car."

"No. Yours is the same, only a different color. We're only going to be here six months, Paul. It would be crazy to buy brand new vehicles. The bank manager recommended the dealer, said he was honest and would sell me good vehicles."

"If you think I'm going to drive around in a stupid beetle bug, you've got to be kidding."

"Well, I'm canceling the rental car, so it's up to you if you return it or not."

Her head throbbed, his arguing getting on her nerves and making her headache worse. "Let's get going. We have a lot of shopping to do before the day is over."

Still grumbling he gave in and got into the rental car. After she paid the bill, she drove him to the dealer and dropped him off. "Just tell him who you are," she called after him.

He came running back to her car. "How about some cash? I can't drive that thing on water."

"Oh, sorry. Here is some cash. Don't ask me how much it is. I've got no idea. Just go and order the appliances and whatever else we need and tell them I'll pay upon delivery. I'll see you back at the castle."

As she pulled away from the curb, she looked in her rearview mirror and saw Paul's angry face and his lips forming words. Shrugging her shoulders, she drove away to find the department stores.

Several times Johanna stumbled as she wandered through the stores laden with parcels. It was as if her brain wasn't sending the message to her legs. It worried her. The symptoms weren't those of a regular flu. She rubbed her neck for a moment to ease the tension and her nurses training suddenly reminded her of meningitis. A pang of fear caused a knot in her stomach. If she didn't get any better, it would be best to fly home, although she doubted Paul would take that suggestion well. She decided to go back to the castle. When she felt better she could go back to Zurich to buy more supplies and needed items.

Just as she was packing the parcels in the backseat of the car, the trunk already stuffed full, a tall man walked by. Her heart somersaulted for a moment, the man resembled Tristan. But of course it wasn't him. It couldn't be.

Once she was behind the wheel and on her way home she thought about him. Why, oh why, didn't I meet him first? Was it fate that I married Paul or was it my impulsive nature? Tristan, I wish you were here...

CHAPTER FIFTEEN

TRISTAN SPENT HALF THE NIGHT DEVELOPING THE PICTURES HE'D taken. He'd shot two rolls of film full, which was very unusual when covering a wedding for a local paper. Which, as it was, was not a regular assignment for him. Usually one of the female reporters covered weddings, but this one was so sudden that no one was available, so the chief asked him to do it. And he was glad he did.

Several pictures would have sufficed for the paper, but he wanted them for his own personal collection. Ever since he met Johanna Von Hertzenberg, he knew she was his soul mate, the woman he was meant to marry. The kiss at the reception had sealed it. He touched his lips where her kiss still lingered. It was as if her perfume clung to him, he could smell it everywhere he moved. Johanna married the wrong man and there wasn't much he could do about it at this point. He was almost sure she returned his feelings. Her eyes had glowed with love for him, yet when she looked at her new husband, she gazed at him with nothing but cool disinterest, as if she was dealing with a cumbersome child. What prompted her to marry the man in such a hurry? Could she be pregnant?

One of the close-ups of Paul Blake surfaced on the paper and he fished it out of the solution. For a moment he was tempted to crumple the picture. His fingers were ready, already crumpling the edges, but he contained his jealousy. Gazing at it, he had the same gut feeling as before. There was something odd about this man, and he just couldn't pinpoint it. He looked at the clock. It was almost three in the morning. He didn't dare call Dick, his detective friend, now. Dick's wife would kill him, especially if he asked Dick to go to the station and do a computer search.

He fished the other pictures out of the solution and hung them up to dry. Johanna's face stared at him from each one, she smiled, but the smile didn't reach her eyes, except in the ones where she was looking at him rather than the camera. He gazed at those pictures a long time before leaving his dark room, turbulent emotions racing through his heart. When an image of Paul and Johanna making love that night floated before his eyes, he angrily turned around and strode from the dark room. Bitterness gnawed at him, rising like bile in his throat, at the thought that he had met his soul mate and could never be with her.

He sank down in a chair in the living room, still holding the picture of Paul Blake. A thought occurred to him. Dick could be working graveyard shift. He quite often changed shifts with fellow policemen because he needed the extra money. Dick had mortgage payments and a young family to feed and clothe. He accepted overtime eagerly and when other officers protested against working on Christmas Day, Dick would jump in and offer to change shifts. He'd give it a go. It was a chance...

Waiting impatiently for the receptionist to answer the phone he kept gazing at the picture as if it could give him the answer he sought. Finally, she answered.

"Hi, this is Tristan MacDonald. Would Dick Fisher be working?"

"Yes, he is. I'll try his line for you."

The girls at the police station knew him well. His hunch had paid off. Dick was indeed working the late shift. "Dick?"

"Tristan, why are you calling me in the middle of the night? Merry Christmas!"

"Merry Christmas. Listen, man, I need a favor. I've got a picture here of a guy. Can you run a fast check on it?"

"Now?"

"Why not? Are you busy?"

"No, thank God not. It's a relatively quiet night."

"Good. I'll come over right away."

It took him longer than usual to get to the police station. Going up the hill was murder because the snow was settling and the few cars that were out this late were spinning and sliding out of control. The drivers had not prepared their vehicles for winter, or they weren't used to driving in snowy conditions, like so many people in the area. More than often they had a mild winter.

He shivered when getting out of his car and rushing to the station. He pushed the buzzer, impatiently waiting for someone to open the door.

"Hi Tristan. What brings you out in this weather at this time of night?" The receptionist, a sexy brunette in her early twenties batted her eyelashes at him, flirting openly.

"A business matter. I'm here to see Dick."

"Oh, you'll find him in his office," she said in a disappointed tone. "Ready for Christmas, Tristan?"

"I guess."

"Where are you having Christmas dinner?"

"Oh, with friends." He knew where her questions were leading and he had no intention of spending Christmas with Tracy Vanderveen.

He waited for someone to let him through the security door and quickly headed for Dick's office. He found the detective with his feet up on the desk reading a magazine. "Man, you look busy."

"Trist, I didn't think you were serious."

"I damn well am. By the way, there are a number of cars slipping and sliding on the on the hill on the Fraser Highway."

"Okay, I'll send a patrol car out. I'm sure the boys will appreciate this," he said with a grin. "I'll be back in a minute."

When he walked back into the office, he offered Tristan a cookie. "Home baked. Try one."

"No thanks. I'm not hungry right now. Attended a wedding tonight and had plenty to eat."

"Tonight or last night?"

"Last night, dammit."

"Boy, you're touchy. What can I do for you?"

"Here is the picture I told you about. Can you run a check on it?"

"I can try. Let's scan it into the computer."

While Tristan scanned the picture, Dick ran a name check on Paul Blake and came up with nothing. "The guy is from the States, you said?"

"Yes."

"That's like searching for a needle in a haystack."

"I've finished scanning the picture."

"Good. Maybe that will tell us something. What makes you want to check out this guy?"

"I don't know. Call it a reporter's hunch."

A few minutes later the computer found a match. Tristan was busy on another computer running name checks. Dick called out to him, "Trist, I've got a match."

"You're kidding. Already?"

"Yes. This guy is wanted in several states. Come take a look."

Tristan was already standing behind Dick and gazing at the monitor. "You sure that's the same guy?"

"According to the computer it is. Hair color is different, he's got a beard here, on that one he has red hair and a moustache, but if you look closely, the face is the same shape. Let's read up what the file says."

"Holy shit," Tristan muttered. "This guy is a master of disguises."

"And wanted for bigamy in one state and suspicion of murder in several others. Read this. Four of his wives died under suspicious circumstances. Supposed accidents, but the police have gathered enough evidence now to suspect murder. Each time the guy disappeared without a trace. Just recently they linked the four deaths to the same man."

"I can read," Tristan said testily. "Go back to the first screen. Do they have a real name for him?"

Dick scrolled back to the first screen. "Roger Fitzgerald. He's got a juvenile record a mile long." He kept scrolling back and forth. "Seems the guy inherited a small fortune from his respective wives. He left his first wife behind in Tennessee with a couple of kids to raise. She hasn't divorced him. Look here, he's been spotted in Reno too! Probably lost all his money and is looking for more victims."

"Oh my God! Do you realize he just married an heiress? I covered the wedding yesterday of Johanna Von Hertzenberg. I'm sure you heard of it."

"The famous castle owner. Yes, of course I heard."

"Well, he's posing as Paul Blake. They're off on their honeymoon now. I have to warn her."

"Don't get involved, Trist. Let us handle it. Where did they go?"

"Hawaii," he lied, not wanting to break his promise to Johanna just yet.

"The heiress will be safe for a while. He doesn't kill his wives until about a year after the marriage."

"Nevertheless, I don't trust him for a minute. She needs to be warned."

"I'll get in contact with the States. So far, Canada has no beef with the guy."

"That's going to take time. She needs to know and soon."

"Don't do anything stupid, man. What's your interest in this woman?"

"She's a friend."

Dick observed Tristan for a moment. The changing tone of voice when talking about the heiress, had not escaped him, or the softening and worried expression in Tristan's eyes. "I detect more than just friendly interest here. I've known you long enough, and..."

Tristan hardly heard his friend's words. He was busy printing the pictures of Roger Fitzgerald and copying the papers in the file. He waited impatiently for the printer to finish. When it was done, he grabbed the papers and turned to Dick. "Thanks, mate. I owe you one."

"What the hell are you doing? You're not supposed to take that stuff, you know better than that. Give them to me!" But his words were ignored. Tristan was on his way out so Dick ran after him. "Tristan, don't be stupid. What are you going to do?" He was already out the door. Dick shook his head and hoped Tristan wouldn't let emotions override common sense.

HE DROVE AS FAST as he possibly could on the slippery roads back to his apartment. After throwing clothes and toiletries into a duffel bag he quickly dialed the airport's number and booked a seat on the next flight to Zurich. Luckily the plane was half empty so his first fear that he couldn't get a seat was quickly stilled. As an afterthought he wrote several post-dated checks for his rent and stuffed them in an envelope. Hurriedly he called the office and left a message with the editor that he would be out of town for a few weeks chasing a hot lead. After checking the windows, the sliding door, and throwing a hurried glance over his paper scattered apartment, he locked the door and ran down the stairs to the manager's apartment to deposit the envelope through the slot.

Though he had plenty of time to get to the airport, he drove as fast as he could. Fortunately, the main roads were cleared and salted and it had stopped snowing.

THE PLANE LANDED IN Zurich airport. He sighed with relief. The journey seemed to take days instead of hours. He'd been unable to sleep because his mind was constantly busy with the danger Johanna was in.

The car he'd reserved at Vancouver airport was ready and waiting for him. It was a red Opel. But before he took off to head for the autobahn he carefully studied the map he'd bought. Johanna told him that the castle was located in the Alps somewhere near the Italian border. He couldn't find the castle on the map but the township of Hertzenberg was there. The nearest large town to it was Zurich.

He was glad that it wasn't snowing. It was cold, frosty, and the roads were clear. The countryside flew by as he sped down the autobahn, the speed limit much higher here than back home. The morning sun painted the sky in vivid pastels turning the snow-capped mountains into pink snow cones. Slowly the sky turned a brilliant blue, the frosty sun bathing the landscape in lukewarm rays.

Zurich had woken early. Traffic was already busy and pedestrians dotted the narrow sidewalks, hurrying to their place of employment.

Though it was Boxing Day, Tristan presumed some stores and restaurants were open. The sun shone through the windshield and for a moment he had to shake his head as exhaustion and lack of sleep threatened to overcome him. He knew he had to stop and drink a coffee or he'd fall asleep behind the wheel. His body also needed fuel for the drive ahead of him through the Alps. He could not chance getting into an accident now that he was so close to his destination.

He found a small bistro that served coffee and breakfast. It was quite full. Customers sipped their coffee or ate a quick breakfast while studying the morning paper. Tristan scanned the tables for an empty spot, but there were none. He approached a table with only one occupant. She was an older woman. "Excuse me, may I share your table?" he asked politely.

"Bitte?"

Tristan pointed at the chair. The woman nodded so he sat down and studied the menu. His knowledge of the language was very limited but the word coffee was almost universal and easily recognized. He noticed a word that resembled bread, underneath it bratwurst. When the waitress came to take his order, he pointed at it.

His order was served quite fast. The sausages smelled appetizing and set his stomach growling. The plate also held some form of scrambled eggs and fried potatoes. It looked delicious. On the side sat a small plate with several slices of fresh baked bread and real butter. He hadn't realized how hungry he was until he took the first bite. After drinking several cups of black coffee he felt refreshed and invigorated.

He paid his bill and left the bistro. He stood for a moment gazing at the small, cozy shops, but most of them were closed. His gaze fell on a flower shop that looked like it was open. Quickly he crossed the cobble stoned street. He was gratified that the girl behind the counter knew some English. He ordered a large bouquet of red roses and asked them to be delivered to the castle that afternoon. He signed the card, compliments of the Langley Advance, hoping Johanna would know who sent her the flowers.

He drove the narrow winding road through the Alps carefully as it was covered with icy patches and loose snow in some places. At times, when he had to fight a patch of black ice and keep the small vehicle under control, he'd grimace and think about the speed with which the salt trucks and snowplows looked after the roads back home in Canada.

Late afternoon he drove into Hertzenberg. The town was small, quaint. He imagined it in summer when window boxes were filled with red geraniums, and tables and chairs were set up outside the small bistros and restaurants. Most of the houses were white with red tiled roofs. It took him just a few minutes to drive up and down the main drag. Finally, he stopped and asked a pedestrian where to find a hotel. The man didn't understand much except the word hotel. He pointed to a turnoff and somehow, Tristan understood he had to drive a little ways to get to the hotel.

He took the turnoff and drove for at least ten minutes before he spotted it. It hardly looked like a hotel, more like a house. It, like the others, was whitewashed with green shutters and window boxes. The roof was red. He parked the Opel, got out and walked to the front door. It too was painted an emerald green with a small stained glass window in the center. The bell, doorknob and mail slot were all solid, highly polished brass.

He pulled the chain hanging from the bell and waited. A young woman opened the door. Long blonde braids hung over her shoulders almost to her waist. She wore the traditional Swiss costume, a red skirt trimmed with colored edging and gathered at the waist. Her shapely legs were clad in white stockings and she wore black shoes. A frilly white blouse with puffy sleeves offset a black vest that was laced in the front. Her round, rosy face beamed as she smiled at him and in German asked him to enter.

He understood the beckoning rather than the language and followed her inside. A stout buxom woman stood behind the reception desk. She eyed him with interest.

"Good afternoon. I'd like to rent a room here if you have any vacancies?" He hoped that at least one of them could understand English.

"The woman's gaze traveled to the girl. " Heidi? Bitte?"

Tristan grinned. The girl's name, Heidi, finished off the picture. He was sure he'd met Heidi from the well-known tale.

Heidi spoke to the woman in swift German. "Deise Herr wollte ein zimmer zu mieten."

"Ah, jawohl. Wie lange?"

Heidi turned to Tristan. "My mother ask how long you stay?"

He sighed with relief. "I'm glad you speak English. I don't know yet. I can pay for a week in advance."

Heidi translated for her mother who nodded and left the reception desk to join Tristan. She extended her hand. "Frau Brunhaber."

He shook her hand. "I'm Tristan MacDonald."

Though she was quite stout, the woman was amazingly swift on her feet. Quickly, she walked toward the stairs and motioned for Tristan to follow. "Folgen Sie mich," she said with a wide smile.

The room was small but cozy. He nodded his acceptance and followed her back downstairs to sign the register and pay for his week's lodging.

After bringing his bag up to the room, he fell onto the bed, hands under his head and stared up at the ceiling. The urge to go to the castle right now was great, but he decided against it. He had no idea how Johanna would receive him or that it was just his imagination that she returned his feelings. She was after all a newlywed and could resent him showing up. If he told her too soon, she could resent him saying bad things about Paul, though he had the papers with him to back him up. No, he'd go to the castle in the morning on the pretense that he was doing a follow up story. But how would Paul act toward him? The man clearly resented him at the reception. What if he threw him out?

AFTER A RESTLESS NIGHT, still suffering from jetlag, he set out to the castle late that afternoon. The road leading to it was even narrower than the one through the mountains, windy and covered with quite a lot of snow. Driving was difficult. Several times branches dumped their load of snow onto the little car. Going up fairly steep inclines, the tires spun uselessly on the icy road and he had to back up and try driving up again taking it very slow.

He drove by the road leading to the castle twice before he spotted it. He saw the tire tracks and knew another car had traveled the road that morning. He hoped Johanna and Paul hadn't gone out. For a little while he thought he'd taken the wrong turnoff, until he exited the thick forest and the castle gates suddenly loomed before him. His breath emerged in small puffs as he got out of the car to open the gates. But he didn't have to. An old man plodded through the snow toward the gates to open them. Tristan hurried back into the car and shivered. His spine was telling him there would be more snow that day or evening.

The old man greeted him by touching his cap as Tristan drove through the gates. He smiled and waved and drove slowly toward the castle. It looked picturesque against the backdrop of snow covered mountains surrounded by snow laden pine trees and its towers he could see were red and gray though they were partially covered with snow, too.

He noticed a blue VW parked at the bottom of the steps and parked his car behind it. Feeling relieved the newlyweds were home he grabbed his camera and got out of the car. Carefully, he walked up the slippery steps and took a deep breath before lifting the heavy knocker and letting it fall against the door.

The door opened slowly. It was Johanna.

"Tristan!" she said in a loud whisper and fell into his arms.

Quickly, he shoved the camera into his coat pocket and embraced her. He heard her weeping softly on his shoulder and patted her back. "Johanna, why don't we go inside? It's freezing out here."

"I'm—I'm sorry," she said and stepped back. "Come in. I'm just so happy to see you."

He knew immediately that something was desperately wrong. This was hardly the welcome he'd expected from a newlywed.

CHAPTER SIXTEEN

JOHANNA LED TRISTAN TO THE PARLOR WHERE THE FIRE CRACKLED and it was snug and warm. She closed the door behind them and turned to face him. "Give me your coat, Tristan. I'll hang it up." She held out her hand.

He took her small hand in his and squeezed it. "Are you okay?"

"I'm not sure. I don't feel well and everything is wrong."

"Wrong?"

"I shouldn't have married Paul. I made a big mistake," she blurted out.

"What makes you think that?"

"I'm sorry. Would you like something warm? Coffee? Hot chocolate? Let me..."

"I'm fine for now. Why don't you sit down and tell me all about it," he said while taking off his jacket and hanging it on the corner of a chair. He waited till she sat down and sat opposite her. Every instinct urged him to take her in his arms again, but until he knew what was going on, he fought it.

"I don't know what there really is to tell. Maybe it's all my imagination, I don't know. Paul has behaved strangely ever since we got married. He's ornery, argues about everything and he's so demanding."

"Demanding as in making love all the time? That's natural you know for honeymooners."

"No, we haven't had sex."

"You haven't? That's strange. Is that what bothers you, Johanna? That he hasn't made love to you?"

She hesitated, looked down at her feet and shifted uncomfortably.

"Eh—you don't know how difficult this is for me. I'm not very good at admitting a mistake, but here goes." She took a deep breath and said with a rush, "I—I—made a terrible mistake in marrying Paul. What bothers me the most is that I'm already thinking about divorce. I don't love the man I married. And now—now I don't even like him anymore." She wanted so badly to tell Tristan how she felt about him but she was not sure of his feelings for her.

But when she looked into his eyes and their gazes locked, she did know. He felt the same way about her. "And now to top it all, I feel positively ill. I think I've got the flu."

"Where is Paul?"

"He's still in Zurich buying more supplies. I felt ill so I came back. I'm renovating the castle. Unfortunately, due to the road conditions, the crew couldn't get here today or the staff I hired."

Tristan glanced at the window. Even through the dirty glass, he could see the snow whipping against the window. "The blizzard has started. I should have waited to come here."

"I'm glad you came, Tristan. I've never felt so alone in my whole life."

"Johanna, where are you? Come and help me with stuff! It's bloody awful out there! I almost got lost!" Paul's loud voice echoed back to them.

"Johanna, there is something I have to tell you..." Tristan got no further. The door opened and Paul stalked into the room.

"What the hell are you doing here?" he shouted.

"Eh—I came to do a follow-up story. The paper asked me to take pictures of the happy couple living in the castle and all."

"Great. That's just what we need. Visitors on our honeymoon. Don't you know what the word privacy means? How would you like it if someone intruded on your private life all the time?"

"I'm sorry. I told the chief I wouldn't be very welcome, but he wouldn't take no for an answer. I won't take up too much of your time."

"Where are you staying, Tristan?" Johanna asked.

"In a small hotel in Hertzenberg."

"Why don't you fetch your luggage and stay at the castle then? That will get the story over and done with faster."

"Are you crazy?" Paul yelled. "Like I want company on my honeymoon."

"I don't want to create problems," Tristan said.

"It's no problem, Tristan," Johanna said quickly. "I'm sure Paul understands that if you stay in the castle a few nights, you'll get a feel of the place for your story and you can snap pictures. It's a big place. I haven't even seen all of it yet."

"A few days? Are you nuts? I forbid it."

Johanna stood up, her eyes flashing daggers at her husband. "Don't order me around, Paul. It's my castle and I'm opening the door to Tristan." For some reason she felt it was important that Tristan come and stayed there.

"I'm sorry, honey," Paul said in a softer voice. "It's just that I so hoped to be alone with you tonight before the work crews arrive. Okay, the reporter can stay, but just for a couple of days."

"Thank you, Paul. Tristan, would you like to drive back to the village to pick up your things?"

"Yes, I'd better do that before the snow gets worse."

She stood up to see him to the door. Paul sank into one of the chairs, a sulky expression on his face. "And don't hurry back," he muttered.

But when Johanna opened the front door, they faced a blinding blizzard. "You can't drive in that!" she exclaimed.

"No, I don't think the little car could handle it."

"Looks like you're stuck here."

"Do I look sorry? I don't like leaving you alone with that monster."

"He's really harmless."

"You don't know..." He reached out to touch her cheek.

Realizing that the door was still open, the icy snow biting into the side of her face, she quickly shut the door. "Tristan, I..."

"I know. I want nothing more than to take you in my arms right now, but we have to wait. Johanna, while we're alone there's something

I need to tell you about Paul."

"What?" Unconsciously she took a step toward him, wishing, wanting to feel his strong arms about her.

"I did a background search on him with the help of a friend of mine, an RCM.P officer in Langley. Paul is..." he got not further. The door opened and Paul joined them.

"What is going on here? I thought you were going to Hertzenberg?" Paul eyed them both suspiciously.

"There's a blizzard. He can't drive in that."

"As if I didn't know that. It started just when I got back."

"Well, let's make the best of it then. Paul, why don't you fetch a bottle of wine from the cellar? We can play cards or something."

"Good idea." Tristan smiled, trying to lighten the mood.

"Okay, I'll go and get some wine and glasses. Johanna, why don't you make us something to eat? I'm starving."

PAUl STOPPED FOR A moment before one of the doors they'd not yet opened. He turned the knob and stepped into a study. Shining his flashlight around, he'd just decided to investigate the study further later on, when his glance fell on a gun cabinet. It held shotguns, rifles, and a few old fashioned pistols. Grinning to himself, he softly closed the door, headed for the kitchen and went down to the cellar, all the while thinking about Tristan's sudden arrival. He waded through the cobwebs and layers of dust until he found the bottle of wine he wanted. Because there were three of them now, he took two bottles of the rack and dusted them off with his sleeve. A large spider crawled on the cement floor where he had disturbed the dust. He stepped on it and squashed it. "There, that's you Johanna, and a lot sooner than planned. I don't trust the reporter. He suspects or knows something. From what I caught of the conversation between those two, he's onto me. I'll have to get rid of him, too. I think I'll set my plan in action tonight. What difference does it make anyway? Now or later..."

Quickly he approached the wall and pushed against it. At first the secret panel wouldn't open for him, but then his fingers found a ridge. As he ran his fingers along it the stone wall creaked and swung open. He shone the torch both ways and swinging at the cobwebs and spiders made his way through one narrow passage. He came to another flight of stone stairs. Some of them were crumbly. Carefully, he navigated them. He reached the bottom and let the torch play around a chamber. Rusty armor lay scattered on the floor, in the center a large wooden table with rusty shackles attached to it. A large wooden chair with leather straps attached to the arms stood in a corner. Rusty tools hung on the walls. He'd entered what looked like some kind of torture chamber.

The torch picked up another door. It was made of thick wood. Large iron hinges were rusted as was the lock. A huge ring with keys hung beside it. He took the ring of keys off the nail and started trying them. One of them fit but at first the door wouldn't budge. After pulling it with all his strength, it started to open. Rust flaked off the hinges as he pulled and tugged. Dust hung in clouds around him causing him to cough repeatedly.

Finally, he could squeeze through the opening. He shone his torch and spotted a number of cells, rusty shackles attached to the walls. Several skeletons lay scattered on the floor. A shiver ran down his spine but he felt satisfied. The castle would give him more than the inheritance—it would help him get rid of the woman and the nosy reporter and no one would ever find them.

Quickly, he made his way back to the wine cellar and grabbed three bottles of wine. He didn't bother looking at the labels. All he needed was to get the reporter drunk. He'd slip a sedative into the wine bottle and feed Johanna more of the powder. That evening would be the last for both of them...

AS THEY ENTERED THE parlor, Tristan could no longer help himself and leaning against the door he reached out for Johanna and pulled her into his arms. He felt her body shake with silent sobs. When she looked up into his eyes her eyes pooled suspiciously. He stroked her hair and kissed the top of her head. "Don't worry, my love. I'll get you out of this mess."

"But how?"

"Very soon. He's dangerous."

"Dangerous? What do you mean?"

"There are things you don't know about Paul. That's not even his real name. Just remember that I love you and I won't let him hurt you."

"How do you..." she got no further. Footsteps sounded behind the door and Tristan released her quickly and pushed her gently toward a chair. "He's back. Ssh, don't say a word," he whispered and stood aside before the door opened.

Her heart sang. Tristan loved her... His warning, that Paul was dangerous, hung in her mind. She had no idea what he meant and longed for some time alone with him so he could explain. But how could she get Paul to leave? Tomorrow—after the blizzard stopped, maybe Paul would find another excuse to go into the village or drive to Zurich and she'd be alone with Tristan...

CHAPTER SEVENTEEN

THEY PLAYED CARDS BEFORE DINNER, PAUL BECOMING QUITE inebriated as he drank one glass of wine after another. Tristan had hardly touched his. He needed to keep his head clear. The more Paul drank, the more uncouth he became. It irritated Johanna though she didn't say anything. It annoyed Tristan who felt like punching the guy. Each time he stood up to pour another glass of wine he almost forced Johanna to drink hers. She'd only had two glasses and now he was pouring her a third. Neither of them noticed that Paul had poured her and Tristan's wine from a different bottle.

"I don't want any more, Paul," she said carefully, hoping not to upset him.

"Why not? This is such a cozy gathering," he answered sarcastically and poured the wine anyway. "How about you, Tristan?"

Tristan shook his head. The first glass of wine was still full. He'd made pretense of sipping it, but didn't drink. He wanted to stay sober and keep and eye on Paul. "No thanks. I'm not much of a wine drinker."

"I bought some whiskey. Want some?"

"No thanks."

Paul proceeded to fill Johanna's glass.

"Paul, please, I don't feel well and the wine isn't helping any."

Tristan heard the slur in her speech and wondered about it. "Just one more before dinner," Paul urged and handed her the glass. "I think we should go skiing after dinner. How about it?"

"In this weather?"

"Haven't you looked outside lately? The blizzard has stopped. It's just snowing a bit now. There's a private slope near here. I investigated today."

"Oh, I thought you went shopping."

"I did a bit of that, but then I scouted the countryside. I'm in the mood. Tristan, I guess you didn't bring skis?"

"Hardly. I didn't come here to ski. It's not wise to go skiing after drinking, Paul."

"I don't need your advice."

Johanna heard their voices fading into the distance. A bout of nausea attacked her so she stood up to go to the bathroom. For a moment the room spun around and she steadied herself on a chair. "Paul, I don't feel good. I'm hardly in the mood or condition to go skiing. Matter of fact, I think I'd like to lie down for a while. Tristan, do you mind?"

"No, of course not." He stood up, his first instinct was to scoop her into his arms and take her to her bedroom, but Paul was ahead of him.

"Sweetie, what's wrong? Let me help you."

Tightening his lips, Tristan watched them leave the room. He frowned, worry consuming his thoughts. Idly, he flipped through the pages of a book Johanna was reading. After half an hour Paul and Johanna still had not returned and he was even more worried. What was Paul doing to her? Should he go upstairs and check it out?

He jumped up and just as he opened the door he saw them both coming down the stairs, dressed in ski clothing. "You're going skiing anyway?"

"I feel better."

Her voice sounded monotonic, robot like. He watched her walk stiffly to the front door. Paul followed carrying their skis and boots. He dropped them on the floor and walked into the parlor soon coming back with a glass of wine. "We'll be back in a bit," he said in a friendlier tone. "Johanna changed her mind. Just make yourself at home. Matter of fact, if you can cook, why don't you make us some dinner? We stocked up on groceries and even bought a fridge and a stove. Here, honey, drink the last of your wine," he urged and held the glass to her lips.

Her mind wouldn't work, her brain numb. She wanted to refuse, didn't want the wine, but automatically she drank as he almost poured it down her throat.

THE DOOR SHUT BEHIND them and Tristan stood staring at it. "My God, a drunkard and a woman who's not feeling well. What the hell are they thinking of going skiing?" he said angrily. "And me staying here and cooking dinner? Like hell I will. I don't trust that bastard for two seconds. I'm going after them."

He ran to the parlor and put on his jacket then sprinted to the front door and quickly to his car. He turned the key, but it was dead. Not even a click sounded as he tried several times while watching the taillights of Paul's car disappear. "I'm sure I turned off the headlights, so it can't be a dead battery. Damn, now what? I wonder where the ski slope is," he muttered. His gaze fell on the smoke coming from the chimney on the roof of the small cottage and the lights. He quickly got out of the car. "That must be the caretaker's cottage. Maybe he knows where they've gone," he muttered and plowed through the snow toward it.

Jakob nodded when Tristan asked him about the ski slope. "Jawohl, you drive the road. Left and left and up mountain. Not far."

"Thanks," Tristan yelled over his shoulder, already on his way. The old man called something after him, but he couldn't understand it. As he plodded through the snow his feet slowly turning to ice cubes a feeling of doom came over him. He tried to go faster, but the snow hampered him. Suddenly he had an idea. The forest was so thick with trees that the snow settled on the branches but not so much on the ground. He entered the forest and continued on there, but only so far so that he could still see the road.

It seemed to take him forever as he continually followed the tire tracks, but he eventually found the ski slope. Dusk had gonc, it was dark but the pristine snow lit the way for him. He was about fifty feet away when he saw Johanna poised at the top of the slope. Paul stood just behind her. Tristan heard his manic laughter and he tried to hurry.

His breath whistled, his lungs pumping for air as he labored up the incline, tripping over broken branches sticking out of the snow, falling headlong several times when his feet encountered rocks, and just as he came close enough to call out to her, he saw Paul reach and push Johanna over the edge.

It almost seemed to happen in slow motion, she disappeared so slowly over the edge. Tristan screamed then, "Noooooo, Johanna..."

Paul wildly looked around and spotted the dark figure coming toward him. He reached inside his ski jacket and pulled out a rifle.

Tristan saw the arm and rifle silhouetted against the dark sky. He ducked as a bullet whistled overhead and another, and then he felt a sharp pain in his shoulder. His mind swam as everything around him grew hazy and the impact of the bullet felled him to the snow. "Johanna," he whispered. "I have to save her."

He concentrated on staying awake, to keep his consciousness. After a while the dizziness passed and he stumbled up, grasping his shoulder. He felt hot blood seep through his cold fingers. For just a moment he saw Paul silhouetted against the dark snow. He was carrying the rifle and seemed to be headed straight for him. The man slid and fell, the rifle slipping from his hands and sliding down the slope. A loud groan reached Tristan's ears. He watched Paul scramble up, hesitate for a moment, then limp to the side. He disappeared into the forest. Tristan continued his climb. When he reached the top, he looked around carefully, but saw no sign of Paul up on the edge of the slope. He breathed fast, his lungs smarting as he hastened to the edge. Just beside it stood a big white sign with large red letters painted on it. VERBOTEN! ACHTUNG! GEFÄHRLICH! Beneath it, DANGER! SLOPE CLOSED DUE TO AVALANCHE! He peered over the edge and not too far down saw Johanna lying like a crumpled doll against a tree trunk, her leg twisted in an awkward angle.

It was a steep slope and difficult to descend. He had no idea why Johanna had agreed to this crazy venture, unless the wine had dulled her mind so much that she was powerless to resist. "Damn, if only I'd told her right away," he muttered as he carefully slid down the slope, grabbing branches to steady his descend. "Dick was wrong. He doesn't wait a year to kill his wives. At least not this one!"

When he reached her, his fingers pushed aside the heavy collar of her sweater and felt for a pulse. "She's alive—thank God—I have to get help," he said softly. "Johanna, can you hear me? Johanna..." his breath came out in puffs of mist, his heart hammered against his aching ribs. Her leg was twisted awkwardly and appeared to be broken. Carefully, he straightened her head, afraid to move her, knowing from his first-aid course that one shouldn't move an injured person. But he couldn't leave here there to go for help, and if they both stayed on the slope, they'd freeze to death before dawn. His mind worked frantically trying to recall his first-aid training. A brace—but how? Something stiff, but something he could bend—he picked up a branch but knew it was useless. Then he remembered the magazine he had stuffed into his inside pocket. Quickly he retrieved it and folded it double, then carefully bent it around her neck. With effort he lifted his bad arm and held the brace in place while he undid his belt and yanked it out of the loops. He wound the belt around the magazine and fastened it. It was a makeshift brace, but it would have to do. Mentally he chastened himself for having moved her head at all, but it was too late now.

"Johanna? Honey, I need your help desperately. Please wake up..."But she didn't answer. Her eyelids remained closed. "I can't leave her here while I get help. She'll die. If only I'd brought my cellular," he chided himself aloud, looking around wildly as if expecting help to appear from the darkness of the forest. Measuring the distance to the top, he carefully gathered her in his good arm and awkwardly lay her over his good shoulder and started to climb, being careful to find support from tree trunks and rocks. His shoulder smarted, his shirt felt wet, soaked with his blood. He could feel it running down to his waist. If he didn't get help soon, they would both die.

Once on top, he held her with his good arm and slowly started the descend to the road. It was difficult not to slide and fall so he sat and slid most of the way. When he neared the bottom, he spotted Paul's car.

He frowned. Why hadn't Paul taken the car? Where was he? Now that his plans were foiled, the man was more than dangerous.

I hope he's fallen and broken his damned neck, he thought, shocked at his own evil thoughts. Where to take her? Hertzenberg had no hospital. The village was too small. He'd have to take her to Zurich.

As he reached the car he looked around wildly for any sign of Paul, but all was quiet. He tried the door and found it unlocked. He lay her carefully on the backseat and took off his jacket to cover her.

He wasn't so lucky to find keys in the ignition. After turning on the interior light, with numbed fingers he searched for the wires beneath the dashboard. Within seconds the engine roared to life and he turned the heater on full blast and glanced at the dashboard to check the fuel level. It had a full tank. He was in luck. Before driving off, he leaned back to check Johanna to make sure she was comfortable and still breathing. Adjusting her head so it wouldn't hit the sides as he drove, his fingers came away sticky. She'd hit her head rendering her unconscious. He just prayed she didn't have a skull fracture, that it was only concussion, her unconsciousness brought on by her state of mind and her illness. The only option he had was to drive to Zurich, at least a two-hour drive under normal conditions. He hoped the autobahn was cleared and salted.

He was lucky, the autobahn was clear. Obviously it had not snowed yet in the lower elevations. He pushed the gas pedal to the floor and drove as fast as the car allowed, breaking all the speed limits. Dizziness overwhelmed him several times but he didn't dare slow down. He shook his head to ward off the fog in his brain, and prayed they would arrive in Zurich safely.

He sighed with relief when he spotted the turn-off sign into Zurich. Just like back home, there were signs with a big H and arrows so the hospital was easy to find.

The emergency at Zurich University Hospital was busy, but when Tristan carried Johanna in, nurses rushed toward him, one pushing a stretcher. No sooner had he laid her down on the stretcher, or he collapsed himself, shock finally taking its toll.

CHAPTER EIGHTEEN

SIR, ARE YOU AWAKE?" A FEMALE VOICE SOUNDED CLOSE TO HIS EAR. Tristan struggled to open his eyes and felt disoriented for a moment. "Where am I?" he asked the nurse standing next to him. "What happened?"

"You very lucky. Bullet not stay in body. Only flesh wound und shock. Police want talk with you."

"Bullet?" he tried to sit up and winced and then he remembered. "Johanna? Is she okay?"

"Girl very hurt. You must talk police first."

"Damn the police. I want to see her," but then he realized he had to tell the police about Paul. "Okay," he said reluctantly. "Where are they?"

"Waiting outside door."

He sat up ignoring the spinning sensation in his head. IV tubes were attached to his arm.

A tall policeman entered followed by a plain clothed man, possibly a detective. "I hope you speak English," Tristan said.

"Yes, I do, said the plain clothed man. My name is Detective Bernard Goelitz. We would like to ask you some questions."

"Fire away."

"What is your name?"

"Tristan MacDonald. I'm a reporter and a friend of the girl I brought here."

"Where do you live?"

"In Canada. We both do."

"Who shot you?"

"The girl's husband, Paul Blake. He is a wanted criminal in the United States. I came here to warn Ms Von Hertzenberg about the man."

"And you had no time to warn her?"

"No. I thought I had plenty of time because he didn't kill his other victims quite this soon. He tried to kill her and I was too late to stop it. He pushed her from a ski slope that had a danger sign on it. She fell and hit her head on something. Then he came after me and shot me. He disappeared after that and abandoned his car. I hotwired the car and drove to this hospital."

"It is a miracle you drove all this way without passing out. You were in shock and though the wound was superficial, it was a deep cut and must have been quite painful."

"Your English is very good, detective."

"I lived in America for a few years. I will translate for the officer so he can take notes. So Paul Blake is still at large then?"

"Yes. That's all I can tell you for now. I want to go and see Ms Von Hertzenberg. Is she conscious?"

"You will have to talk with the doctor about her. Her family must be informed. Do you have a phone number?"

"Not with me. It's in my bag at the hotel in Hertzenberg."

"We will contact the United States authorities about this man Paul Blake."

"They won't find anything under that name. Try Roger Fitzgerald. That's his real name. He uses different names and disguises. So far he has killed four wives. At least—four that they know of."

"Why didn't you stop Ms Von Hertzenberg from coming to Switzerland with this man? If you are her friend..."

"She just married him, December twenty-fourth. I found out the next day. I didn't trust the man for some reason and after taking pictures at the wedding I asked a detective friend of mine to run the man's picture through the computer. I got on the first available plane."

"I see. The man cannot have gone far. The weather is bad."

"Maybe he took Johanna's car. Who knows?"

"We will go to the castle and search for him. With your permission, we will also fetch your luggage from the hotel. We need to speak with her family, or—perhaps you would prefer to do it?"

The idea of calling her parents didn't appeal to Tristan, but he knew it was his duty. "Yes, I will. Now can I go and see her?"

"I will send her doctor to see you."

They left the room and Tristan waited impatiently. Finally, an older doctor entered.

"Mr. MacDonald?"

"Yes. Are you Johanna's doctor?"

"Yes. You are a close friend?"

"I am. How is she?"

"She is in a deep coma. Her leg is broken, but that is not too much worry about. Her head injury is of more concern. She suffered a heavy concussion and lacerations to the head and some broken ribs. During surgery to set the leg, her heart stopped. We administered cardiac massage and restored a spontaneous effective heartbeat, but could not effect spontaneous respiration. We had to intubate the trachea and pass a large cuffed endotracheal tube and attach the airway to an oxygen-powered mechanical breathing device. We're continuously monitoring her cardiac activity. What caused her to go into cardiac arrest is a mystery, as is the failure of her CNS functions, we don't know. We've done an ECG and can't find anything wrong with her heart."

Deep concern laced Tristan's voice. "She will come out of the coma, won't she?"

"We hope so. A coma can last from days to weeks, depending on the patient's emotional state at the time of the accident, but I must warn you, the EEG showed very little brain activity."

Tristan swallowed hard, his heart a lump of fear for the woman he loved speeding up his heart rate. "How long do I have to stay hooked up to these things? I want to be with her."

The doctor glanced at the bags of antibiotics and blood, which were almost empty. "We can release you very soon. You are a strong man."

"How long was I unconscious?"

"You came in late last evening. It is now the next afternoon. Fortunately the bullet just caused a superficial flesh wound. We did some repair but you are fine. Now I must return to my patients. Your friend is in room 403 on the next floor."

"Thank you."

He almost willed the fluids to go through the tubes faster, he was so impatient to go and be with Johanna. When the bags were completely empty, he buzzed the nurse. It took a few minutes before she walked in, but when she saw the empty bags, she quickly took the IV out of his arm and put a bandage over it.

Walking to the cupboard in the corner of the room, she took out a plastic bag and handed it to him with a smile. Obviously, she couldn't speak English.

The bag contained his clothes. "My wallet and watch?" he asked, pointing at his wrist.

She nodded and left the room. He dressed, wincing at the shooting pain through his left arm. His shirt was ruined but he had nothing else to wear so he put on his leather jacket and zipped it up, throwing the shirt in the garbage container.

The nurse returned and handed him an envelope. "Thank you," he said again and took out his wallet and watch. He noticed he'd not yet set it to Swiss time and quickly set it to the time of the clock on the wall.

Though he still felt a bit wobbly, he felt his strength returning and he almost ran out the room and into the corridor wildly looking for an elevator.

CHAPTER NINETEEN

"HALT!"

Tristan almost slid on the highly polished floor as he came to a stop in front of Johanna's room. "I'm Tristan MacDonald, Ms Von Hertzenberg's friend," he told the police officer guarding her door.

"Ah, okay." The policeman stepped aside to allow Tristan to enter the room.

She looked so pale. A white bandage was wound around her head, her hair still matted with some blood from her head wound, though the nurses had obviously tried to clean it up. She was on life support, tubes everywhere. Her face distorted from the large breathing tube inserted in her mouth and down her throat. The heart monitor beeped steadily. Softly he approached the bed and pulled the chair up. He sat down and took her hand in his. "Johanna, if you can hear me, I'm so sorry. I should have stopped you from going to the ski slope. What was wrong with me to allow that? I just didn't want to confront Paul right there and then, didn't think he'd try anything just yet. He didn't kill his other wives till a year later. What prompted him to act so fast with you?"

He paused for a moment swallowing hard. His heart ached to see the girl he'd fallen in love with, so sick, so still.

He remained by her bedside, holding her hand, talking to her softly and searching her face for any sign of life. When the detective came to see him late afternoon and gave him his luggage he almost resented the intrusion.

"Mr. MacDonald, you need to rest. Believe me, she's in good hands here. Why don't you find a hotel? You also need to call her family now that you have your personal belongings."

Tristan knew he was right but reluctant to leave Johanna. "Back home it's possible to stay with a patient. They put a cot in the room. Can that be done here?"

"I'm sorry. The hospital isn't set up for that. There is a hotel very close by. I assure you they will call the moment there is any change. You really need to call Canada. Or would you prefer me to do it?"

He didn't look forward to such a terrible task, but at least he could be kinder than the business like detective. "Okay, I'll go and do that. I'll freshen up, will try and rest for a while and then I'll come back. Any sign of Paul Blake?"

"We have combed the area all day and found nothing. The fresh snow that fell overnight didn't help matters. There were no tracks left by the time we got there. Ms Von Hertzenberg's car is still parked in front of the castle. My men are searching the ski slope area as well as the castle. Don't worry, he won't get far."

"Detective, don't go yet," Tristan said as the detective turned to leave. "I have the file on Paul Blake in my bag. If you don't mind, I'd like it back after you've photocopied all the paperwork."

The detective's face lit up. "That would be a big help. Would it be too much to hope for a picture?"

"There are several."

After the detective left, he stayed with Johanna a while longer, barely unable to tear himself away just in case she came out of the coma. But, it didn't happen.

WEARILY, HE WALKED INTO the hotel room, threw his bag down and sank onto the bed. He gazed at the phone for a while before finally picking up the horn and dialing the operator.

Johanna's father answered. "Tristan MacDonald? Ah, yes, the reporter. What can I do for you?"

"I'm calling from Switzerland." He paused for a moment and swallowed hard. "I'm afraid I have bad news for you."

"You're in Switzerland, too? Johanna? Is she okay?"

"I'm sorry. She had a bad skiing accident last night and is in a coma in the hospital here in Zurich."

"What the hell happened and what are you doing there? Johanna is an excellent skier."

"It's a long story. I think you and your wife should come as fast as possible. If the doctors want to take her off life support they need permission from her next of kin."

"I'll call the airport right away. Is her husband with her? If that bastard gives permission, I'll..."

"No. He's gone."

"Gone? What—how..."

"I'll tell you about all that after you arrive. Please come right away. Your daughter is in critical condition."

"How critical? Damn it, man, talk to me!"

Tristan hesitated. "During surgery Johanna's heart stopped. When they revived her, she wouldn't breathe on her own. They fear if they remove the life support, she won't breathe."

"Why for God's sake? What's wrong with her?"

"The doctors don't know except that she has a heavy concussion. She's in deep shock. Maybe the trauma of everything that happened..."

"But what happened? Dammit, tell me!"

"Paul tried to kill her." There was silence at the other end for a few moments while John digested this news. Then he spoke brusquely, a noticeable tremor in his voice.

"What's the name of the hospital?"

"Zurich University Hospital."

"Thank you for calling us. We will see you soon."

Tristan replaced the horn and lay on the bed. His eyes burned from lack of sleep but his mind was too restless, his heart filled with worry.

He hardly took time to have a bath, a shower impossible because of his shoulder. When he had on clean clothes, he felt a little better and rushed back to the hospital to sit with her, to pray and wait...

CHAPTER TWENTY

JOHN AND LESLIE HURRIED INTO THE ROOM, LESLIE THE FIRST TO reach the bed. "Oh my God, my baby—my little girl..." she sobbed and lifted Johanna's hand to her face. John stood behind her, his face drawn and pale.

Tristan woke with a start. He'd fought sleep all night, but finally his head sank to the bed and still holding her hand he'd drifted off. "Mr. and Mrs. Von Hertzenberg, you're here already. I'm so glad."

"We left soon as I got off the phone. The flight was filled, but they squeezed us in somehow because it was an emergency." His voice was filled with emotion, his eyes dark with worry as he gazed down at his only child. He placed an arm around Leslie's shaking shoulders. "Ssh, honey, everything will be all right."

"Look at her, John. She's so pale. How could this have happened?"

"I'm sure Tristan can enlighten us, you don't mind if I call you that? And please, call us John and Leslie. I'd like to talk to a doctor, too. Can they speak English?"

"Yes. Her doctor speaks very good English."

"Good." He stroked Johanna's arm, then walked around the bed and faced Tristan. "Now would you tell me what the hell happened here? Where's that useless piece of shit she married? You told me he's gone. What do you mean, gone?"

"Why don't you and I go to the cafeteria for a coffee, rather than talk about it here. They say that comatose people can hear everything that goes on around them. I don't want to jeopardize Johanna's recovery with this upsetting information."

"My wife needs to know, too," John said, his face grim.

"You can fill her in later. I don't really want Johanna to be alone."

John studied Tristan's face and his eyes and knew that this man really cared about his daughter. "You've fallen in love with her," he said softly as they left the room.

"And that I have. I fell for her hard, even before she got married."

"Then why didn't you do something about it?"

"I was too late. She was already engaged to Paul Blake and making wedding plans."

"Yes. And a rushed wedding it was. I was against it, so was her mother. She wouldn't listen to us."

The cafeteria was busy but they managed to find an empty table. Sipping his coffee, Tristan told John everything he discovered the night of Johanna's wedding, his decision to travel to Switzerland to warn Johanna and possibly bring her back and his love for her. "I'm sorry, John, I never got the chance to warn her. The guy doesn't kill his wives until after a year or so. Maybe my arrival sped up his plans. And I feel guilty as hell. I should have tried to stop Johanna from going skiing, even if I had to punch the bastard out."

"You put yourself in a tough position. You say the authorities in the States were contacted?"

"Yes, Dick said he would do that right away. What puzzles me is that the cops haven't found him. If the other car is still there he has to be in that area somewhere."

"Unless he had an accident himself. And I hope not. I want the bastard to suffer for what he did."

"Can you tell me what the doctor said? Did you speak with a doctor?"

"Yes. She has a heavy concussion, couple of broken ribs and a broken leg. During surgery to set the bone, her heart stopped and when they revived her, she wouldn't breathe on her own. The coma is probably partially induced by the trauma she experienced before the accident. She wasn't happy and knew she'd made a mistake. The doctor said she could stay in the coma for a few days, or it could take weeks. We need to keep talking to her so she feels secure even in her subconscious level.

You'll have to talk to the doctor to get all the medical details. I can't remember all those fancy words."

"Your interest in my daughter, how did it happen?"

Tristan waited for a moment before answering, his pain almost too great to talk about the deep love he felt for Johanna. But he owed her father an explanation. "I fell in love with her the moment we met, when I interviewed her about her inheritance. " He looked into the older man's eyes and sighed. "I knew deep down we were meant for each other. I'm such a fool. I should have fought for her, done something to stop her. When she comes out of this, if she'll have me, I want to marry her. She's free after all since Paul Blake was already married."

John reached across the table and grasped Tristan's restless hand. "Don't blame yourself. Johanna is a very impulsive and willful young woman. Once she's set on a course, nothing will budge her. Her whole life she's had to learn through trial and error. This was just a harder lesson than she needed, anyone would need."

"I'll say. Now that you and your wife are with her, I think I'll go and get some rest and then I'm going to the castle to help in the search. If I lay my hands on that monster..."

"Let the police handle it. You won't be much good to Johanna if you get hurt as well."

"I can take care of myself. I'll be fine."

"Mm, you two will make a good pair, just as stubborn and determined. Be careful."

But Tristan didn't need to go to the castle. As he and John left the cafeteria, they ran into the detective.

"Mr. MacDonald, can we have a few words?"

"Yes, of course. This is Johanna's father."

They shook hands and walked to a nearby waiting room. "Any further developments?" Tristan asked.

"We have reason to believe Paul Blake is dead. After you left the scene of the crime last night, there was another avalanche and we found scraps of clothing stained with fresh blood. They don't belong to Johanna's clothes or yours so we think he was overcome by the avalanche."

"It could be just another escape ruse. I don't believe it," Tristan said with a frown. "The guy's too smart."

"We would have found him by now if he were still alive. We've had helicopters searching the area all day, men on foot, and we haven't seen a sign of him. I think in spring or summer we'll probably find his body beneath that mountain of snow. It's impossible to dig for him now. The danger of more avalanches is too great."

"So you're giving up the search?"

"To a degree. His picture has been sent to all the airports in Europe. If you're right and he did manage to escape somehow, he'll be picked up when trying to leave the country."

"Unless he has another disguise and false identification," Tristan muttered.

"I'm sorry. We did our best. We combed the countryside and the castle."

John shook his head and growled, "I hope he's dead, because if he's not, I'll surely kill the bastard myself! Tristan, go and rest for a while. Give me the name of your hotel and tell me where it is and if there's any change, I'll get in touch with you right away."

BUT THERE WAS NO change. After three weeks of bedside vigilance by John, Leslie and Tristan, Johanna remained in the deep coma. Tests had shown very little brain activity. Everything hung in the balance now if she'd breathe on her own when they removed the tube. The three of them sat by her bed talking to her, watching for a flicker of her eyelids, a movement of her fingers, but there was none. They took turns resting, promising to alert if there was any change.

Tristan stood up, stretched and walked to the window to gaze out at the snowy landscape. Hope was slowly fading for her. He knew that today the doctor would ask her parents to make the decision to take her off life support. His chest ached, his heart resembling a heavy stone. He'd lose her before he ever had the chance to tell her how much he loved her and to make her his wife. So much he wanted to make her happy, to erase this blemish on her young life.

A discreet cough sounded behind him and he swung to face the doctor. Leslie turned pale and leaned heavily on John whose face remained a mask.

"I'm sorry I have to ask you this, but have you made your decision?"

John's voice was rough as he answered. "The last thing my daughter would have wanted is to be kept alive as a vegetable. We've discussed such situations in the past. Yes, it's time to remove the life support and let her rest in peace."

Tristan clamped his lips together. He wanted to scream out to not allow it, to keep her for just a little while longer, but he had no rights. He listened to Leslie's soft sobs. Glancing at John, he saw a tear trickle down the man's lined face as he gazed at his daughter.

A nurse came into the room and the doctor instructed her in German. It only took seconds to remove the endotracheal tube and turn off the ventilator. The only machine that was left on was the heart monitor. The steady beat of her heart was the only sound in the room as they waited. John held one hand, Leslie the other. Tristan had no choice but stand at the foot end of the bed and stroke her good leg.

But to the doctor's amazement, Johanna's lips opened. She inhaled and inhaled again, her breath sounding like small gasps. Shortly after, her eyelids opened.

"John, she's awake—she's breathing," Leslie cried out in between sobs. "Johanna, can you hear me? Missy, it's Mom. Johanna..."

She didn't stir, her eyes gazing sightlessly at the ceiling.

The doctor asked them to step aside while he quickly shone a light into her eyes. Her pupils didn't dilate or contract and her eyes remained fixed. "I don't understand. She is out of the coma but there is no reaction. We will have to run some tests as soon as we know she's stable," he said. "Perhaps she will be alert later."

AFTER ANOTHER WEEK AND more tests, the diagnosis was that Johanna had become catatonic. Her brain showed a little more activity than before, but there was nothing further they could do for her. John consulted with the doctor and the specialists and asked if she could be transported back to Canada and they agreed, so he made the arrangements.

It was a somber group that traveled back to their homeland.

Little did they know that she could hear, see everything that was right in front of her. Her brain just wouldn't command her body, her speech. She felt helpless, caged and frustrated.

CHAPTER TWENTY-ONE

THE NURSE COMING IN TO CHECK ON HER STARTLED HER OUT OF her thoughts, the memories of what had brought her to this state. She almost resented the intrusion, the constant pulling at her body, telling her to go to the bathroom when she didn't need to, making her eat when she didn't want to.

Tristan, where are you? Why did you leave so soon? You said you had a lead. What lead? You're still convinced that Paul is alive, but I don't want you to get hurt. Tristan, I wish you'd come back...

The nurse finished pulling up her panties and led her back to the chair. After she left the room, Johanna wanted to sink back into thought. The journeys of her mind were her only escape, that's where she led her life now by concentrating on memories. The door opened and closed interrupting her thoughts, but when her father's face appeared before hers and he kissed her on the forehead she didn't mind the intrusion and she knew it was dinnertime.

"Johanna, your dinner looks delicious. Mom brought you some of her homemade soup," John said as he slowly fed her.

I can hear you, Dad—if only you knew how tired I am of soup and the other slop they give me...

"Sweetie, I bought you a new dressing gown. I'm sure you'll love it," her mother spoke behind her.

Move in front of me, Mom, so I can see you—tell me where Tristan is—talk to me...

TRISTAN DROVE HOME AS fast as traffic would allow. Impatiently he waited for the traffic lights to change, his mind busy with the information he'd spotted on the Internet. The lights at the main intersection took forever to change. He drummed his fingers on the steering wheel almost willing the traffic to move. He cursed softly when the lights turned red again and he didn't get through. Langley had changed so much over the last years. When he first lived there it was a small quiet community. Now it was a city. He hated the changes and often thought back to the past when farms graced the land where there were now malls.

The lights changed to green and he quickly shot through the intersection and drove South to his street. Ten years ago, when his father was transferred to Ontario and his parents moved there, he'd rented a one-bedroom apartment in Happy Lodge. It wasn't a fancy apartment, but it was home, cheap and convenient for work.

After he parked his car in the underground parking he dashed to the elevator and stabbed impatiently at the button. It took too long so he decided to take the stairs and ascended them three at a time.

Ignoring his beeping answering machine, he threw his jacket and briefcase on the couch. He dove to the floor to search through the information he'd printed out from the Internet relating to catatonic conditions. The pile of papers did not contain what he wanted. Yet somewhere in his mind he recalled that he'd read something about zombies during his search on the net of the last few months.

Quickly, he turned the computer on and brought up Explorer. He typed catatonic in the search box, once again it bringing up thousands of websites. He'd already printed out all the files relating to Johanna's condition.

Impatiently he ran through the long lists reading each title, until finally, there it was! 'Medicine Returns the Zombie Stare.' He thought it irrelevant to Johanna's condition so he'd always passed it by.

He clicked on the URL. The website took an infinite time to load, though he noticed that the digital clock on the bottom of the screen had advanced by no more than half a minute. Eagerly he started to read.

Some of it didn't make sense. According to the article, zombies were recognized in Haiti. Voodoo sorcerers, called bokos, would secretly poison or curse and individual. After burial the boko would steal the body from the tomb and return it to a catatonic form of life.

But Johanna had not died and there was no diagnosis of apparent but temporary death caused by a poison. The next paragraph prompted Tristan to print the article quickly. He snatched the papers form the printer and eagerly read the article again. He tossed the first few sheets over his shoulders. They landed silently among the mess on the floor, a silent monument attesting to his research into Johanna's condition. He concentrated on the last page, that one paragraph that had caught his attention.

Datura stramonium, an extract of the thorn apple is used to awaken victims. Its possible repeated administration could produce a state of psychological passivity...

Rubbing the day's growth on his chin, he thought, is it possible? Could Paul Blake have gotten hold of such a drug to turn Johanna into the zombie state she was in now? Was the man ever in Haiti? The author wrote in the last paragraph that many details of the mysteries of voodoo remained unexplained.

He had to go and see Dick and find out more about Roger Fitzgerald, how his former wives died. He'd also run a check to see if Paul Blake traveled anywhere before his marriage to Johanna.

The phone rang again. He let the answering machine catch the call. Dick's voice sounded through the apartment. "Trist, I've got some news. Call me back."

Quickly he grabbed the phone and shut off the answering machine. "What's the news?"

"Dammit, Trist, answer your phone for a change instead of letting me talk to that stupid machine. Where have you been? I've left several messages."

"I haven't listened to them yet. So what is this important news?"

"They've spotted a guy resembling Paul Blake in England. He's got red hair and a beard. They caught him trying to sell some very old silverware. Probably stolen from the castle."

"I thought he was dead."

"They never did find a body, and remember, you were suspicious about those scraps of clothing."

"Yes, but they had all airports covered. How the hell did he get through? And where's he been hiding all this time?"

"Who knows. The FBI called me and they've been in touch with Interpol. They're on their way to England."

"Thanks a million, friend! I'll talk to you later," Tristan almost shouted into the mouthpiece and slammed the phone down.

Within seconds it rang again and Dick's voice boomed through the apartment. "Trist, don't do anything stupid. Let the FBI and Interpol handle it. Dammit—Tristan, I know you're there. Answer the damn phone..."

"Sorry, Dick. I have to do this." He shut off the answering machine, picked up the phone and called the paper. "I'm on a hot lead. I'll be out of town for a while," he told them.

While he packed his bag the phone rang constantly. Finally, it stopped for a while. He erased the messages and turned the answering machine back on. After a final glance through the apartment, he locked the door and headed for the elevator. As he was waiting, he heard his phone ring and Dick's loud voice echoing into the hallway. "Dick, sorry. I'm onto something I can't share just yet. You'd declare me nuts if I told you. And I mean to catch that bastard!" he stepped into the elevator and pushed the button for the garage. He'd go to London first, though he'd have to be on standby. He didn't allow himself the time to book a seat. After London, he'd go to Haiti. It was a slim hope he'd find Paul Blake so he could beat the truth out of him. But he had to try.

BEFORE HE DROVE TO THE airport, he stopped at the extended care home to visit Johanna. The nurse had already prepared her for the night. She lay propped up against pillows, her eyes gazing at the wall opposite. She looked so pretty in her frilly nightie, her neatly braided hair hanging in two long braids over her shoulders, almost like a little girl.

He gathered her into his arms. "Sweetheart, I told you about the lead. It's an avenue we haven't thought of before but I'm going to investigate it so I'll be away for a little while. Dick also called me and told me that Paul was spotted in England. I'm going after him. I hope to catch the prick and beat the truth out of him, what he did to you to put you in this state. I'll be back soon, honey, hopefully with a cure for you." He kissed her on the lips and murmured softly against them, "I love you."

Was it his imagination or did he feel a slight tremor go through her body? He gazed into her eyes but they stared back at him without recognition. "I love you so much, sweet girl. I'll be back soon, I promise."

When he finally broke away from her his sleeve caught on the brooch pinned to her nightie. From it dangled a very old locket, given to her by her grandmother just before she died, Leslie told him.

He knew how much she treasured the brooch. She'd worn it the day of the accident. So he'd brought it to the hospital and asked the nurses to pin it on everything she wore, night and day, hoping it would help restore her, trigger something. But it had not woken her out of her trance.

Carefully, he unhooked the loop that had caught the little gold, sapphire studded bow from which the locket dangled. He lifted her hand and placed it over the brooch. "Honey, I have to leave now. I'll see you soon," one last kiss and he left the room.

Oh my God, he's going after Paul, she thought, fear for him putting knots in her stomach. I don't want him to go. I want him to stay here with me—Paul is dangerous...

CHAPTER TWENTY-TWO

TRISTAN WAS SURPRISED THAT HE DIDN'T HAVE TO GO ON STANDBY in peak holiday season, that the plane was only three quarters full and he even had a window seat. Once they were airborne, he thought about his impulsive decision to go after Paul in England and called himself a fool. London was a large city and what could he do? He wasn't even an investigative reporter. It was too late. He was on his way to England and nothing he could do about it. Dick was right. The FBI wouldn't appreciate his interference. He frowned and thought about his hunch that Paul could have visited Haiti and decided once he got to London, he'd fly straight to Haiti from there. Best to let the police handle the rest of the investigation. His main interest was to find a cure for Johanna.

"SIR, I'M AFRAID I have to take your breakfast tray. We'll be landing at Heathrow airport shortly," the stewardess said loudly.

Tristan startled awake. "Huh? What time is it? We're there already?" He'd fallen asleep to the steady humming of the engines and slept so soundly that he hadn't even heard the stewardess serve breakfast.

"I tried to wake you," she said apologetically.

"That's okay. I'm not hungry right now," he reassured her.

Disembarking was painfully slow, his luggage arriving on the turnstile even slower. Once he'd grabbed his duffel bag, he searched for a phone. The airport was bustling with activity, people arriving, happy reunions, tourists wandering around lost. He kept bumping into people in his haste. Finally, he found a payphone. But of course he had no

English currency so he reversed the charges to his home phone number. He cursed at having forgotten his calling card. He'd used it the night before and left it on the coffee table. Dick wasn't at the station, so he tried his home. His wife said he was asleep, but Tristan told her to wake him up. "It's important," he said.

"He's not going to like it."

A groggy Dick answered the phone. "Tristan, what the hell are you doing waking me up? I've worked ten nights straight."

"Any more news about Paul Blake alias Roger Fitzgerald?"

"No. The FBI and Interpol have a net over all of Europe but he's disappeared. Probably disguised himself and has new fake ID. You know he's been on America's Most Wanted? That didn't bring in any clues, just false leads."

"Great. So he's probably not even in London anymore."

"Where are you calling from? You sound awfully far away."

"I am. I'll call you later. Go back to sleep."

"Trist, if you're in London..."

But Tristan hung up the phone. "That was a waste of money," he muttered. "What the hell am I doing here? Never mind Johanna being so impulsive, I'm just as bad."

"I beg your pardon?" an elderly lady said while trying to access the phone.

"I'm sorry. Just talking to myself," he said, sending her a grin while moving aside.

For a while he roamed the airport wondering what to do and cursing himself for the stupid move he'd made until he made up his mind to fly to Haiti and do some investigation into the zombie process. He searched for Haiti flights and saw there was one that afternoon. After purchasing a ticket, he decided to hang out at the airport and get his thoughts together. His impulsiveness had sent him on a wild goose chase. He had to act calmly and with wisdom if he was going to get anywhere. I should have at least tried to find out if the guy has even been to Haiti, he thought. But with so many aliases, he could have gone under any name. Well, I'll follow my hunch and see where it brings me.

CHAPTER TWENTY-THREE

THAT SAME AFTERNOON HE ARRIVED IN HAITI. IT WAS ONE PLACE he'd never been before. Just like in London the airport teemed with tourists. He left the airport and within seconds was surrounded by Haitians offering to guide him. Shaking his head he tried to get away from their shouting and shoving. A taxi pulled up and the driver got out. He grinned at Tristan from ear to ear, his teeth showing white against his black face.

"Taxi, sir?"

"If you can get this mob away from me, yes!" Tristan shouted, hoping the driver understood sufficient English to grasp the meaning.

The driver clad in a colorful unbuttoned shirt and baggy shorts shouted in Creole Haitian and the crowd fell back, some shaking their fist at the driver. He quickly grabbed Tristan's duffel bag and put it in the trunk then opened the back door of the taxi.

Tristan climbed into it, the sweltering heat already starting to affect him. He wasn't dressed for the tropics.

"Hotel?" the driver asked, turning around to look at Tristan.

Tristan studied the man for a moment. His black face was leathered as if spending a lot of time in the sun, his coal black eyes curious. A little cap sat backward on his head. "No, I want to see a voodoo priest or priestess. Someone who can tell me about zombies."

The smile disappeared and the driver threw him a strange look. "What white man want with voodoo and zombies? You come right time. We go festival of Ryej Mirak in Ville Bonheur. It very far," he said in with a thick accent.

Tristan wished the man would just drive and then do the talking. All this talk was wasting precious time. “I don’t care how far it is. I need to fine a cure for the woman I love. She is very sick and I think it might have to do with voodoo and the making of zombies. Can we go now?”

“What wrong with your woman?”

“She sits in her chair the whole day and doesn’t move, but if someone tells her to eat, she will eat, or go to the bathroom, and she will walk to the bathroom. She doesn’t talk.”

“Maybe someone poison her, put bad voodoo curse on woman.”

It bothered him to talk to a total stranger about Johanna, but he had no choice if he wanted the man to take him to a voodoo priest or priestess. “I’ve never believed in that sort of stuff, but I don’t know what else to do to make her better. This is just a blind guess because the doctors don’t understand what is wrong with her.”

“I take you to famous Mambo. She very good, better than Bokor, he black magic and sorcery.”

“Maybe you can tell me about voodoo and zombies?” Tristan asked, glad that the driver finally pulled away from the curb and drove away from the airport.

“Much powerful magic. Mambo will explain. I translator,” the driver said, obviously proud of his knowledge of the English language.

After they left the capital, Port-au-Prince, they followed a road dotted with potholes. Mapou trees nodded in silent witness as thousands of pilgrims made their way to Ville Bonheur. Many were on foot, some on bikes, others in cars that could only drive at a slow pace.

“Isn’t there another road to this place?” Tristan asked, annoyed at the slowness of his journey.

“No. One road go to Ville Bonheur.” He honked several times so that people would move out of the way to let them through.

Tristan sighed. “How many miles to this Ville?”

“Maybe sixty.”

“At this rate, it will take us hours to get there.”

“Road small. Many people go to sacred waterfalls. Your woman, she dead first?”

“No. She acted strangely, as if she was under hypnosis, and then a man tried to kill her. She was in a coma for a few weeks and when she woke up, she became like a zombie."

"If she no dead, she not zombie. Maybe poison, voodoo spell. Me think you waste trip."

"Pardon?"

"Maman, the priestess, she tell you bring woman."

"That's impossible."

"You want woman no more sick, you bring."

"Just take me to this Maman and we'll see if she can give me medicine to take home."

The driver shook his head and concentrated on the road.

Tristan gazed at the crowd snaking along the road. They were an odd assortment. A young man on a donkey, an old woman carrying a naked toddler, children, people from all over Haiti seeking to celebrate and worship. Poverty was evident in many of them.

"They are go to sacred falls, Saut d'Eau."

"Is that where we're going, too?"

"No. We find Maman. I hope she home."

"I hope so, too," Tristan murmured and closed his eyes, his thoughts dwelling on Johanna and the cure he hoped to find for her here.

The heat, monotonous humming of the car's motor lulled him to sleep. When the driver woke him, it seemed he'd only slept minutes but when he looked out the window, he knew he'd slept for a couple of hours. "We're here?"

"Yes, sir. I see if Maman home."

Tristan watched him walk to a small shack and disappear through an opening covered by a colorful curtain. He seemed to be gone a long time before he finally returned. "Maman see you now. You have American dollars?"

Shit, Tristan thought. I wonder if Canadian cash will do... "I have Canadian dollars. Same thing."

The driver looked dubious. "I ask Maman."

Again he was gone for quite a while before he came back and smiled. "Maman say yes."

"Good. Let's go and meet this Maman then."

Candles lit the interior of the hut. Their flames flickered uneasily when he entered sending creepy shadows over the walls. A stout woman sat Buddha style on the floor, surrounded by a few dozen candles. She had her hands flat against each other and raised as if in prayer. Her eyes were closed. Tristan cleared his throat to announce his presence and saw her eyelids flicker open. She regarded him with coal black eyes that seemed to look straight through his body. Her kindly round black face remained passive, not a muscle twitching.

He'd not heard the driver come in behind him. "You tell Maman."

"How do you do," he said awkwardly. "I am from Canada and I come to seek medicine to heal the woman I love."

The driver translated softly and waited for Tristan to explain Johanna's illness. When he was finished and the driver finished the last translation, the woman nodded. She said something in clipped tones sounding like an order.

The driver told him just what he'd told Tristan himself, that he needed to bring Johanna to Haiti.

"Can't she give me medicine for her?"

"No. Maman say woman possessed by evil spirit. She do ceremony."

Maman spoke again looking directly at Tristan.

"She say you much trouble, danger. You careful. You go now. Come back with woman."

Maman closed her eyes and started to chant. The atmosphere gave Tristan chills down his spine, his skin puckering. He felt the driver tug at his sleeve and reluctantly turned to leave. What had he accomplished but nothing? How could he bring Johanna here?

"You want tour?" the driver asked while holding open the door.

"No. Take me back to the airport. Your Maman can't help me. Isn't there anyone else?"

"She is best. You bring woman."

Exasperated, he got into the taxi. The drive back to the airport took just as long and he had no idea if there would be a flight back to Canada that night. As they drove over the potholed road he thought about the possibility of bringing Johanna to Haiti and slowly a plan formed in his mind. Every afternoon, weather permitting, someone took her for a walk outside depending on who was with her at the time. If he stayed with her after lunch, took her for her walk, then maybe...

CHAPTER TWENTY-FOUR

JOHANNA FELT HAPPY THAT TRISTAN RETURNED SO SOON. SHE FELT so safe when he was there with her. His soft voice was like a caress as he talked to her, his touch soothing as balm.

"I didn't find Paul, Johanna. Matter of fact, I gave up when I got to London. I thought it better to leave it to the FBI. But I have a plan for you, to make you better. Soon as you finish your lunch you and I are going for a walk."

Make me better? How?

"I can't call your parents and tell them. They would never allow it and sign the discharge forms," he whispered close to her cheek. "They're such devout Christians, they'd be horrified if I mentioned voodoo."

I don't care, Tristan. I allow it. Anything to get me out of this prison...

"You see, I think Paul gave you something before you went skiing. At first I thought he tried to turn you into a zombie, but for that you have to die first and you didn't die. I went to Haiti and saw a priestess, but she can't do anything for you unless you're there. She thinks there's a spell on you, that you're possessed by an evil spirit, perhaps poisoned."

I know now that Paul put something in my wine. That's why I felt so sick, so strange...

"So, how about it, my love? Are you game?"

He gazed into her eyes trying to find an answer but there was nothing. Yet somehow he sensed that she wanted him to do this. "Okay, last little bit," he said tenderly while feeding her the last of her pudding. "And then we'll wait until the nurse comes to take you to the bathroom. After that I'll take you for your walk, but instead, I'll take you to the car. By the time they realize you're gone we'll be well on our way to Haiti. They've got phones on the plane, I'll call your parents once we're on our way."

She felt impatient, willing him, urging him to hurry, but she knew he had to be careful.

The nurse came in. "All finished?"

"Yes, she ate all of it."

"She always does," she said while taking away the tray. "Come, Johanna, let's go to the bathroom."

It always felt so strange. When urged, led, her legs moved. Yet when she tried to move them herself, they wouldn't.

Tristan stood up and walked to the window. It was a glorious day, the sky a vivid blue, birds singing in the trees. The grounds of the care home alive with vibrant color, the flowerbeds beautifully tended by gardeners. The door clicked behind him and he heard the shuffling of Johanna's slippers.

"She's all done. We'll take you for a walk later, Johanna."

"I'll take her for a walk this time. I took the afternoon off work," he lied.

Work, he thought. If I don't call the paper, I won't have a job anymore...

The nurse nodded. "Okay, we're really busy so that would help us out." She put on Johanna's slippers. "Do you think she needs a sweater?"

"No, it's quite warm. The wind has settled."

The nurse left. No sooner had the door closed behind her or Tristan quickly opened the drawers of her night table, pulled out some clothes and stuffed them behind her. He wheeled Johanna out of the room and into the corridor. He held in his stride and pretended to stroll once he got outside the doors. Inwardly, he wanted to run. Glancing over the grounds he saw there were very few people outside. Most of them were in their rooms and getting ready for an afternoon nap. Johanna was one of the youngest patients in the home.

Instead of helping her out of the wheelchair and walking with her, he left her in it and casually strolled to the parking lot and opened the passenger door. He quickly looked around to make sure no one was near and watching. Scooping her into his arms he set her on the seat and fastened the seat belt around her. He parked the wheelchair near some bushes, gathered her clothes, hurried back to the car and threw her possessions into the back prayed no one that knew Johanna would see them.

His fingers shook as he unlocked his door and got into the driver's seat and started the car. After he drove down the long driveway and drove through the gates, he held his breath. As he turned onto the street, a sigh escaped his lips that came from the depths of his soul. He sped up, being careful not to exceed the speed limit and headed for the freeway. "Sweetheart, we're on our way," he said with a nervous smile and gave her knee a loving pat.

Soon as he'd arrived in Vancouver that morning, he'd bought two return tickets for the afternoon flight to Haiti hoping his plan would succeed. And so far, it had. Oh, God, don't let anyone visit early this afternoon to set off the alarm and alert the police, he thought. I'll have to phone her parents before dinnertime. They'll freak if they find out she's missing. I can't do that to them. But what if they have the police meet the plane in Haiti? I hope they'll listen to me...

CHAPTER TWENTY-FIVE

"JOHN? THIS IS TRISTAN."

"Where the hell are you? Johanna is missing. The last time someone saw her was with you. You took her for a walk outside. Did you take her back to her room? If Paul Blake..."

"She's with me, John."

"What?"

"I felt she needed to get out of that home for a while, to have a change of scenery. Maybe that will help to revive her. So, I took her for a long drive and I've booked a hotel room for her and one for me. We're not that far away," he lied. He came up with the story while they were waiting to board the plane.

"Why the hell didn't you discuss this with us first? What's that strange noise in the background?"

"It's the air-conditioner. I was afraid you wouldn't give your permission. I'll try anything to bring her out of this catatonic state."

John's tone softened. "I'm sorry. I shouldn't have yelled at you. Hearing that Johanna was missing was quite a shock. You know, you could be right. It's something we never thought of doing. We should have brought her home on Sundays so she could be in an environment she knew. We discussed keeping her at home, but thought it better she was in professional care. Little good that has done. I'm going to talk with Leslie. I think we should bring her home after all and hire a private nurse."

"Good idea," Tristan said, grinning at Johanna who sat quietly beside him staring at the back of the seat in front of her. "I'll keep her on this little holiday for a day or two and then I'll bring her back."

"How can you take care of her?"

"I hired a nurse," he lied.

"Oh, good idea. Give me a call tomorrow morning how things are going and if there's any sign of improvement?"

"I will. Say hello to Leslie and tell her not to worry. I love Johanna more than life itself and will do anything and everything to protect her and make sure she's safe."

"Thanks, Tristan. You're a good man. Bye for now."

Tristan put the phone down, smiled and continued to feed Johanna the mashed potatoes served with dinner and held the cup of milk to her lips. He took her to the bathroom once, closing his eyes as he pulled her panties down and helped her sit on the toilet. It was after an invasion of her privacy, one she normally wouldn't appreciate.

I wish you could always look after me like this—your hands on my body are so gentle, the touch of your fingers filled with love—oh Tristan, I hope this woman can cure me...

THEY ARRIVED IN HAITI right on time and the taxi driver was waiting as Tristan had instructed him. At the airport, he'd sat Johanna down on a chair while he exchanged Canadian dollars for American He felt in his pocket to make sure the American money was secure and safe. He handed the driver a one hundred dollar bill. "You'll get the rest when we come back," he said.

"This your woman?"

"Yes." Tristan glanced at Johanna who walked slowly beside him. He held her arm tightly, afraid she'd fall, watching for anything that could trip her. Some people looked at them strangely when he lifted her in his arms and set her on the back seat, but he didn't care. He climbed in beside her. She sat stiff, unmoving, resembling a mannequin, but nevertheless, it felt good to have her next to him.

The taxi took off and before long they had left the bustling city for the country and the same road. The driver glanced at him in his rearview mirror.

"She beautiful."

"Yes, that she is," Tristan pushed a lock of hair away from her forehead. He placed an arm around her shoulders and pulled her to lean against him, and cupping her head, pushed it onto his shoulder. To anyone glancing at the passengers in the taxi, they looked like a normal tourist couple.

The road was just as busy as before, if not busier. Dozens of people were trooping to Ville Bonheur. Tristan closed his eyes, happy to feel the warmth of her body.

Oh Tristan, if only this were our honeymoon, she thought. I see all this wondrous scenery, the people—when I'm well this is where I want us to go...

It was stop and start all the way. Tristan thought they'd never get to Maman's hut. Under normal conditions he would have enjoyed this experience, listening to the song of the people, their melodious chanting, the lush vegetation, the beauty of the land.

"We here, Maman's hounfo," the driver said. "Maman know you come."

Tristan didn't ask how the woman knew. He presumed by the driver's pointing, a hounfo was her hut. This was a mysterious land filled with folklore, legends and mystic practices.

After he got out of the taxi he carefully scooped Johanna into his arms and carried her to the hut. The driver followed close behind them as they entered. As before Maman sat in Buddha position on the dirt floor, surrounded by dozens of candles. She was not alone. Tristan looked at the driver. "Who is that?"

"He is Houngan. He help Maman perform sacred ceremony."

When his eyes became accustomed to the dim interior, Tristan noticed a pentagram marked into the dirt on the ground with strange symbols. Maman spoke in quick syllables to the driver who turned to Tristan.

"You give money to Maman so she can pay serviteurs for goat."

"Goat?"

"You do as Maman say. Put woman on ground."

He took the money out of his pocket and handed it to the driver who in turn handed it to the priestess. She nodded and spoke to the man.

"Maman say take clothes off woman."

"Now wait a minute..."

"No clothes."

He felt like canceling the whole procedure right there and then, but then thought, I didn't make this trip for nothing. If she has to be naked, so be it.

Oh my God, he's exposing my body to those strangers, Johanna thought as she felt Tristan take off her long skirt, her top, her panties, until she lay naked.

He folded her clothes neatly and put them in the far corner of the hut and returned to stand just outside the pentagram.

They waited. Tristan didn't know for what, because no one spoke. When he tried to ask a question, the driver hushed him. Maman was humming softly and swaying back and forth. She seemed to be meditating. Next to her burned a small fire, above it hung a small, iron pot. Some liquid bubbled inside the pot, its steam spiraling up toward the ceiling. He presumed it to be incense because the air was thick with a heavy musky scent.

Tristan gazed down at Johanna as she lay in the center of the pentagram. She looked so helpless. For a moment he felt regret but quickly squashed it. This was a last desperate attempt to restore the girl he had fallen in love with. She looked so helpless, so innocent and vulnerable. Under normal circumstances he would have been turned on by her beautiful body, but the turmoil within him, the worry that gnawed at his heart and mind, left his libido dormant.

The bleating of a goat sounded behind him. He turned to look and saw several people entering, one of them leading a goat into the hut two others carrying small drums. From somewhere, Maman, who had come out of her trance, produced a live chicken and handed it to the Houngan who stood beside her. Maman carefully lay a circle of stones in front of her on the ground and put some twigs in its center, then she lit it and watched the twigs crackle and catch flame. Then she threw some powder on the flames and as they flared up into a greenish bluish color she gazed into them.

Nodding, she stood up and walked to the back wall of the hut that had a few shelves leaning on rough rocks and potions and powders in bottles and jars on the shelves. Her deft fingers grabbed jars, threw pinches of powders in a clay bowl and added drops of liquids to it. She mixed it and nodded to the Houngan.

Tristan watched in horror as the Houngan grasped the chicken by the legs and began swinging it around in a wide circle, the chicken squawking loudly, protesting at this cruel treatment. He kept swinging it until its neck cracked. He twisted it and wrenched it off the body. Blood spurted from the stump. He threw the head on the fire and held the chicken above Johanna and proceeded to paint her body with its blood. The fire increased in intensity sending smoke spiraling like gnarly fingers through the hut. It swirled and feathered, concentrating on Johanna, as if some unseen entity directed it toward her. The candles flickered, a strange warm breeze brushed Tristan's face, his arms.

Shuddering, he watched the ritual, listened to the chanting of both Maman and the Houngan, accompanied by the rhythm of eerie drums. It got louder and louder and wilder mixed with something in her hand that she shook wildly, rattling, until all of them danced around Johanna, the chicken still swinging from the man's hand. He glanced at the driver who said, "Is ason, Maman's magic rattle. Sssh..."

Suddenly, Maman held up her hand and they stopped dancing. She fetched the clay bowl, held it under the chicken's neck and squeezed blood from it into the bowl. Then she mixed it with the potion. Using a wooden spoon she ladled the liquid into Johanna's mouth.

Tristan felt sick and was glad Johanna didn't know what was happening.

But she did know and her stomach churned. She had no power to refuse, couldn't even spit out the vile tasting concoction. She had no choice but to let it slide down her throat. Even her choking reflexes didn't work.

Maman returned to her dancing accompanied by the Houngan and the serviteurs. They chanted, Maman's eyes rolling until only the whites showed. Then she pointed and the Houngan lurched for the goat. He produced a long knife with a broad blade from underneath his shirt and slit the goat's throat. Then he proceeded to hack it to pieces. The blood that poured from the animal's throat was caught in a bowl by Maman.

She stood and handed Tristan the bowl. They expected him to drink... Well, I subjected Johanna to this ritual, so I'd better drink the stuff, he thought, and took a swallow from the bowl. It tasted sickly warm and bitter sweet. He almost gagged but managed to control it. The bowl passed to the driver, then to the Houngan, to the man who had brought the goat and the serviteurs, Maman, and last of all she ladled the blood into Johanna's mouth. The bowl dropped to the floor and they continued their dance. Tristan stood rooted to the ground, hardly believing he'd subjected his beloved to this pagan ritual. He felt like grabbing her, running outside with her, but something held him back, kept him immobile as he watched the ritual continue.

Someone coughed. It was a woman's cough. He looked behind him to see who else had entered the hut, but there was no one. Maman's chanting turned to singing accompanied by the Houngan and the serviteurs, louder and louder. Tristan's gaze was pasted to their faces, their actions, wondering what they would do next.

Something touched his feet. Hardly daring to see what it was he carefully looked down to see Johanna's head turned, her eyes gazing into his, tears soaking her cheeks and mixing with the blood.

"Oh my God! Johanna, you're back! Are you really back? I'm not having a hallucination?"

She slowly moved and sat up, gazing around, lifting her arms, wiggling her toes and she started to laugh and cry. Her voice sounded hoarse, six months of not speaking having affected her voice box, but he knew that would heal. She got up on her feet and stood before them. Hesitantly she took a step, then another, still laughing and crying at the same time.

Tristan watched as she slowly started to dance with them, almost like an Indian dance. It was a dance of joy. Right now, she resembled something from a horror movie. Her naked body streaked with blood, her blond hair red and stringy, her face a mass of blood she resembled more a murder victim than his beautiful Johanna. She danced with Maman and the Houngan amidst the serviteurs and then grabbed Maman and hugged her, staining the white gown.

Maman beamed from ear to ear, her teeth gleaming white. It was the first time Tristan had seen her smile. Johanna stopped dancing and became quiet. She turned to him, took one step, then another and ran into his arms to sob quietly on his shoulder. "Thank you," she said in a raspy voice. "Thank you, my love."

Maman held up her hands to silence them all, spoke then and the driver translated.

"Maman drive evil spirit out your woman's body. She give potion to kill poison."

"How did she know there was poison in Johanna's body?"

"Maman talk with spirit. Spirit tell Maman."

"Oh." Tristan didn't question him or the procedure any further. It was enough that he had Johanna in his arms and that she was healed.

"Now you go Saut d'Eau. You wash in sacred waters."

Maman produced a white cotton shift that she gently draped over Johanna's head until it covered her body to the knees.

"Can you walk, Johanna?" Tristan asked.

"Oh, yes. Can I ever. Now that my legs will do what I want them to do, I want to walk, run, jump, swim—you name it!"

Next, Maman handed Johanna a small wooden bowl that contained some white liquid and pointed to Johanna's mouth.

"You drink. Look," the driver said and put his head back and made a gargling sound.

"I think she gave you a gargling concoction for your throat," Tristan said.

"Anything should taste better than that vile stuff she poured down my throat. But who cares, it healed me," she said croakily, with a smile, and took a mouthful of the liquid. Leaning her head back she gargled. It also tasted bitter, but she didn't care. She stopped gargling and holding the liquid in her mouth she looked at Maman questioningly.

"Is she supposed to swallow it?" Tristan asked.

The driver shook his head. "No, spit now."

Gratefully, Johanna spit the liquid into the empty bowl Maman handed her. When she spoke again and said, "thank you," her voice sounded almost normal. She had to repeat the procedure several times until her voice was back.

Then they left the hut, followed by Maman and her assistants, and barefooted walked through the village to a steep slope. They had to descend rough terrain to get to the falls. For moments, Tristan and Johanna were awed at the magnificence of God's creation. Encased in verdant greenery, the Tombe River plunged more than a hundred feet, producing three rainbow waterfalls. In the pool below were dozens of people already bathing, worshipping and chanting—their hands raised in prayer. Some were dressed, others were naked or half naked, not caring who saw them, exposing themselves before their gods, baring their souls.

Johanna felt the serenity invade her heart, her soul. Slowly, she kneeled and pulled Tristan down with her. She raised her face to the sky above and raised her hands and prayed silently, Thank you, God, for this wonder, this miracle. Thank You for this man, for Tristan, Thank You for this wonderful day, for my life...

Tristan too, prayed silently and thanked God for the miracle he had just witnessed. When Johanna stood up, the driver indicated they were expected to bathe in the pool below. After Tristan removed his running shoes and socks, took off his shorts and shirt, they descended the slope and fell into the water. It was icy, but they didn't care about the cold as they splashed and laughed prayed and sang. Johanna cried, but they were happy tears this time.

When they left the pool, they took one last look behind them as they walked back to Maman's hut. Once there, Johanna changed into her clothes and Tristan put on his clothes again that he'd grabbed after leaving the pool. She felt wonderfully clean, not only her body, but her soul felt cleansed, her spirit serene. "I don't know what to say to her," she told Tristan. "I'm so grateful."

"She know," the driver said from the door. "We go now. Airport?"

Tristan looked at Johanna who shook her head.

"I think I'd like to stay in Haiti a couple of days if it's okay with you."

"Yes, of course. Take us to the best hotel," he told the driver and put his arm around Johanna's waist.

"I guess you didn't bring my wallet, my toiletries," Johanna said.

"Typical woman. No, of course not. If you knew the way I had to get you out of the nursing home..."

"But I do know. I heard everything you said, always. I was trapped inside my body, nothing would obey me, my voice, my limbs..."

"My God, so when I talked to you, you understood every word?"

"Yes."

"Then you know I want to marry you, that Paul is a bigamist."

"Yes."

"Yes to Paul, or yes you'll marry me?"

She grinned. "Yes, I'll marry you. Soon as we've found the bastard who did this to me."

"They may never find him."

She just smiled and moved out of his arm to go to Maman. "Thank you so much." She reached up to kiss the smiling priestess on the cheek. "And you, too," she told the Houngan and shook his hand. "All of you," she shouted joyfully, "Thank you!"

Tristan joined her and taking the wad of American dollars out of his pocket, shoved them into Maman's hand. "I don't know what to say to express my gratitude," he said, his voice hoarse with emotion. All he could do was pump her hand while putting his other arm around Johanna.

The driver waited impatiently by the taxi. When they appeared, hand in hand, he opened the back door for them. They climbed into the taxi and sat, arms around each other, on the backseat. "You know, I suddenly feel exhausted," she said.

"I can imagine. This has been quite an emotional experience."

"If I fall asleep on the way to the hotel, will you mind?"

"No, as long as you'll let me wake you every now and then to make sure I'm not dreaming all this."

"Okay! Deal!" she sealed it with a lingering kiss. "Soon as we get to the hotel I need to call my parents. You told them we weren't far away from them and staying in a hotel. And I need to buy some things. If you can lend me the money I'll pay you back as soon as we're home."

"Women," Tristan sighed, "they can't think about anything else but shopping! And it's okay. I'll pay for whatever you need and want. No one will accuse me of marrying you for your castle."

But she didn't hear him. Her eyes were closed, her head resting quietly on his shoulder.

He looked down at her and rested his cheek on her damp hair. "How much I love you," he whispered. He too closed his eyes, now realizing how taxing this day had been.

CHAPTER TWENTY-SIX

"JOHN? CAN YOU GET LESLIE ON THE PHONE?" TRISTAN ASKED. "There's something I need to tell you both."

"Is Johanna okay?"

"Yes, she's fine." He heard John calling Leslie to the phone and waited until he heard the click of the extension. He handed the phone to Johanna.

"Mom—Dad..." Her voice broke for a moment. "Are—are you there?"

"Oh my God, John did you hear that?"

"Yes. I don't think it's funny."

"John, that's our girl. She's back."

"How's that possible? I spoke to Tristan hours ago and he was taking her to a hotel."

"Dad, it's me. Really. I'm here, talking to you."

"Johanna?"

"Yes, it's me. I'm better, Dad."

"How? What happened? Tristan..."

"Is the most wonderful man on Earth. We're going to stay here for a couple of days and then I'll be home."

"I want to see you *now*, make sure it's real."

"It's real. I'll call you again tomorrow."

"But how did all this happen? Where did Tristan take you?"

"Haiti."

"What?"

"Haiti and I'd like to stay here for a few days. This is where he found a cure for me."

"In Haiti of all places. But how? What kind of cure?"

"We'll tell you all about it when we return. I have to hang up now."

"Can't you talk a while longer, honey?" Leslie asked in a shaky voice.

"Mom, I promise I'll call tomorrow. Right now I want to enjoy a good soak in a tub and I'm starving. I need some real food, like the juiciest steak I can find or even a burger and fries if they have those here. After all that soup and pudding, I feel like I look like one. I have to go now. I love you both."

She hung up the phone and sent Tristan, who was standing by the sliding doors, a wide grin. "They wouldn't believe me at first."

"I bet. We'd better not keep them waiting too long."

"Just a couple of days. I really need this, Tristan. I need to think and I need to rest. I feel emotionally exhausted."

"I would think you'd be physically exhausted. You haven't really been normally mobile in months. What do you want to think about?"

"Our future," she told him, but it was a half lie. She also wanted to think about how she could find Paul and punish him for what he did to her. "And yes, I am a bit tired, but don't forget—every day I received intensive therapy. Mom and Dad hired a private therapist and that woman was relentless. I didn't mind. It broke the monotony of the endless hours. So, my body didn't waste away, contrary to many such patients. But now, first things first. A bath!"

"That makes two of us! Ladies first."

As the tub filled and she took off her skirt and T-shirt she wished for her toiletries. But, they were back home. All Tristan had stuffed in the bag was a hairbrush. She noticed some small bottles on the vanity. One of them was shampoo. Grimacing, she took off the lid and sniffed it. It was better than nothing. And at least he'd grabbed some underwear she noticed.

The water felt hot after the icy experience she just had at the falls, but once she relaxed, it felt heavenly—fact, it felt heavenly just to be able to move at will, to dunk her head, to swish her arms and legs through the water. After splashing a while, she lay back and relaxed and closed her eyes. At first her thoughts dwelled on the strange ceremony that healed her, but slowly they drifted to Paul and what he'd done to her and her gut feeling that he was still alive and probably up to his old tricks. Her father's hunting rifles ran through her thoughts, but she shook that idea aside. She'd been incarcerated in her body all these months—the man wasn't worth going to jail for and being trapped again. Voodoo—could she do to him what he'd done to her? She pondered about her resolution to catch Paul and before handing him over to the authorities to make him suffer, but she couldn't come up with a plan. Not yet.

"Are you okay?"

Tristan's voice startled her out of her thoughts. She sat up and called out, "Almost. I still need to wash my hair."

"Better hurry, or I'll join you!"

It was on the tip of her tongue to tell him to come in, but she didn't. Just the thought of him in the tub with her set the blood racing through her veins. While she washed her hair, wild thoughts raced through her mind of Tristan making love to her. They were soon replaced by another picture, a far away voice that told her to be still, of Paul having sex with her and she was unable to respond... Shaking her head at the thought she dunked and rinsed the suds off her hair. But it wouldn't leave her mind. Consciously, she couldn't remember them making love, but her mind kept sending her different pictures. They were unwelcome images. Nevertheless, she needed to remember, to know everything he did to her.

Annoyed at the memory of Paul overpowering her thoughts about Tristan she stepped out of the tub and wrapped a towel around her head and another around her body. Before leaving the bathroom she filled the tub for Tristan.

When she entered the room wrapped only in the towel, Tristan turned away from the window and grinned. "You look delectable enough to eat."

She nestled into his embrace and leaned her head against his broad chest. His heartbeat was loud and steady. It matched the beat of her own as it sped up. Gazing up at him, she saw the love shine from his eyes. She reached up and traced the outline of his lips, longing for them to claim hers, waiting...

"I think I'll take that bath first," he murmured, his voice husky.

"Why don't you do that while I brush the tangles out of my hair," she said, the magic moment broken now.

Reluctantly he released her and disappeared into the bathroom. She stood before the mirror and unwound the towel. As she brushed her hair, the other towel fell from her body. Gazing at herself in the mirror, she noticed she lost some weight. It didn't matter. Those few extra pounds needed to come off anyway.

She was about to pull the T-shirt over her head when Tristan emerged from the bathroom followed by a cloud of steam. "Now that's something I'd like to greet me every day after I have a shower," he said softly and with two big strides joined her scooped her into his arms and carried her to the bed.

He lay her down gently and gazed down at her. "I want you so much, my darling, but maybe it's too soon. You need to rest," he said, his voice laced with passion.

"I've rested for seven months," she murmured, devouring his lean body, his chest sprinkled with black curly hair, his strong thighs, slim hips and finally her gaze rested on his erection jutting out from a bed of dark curls. She reached up to touch it, running her fingers along the velvety shaft, finally to encase it and stroke it.

He groaned and fell onto the bed beside her. "You know what you're doing to me?" he asked against her moist lips.

"Yes, you're making me suffer," she whispered. "Make love to me, Tristan?"

His need was too great and he sensed hers. While his lips drank from the sweet nectar of her mouth, his hands wandered to her breasts, her nipples, then down to the silken softness of the folds between her legs. He felt her legs open wider, inviting his wandering fingers to explore further, to enter her hidden domain. A drum sounded in his ears, his heart beat a crescendo and his loins felt as if they were on fire as he explored, felt, entered her. Her hand crept down, reached for him and he knew unless he took her now he wouldn't be able to control his need for release. Still clinging to her lips, he rolled her onto her back. Automatically, his throbbing erection found entry. Pulling away from her lips for a moment, he took a deep breath, gazed down into her eyes, now a midnight blue. Her hands circled his neck, pulled his face down to her breasts. He took a nipple between his lips and sucked gently and slowly started to move within her.

Johanna arched her hips and wound her legs around his body to encase him, to pull him further into her. She met him stroke for stroke until she cried out in ecstasy as she felt the urgency to release.

Tristan couldn't hold back any longer. Driving into her harder and faster, his breathing heavy, he once more claimed her lips. A roaring tide thundered in his ears. Vaguely he heard her moan in response, felt her legs tighten even more around his body, her fingers dig into his back. Her body tensed beneath his as his lips claimed hers again and he explored the honey sweetness of her mouth. A great shudder ran through his body as the last of his release left it. He heard her groan in return and hoped he'd satisfied her.

She took his face between her hands and forced him away from her lips. Gazing deep into his eyes she murmured, "I love you more than life itself, my darling. It's never been like this before for me."

He kissed her tenderly on the nose, on her forehead and rested his head on the pillow next to her, their cheeks touching. "Or for me."

"Will it always be like this?"

"Yes, oh yes. We belong together, my sweet. I knew that from the moment we met."

Spent, they lay in each other's arms quietly just drinking from each other's presence and the great love they felt.

After a while, Tristan finally moved. He pushed her still wet hair back from her face and kissed the tip of her nose. "Sweet, how about we go find a place to eat?"

"Shopping first. I haven't a thing to wear. Tristan, I never knew it could be like this."

"Neither did I. I've been with other women and it wasn't the same."

"For me there was only one man before Paul, and that was some years ago. No, it wasn't the same. Paul didn't touch me before we married. Now I keep getting images in my mind that when we were in the castle, he forced sex on me. But I don't remember it."

"It's your subconscious telling you things."

"Probably. Tristan, I just realized. I barely know anything about you. I don't even know how old you are."

He laughed. "Old compared to you. Thirty-two."

"That's not old, silly."

When she moved out of his arms and sat up on the side of the bed, he reached for her to pull her back.

Johanna evaded his hands and stood up. She retrieved the towel and wrapped it around herself, then walked to the balcony and gazed out at the magnificent sunset, reflected in the turquoise waters of the Caribbean. "Tristan, come look at this. Looks like an artist has gone to town on the sky with his pastel paints."

He joined her on the balcony. "It's beautiful, just like you," he said while placing an arm around her shoulders. "I wonder if any stores will be open. I didn't realize it was this late."

"Well, if we stand here talking we won't know, will we?" she tickled him, which caused him to chase her into the room. They playfully wrestled for a few minutes until she grabbed her clothes and walked into the bathroom.

"I'm going to look stupid walking around on these silly slippers," she muttered when she came out to find Tristan dressed too.

"We'd better go and find you some shoes then. Let's go," he said taking hold of her hand and placing a kiss on her forehead.

CHAPTER TWENTY-SEVEN

THEY SPENT THREE DAYS IN HAITI EXPLORING PORT-AU-PRINCE, bargaining at the marketplaces for items that interested them, the local art was magnificent and Johanna bought several paintings she fell in love with. Tristan had rented a car and the toured the countryside, driving along the golden beaches and swimming in the crystal-clear turquoise water of the Caribbean. Johanna fell in love with Petionville. In the shelter of its green vegetation and flowers they saw the villas of the rich and several good hotels. They decided when they returned to Haiti for their honeymoon, they would stay in one of those hotels. Last of all they visited Boutilliers, still higher in the mountains from where they admired the sunset and Port-au-Prince tumbling down the mountainsides toward the sea. The city was a spread-out sprinkle of white confetti, enhancing the aquamarine of the one of the most beautiful bays in the world. They drove through the brazen mountains, finding the air light and refreshing as they left the car and climbed. Though Johanna felt quite strong, climbing was an effort so Tristan piggybacked her part of the way. They packed as much exploration into those three days as they could, finding Haiti a patchwork of velvety green montaine forests and barren, treeless hillsides occupying the western end of Hispaniola, the Caribbean's second largest island.

They were days filled with wonder in the discovery of each other's minds and bodies as if they were already on a honeymoon. Both had shoved Paul into the farthest recesses of their minds, until Johanna phoned her parents and they mentioned that his face had appeared on America's most wanted list again.

"That's it. As much as I hate it, we have to go home," Johanna said.

"Yes, I guess we do. If I don't show up for work I'll be out of a job."

"And my parents are anxious to see me and find out exactly what all happened. I'm also eager to surprise Jen, Shawna and Paula. They truly proved themselves the best friends a girl can ever have. They never abandoned me."

"You'll shock the living daylights out of them. Unless of course your parents told them."

"I asked them specifically not to say anything. They think I'm still with you holed up in some hotel."

"Well, I guess we'd better pack then and head for home, but before we do I want to hold you in my arms one more time."

"There will be lots more times, Tristan. We're going to spend the rest of our lives together."

"But for the present, for a while we'll be living apart. And Lord knows where the paper will send me next."

"True," she said softly while she moved toward him, her body already yearning for his. It was as if they couldn't get enough of each other.

WHEN THEY ARRIVED AT the Von Hertzenberg house her parents were working in the greenhouse. Johanna pushed the intercom and her father answered. "Dad, we're home!"

Within seconds her parents came rushing into the house, her mother hot and disheveled, tears already soaking her face as she laid eyes on her daughter.

Tristan left the kitchen quietly and went to the living room to call the editor in chief. As he suspected they had several assignments ready for him. Patiently he listened to the reprimand but after he told them that his absence would produce one hell of a story, the editor calmed down.

"I want you to fly to Edmonton tomorrow to cover the figure skating competitions," the editor told him.

"That means staying there for a couple of weeks. I told you I want to stay close to home for the time being."

"I've got no one else available and you're the best. Sorry. It's your gig."

He gazed into space for a moment wondering how to tell Johanna that he'd be away for a few weeks. But since it was his job it was something she would have to get used to. He heard her voice in the kitchen telling her parents about the trip to Haiti and her healing and smiled. He waited for a while before joining them, giving her a chance to be alone with her parents. Meanwhile he looked at the pictures of Johanna scattered throughout the living and dining room.

"Tristan, where are you? Mom made coffee. Come join us," Johanna called from the kitchen.

Quickly he joined them to be clasped in a bear hug by John. "I don't know how to thank you," John muttered in a voice filled with emotion.

"I took a hell of a risk," Tristan mumbled awkwardly.

Leslie was still too emotional to say much. Once she poured the coffee all she could do was gaze at her daughter as if she were an apparition from outer space.

The conversation finally slowed down. Tristan took Johanna's hand in his and asked, "Did you tell them about us?"

"Of course. Mom and Dad apparently already talked to the minister months ago and the marriage to Paul was annulled. I'm free, Tristan."

"Then we'd better set a date."

"No rushing this time around," John interjected. "Though you already have my approval in your choice of mate."

"Thanks, Dad. What about you, Mom? You're not saying anything."

"I'd like you to stay home for just a little while. We've missed you so much..."

Johanna leaned over to give her mother a quick embrace. "Okay, just a little while, but don't forget there are things I need to tie up. Like the castle for instance."

"You're not going back there?"

"Why not? The danger is gone and I need to renovate the castle and set my plan into action."

"And what's that?"

"You don't know yet, but it seems I'm a multi millionairess. Of course, now that I'm no longer married, I probably can't touch the money. I want to turn the castle into a holiday retreat for needy children from all over the world. I'll get charities involved and I'll hire staff. I'll turn part of the castle into our private quarters in case we want to go there for holidays."

"That's a marvelous idea," Tristan said. "I'm all for it, and you'll be married again soon. Maybe you should call your lawyer in Switzerland and see where you stand."

"I'm all for it too," Leslie said. "Maybe your father and I can go there for our second honeymoon once you've finished the renovations."

"That's settled then."

"Honey, I just talked to my boss and I have to go away for a few weeks to Edmonton on an assignment. And—I have to write a story about your healing of course."

"Do you have to? I'm so tired of being in the news."

"Look, there were all kind of stories about your illness, so it's best we kill all that. Don't worry, I won't go into the wrong kinds of detail," he said with a grin. "And then off to Edmonton."

In a way she was disappointed but on the other hand, she needed some time alone to think about her plan of revenge. First she had to find out where Paul was, if she even could...

"I'll go and call the lawyer now. What time is it over there?" she said looking at her watch. "Darn, it's too early. It's the middle of the night over there. I'll call them late tonight."

Tristan stayed with her to wait until past midnight to call Switzerland. They sat quietly in the living room on the couch, Johanna stretched out on the couch. He looked down at her head resting on his legs and stroked her hair. She was so determined seemed so strong, yet he was afraid that she was overdoing it, lying about her feeling of well-being. He had already learned that she was stubborn and willful, that she would often stumble throughout life, but stubbornly pick herself up again and go on. Glancing at his watch he noticed it was near one.

Gently, he woke her. "Honey, it's time to call the lawyer."

"Huh? Oh, I must have zonked out."

"You sure did. It's okay, you need to rest."

Her chin set stubbornly. "How many times do I have to tell everyone that I'm fine?"

"I know, honey. Call the lawyer," he said patiently while planting a kiss on her temple.

She need not have worried. Mr. Schneider told her that since everything had been transferred into her name and she was getting married to Tristan anyway, he would not change anything.

"I'LL COME BACK FAST as I can," Tristan told her as she saw him off at the airport.

"It's okay, Tristan. You're a reporter and I'd better get used to your absences," she answered in a matter of fact tone.

"True. But our love is so new, so precious, I want to spend every minute with you."

"Right now that's not possible. Anyway, there's your last call. You'd better go." She waved until he was out of sight and hurried out of the airport back to her car. Today she would surprise her friends. She'd already phoned the hospital and found out the three of them were off. Hopefully, they were all gathered at Shawna's place.

The hour's drive back to Langley seemed to take forever. Traffic was heavy, the highway congested with peak hour traffic. When she eventually pulled up in front of Shawna's apartment building she glanced up and saw the sliding door open. She knew at least someone was there because Shawna always meticulously locked everything if she was out.

She pushed the buzzer. Paula answered. "Avon calling," she said in an affected tone hoping they'd fall for it. Both Jen and Paula occasionally bought Avon ornaments from the Avon lady and Shawna collected their ceramic beer mugs. The ruse worked. After a few moments of silence the door clicked open.

Shawna opened the door of the apartment took a step back, then rushed forward and embraced Johanna. "My God," she sobbed. "It's really you!"

"What's taking you so long, Shawna? Invite the woman inside for crying out loud," Paula called out in a loud voice.

Shawna put her finger to her lips. "Ssh, don't say a word," and she pulled Johanna along to the living room.

Paula screamed and feigned a swoon as she sank back onto the chair. Jen just stared and turned very pale. There was utter silence for a few moments until the girls squealed and ran to embrace their friend.

"My God, JoJo, you had us all worried sick at first running off like that," Shawna said when they finally dried their happy tears and sat down.

Johanna laughed. "First of all, I didn't run off. Tristan abducted me!"

"Your mother told us. We went to visit you just after the nurses discovered you were missing. Man, what a panic! First we all ran around the home like idiots looking for you, and then when no one could find you, the administrator called your parents and then the police. We didn't know what to do, so we went to your house. We were there when Tristan called," Jen said.

"It's so romantic," Paula sighed. "I wish some handsome hunk would swoon over me the way Tristan does over you. You're so lucky!"

"Yes, very lucky," Johanna said softly. "He's a wonderful man."

"You should never have married that loser," Jen said in a reproving tone.

"Jen, if you say I told you so, I'll..."

"You'll what? I can't believe you were ill for so many months and now you're sitting here as if nothing has ever happened. Tell us what happened, Jojo. We're dying to hear the whole story."

They talked for hours till deep into the next morning when the four of them finally fell asleep.

AFTER THEY WOKE UP the next morning and had coffee Johanna asked them, "When are you guys taking your holidays?"

"I haven't thought about it yet," said Paula and Jen and Shawna echoed her.

"How about you take them soon?"

"I don't know if we'll be able to all take them together," Paula said.

"Well, try. I'd like you to go to Switzerland with me to the castle."

Paula squealed again and excitedly already started making plans. "When?"

"Next week."

"Oh Lord, I'll have to buy a whole new wardrobe. What do people wear over there?"

"Don't be silly, Paula. The castle is quite isolated. No one to see you but the old caretaker and the birds. I'll pay for your tickets of course. But I think it would be fun if the four of us supervised the renovations and helped me set my plan into action."

"Plan?" they echoed.

She told them what she wanted to do with the castle. But she kept quiet about her resolve to hunt down Paul and about her plans for him. After all, she wasn't quite sure yet how she'd proceed. Once she found him, what kind of punishment could she as a woman mete out?"

"Okay, that's settled then. Let's just hope the three of you can take your holidays that soon. Failing that, just take leave of absence for a month and I'll pay your wages. Three weeks is hardly enough anyway."

"What about Tristan? What will he say?" thoughtful Jen asked.

"He's gone for a few weeks on an assignment to Edmonton. I won't tell him until he's finished it."

"But he'll find out when he calls your house," Shawna said.

"Took care of that, too," Johanna told them and produced the cellular phone she'd purchased that morning from her purse. "He'll call me on this."

"You're devious. I don't know if it's good to start a relationship on lies," Jen said.

"It's not a lie. I don't want him to know because he'd worry. In a couple of weeks will be time enough to tell him."

"What about your parents? What will they say?" Jen asked.

"They already know and don't exactly approve, but I'm a big girl. And I told them I'd try and take your three along. That pacified them."

"Great. Let's call the hospital right now and see if we can do it," Shawna suggested.

CHAPTER TWENTY-EIGHT

JOHANNA DROVE HOME HUMMING TO HERSELF. NOW SHE COULD finally concentrate on her plan of revenge and find Paul although she didn't have a clue how to go about it. Her parents were working in the greenhouse when she got home so she went straight up to her room to think. As she sat down on her bed her eye fell on her grandmother's jewelry box. It reminded her of the diary she had found in the jewelry box in the castle and took to a translator to have translated into English. She made a mental note to pick it up before going to the castle.

For the first time since her grandmother's death she opened the jewelry box. Inside were the cameo brooch, necklace and earrings for her mother but there was also an array of other gold necklaces. Some were set with stones while others were just plain gold with either crosses or lockets on the chains. Below the tangled mess of necklaces were two velvet boxes. She dug them out, opened them and gasped at the ruby and emerald sets. Wondering if they were real or paste she replaced them carefully and sat on the bed untangling the chains. While doing this, she thought about the desk and the secret panel. It was time she moved the desk to her room and investigated what was hidden there.

After untangling most of the chains she put them back into the jewelry box and read her grandmother's letter again. She still couldn't read it without feeling a tight lump in her throat. Folding it carefully, she placed it inside the jewelry box and went to the cottage. It was also the first time she'd entered it since she'd found her grandmother that day.

The cottage seemed empty, as if it had died along with her grandmother. No aroma of coffee or tea greeted her, no clicking of knitting needles. More than ever she missed her grandmother and tears ran unheeded down her cheeks. She stood for quite a while in the center of the living room. It was the same as always and exactly as her grandmother had left it that day. Her mother kept it clean and dust free but left everything in place.

When she entered her grandmother's bedroom and approached the desk it felt like an invasion of her grandmother's privacy. But she needed to do this. It was her grandmother's wish. She tried moving the desk but its solid oak structure made it far too heavy. She'd have to get her father to help her move it to the house. Remembering the instructions in the letter, she pulled out the drawers and set them on the floor beside her. Her fingers searched the smooth wood for the mechanism that would open the secret panel. It was just a thin piece of wood attached to the side. She turned it carefully and watched the panel slide open. She peered inside the dark compartment and saw the jewelry box. It was the twin of the one in her bedroom and the large one in the castle, just a tad smaller. Reaching inside she took it out carefully and sat on the side of the bed with it. Stroking it for a moment, wondering what secret wonders it held, she thought about Gran and the letter. The contents would fascinate her, Gran had told her in the letter. A small key stuck out of the copper lock. She turned it and the lid clicked open. Inside were some yellowed letters and a small scroll, the ends made of carved wood. She took out the scroll and after unclipping the small gold catch, unrolled it carefully. The parchment was old and brittle. Afraid to tear it, she unrolled some of it. 'Hertzenberg' it said in large letters with a faint drawing of the castle below them. Unrolling it a little further she noticed it was basically similar to a blueprint of a house, but drawn on parchment. The lines were faded but she could still see them although some of the lettering was illegible.

Carefully, she unrolled it further until it lay the entire length of the bed. Sitting cross-legged on the bed, she studied the parchment carefully. She recognized the parlor, the stairs and the master bedroom. As she gazed at the drawings she noticed spaces in between them like hallways. But she knew there weren't any hallways there. In the parlor they had drawn in the large fireplace but again, behind that wall and fireplace was a drawing of a corridor and a door leading into it. She frowned. There was no door on that wall. She was sure of it.

It dawned on her. The castle possessed secret passages and rooms. Excited at her find she rolled the scroll and unrolled the rest of it. Her great-grandmother's bedroom had just such a corridor hidden behind the wall but also a small room right behind the dressing table.

For a while she mused over the castle's plans until a sudden thought entered her mind when she spotted a passage behind the cellar walls. This passage led to another set of drawings of a floor she had never seen when she inspected the castle room for room, floor by floor. Paul spent an awful lot of time in that cellar, she thought. And the police couldn't find him after my accident. Could it be? Did Paul somehow stumble on the secret passages and hid in them? After all, the heat was on in Europe. She remembered Tristan telling her that Paul was spotted in England and other European countries. It was possible that he'd gone back to the castle to hang low until the heat was off.

Excitement mixed with fear flooded her at this thought. If that were true, then he could still be in the castle since no one in Europe could find him. He could easily sneak out at night in disguise to go and get supplies in the morning and return again the next night. If these passages are underground the caretaker won't notice anything unusual. But what about his footsteps in the snow? Surely the police would have seen them... Unless he waited until the snow was gone. After all, we bought enough supplies to last for months so he wouldn't go hungry and he had a wine cellar filled with bottles of wine. And after sufficient time, when the police give up, he'll probably try to sell more of the antiques and take off to Mexico. Could it be? He can't go back to the States, or to Canada.

She speculated for a while and the more she thought about it, trying to put herself in Paul's position and thoughts, the more plausible her speculations became. She felt like calling her friends to cancel the trip and going on her own, but she knew how much her friends looked forward to it. It would be too dangerous to be there by myself anyway, she thought. With them around, maybe Paul won't try anything. And perhaps this is the perfect set-up for my revenge—but I still don't know how—I'll have to think about it some more. Maybe the castle will give me the answers.

Carefully she rolled up the parchment and after locking the scroll put it back in the jewelry box. She looked at the letters but they all needed translation. When she took out the last letter she found a few very faded pictures. After taking them to the window and studying the first one in the light she thought at first it was a picture of her great-grandmother but upon looking at it closer she noticed differences. Puzzled, she looked at the other pictures. They were of two babies, two toddlers and then two teenagers. They looked alike and it was easy to tell they were sisters. So the original Johanna Von Hertzenberg had a sister—but where was she? No one had ever mentioned this. Was this the secret her grandmother had talked about? She turned one of the pictures over and saw the two names on the back. Juliana und Johanna Von Hertzenberg. So her grandmother was named after the older sister. Maybe she died, Johanna thought. It's strange though that Gran never mentioned anything. Perhaps she was just as puzzled as I am.

CHAPTER TWENTY-NINE

THE GIRLS CHATTERED EXCITEDLY WHEN THEY LEFT ZURICH airport and Johanna hailed a taxi. "Why don't you rent a car?" Paula asked.

"I've got a car. It's at the castle. It should still be there I think."

"What if it's not?"

"I doubt Paul would try anything so stupid as to sell the car. The police would arrest him immediately."

"I suppose. You always talk as if he's still alive. You don't think he's dead?"

"I don't know, Paula. The police never found a body under all that snow. They dug for him after most of it melted but came up with empty hands."

"Then if he's not dead where could he be?"

"Who knows. He's probably far away by now, hiding in a foreign country," she said, a little voice deep down telling her, he's probably alive and hiding in the castle...

"I hope so. Just thinking about the guy gives me the creeps," Jen said while climbing into the taxi that just pulled up.

Paula had gone overboard as usual. Johanna grimaced as the driver tried to fit their luggage in the trunk. Shawna and Jen had each just brought one suitcase and a shoulder bag. All she had brought herself was a shoulder bag because her clothes were still at the castle. After they piled into the taxi and the driver had finished loading their luggage, they talked excitedly and made plans, pointing at buildings they passed, stores and Paula squealing in delight at how handsome the Swiss men were.

Johanna let it all slide by. Her thoughts were on the first journey to the castle. Only when they left the rural area and drove through the countryside did she take notice. "Look at all that beauty, those mountains," she said to the girls. "It's like a picture postcard."

Miles of verdant green meadows stretched to the mountains, cows, sheep and horses grazing contently in the warm summer sun. Wild flowers of all descriptions and color made a bright splash against the green. She could see just a splattering of snow on the highest mountains, but most of it was gone.

Before she realized, they arrived at the castle. It, too, looked very different in the bright summer sun. Though the lawns were unkempt, everything surrounding the castle was green and flowers grew abundantly, wildly, among the grass and weeds. Roses and ivy crept up the walls of the castle. She noticed what must have been a rose garden once and made a mental note to hire gardeners to landscape and tidy up. The fountain was still stagnant. Maybe the mechanism for the fountain was broken.

"Oh my God, it's huge!" Paula exclaimed.

"It's beautiful," Jen said softly. "Like a castle from a fairytale."

"Is it haunted?" Shawna asked.

Johanna grinned. "It's big, it's beautiful and yes, there's a legend that it's haunted," she answered all three at once at the same time thinking about the mysterious voice that had called her name several times. It could have been the drug— she thought. But after I first got there, I heard the voice too...

To her gratification, the VW was still parked in front of the castle. She wondered if it even ran and where the keys were.

After the taxi driver had unloaded the luggage and taken all the suitcases and bags inside the castle, she tipped him handsomely and opened the door wide. "Entrée, fair ladies. Enter my realm of magic," she said with a wide sweep of arm.

"It reeks," Paula said wrinkling her nose.

"It's musty. It needed to be aired when I had the accident but it was too cold at the time. I was only here for a couple of days anyway." She picked up her bag and started up the stairs. "I can give you each a separate room or we can bunk together. We'll have to clean up a couple of rooms though. When Paul and I got here the caretaker had only cleaned the master bedroom."

"Hey, I didn't come here to work," Paula grumbled.

"We just arrived Paula. How can you expect Johanna to have a cleaning crew in here already? Don't be unreasonable," Shawna snapped.

"Now, girls, we came here to have a good time. A bit of elbow grease won't hurt us," Johanna said. "Let's take our stuff upstairs and I'll give you the grand tour first. After that you can choose your rooms and decide if you want a bedroom to yourself."

"I don't know if I want to sleep alone," Shawna said while opening the door to the parlor and glancing inside. "This place is creepy."

Jen shuddered. "Maybe when all the drapes are open it'll be better," Jen said. "Let's open the drapes first."

"It looks different in the light," said Johanna. "Come on. We can open the drapes after we've taken the suitcases upstairs."

"How come you only brought one bag?" Jen asked her.

"After I had the accident no one thought to come and pick up my stuff here. It should all still be in the master bedroom."

"Ssh," Paula put a finger to her lips and listened intently. "I thought I heard something. Maybe it's the ghost."

Johanna had heard the slight sound, too. It seemed to come from the walls in the hall. "It's just creaking and groaning. Remember, this place is old."

"Well, I think I'd rather stay in a hotel in the village," Shawna said. "I don't like ghosts."

Paula giggled. "Don't be silly, Shawna. Think about it as an adventure you can look back on when you get old. You can tell your grandchildren that you slept with The Von Hertzenberg ghost."

"Shut-up, Paula. Come on, we can't hang around the hall forever," Johanna urged.

Arguing, bickering and stumbling, the girls followed her up the stairs and to the master bedroom. It was still in the exact state she'd seen it before the accident. Her clothes lay strewn on the bed where Paul chucked them as he helped her into her ski gear. With disgust she noticed Paul's clothes hanging over a chair. Maybe he wasn't in the castle after all. Surely he would have gone to the bedroom to get his clothes? "This is my room. How about you three take the rooms next to this one and the one opposite? That way we'll be close together," she told the girls while grabbing Paul's clothes and throwing them into the hallway.

They left to go to their own rooms. She smiled as she heard them grossing out at the dust when they removed the dust covers. They'd be busy for a while. She opened her bag, took out the jewelry box and set it on the dressing table. Now was not the time to study the scroll. She'd do that in private when her friends were busy. Sitting on the side of the bed she scanned the walls wondering if this room, too, had a secret panel. She'd have to find out soon because if Paul was indeed hiding in the secret passages she didn't want unwelcome visits in the middle of the night. She had to find him as soon as possible. At the thought of Paul, she stood up and inspected the wardrobe. Paul's clothes hung exactly as they were when he'd put them in there. After opening each drawer of the dresser, she couldn't be sure if anything was missing or not. He could easily have fetched just enough clothes from the bedroom not to make it obvious. His suitcase still stood next to the wardrobe.

Johanna—Johanna...

A shiver ran down her spine. The familiar whisper that haunted her thoughts during her illness welcomed her back to the castle. After discovering the secret of the passages she thought it might have been Paul trying to freak her out. But she'd heard the voice soon after their arrival at the castle so that couldn't be. And it sounded like a female voice.

A faint breeze wafted past her face. She shivered and set about unpacking her bag and tidying up the clothes on the bed. Soon as she could she'd deal with the Paul issue...

CHAPTER THIRTY

PAUL HEARD FOOTSTEPS FROM FAR AWAY. HE FROWNED. "WHO THE hell could that be?" he muttered while dousing the oil lamp he'd purchased on one of his excursions and grabbing his flashlight. He headed for the passages. Boredom had caused him to explore them all and he knew his way well by now.

Trying to go up the crumbly stone stairs without making a sound was not easy. He cursed softly when a stone broke loose and tumbled to the ground below. Moving quickly through the passages he followed the sounds. A narrow flight of wooden steps led to the floor where the bedrooms were. Again he had to be careful. The steps were old, some of them rotten and they creaked in places. He scaled them three at a time trying not to put too much weight on them.

The sounds came from the area of the master bedroom. He peeked through the peephole of the bedroom next to it and saw Paula just as she was changing. Damn, what the hell is she doing here, he thought, at the same time ogling her body as she waltzed around the room in her g-string and bra. Pity I blew it this time. Can't ever go back to Canada now.

He saw Paula stop suddenly and stare suspiciously at the wall. Have to be careful, he thought. I think she heard something.

He moved on to the master bedroom and slid away the small partition that hid the peephole. When he saw Johanna moving around the room he cursed under his breath. Damn, when I went to that little bar and manipulated the conversation to Hertzenberg and the heiress, they told me she was dead. Should never listen to an old drunk... With consternation he saw Jen and Shawna enter the room.

Quickly, he went back to his hiding place. He had planned to stay there until the heat was off. The few times he'd disguised himself and gone into Zurich he made some discreet inquiries and knew the FBI had found out about his excursion to England and the sale of the silver and crystal. So that was another disguise he couldn't use anymore. Three times after that he'd planned an escape and left, but the attempted sale of a painting in France, had caused the FBI to be hot on his trail again. He'd rented another car and driven, but when he tried to sell the painting in a small antique store, the antique dealer recognized him and again the chase was on. When he got to Spain, he managed to elude the FBI, and made his way back to Switzerland and the castle. It was the ideal hiding place. He waited until the news of Johanna's misfortune had died down and her pictures no longer appeared in the papers. Often, he cursed the German language, wishing he knew what the papers said about Johanna and about him. Now, the arrival of the girls had upset his new plans to leave the country and make his way to the Italian coast and then on to Mexico by boat.

He had to get rid of them. But how? Killing all four of them wouldn't do. If all four girls went missing, then the FBI would be so hot on his trail he'd have no life left at all, he'd be on the run all the time. And they'd surely catch him and he'd rot in jail.

There had to be another way to make them leave. For a moment he thought about donning one of his disguises and leaving the castle but he wasn't quite ready. Plastic surgery was his only answer. But for that, he needed money and a lot of it. And the only way to get money, since the bitch had not put the Swiss account in both names, was to sell the valuables in the castle. And even if the account was in both names, he wouldn't have been able to access it. The police would surely have frozen the account. He needed more time to plan the perfect escape and leave with a fat wallet, and the arrival of Johanna and her friends had loused that up. Unless they were only here for a short holiday...

He stalked the dirt floor, back and forth, cursing. Punching the walls didn't dim his anger and frustration. It just hurt his knuckles. He kicked one of the skulls angrily and watched it shatter against the wall. Suddenly a thought occurred to him. Ghosts—I can haunt them. They'll be out of here in no time—and in the meantime I can have some fun with them too. He felt inside his pocket and fingered the little bottles filled with powders he'd brought back from Haiti. Pulling them out, he chose a small vial with a blue lid. That one was just a hallucinatory drug and wouldn't really do any harm. He grinned evilly as he opened a bottle of wine and put it to his lips. He gulped half a bottle down and felt it calm his frustrations. Satisfied, a plan slowly forming on his mind, he fell down onto the cot and lay back, drowsiness caused by the fast consumption of the wine, overwhelming his thoughts. He drank the rest of the wine and threw the bottle on the floor. Still grinning evilly, he said softly, "I should be thankful the little troupe arrived. It'll break the monotony and boredom and I'll have some fun. I'll start with the black-haired bitch and then I'll..." his slurred words trailed off as the wine did its job.

CHAPTER THIRTY-ONE

JOHANNA OPENED THE PANTRY AND GLANCED AT THE SHELVES. SHE frowned. The groceries she and Paul had bought were mostly gone. She'd have to talk to Jakob and ask him some questions. Maybe he took them, thinking she wouldn't be back. *Or—maybe my suspicions are right on and Paul is in the castle and he has been eating them...*

"We'll have to go grocery shopping, guys."

"I noticed," Paula said while inspecting the fridge. "This milk must have turned into cheese by now." She took out the bottle of milk and sniffed it. "Strange, it doesn't smell off at all and it looks normal."

More proof, Johanna thought, a pang of fear and apprehension causing a strange knot in her stomach. "Maybe the caretaker put it in there. He probably doesn't have a fridge," she excused the fresh milk so not to make her friends suspicious. When she opened the door to the freezing compartment she noticed frozen meat, ice cream and sausages. *He's been living well. I've got to get other people in here as soon as possible.* "First things first. Let's go to the village to buy groceries and inquire about hiring people to clean on a daily basis. We'll stop at the cottage on the way out. Maybe Jakob is home now."

Her coat still hung on the coat rack where she'd left it months before. She dug in the pocket but the keys weren't in it. "Mm, wonder where the car keys are. Maybe Jakob has those too. Let's walk to the cottage."

Jen decided to go with her. Paula and Shawna chose to stay behind to unpack their suitcases. They walked to the cottage, Jen unusually quiet. "What's wrong, Jen? You're not talking."

"I have this weird feeling," Jen started.

"You and your feelings. For goodness sake, what would you have a feeling about now?"

"I don't know. Just that something isn't right."

"You said the same thing when I married Paul and you were right then. I should have listened to you."

"This is a different feeling. I can't quite put my finger on it, but I've had these creepy chills down my spine ever since we arrived here."

"Probably the dampness in the castle. We'll soon take care of that," Johanna said making excuses. She, too, felt the chills down her spine and knew they were coming from sources other than dampness. She knocked on Jakob's front door. To her delight he was home.

"Frau Von Hertzenberg..." he said in a shocked tone. "I happy—but..."

"You probably thought I was still in the hospital. Right? Is that what the police told you?"

"Jawohl. Police tell Jakob you much sick. Go back Canada. Herr Blake?"

"He is gone. He was a very bad man. My friends and I came for a holiday and I want to renovate the castle just like I planned. Can you find the work crews for me again? I'd like them to start right away."

"Jawohl." He smiled broadly and pumped her hand. "Jawohl, ich machen das schnell."

"I guess that means he'll do it," Jen said softly.

"I remember that word. It means fast. Jakob, do you have the car keys?"

"Jawohl. Ich machen die auto." He disappeared inside the cottage and returned with the keys.

"Thank you, Jakob." Johanna took the keys and told him they were going to the village to buy groceries.

"Do you know what he said?" Jen asked.

"No. My grandmother taught me a little bit of the language, but not to the extent that I can understand it when spoken."

"Why didn't you ask him about the groceries?"

"He probably wouldn't understand. Like me with his language, he probably understands just a few words of English."

Johanna unlocked the doors and got into the VW. She started it. At first it spluttered, but then it kicked in and they drove off to Hertzenberg.

PAULA RAN INTO SHAWNA'S room and grabbed her friend. "I swear this place is haunted. I just heard the strangest sounds."

"Don't be silly. The castle is old and creaky. You're bound to hear noises."

"Shawna, share my room? I don't want to sleep by myself."

"No, I want to..." she stopped short when a distant howling echoed through the room, the hallway. "What the hell is that? Sounds like wolves."

"There's a forest nearby. Do you think there are wolves in it?"

"Who knows. I'm staying in my own room. Have you examined the furnishings? Beautiful antiques."

"Before I unpack more I want to dust and clean first. There's a hundred years of dust in that room."

"Then go and do it and let me deal with my stuff," Shawna said impatiently.

Paula returned to her room and took a T-shirt she didn't like anyway out of her suitcase. While she was busy dusting and thinking how she could meet men in this isolated place, she heard it again. Only this time it was louder. Her heart pounded as she sank onto the bare mattress and gazed at the walls.

Paula—Paula—Paula—go away...

It was a hoarse male voice coming from far away. It sounded hollow. Terrified, her eyes blacker then they already were, she ran from the room back to Shawna. "My God, it's talking to me now."

"Paula, your imagination is running overtime. Go clean your room. I'm busy," Shawna snapped, fed up with Paula's games.

"But I heard it. I swear."

"You heard it in your mind because you believe there are ghosts here.

I don't believe in any such thing. Ghosts don't exist."

"They do, and whatever it is, it's picked on me to haunt."

PAUL LISTENED INTENTLY TO the two girls and suppressed his mirth at Paula's discomfort. Before the week was over he'd have had his fun with them. They'd all be gone and he'd have the place to himself again. Deciding it was enough for now, he returned to his hiding place to plan and plot further ghostly acts to chase the girls away. He grabbed a bottle of wine off the table, uncorked it and paced back and forth. While gulping down the wine he envisioned Paula in his mind. She was the first one he'd have his fun with. He could already see her strapped to the bed, immobile, passive, her black eyes filled with lust for him yet totally submissive and quiet. At that thought, while imagining her breasts bared for him, her legs spread exposing her private parts, he could feel the sexual tension rising within his body, his loins starting to throb. That evening, he'd put the drug in their wine. He was sure the girls would have a few drinks that evening.

CHAPTER THIRTY-TWO

JOHANNA COULD HARDLY WAIT UNTIL HER FRIENDS WENT TO BED. They spent the whole day cleaning and dusting their rooms and putting their things away. Dinner was simple that night. She had picked up take-out food when they did their shopping in Hertzenberg. Tomorrow, a cleaning crew would arrive and hopefully the work crews she'd asked Jakob to arrange for.

"Go and get another bottle of wine, Jo. That stuff is damn good," Shawna said.

"Don't you think it's time we hit the sack?"

"I can stand another glass of wine," Paula said. "Maybe I'll pass out and won't hear the ghost."

"Paula, stop it. There are no such things as ghosts. Who wants to come down to the cellar with me?"

Jen stood up. "I'll come. Where's the flashlight, Jo?" Johanna left the parlor and went to the kitchen to fetch the flashlight. She opened the creaky door to the cellar and started down the steps, followed closely by Jennifer.

"It's even more creepier down here, Jo," Jen said while shining the flashlight at the wine racks.

"I know, that's why I wanted one of you to come with me. This will do. Let's go back to the parlor," Johanna said, while grabbing a bottle off the first rack.

"You need to have proper lighting installed. Are you going to get them to clean the wine cellar, too?"

"Definitely. I'm tired of fighting spiders and cobwebs."

"At least there aren't any cockroaches."

"That's all I'd need," Johanna sighed.

When they returned to the parlor Paula was already half asleep. "You don't need any more, Paula. Why don't you go to bed?" Johanna said.

She sat up with a start. "No, I'll have one more glass of wine. That will make me pass out for sure."

"Me too," Shawna said, "Although I don't believe in ghosts. I just don't like all the creaks and groans. I bet we'll hear even more throughout the night. When you were here before, Jo, did you hear them?"

"Not that I can remember," Johanna said while pouring them another glass of wine. She was still sipping the first glass herself, wanting her head to stay clear after her friends were asleep so she could study the blueprints. To her relief they finally decided to go to bed.

"Let me give you sheets and blankets. You haven't made your beds yet," she said while leading the way up the stairs.

"Are they dust free?" Paula asked.

"Yes. They are all wrapped in plastic." She took out sheets, blankets and towels and handed them to the girls.

"I don't feel like making my bed. How about we all sleep together in your room tonight?" Paula slurred.

"No way. I'm going to read for a while." Normally, she wouldn't have minded, but she had a task to complete and needed to be alone. "Your doors have keys in them. Lock them if you feel uncomfortable. I'll help you make your beds."

She helped them make their beds and said goodnight. After turning the large brass key and locking her own door she leaned against it for a moment. Tristan, she thought. I haven't called him and my cell isn't turned on... Now that everything was quiet she could safely call him. She took the cell phone out of her purse and activated it. No sooner had she pushed the on button or it rang.

"Johanna? Where have you been? I've been trying to ring you for hours."

"Hi, Tristan. Sorry. Guess I'm not used to carrying a cell phone yet."

"I miss you, honey."

"I miss you too. When do you think you'll be back?"

"Probably sooner than expected. I've asked them to assign someone else to this one."

Damn, she thought. That's not part of the plan. "Have they done that yet?"

"No. But I expect to hear from my boss any day now."

They chatted for a while about wedding plans until Tristan said he had another call coming in. "That could be my boss right now. I'll call you back."

"I'm going out for a while, hon," she lied. "I'll call you tomorrow."

"I love you."

"I love you, too."

Feeling rather guilty for deceiving him, she turned off the cell and looked at her watch. It was past one in the morning so it would be close to lunchtime in Canada. She'd have to calculate the time difference tomorrow morning and remember to call him. Though her heart burned with love for him, foremost on her mind now was to find Paul and make him pay, and she had to do that on her own. Stilling the pangs of fear, of slight regret, and squashing the thought of calling the police, she quickly she took the scroll out of the jewelry box and spread it on the bed. The light was dim so she turned on her flashlight. After locating her great-grandmother's bedroom on the map she inspected it and studied the secret passages carefully and the small room behind the walls. She rolled the scroll and put it back in the jewelry box then quickly left her room and noticed Jen, Paula and Shawna had left the doors to their rooms open. Peeking in, she saw they were fast asleep, Paula snoring softly, Shawna sprawled over the bed without covers.

She hurried to her great-grandmother's room while holding the bunch of keys tight in her hand so they wouldn't jingle. Carefully, she turned the key in the rusty lock. The last thing she wanted was for the girls to wake up. Locking the door behind her, she turned on the light.

The dressing table weighed a ton but she managed to move it away from the wall. She searched for something to push, any kind of mechanism that would open up the secret panel to the small room beyond, but she saw nothing, felt nothing. Then suddenly she noticed that one of the boards was lighter than the others. Running her fingers over it, it felt no different. Frustrated, she punched the board and suddenly, silently, the panel swung open to reveal the secret room. It was small. No bigger than a large walk-in closet. Turning on the flashlight she peered inside. She could hardly see through the sheet of cobwebs. She swiped at them with the flashlight and almost choked at the cloud of dust she disturbed. Portraits stood against the wall. She pulled them out and using her sleeve wiped the dust away, revealing paintings of the same two girls as the ones on the pictures in the jewelry box. Because they'd been hidden away from damaging light for so long, the pictures were clearer. She wondered why they were hidden in the secret room and put them on the bed deciding to hang them on the walls.

By the time she had removed a lot of the dust with one of the dust covers she felt like a dust bunny herself. The room contained memorabilia of a young girl. Old toys, dolls, some embroidery started but not completed and another jewelry box. It belonged to the set of three, her grandmother's, the one she found on the dressing table in this room and the one hidden inside her grandmother's desk. This one was the largest of all. As she lifted the lid she wondered if there was a fifth, perhaps one belonging to Johanna and Juliana's mother. Where could it be though? She occupied what she thought to be the master bedroom but maybe it wasn't. And where was Juliana's room? Making up her mind to inspect all the rooms in the castle the next day, she played with the jewelry inside. Some of the bracelets were very small, probably belonging to one of the girls when they were little. Necklaces, childish paraphernalia, but the jewelry box held nothing of value or anything that could tell her more about the mysterious sister.

Disappointed, she went back into the bedroom and sat on the bed gazing at the portrait of her great-grandmother on the wall. Or was it? Could this be the sister perhaps? Totally confused, she went back to the secret room and wondered how she would get into the passages.

Running her flashlight through it again, she saw shelves of old books on both sides and the back. She started to remove the books from the back shelves when one seemed to be stuck. She tugged it, tugged it again, but the bottom was stuck to the shelf. When she yanked it forward, part of the wall, including the shelves, swung open to reveal a passage beyond. "That's it," she mumbled and shone the flashlight into the passage. It ran to the end of the room, stopped at the other end, but it looked like at the far end was another passage.

At first she was tempted to explore, but then decided against it. If she got lost, it would take her hours to find her way back and there was always the chance of running into Paul, if he was indeed hiding out somewhere in the depths of the castle of which she was almost a hundred percent sure now. The last thing she needed was for him to have the advantage over her. First thing she had to do is give her friends some tasks. Maybe send them to Zurich to buy some supplies or something, while she copied the passageways from the blueprint and made a map.

Just as she was about to close the panel she heard a sound. It seemed to come from within the passages. Listening intently, she dashed into the secret room and closed the panel hoping she'd find the mechanism again to get out. Then she shut off the flashlight and waited. Far in the distance she heard footsteps, a man's cough. It sounded like Paul's but she couldn't be sure. The footsteps came closer. Wondering if she should close the panel to the passages she waited but the footsteps stopped not far from her, maybe near her bedroom. She heard a man clearing his throat and cough softly again then an unearthly howling echoed toward her. Shuddering, she slunk even more back against the wall. Wishing she had x-rays eyes, she waited. The man called her name. Disguised, lower, but she distinctly recognized Paul's voice. So she had been right all along. Paul was hiding within the secret passages of the castle, maybe another secret room somewhere and he knew she and the girls were there. And now he was acting like a ghost to chase them away. She grinned. If he knew she was onto him...

Obviously, he had not found this secret room because the cobwebs and dust were not disturbed. The footsteps receded, shuffled, until they stopped again. This time he called out Paula's name. Johanna's mind worked desperately as to what kind of story she could come up with for her friends. If they woke up from Paul's supposed haunting, they would surely leave. Maybe they would sleep through the night after all the wine they consumed that evening. She hoped so.

Eventually, Paul stopped and she heard his footsteps shuffle away, far into the distance, until she heard nothing. She closed the panel and heard it creak slightly. Glad that she had not closed it before and revealed herself, she turned to face the back of the bedroom wall. A small hole let through a tiny beam of light. Without turning the flashlight on, she moved closer and peered through the hole. It was so small it would hardly be noticeable from the other side, but it was big enough for someone to spy through. Wondering if the other rooms, her own bedroom, had such a hole, she shone the flashlight on the wall to search for the mechanism. She didn't need to look far. On this side was an ordinary doorknob. When turned, the panel swung open and she stepped back into the bedroom.

Glancing at her watch she noticed it was near four in the morning. Quickly, she put the dressing table back, turned off the light and after locking the door behind her hurried to the bathroom to wash off the dust. Tomorrow she would thoroughly inspect the other rooms and the turrets she'd not had a chance to look at the few days she spent at the castle with Paul.

Soon as she was back in her bedroom she felt the walls for tiny holes but she couldn't find any at this point. Crawling under the covers her flesh puckered at the thought that Paul could be watching her right now, could even kill her while she slept...

PAUL WAS ANNOYED THAT Johanna stayed up so late. He had watched Paula take off her clothes and then Shawna and Jen. After inspecting their bodies, his first choice was still Paula. She slept naked and had not bothered to crawl under the covers. He'd heard them fetch wine from the cellar several times, so he knew they drank a fair amount. He kept checking on Johanna and to his consternation found her gone from the room. It made him uneasy. He listened for sounds in the passages. But then again, Johanna didn't know about the passages, so why should he worry? Eventually, he got tired of watching a sleeping woman and waiting for Johanna to go to bed, so he returned to the cellar for a while. He could try again in half an hour, after he'd had a few glasses of wine. Maybe tonight the drug wasn't even necessary. Paula's voice had sounded slurred and she'd passed out as soon as she fell onto the bed.

His libido was working overtime as he concentrated on the picture of Paula's nakedness that hovered in his mind. Impatiently he drank some more wine and kept glancing at his watch. Surely Johanna would be in bed by now?

He set the empty bottle on the table and took off his clothes. "Might as well be ready," he muttered. He took the leather straps out of the metal loops on the torture chair and tore one of his shirts into strips, just in case she did wake up. Quickly he headed back up the stairs and through the passages to Paula's room. He peered through the peephole and saw her lying in the exact position as before. Then he ran to Johanna's room and with satisfaction saw her sleeping soundly.

The grooves in the walls had become familiar friends to him. It didn't take him long to find the ridge to push that opened the panel into Paula's room. The panel creaked loudly, causing him to stop short. He held his breath and watched her carefully, but she didn't stir.

Leaving the panel open so he could escape easily, he advanced to the bed. He touched her foot, then moved closer and grasped a breast. He squeezed, but she was out stone cold and didn't utter a sound. Thoroughly excited now, he quickly tied her wrists and ankles to the four posts of the bed. As he lifted her head to gag her, she groaned softly. Afraid she'd wake up and spoil his mood, he let go of her head and waited, but she snored softly and didn't wake. He decided not to gag her and take the risk. Having her mouth bound would surely bring her out of her drunken stupor.

He climbed onto the bed and sat on his knees between her legs. He knew she didn't have a boyfriend and vaguely wondered if she was a virgin. That thought excited him even more. Leaning forward, he kneaded her breasts, pinched her nipples, then took a breast in each hand and squeezed as hard as he dared. The nipples almost looked like they'd pop off, her breasts resembling ripe melons ready to burst.

Tired of her breasts he moved down to her private parts parting her roughly and exploring. His breath came fast as he felt deep inside. Never before had he wanted a woman as much as he desired this one. The black triangle between her legs was soft as velvet. His lips brushed across it, allowing it to stroke them for a moment. Inhaling her feminine scent, he bit, but not too hard. She started to squirm a little under this rough treatment so he stopped. I have to find a way to put the drug in their drinks, he thought, as he positioned himself.

He slammed into her with one thrust. For a moment he felt disappointment when he encountered no barrier, but his desire was too great. He'd worked up to this moment the whole day and though he tried to contain his lust to make it last at least a little while, he was spent after a few swift strokes. He groaned softly and collapsed on top of her, a breast in each hand. It was his weight that caused her to stir, to try and turn over onto her side.

Still breathing heavily, he quickly jumped off the bed and untied the straps. Her eyelids half opened, but then she curled up and hugged the pillow.

It was enough for one night, he decided. He could have more fun with her and the others once they were drugged. And... if they went to bed in decent time. After picking up the straps and his flashlight, he quickly left the room, closed the panel and returned to the cellar. Still naked, he lay on the cot and drifted off while dreaming which girl he'd take next and what he could do to them while they were under the influence of the drug.

CHAPTER THIRTY-THREE

"MAN, I'M STILL TIRED," PAULA SAID WHILE YAWNING .

"That's what you get if you drink so much," Shawna retorted.

"You needn't talk. We all drank a lot. I think Johanna must have fetched at least six bottles of wine from the cellar. I remember she went down there at least three times."

"Who cares?" Jen said. "We're here to have a good time.

"I passed out soon as I hit the bed, but I had the weirdest dreams. This handsome hunk made love to me. He was quite rough," Paula said with an exaggerated sigh. "It was so real, I even feel sore this morning."

Johanna looked at Paula suspiciously. Paula was quite inebriated the night before and when drunk, it was almost impossible to wake her. .Surely Paul wouldn't dare? Yes, he would, she thought. My God, if he's starting to play sex games with my friends, I'll have to speed up my plan. He's a cold-blooded killer. I can't risk their lives. A vivid picture floated before her eyes for a moment, a suppressed memory surfaced of Paul raping her while she was drugged. She shuddered at the thought of what he could do to her friends while they were sleeping. The sooner she had a full working crew in the castle, the better. But then there were still the nights...

"Do you ever have anything else but sex on your mind, Paula?" she asked, trying to make light of the supposed dream. "Why don't the three of you take the car and go to Zurich?" Johanna asked her friends. "There are quite a lot of things I need and I can trust you to buy the right colors. I'll give you my visa card."

"You'd trust us with your visa?" Paula asked with a mischievous grin. "That could be dangerous."

"Sure," Jen said. "Might be fun. That's if we don't get lost."

"I have a road map and a map of Zurich. I've also got a list of stores the bank manager gave me."

"Okay, let's go then," Shawna said. "Sure you don't want us here, Jojo?"

"I'll be fine. Oh, there's something I need you to pick up for me." She dug in her purse for the card the translator had given her. "Here is the card with the name and address. He has something for me I really need."

"What is it?"

"Just something I asked him to translate," Johanna said, handing Jen the card.

"Well, let's get cracking then. Do I have to pay this man?"

"No, I've already paid him in advance. Here is the receipt."

After they were gone, Johanna washed the dishes and then thought about where she should start first. Just as she was about to go and find the entrances to the turrets, the knocker announced visitors.

She opened the door and faced a group of people. Jakob's work crews had arrived. Happy to find out that one of the cleaning ladies spoke fairly good English, she gave them instructions. They would start with the main floor. Jakob had the woman translate for him that the landscapers would arrive soon, too. Now, she could explore and feel safer. With so many people busy in the castle, Paul wouldn't try anything. It was the night that worried her...

Soon, there were people everywhere, cleaning, scrubbing and polishing. Drapes were taken down and hung outside. She smiled at the women beating the dust out of them. They should really go to the cleaners but she could do that later. Without the drapes, the rooms now flooded with light, the castle already looked a much friendlier place. Windows she'd not been able to see out of started to sparkle. The covers came off the chandeliers, sunshine playing with the crystal facets, sending dozens of colored lights through the hall and the rooms.

She'd never inspected the ballroom. When she entered it, she gasped. It was magnificent, almost royal in its splendor with its rich red velvet drapes held by golden tassels, gilded chairs and chaises covered in red velvet, rich mahogany tables and a shining marble dance floor. Huge paintings in gilded frames graced the walls. They were of her ancestors. She walked by them slowly, seeing resemblances. Especially the blond hair and blue eyes were predominant.

Leaving the cleaning crews to their work, she headed for the turrets. The large key ring with brass keys jingled in her fingers as she sprinted down the long hallways. She had to try a dozen keys before one unlocked the door to one of the turrets. A solid oak spiral staircase faced her and of course everything wore the forever cobwebs. She swiped at them gingerly as she cautiously climbed the steps, coughing at the dust she sparked up.

Disappointed, she looked around the large circular room. Its floor was plain wooden planks, now covered with a thick layer of undisturbed dust, the furniture sparse. A cot stood next to the wall with a bare mattress. A solitary desk sat beneath the small window.

After inspecting all the turrets but one, she almost decided to leave the last one. She'd left all the doors to them open so the cleaning people could get in there to clean. She had to try almost all the keys to unlock this door, the last key, which seemed newer than the rest, finally unlocked it. After opening the door she hesitated, then resolutely swiped at the cobwebs and climbed the stairs.

She'd found what she was looking for. This had to be either Johanna's or Juliana's room. The furniture was similar to the one she thought to be Johanna's room. The wooden floor did nothing to enhance it, the furniture, not covered with dust covers gray with dust. The bed did not have a canopy and the mattress was bare of covers. Through the layer of dust she noticed a vague stain. Holding her breath, she wiped some of the dust away, coughing from the cloud she created around her. The stain was old, rusty looking, but it resembled blood. Sharply, she drew in her breath. A shiver ran down her spine. A gut feeling told her that something had happened in this room that wasn't right.

A wardrobe stood against the wall. She opened it and saw a few dresses and nightgowns for a young woman, but nothing of importance. The drawer at the bottom of the wardrobe held some nightgowns. When she turned around she saw the chamber pot beneath the bed and grimaced. A nightstand next to the bed revealed nothing either. On top of it stood a beautiful bowl and pitcher edged with gold. Underneath the tiny window stood a desk, holding a silver inkbottle, a piece of paper and a pen. She walked to it and picked up the paper. After blowing off the dust she noticed it was the start of a letter. Liebe Johanna, Ich... That's all it said. Black ink splatters stained the rest of the sheet of paper as if the writer had been interrupted. She knew what Liebe meant. Her grandmother had called her liebling occasionally. It meant dearest. The note was meant for Johanna but never completed or given to her. She wondered about the notes she'd found in the jewelry box, if they were from the same writer.

Johanna...

The voice was stronger now, anxious. Johanna glanced around the room nervously. Could Paul be haunting her even here? Were there passages in the turrets, too? She tried to remember the blueprints but couldn't recall passages near the turrets.

Johanna...

Again the voice called her name. It sounded more like a young woman's voice. Could Paul do such good imitations?

Help me...

Johanna ran from the room and down the stairs fast as she could. She locked the door firmly behind her determining to clean that one herself and to go study the scroll again. She almost tripped over a rolled up carpet runner as she hurried to her bedroom hardly hearing the apologies from the woman waxing the floor.

Shutting the door firmly behind her and locking it, she pulled the bed away from the wall took the scroll out of the jewelry box and sat behind the bed with it. She didn't trust the walls. In this place they had eyes and ears and the last thing she wanted was for Paul to see that she knew about the secret passages.

Danger...

The voice whispered close to her ear so she knew it couldn't come from the walls. Trying to ignore it, she studied the blueprints and especially her room. There was indeed a passage behind the far wall. Opening the curtains wide, allowing the sun to filter into the room she went over the wall inch by inch and finally found the tiny peephole. It was only a few millimeters but large enough for someone to spy through. Centered in a knot in the wood it was hardly visible to the naked eye.

She opened her purse and took out some chewing gum. After chewing it for a few minutes, she took the wad of gum and stuffed it into the hole and over it. "There. Now at least he can't spy on me," she muttered softly. "As long as he doesn't push it out. I'll ask the carpenters for some putty to plug it."

Feeling safer now to sit on the bed with the scroll, she spread it out and looked for the turrets. She was right. There were no passages behind the turret walls. The voice couldn't have been Paul's. If it wasn't his voice then whose was it? Again chills ran down her spine. Maybe the rumors in the village were right and there really was a castle ghost...

As she was studying the blueprints, every now and then she'd glance at the chewing gum to make sure it was still in place. Thankful that Paul's haunting had not woken her friends that night, she rolled up the scroll and looked around for a hiding place for it. She placed it beneath the mattress and when leaving the room locked the door.

Wondering why Juliana's jewelry box was in Johanna's bedroom and about the diary she went downstairs to see how the cleaning was coming along. The renovations, she had decided, had to start immediately. And she had to corner Paul somehow and punish him. A gun, she thought, but where do I get one? Maybe Jakob knows.

Hurrying out of the castle and to Jakob's cottage she noticed him outside supervising the landscapers. She smiled. The old man was obviously in his element and enjoying the restoration of the gardens. She noticed the rose garden was already cleaned up, its bushes in full bloom now displayed in their full glory. Making a mental note to cut some roses, knowing the bushes would bloom more if she cut them regularly, she hurried to Jakob.

"Jakob," she called out. He looked at her with a smile.

"Jawohl?"

Panting, she stood before him. When she asked him about a gun he didn't understand but when she imitated shooting, he did. He frowned at her and shook his head. It was obvious he didn't approve of guns for women. She gave up. It was no use talking to Jakob. Maybe if she went to Zurich she could buy one there.

The cleaning would not be done in one day, she knew. There were the East and West wings she had not even explored yet. It was her next task. In the East wing she found another master bedroom. It was three times as big as the one she occupied now and what she thought was the master bedroom. She opened door after door and left them ajar for the cleaning people. She'd asked them to pack any clothes found in the rooms and bring them to the attic. Sighing, she thought about the attic. She'd glanced into it but had not explored it. It had more dust than any other place in the castle and the cobwebs were so thick one could hardly see what was there. She was sure she'd find some interesting things there eventually.

When she ran down the stairs, back to the main floor, the interpreter approached her and asked her to open two locked doors. She thought she'd seen all the rooms on the main floor but she had not. One door opened to a large study, its walls lined with beautiful oak bookcases covered with glass. A large oak desk stood in the center, a Persian rug on the oak floor. Several antique chairs stood in corners. On the one wall a large painting of a couple, newlyweds, obviously Johanna and Juliana's parents, the Baron and Baroness Von Hertzenberg. They looked proud and stiff, their faces stern and unsmiling. Next to the painting was a glass cabinet, in which hung several antique hunting rifles and a pistol. The cabinet was locked. She wondered about the key for it and went to the desk. Sitting behind it she felt almost as regal as the original Baroness. She opened several drawers but found nothing. The center drawer was also locked. Frowning, she wondered where to find the small keys to fit those locks. Maybe in the master bedroom, she thought and left the study to go back to it. She was right. She found the keys in the drawer of a nightstand next to the bed, along with an antique pocket watch and some other male items.

Hurrying back to the study she tried them and easily unlocked the gun cabinet. She grinned as she carefully lifted a rifle from the cabinet. There was no need to buy a weapon. This one was old-fashioned, but she didn't care. Paul wouldn't know that it wasn't loaded. As she gazed at the other weapons displayed in the cabinet, she noticed an empty space. "That's where Paul got the rifle he shot Tristan with, but why did he bother returning the keys to the drawer in the master bedroom? Where did he get the bullets?" she wondered aloud. At the base of the cabinet was a drawer, also locked. The same key opened it. It contained several boxes of bullets and magazines. She locked the drawer again. It was bad enough that she'd use a rifle, a weapon she'd always hated, without loading it as well.

Soon, she'd set her plan into action, after she'd figured out all the details. It would have to be on a day that Jen, Shawna and Paula were busy. She glanced at her watch and saw with consternation that it was almost dinnertime and they weren't back yet. It was also time to call Tristan. She closed the study door to shut out the cleaning noise and sat on the dusty chair. By now she felt like a dust ball herself. She couldn't get an answer. Twice, the answering service clicked in. Instead, she called her parents to reassure them that she was okay. She'd promised them to call faithfully.

"Johanna, Tristan called. He was so surprised when I told him where you were. How come you didn't tell him?"

"Mom, you shouldn't have done that. Damn, now he's probably on his way here."

"I don't know about that. He sounded disappointed. Almost angry."

"I lied to him. Of course he's angry."

"But why on Earth the big secret?"

"I didn't want to jeopardize his job because he would have gone with me," she lied, hating herself for these white lies but she knew she'd get all kinds of opposition should she tell them the truth for her visit to the castle.

"I'm sure Tristan knows his responsibilities. I dare say he would have forbidden you to go."

"No man forbids me to do anything and to avoid an argument, I didn't tell him. It was the most logical thing to do."

"Your logic and mine are two different things."

"Let's stop arguing, Mom. This is long distance." She chatted for a while about the castle, her plans for it and how it was starting to look different already with just cleaning and finally, after talking to her father for a few minutes, she hung up.

"Dammit, if Tristan shows up, that'll spoil my plans. I want to be with him, but I have to do this first. I'll have to hunt for Paul tonight when the girls are asleep."

CHAPTER THIRTY-FOUR

JEN, SHAWNA AND PAULA ARRIVED BACK WELL AFTER DINNER. "DID you guys get lost?" Johanna asked with a smirk.

"No, we stayed till the last store closed," Paula said.

"And we stopped for something to eat," Jen added. "Shawna, give Johanna her dinner. That'll lighten her mood."

Shawna grinned and handed Johanna a bag. "The Chinese food is different but it's delicious. Sorry we couldn't keep it hot for you."

Johanna grabbed the food eagerly. She just realized she'd had no lunch and she didn't care if it wasn't hot. Anything would taste good right now. "Did you find everything I asked for?"

"Yes, including this," Jen said and handed her a large envelope.

It was the diary, she knew, but she wanted to read it in the privacy of her room. "Thanks. I'll eat while you guys unload the car."

"Place sure looks different already," Paula said carrying in a pile of parcels. "The rose garden is beautiful."

"They've worked hard all day, but it's going to take a couple of weeks before it's all finished."

"I can imagine. Have you counted all the rooms yet?"

"No. I just opened them all today and investigated them. Found some interesting things."

"Like what?"

"A library filled with old books. Whole sets that have to be worth a fortune. The study, the master bedroom, the turrets..."

"You look like a cleaning lady yourself," Paula said.

"I feel like one. A hundred years of dust everywhere. Honestly, no wonder I wasn't hungry. By the way, I have a feeling Tristan might be on his way here."

"Really? That will be nice for you, but I'd hoped we could spend some time with just the four of us before you settle into marital bliss again," Jen said.

"Well, it's my fault really because I didn't tell him we were coming here. I knew he'd disapprove."

"As if you would let you stop that," Shawna said.

"I know. I just wanted to avoid the argument. Mom went and told him. I never thought he'd phone there. That's why I got the cell phone."

"Maybe he tried your cell and it was turned off again."

"That could be. I don't want to run the battery dead by having it turned on all the time. I guess I should have bought an extra battery for it."

They finished unloaded the parcels and Johanna regarded the pile in the hall with a frown. "What did you do? Pile them all on the roof of the car or something? Or did two of you run behind the car..."

Jen laughed. "I hope you don't mind but we noticed the hitch on the back and we rented a small trailer. You'll need to do more shopping and that car is hardly big enough."

"You're right. Now that I've decided what I want to do with the castle I need to buy a few vans to transport the children and their parents in. We can go and do that later this week."

"You've taken on a huge project, Johanna. You won't have time for your regular job anymore," Jen said.

"I know. I think I'll quit the hospital and will concentrate on the castle project."

"Are you going to buy horses?" Paula asked.

"That, too. I'll have to hire stable boys and someone to train and guide the guests. Hertzenberg will once again provide a lot of work for the people in the village. There will be certain areas off limit of course. I plan to have one wing turned into private quarters for Tristan and me and our visitors."

"Does that mean you're going to leave Canada?"

"I haven't thought about that yet. Running this castle as a resort for needy children will take up a lot of time. Maybe I'll spend most of the year here and part of it in Canada."

"I wouldn't mind living here," mused Shawna.

"Well, I'll need competent staff, nurses, so you can think about it," Johanna suggested with a smile. "That's way down the road. I'm going to have a bath now that I've managed to pump down some food. How about you three unpack everything and give it a place? I'll see you in a bit."

SHE RELAXED IN THE steaming water, her thoughts on Tristan and what he was up to. After her bath, she'd try and call him again, she decided. Maybe he was just sulking. Though she loved him with all her heart, he was still a man with male quirks.

Closing her eyes she tried to concentrate on the project but instead, her thoughts dwelled on Johanna and Juliana.

Johanna—help me...

Spluttering, she sat up and peered through the steam at the walls. But the voice was too close, almost as if it was right behind her head. Gingerly she turned to look behind the tub but saw nothing. She shivered at the thought that Paul could be watching her right now. That thought caused her to quickly wash her hair, rinse it and start washing her body. A sound coming from the corner of the bathroom startled her. She thought she saw a vague shape. Now thoroughly alarmed, she jumped up and wound the towel around her body. While stepping out of the tub she hissed, "Who's there? Paul..."

Johanna...

The shape moved closer to her. Her hands searched for something, any kind of weapon, but there was nothing suitable except the cake of soap. Holding the slippery object in her hand wondering what good it would do, she waited until the shadowy figure was close enough. She lashed out at it, the soap tightly clenched in her fist. But she hit thin air.

The shadow vanished, the steam cleared a little and she scanned the wall for panels but saw nothing. She knew for sure she should have hit the person, yet her hand had encountered nothing solid.

Not bothering to put on her robe, she dashed for the door and turned the handle. The door wouldn't open. She yanked, pulled, but it was stuck tight. Wondering if her friends had pulled a trick on her, she beat the door with her fists, the towel falling to the floor. "Paul, Jen, let me out! This isn't funny!" she yelled.

Not a sound from the other side. Something brushed past her arm causing her to jump. "Who's there? Get away from me!" Trying to cover her nakedness with her arms she slunk away until her back touched the far wall.

The steam slowly evaporated and she could almost see clearly. A vague shape hovered in the bathroom just above the tub. It resembled a woman in a long white nightgown, a long blond braid hanging over one shoulder.

"My God, I'm hallucinating," she muttered as lilywhite hands reached out to her entreatingly. As she stepped forward, the hallucination slowly faded.

Dashing for her robe now, she quickly put it on and tried the door again. This time it opened easily. She pulled it shut tightly behind her and breathing heavy, ran to her bedroom.

After she'd dressed and calmed down, she tried to think about the experience rationally. This couldn't be Paul's doing. Even if he had the means to project images, the peepholes were far too small. If there was even a peephole in the bathroom... She'd really seen the castle ghost. She curbed the urge to run downstairs and tell her friends about the experience. They would be gone in a second and she'd be left all alone in the castle with Paul.

Glancing at her watch she saw she hadn't been gone all that long so she decided to read the translated diary and letters.

She started with the letters first. They were printed neatly on white paper and the English translation was very good.

My dear sister,

I have arrived in the convent. The nuns are very kind to me. I like it here very much though I miss you a great deal already. I can't tell you very much yet except that I am happy.

Your loving sister, Juliana.

Johanna folded the paper and looked at the other four letters. They all read much the same, cryptic and to the point as if they were dictated to the writer. The last one read a little different. It spoke of Juliana's return to the castle. But Juliana had never returned. It was as if she had vanished completely.

Sitting on the bed, she opened the diary and started to read the translation, leafing through the diary as she read. Several times she had to smile at the girlish language. Then, the notes became older, more sophisticated and spoke of her great-grandmother's yearning for love. Leafing through the pages she stopped when she saw Juliana's name mentioned. At first the notes were just about sisterly quarrels, petty jealousies. Then, when the girls were in their late teens, Juliana had a lover. Her sister was desperately jealous of the affair. It spoke of the girls' fear of their father, of his violent temper and his strictness, and finally Juliana was found out. She was sent to a convent and it broke Johanna's heart.

Several entries commented on the letters received from Juliana and how Johanna finally heard nothing from her sister.

Near the end of the diary, Johanna spoke of her love for Claus and their plans to elope. The final entry was the day the two lovers left Switzerland in the deep of night.

Johanna sighed as she read about the romance, the love her great-grandparents felt for each other. It reminded her of Tristan and the love she bore for him. Quickly, she grabbed her purse and the cell phone and dialed his number. Would he still be angry with her? Was he really on his way to Switzerland?

To her relief, he answered the phone this time. "Tristan? I've phoned you several times, but no answer." There was silence at the other end and for a moment she thought he'd hung up.

"I'm not very happy with you, Johanna."

"Yes, I know," she said softly.

"Why on Earth didn't you tell me what you were up to?"

"You would have tried to stop me."

"Yes, I don't like the idea of you going to that castle alone."

"I'm not alone. Didn't Mom tell you? Jen, Shawna and Paula are with me."

"Oh? No, she didn't. That makes me feel a bit better, but I still don't know why you deceived me. A relationship can't be built on lies."

"I know. I'm so sorry, Tristan. I do love you with all my heart, you know that. This is just something I needed to do."

"You could have done it with me."

"But you would have lost your job. You've already taken far too much time off because of me."

"The renovation of the castle could have waited a few more months. Why the rush?"

"Tristan, I rushed into marriage with Paul and just needed some time alone, to think things out. I also wanted to spend a few weeks with my friends while I'm still a single woman. Can you understand that?" It was partially true. He didn't sound angry, just very disappointed in her. "Dad warned you that I'm stubborn and willful."

"So he did, but I didn't quite expect this. It was a cold shower for me, let me tell you."

"Do you want to wait to get married?"

"I didn't say I'd changed my mind. But I do want to talk to you in person. I've asked for a replacement and soon as he or she arrives I'm coming over there to join you."

"Okay. Tristan, do you still love me?"

"Yes. If our love can't weather a storm now, then it's not worth going on. I love you more than life itself, but like all relationships, we need to get to know each other and get through rocky bumps. I feel our love can survive anything. Just don't ever lie to me again, my darling."

"I won't." She was thankful he hadn't guessed the real reason for her urge to come to the castle. They talked for a little while until Shawna burst into her room. Quickly, they said goodbye with the promise that she'd leave her cell phone on and he would phone her soon as he was on his way.

"What the heck is taking you so long?" Shawna asked.

"Sorry. I phoned Tristan and we got talking," Johanna said while quickly putting the diary and letters back into the envelope.

"We've unpacked everything. Let's go downstairs and play cards for a while. You know, investing in a TV and VCR wouldn't be a bad idea. We could rent some movies."

"Yes, horror and ghost movies," Johanna grinned. "We're in just the right setting for that kind of stuff."

Shawna shuddered. "Stop it, Jo. You're freaking me already."

If only you knew, Johanna thought.

CHAPTER THIRTY-FIVE

THAT EVENING, THEY ALL DECIDED TO GO TO BED EARLIER THAN the night before. Jen, Shawna and Paula were tired from their excursion to Zurich and Johanna feigned tiredness. They didn't drink any wine that evening and stuck to orange juice instead. She hoped they slept sound enough not to wake if Paul decided to play games again.

Near midnight, she checked to make sure her friends were asleep before she grabbed her flashlight and the rifle from beneath her mattress. She ventured softly to her great-grandmother's room to wait. The wad of chewing gum was still in place. Sitting on the bed, waiting for sounds to come from the walls, she waited impatiently.

It was just after one in the morning when the howling started. She grinned. Paul's imitation of ghostly howling sounded more like a wolf. She heard his feet shuffle through the passages, his cough, clearing his throat. He tried unearthly laughter that echoed through the silence of the castle.

A piercing scream came from the direction of her friends' rooms. Her first urge was to rush to their aid, but she needed to follow Paul, to catch him that night and maybe lock him in one of the turrets.

In the distance she could hear the girls talking excitedly, banging on her door. She'd locked the door and hoped they would quit soon. Paul's haunting continued for a while, interrupted by her friend's squeals of fear. She felt cruel, but she had no choice.

After opening the secret panel, she left it wide open, in fear of not being able to find her way back. She did the same with the bookcase panel at the back of the secret room. Before entering the passage, she lit a large candle and set it in the center of the secret room. She needed a guiding light as the passages were inky black.

Her heart thumping with fear, she held her breath as she started to move toward the sound of Paul's ghostly games. Several times she ran into a dead end and had to feel her way back groping the walls for the opening to another passage.

How she got there, she had no idea. She saw the bright beam of a flashlight on the stone floor, above it the shape of a man. It was Paul, she was sure. She stood very still clutching the flashlight and the rifle to her chest. She hardly dared breathe. What if he came toward her? She wondered which room was behind the wall. Her friend's voices were clear, their conversation heated. Paul was quiet for the moment, just listening.

"Why the hell doesn't Johanna hear this stuff?" Paula said.

"Damned if I know. All I know is that I'm going to sleep in a hotel from now on. First thing tomorrow morning I'm packing my things and getting the hell out of here," Shawna said.

Paul's laugh echoed through the passages. It sounded evil, demonic. The girls screamed. Johanna could almost see them in her mind, huddled on the bed together, their eyes wide with fear. She felt sorry for them, but there was nothing she could do at this point. She needed to proceed with her plan.

It seemed to take forever before Paul decided it was enough. She watched him pick up the flashlight and had to slink back into the passage as it came toward her. Trying not to make a sound she stepped back a few paces away from the advancing light. It disappeared around a corner. Just as she stepped forward, something scurried over her feet. She almost screamed and managed to stop just in time. Not even wanting to think if it was a rat or a mouse, she quickly walked to where the flashlight had disappeared and rounded the corner.

The light was far ahead of her. Stealthily she crept behind him until the light dimmed and disappeared. Carefully she negotiated each step she took, which was just as well because suddenly she stepped into air. Crouching on hands and knees she felt with her hands and encountered stairs. She heard his footsteps in the distance and holding on to the wall she gingerly went down the stone stairs. It was a narrow stairwell, so narrow that it barely fit her body.

When she got to the bottom she saw the light in the far distance. Speeding up a little she followed until it was gone and again she encountered a stairwell. This continued until she felt as if she'd reached the center of the Earth. She'd gone down three stairwells so far. Mentally she pictured the scroll and tried to remember the different levels of the castle and knew there had to be another floor below the cellars.

At the end of the last passage she saw a fairly bright light, too bright for a flashlight. She hurried toward it and stopped at the end of the passage. Carefully, she peeked around the corner and saw a large room. The walls were rock, as if it was an underground cavern of some sort. In its center stood a large, rough wooden table with a bright burning oil lamp on it and a pile of books. An array of empty and full wine bottles stood at the far end of the table and dirty plates and cups. A couple of rough wooden chairs stood around the table. On one of them sat a man with his back toward her. He was twirling the flashlight and humming softly to himself.

It was Paul.

Grimly, she smiled with satisfaction. Her hunch had paid off. Was he armed? Could she do this by herself? Her gaze wandered over the walls and saw the rusty shackles and chains attached to them. On the table lay a bunch of rusty keys. She decided to wait. He had to be asleep before she could do anything. Cursing silently she wished she'd taken some rope along. Suddenly, she spotted the chair with the rings for straps on the arms and the legs and she nodded. That would do for starters. The straps, she noticed, lay on the table.

Paul stood and started pacing the floor. She saw the wild demonic expression in his eyes and shivered. Maybe she shouldn't do this by herself. Wondering if she could enlist the aid of her friends, she slunk back into the passage when he came too close.

"They'll leave now." She heard him say. "Bloody bitches. I'd like to get hold of the dark one again though. Those tits of hers drive me crazy.

Maybe I should go upstairs and put some of the stuff in their wine. I need some food anyway."

Johanna started to back further into the passage but she need not have feared. She saw him walk to the wall and pull a lever. The wall swung open and he disappeared through it. So there was another way out...

She made up her mind then. This was not something she could do alone. Her friends were terrified and deserved an explanation. They would stand by her, she knew that for sure and she finally realized that to tackle Paul alone was far too dangerous. Now to find her way back...

It was like navigating a maze. At least, this time, she could use the flashlight with Paul out of the way. Shining the light on the floor showed her a clear track in the dust where Paul had walked. Eventually she got to the room where her friends were still in an intense argument. The sound of their voices traveled down the passage, guiding her.

Sighing with relief, she stepped into the secret room and shut the bookcase behind her. After blowing out the candle, she headed quickly to Paula's room. It was locked so she knocked loudly to overpower their conversation.

The door opened a crack to reveal Shawna clad in sweats. "Jo, where have you been? You're filthy! You wouldn't believe what happened, and..."

"I know what's happened and you won't believe me either. Let me in, Shawna."

"Sorry."

Johanna walked into the room and looked at Paula's angry face and Jen's teary eyes. "Don't worry, guys. It's not real."

"You know?"

"Of course I know. I'm not deaf. Look, I've got something to tell you and I need you to listen carefully. We have to talk very softly because the walls have eyes and ears."

"So we found out," said Paula sarcastically. "The ghosts are real."

"They're not real. That's what I want to tell you. Now listen carefully..."

In a whisper, she told them everything. Her reason for wanting to come to the castle, her suspicion that Paul could be there. Her discovery of the scroll with the castle blueprints, the secret room, the passages. And her discovery of that night.

"You mean Paul is the one who's been freaking us out?"

"Yes. And believe me, he's as evil as they come. Right now he's in the kitchen putting a drug into the wine in the fridge."

"Oh, my God," Paul said. "He was going to kill us all!"

"No. He was going to drug us all so he could have some perverted fun with us. He was mumbling about Paula's boobs."

"You're kidding. He's never seen my boobs!"

"There's a hole in the wall. He's been spying on us all. I don't want to plug it up with gum right now because he'll get suspicious, so just wear your sweats and don't get changed in here. Listen, I want to punish him with a vengeance and I need your help. I can't do it alone. This is my plan..." she proceeded to tell the girls how she wanted to punish Paul and hoped they'd agree to help her.

They did.

"When do you want to do this, Jo?"

"Tonight. He can't stay awake forever. We'll wait a while and then we'll all go through the passages to where he is. There are more rifles in the study. They're not loaded, but he won't know that. We have to be super quiet though. No freaking out at bugs or cobwebs."

"I don't know if I'm brave enough for that," Jen said in squeaky whisper

"Don't be silly. What can he do against four of us?"

"Plenty. Why don't you just call the police?"

"Because I want him to squirm for a bit. He needs to feel what it's like to be confined. Admittedly I wasn't shackled or anything, but it felt like it being jailed within my own body. Look at the jails nowadays. They even have TV."

"Tristan will be here soon. Let him deal with it," Paula suggested.

"No. Look, if you're not willing to help me, I'll do it alone."

"No, I can't let you do that. I'm scared stiff, but I'm with you," said

Shawna. "But what if he overpowers us and imprisons us somewhere in the castle? No one will ever find us."

"Paul is basically a coward. I was going to deal with him alone, but that would be too dangerous, I realize now. But four of us? I have a feeling we'll scare the pants off him. So how about it? Are you all game?"

Paula and Jen agreed reluctantly. Johanna felt relieved. She'd tell them about the real castle ghost later...

CHAPTER THIRTY-SIX

"DO YOU THINK HE'S FINISHED IN THE KITCHEN?" PAULA ASKED IN a loud whisper.

"Ssh, not so loud. I don't know. It's been more than an hour. I'll go down for a glass of milk," Johanna said. "I'll make enough noise to announce my coming and that will chase him back down. There must be an entrance in the wine cellar too, but we'd better take the other passages."

"Wouldn't it be easier to find the passage in the wine cellar and go from there? I don't fancy going through a maze of tunnels."

"I don't know where the panel is and it would take too long to find it. Plus, it opens directly into that room and he could have the advantage over us because the panel opens rather slowly."

"I feel like we're a SEAL team or something," Paula giggled nervously.

"Okay, let me go check the kitchen."

Johanna hurried down the stairs stomping loud. Her footsteps echoed in the silence of the night. She opened the kitchen door fearfully, but Paul had gone. Opening the fridge, she took out the bottles of wine and poured them down the sink. Returning to the still open fridge, she saw in a glance that a bottle of milk was missing and some of the snacks her friends had bought in Zurich that day. Taking out an unopened carton of orange juice, she took it upstairs with her.

They shared the orange juice and waited a while longer. "Okay, it's time we start," Johanna said while jumping off the bed.

Her friends followed her hesitantly. "Are you sure about this, Johanna?"

"As sure as I'll ever be. Let's go and get the rifles first and hope Paul isn't spying on us."

Shawna eyed the wall suspiciously before she left the room. "Do you think the hallways have peepholes, too?"

"No, they don't. Come on and don't talk. Sounds really carry right now because everything is so quiet. Just follow me."

After giving each of the girls a rifle and helping them to load the bolts and magazines, she led them to Johanna's room and to the secret room.

"I'm scared stiff, but this is so romantic. Like an adventure novel," Paula whispered.

"Ssh, no more talking now. Come on," Johanna whispered and opened the bookcase panel.

"I don't want to go in there," Jen whispered loudly.

"Dammit, Jen, be quiet. Just follow me. Just remember at the end I have to turn off the flashlight. Otherwise he'll see us. I don't know if he still has the rifle he shot Tristan with. Or, he could try to escape and then we'll never find him, nor will the police. He thinks he's smart, but he never reckoned with Johanna Von Hertzenberg. Not another word now, not a squeal, or even a breath."

She led the way hoping her friends were right behind her. It was easier to navigate the passages this time, the bright beam of the flashlight lighting her way. It also caused soft gasps from her friends when they spotted spiders and a mouse scurrying away. At one point Jen stopped them by whispering, "That's it. I'm going back."

Shawna yanked hair. "No way. I'm continuing and you'd have to crawl right over me."

"Ssh, be quiet. One more stairwell and we're there," Johanna whispered over her shoulder. "We don't want him to hear us."

She stopped when she saw the light at the end of the passage and pointed at it. Paula, right behind her, nodded and moved her head so Jen and Shawna could see it. Johanna doused the flashlight. They crept toward the light slowly, softly, until they reached the open door. Johanna stopped and put her fingers to her lips. She peeked carefully around the corner and pulled back right away. Paul was facing her way.

Motioning the girls to follow her, she headed back into the passages.

"What the hell are you doing?" Paula said in a loud whisper.

"Shut up, Paula! You'll give us away!"

She waited until they were back in the bedroom and closed the panel. Perspiration dripped from her forehead and she wiped it away with the back of her hand. "We have to wait until he's had enough to drink. He's too perky yet."

"You mean you want us to go there again?" Jen asked in a shaky voice. "I guarantee I feel spiders crawling up my legs. And I'm sure I saw a rat."

"Don't be such a baby, Jen. I didn't see anything but cobwebs from years of dust."

Shawna shook her head vehemently. "I'm not going back there. What if the guy grabs us all?"

"So you're going to abandon me? Fine. I'll do it alone," Johanna said and started to leave the room.

"Jojo, come on now. We can't do this. Let's call the police and have him picked up," Jen said.

"I can and I will do it. See you later."

"Honestly, I've never seen anyone so pigheaded!" Jen said. "Fine, I'll help you even if Paula and Shawna won't. When do you want to go back?"

"I'll set the alarm for four or so. He should be asleep by then."

"So what are we going to do till four? Sleep? There's no way in hell I can sleep. Twiddle our thumbs?"

"I'm wide awake. Never mind setting the alarm and going to bed. Why don't we go down to the parlor and play cards for a while. That'll pass the time."

"Good idea," Paula said. "I wouldn't mind a glass of wine either to calm my frayed nerves. And I'm in. What about you Shawna?"

Shawna agreed reluctantly. "Very well. But if he kills me, I'll never forgive you, Jojo."

Johanna laughed. "Okay, I'll hold you to that. Come on, let's go. He could be standing behind the wall right now listening to us and he'll know what we're up to."

Fearfully they looked at the wall and followed Johanna out the room and down to the parlor.

They played cards, though none were really into the game. Johanna stopped the girls from drinking wine. They all needed bright minds when tackling Paul.

It was finally getting close to four. "Okay, how about we go check him out now?" Johanna said.

"Oh, God, I hoped you'd given up on the thought," Jen said wistfully. "You never said another word about it while we played."

"Never. And for your information, my mind was on it all the time. Let's go." Grabbing her flashlight, she led the way, more determined than ever though inwardly, she quivered.

They followed the passages and stairs down to the dungeons until they spotted the soft glow of Paul's oil lamp. It was much easier to negotiate the passage this time. "Turn off your flashlights," Johanna whispered. She tiptoed to the door, the sour smell of wine entering her nostrils. Carefully, she peeked around the corner and saw Paul sprawled naked on his bed half covered with one of the expensive satin quilts from upstairs. Motioning her friends to follow, she walked into the dungeon and toward Paul's bed. He seemed in a deep sleep. She hoped he was inebriated enough that he wouldn't wake as they dragged him to the chair.

"Help me," she hissed as she placed her arms under his armpits and sat him upright.

Just as Jen and Paula reached out to help her, Paul woke up.

"What the hell's going on? Get off me!" he yelled and lunged for Johanna as she stepped back. He kicked Paula and sent her sprawling on the ground. Jen tried to help Johanna but he sent her flying too. She landed painfully against the wall. Paula, furious now as she rubbed her chafed arm, lunged for Paul again, but in vain. He sent her sprawling for a second time. This time she fell hard against the table.

Johanna saw her way clear when he concentrated on getting Paula off him. "Take this!" she hissed and quickly reversed the grip on her rifle and struck him on the side of the head with the butt. Paul collapsed back onto the bed unconscious.

Panting, Johanna watched him for a moment to make sure he was out cold. "Okay, he's out. Are you okay, Paula? Jen?"

Shawna helped Paula up who painfully rubbed her knee. "Besides a few bruises and scrapes, I'm okay."

"So am I," Jen said. "Okay, we'd better get him to the chair right now, before he comes out of it."

They dragged him to the chair. He wasn't a big man, but a dead weight. They hoisted him into the chair, his head lolling on his chest.

"Grab those leather straps on the table, Shawna," Johanna said. "Okay, each one of you take a strap and tie him up. Give me one too."

While they were intent on securing the straps, Paul stirred and started to struggle. "Get me hell out of this thing!" he yelled. "You'll pay for this, bitches!" he stopped for a moment to spit in Paula's face. She recoiled and grabbing the edge of her shirt wiped the spit off her face. "You didn't seem to mind my attentions last night," he growled.

"What the hell are you talking about?" Paula said.

"Don't you remember, honey? You were a pretty good lay!"

"Like hell I was!" Paula said and yanked the strap tighter, but his words reminded her of the dream, or what she thought was a dream. Could it be?

"That's enough!" Johanna said. "If you don't shut up, I'll hit you again!" She held the rifle up as if to strike him.

"Honey, I'm so glad you're okay," he said in a slimy voice. "I've missed you so much."

"Yeah, right. And I'm totally blond!" She moved behind him and stood well away from him, the rifle pointed at his back. "Cover him, girls."

They stayed far enough away from him but kept their rifles pointed at him. Paul sat on the chair, a silly grin on his face. "And what do you propose to do now? You wouldn't have the guts to shoot me. None of you would."

"Don't tempt me, asshole! You'd better believe I have the guts after what you did to me."

"It was an accident."

"Accident my foot."

"The police totally misunderstood. That reporter..."

"Is my current fiancé. Since you're already married I'm free and single."

"I divorced her."

"That's another lie and another day of torture. Paula, aren't you finished yet?" Paul didn't seem scared enough for Johanna's taste. But he would be. While the girls finished securing the straps and checked them once more, she held the butt of the rifle up, ready to smash it down on his head. On the back of the chair was a wide leather band that was meant to go around someone's forehead. She pushed the ends of it forward.

"Now his head."

When he was completely secured, she stood back and surveyed their handiwork. "Good."

Paul tried to wiggle the chair. It creaked a bit but was secured to the ground with large, rusty bolts.

Johanna glanced at the torture equipment hanging on the walls and thought about it for a moment, especially when she saw the finger screws, but she thought better of it. He wasn't worth going to jail for.

Jen wiped the perspiration off her forehead. "Phew, now what?"

"Now we leave him here. Shawna, grab that lamp. He can sit here and rot in the dark and think about what he did to me and his other wives."

"He's going to yell all night," Paula said.

"So? We won't hear him. It's far enough in the ground that no one will hear him except the rats."

"What about if he has to go to the bathroom," Shawna said, shivering at the mention of rats.

"Who cares? He's nothing but a piece of shit, so let him wallow in it. Come on, let's go."

"You can't leave me here like this. I'll die," Paul hissed.

"So? Isn't that what you meant for me? No one but us will ever know. Bye, Paul."

"You bloody bitch! You'll pay for this!"

Johanna pulled the lever on the wall. The stone wall opened slowly to reveal the wine cellar. "Just as I thought. Now I know why you were so long down here before getting just a bottle of wine." She checked the straps and bolts one more time. Even though they were rusted, they were still too strong for Paul to break free. She'd check on him regularly anyway. "Come on, let's go."

Shawna grabbed the lamp off the table and Johanna waited till her friends moved into the wine cellar. The wall closed slowly behind her. The last they heard were Paul's curses. Once the wall was in place, they couldn't hear his foul language anymore.

"Phew, that was something else. So now you're just going to leave him there?" Jen asked.

"For a little while. Long enough to punish him and make him squirm a bit."

"I never thought you could be that cruel." As she spoke the words, Jen saw the pain reflected in her friend's eyes. Small dots of perspiration dotted Johanna's forehead and her mouth twitched when she spoke. Though Johanna was a strong person, had refused therapy to overcome any psychological residue from her torturous marriage and illness, it was obvious that the memory of her immobility still lingered strongly causing hate and revenge to fester in her heart and mind.

"Well, you try sitting in your skin for months on end without speech or movement. It's living hell and that's what I want him to experience—a living hell. Jail is too good for him."

"I'm sorry. I know you went through hell, Jojo, but you're taking the law into your own hands now and that's not good."

"I just want him to know what it feels like to be confined and unable to move. Pity he can still talk. I couldn't utter a sound. I'll contact the authorities soon. I promise."

"Maybe he'll get the death penalty in the States," Shawna suggested.

"Maybe he will, but, don't forget appeals. It takes years for a murderer to actually be executed. Anyway, even the death penalty is too good for him. He needs to suffer, to know what it's like to be the victim. And by the way, that dream of yours, Paula?"

"Yes, the one about the hunk having sex with me?"

"I think that happened for real. You were quite drunk and when you're that way, you don't wake up even if we'd drop a bomb next to you. I think it was Paul." She saw Paula's face pale.

"My God, you don't mean that!"

"Yes. Don't you remember saying that you actually felt sore?"

"I feel sick at the thought at him touching me anywhere, let alone have sex with me. I need to go and throw up," Paula said and started to walk away.

"So now do you see my point that jail is too good for the jerk?"

"I do," Jen agreed. "Can we go upstairs now?"

"Yes. Let's take a bottle of wine with us. I think we could use a glass after this night. At least we've got the creep."

"I hope your Tristan gets here soon."

"Not too soon. He'll insist I hand Paul over to the police. I want him to suffer for at least a few days."

"I need a bath," Paula muttered, still wiping her face.

"I think we all need one. How about we quickly take turns bathing and then we'll share a glass of wine to toast to our success. You don't have to be afraid anymore. The mystery ghost is safe and secure downstairs."

"I still have the creeps," Jen said as she opened the bathroom door. "What if he gets loose somehow?"

"I don't know how, but just in case, keep the rifles with you. Maybe we should sleep together for a bit. Jen, you bunk with Paula. Shawna, you bunk with me."

"Good idea. Makes me feel better," Jen said.

After they all bathed and shared a glass of wine they went to bed exhausted though Johanna didn't sleep right away. The events of that evening played through her mind for quite a while, until she forced the thoughts away and thought about Tristan instead. Now that she had fulfilled her plan, she longed for him, for his strong arms around her, his lips on hers. Just as she started to feel drowsy, she heard the voice calling her name again.

Johanna...

She glanced at Shawna, but apparently she had not heard it. Johanna lay with her hands under her head gazing in the direction of the voice. So this was the real castle ghost, except it no longer frightened her. She waited to see if it would speak again, but it didn't. Her thoughts drifted back to Paul and what he must be feeling right now and smiled grimly. Serve you right, she thought. You're getting what you deserve... Smiling happily that her plan had worked, she closed her eyes and tried to sleep.

CHAPTER THIRTY-SEVEN

THE CLEANING CREWS WERE ALREADY HARD AT WORK WHEN THE girls finally woke up and rose to make breakfast. When Johanna glanced out of the window, she noticed a crew of landscapers busy as well.

"How come you're so quiet, Jojo? The eggs not to your liking?" Paula asked. She'd done the cooking this time.

"She's probably thinking about Paul. Shouldn't you bring him some food?"

"No!" she snapped in a steely voice. "I'll bring him some water later. Can't let him dehydrate."

"You're so quiet. What's wrong? Are you feeling guilty?"

"Hell no. Nothing is wrong. There's something else I need to tell you guys and maybe you can help me solve the mystery."

They were all ears. "What mystery?"

"Okay. First of all, the castle does have a real ghost."

Paul and Shawna squirmed uncomfortably. "I'm getting out of here, this is all too crazy for me!" Paula murmured.

"It does? How do you know?" Jen asked.

"I've heard and seen it. Apparently you haven't, otherwise you'd be freaking at me by now. She's not scary anyway. All she does is call my name and once I saw her in a hazy fog sort of."

"She?" Jen said.

"Yes, it's a female voice."

"Maybe it's your grandmother," Paula said, her eyes wide as saucers at the thought that there really was a ghost in the castle, but now quite intrigued.

"No, I don't think so. The voice doesn't sound like Gran's."

"How come we can't hear or see it?" Shawna asked.

"I don't know. Maybe it's just concentrating on me. I don't feel afraid of it anymore. I did at first."

"So what's the mystery?"

"Soon as we finish brunch, I'll show you some letters my grandmother left me and a diary I found. I'll also show you the scroll and some portraits."

"Do we have to go through creepy passages again?" Jen asked while shivering in an exaggerated manner.

"No, silly. The stuff is upstairs in my room and Johanna's."

"Johanna?"

"My great-grandmother. I was named after her."

"Oh."

"I look like her, too."

THEY FINISHED EATING, CLEARED off the table and Johanna led the way to Johanna senior's room. Her friends drooled over the porcelain dolls. Johanna pointed at the portrait on the wall. "That's my great-grandmother Johanna. I guess she must have been about eighteen then. And look at these," she said while opening the panel to the secret room and taking out the portraits hidden in there.

"Wow, they sure look alike. And like you. The three of you could be sisters," Jen said.

"Yes, we could I suppose. Now read these letters and the entries in the diary." She handed the diary and its translation to Paula and gave the letters to Jen and Shawna to read. They were quiet for a while, intent on what they were reading. While they were busy, Johanna rummaged in the secret room. Several boxes were filled with trinkets and old dresses. She pulled the dresses out, grimacing at the style. If they got bored, they could play dress-up.

"So, what I can make out is that this Juliana went to some convent and no one ever heard from her again."

"I don't think she went to a convent at all. I think something happened to her. Come with me to the turret."

Pushing all thoughts of Paul into the very back of her mind, she concentrated fully on the castle mystery—the mysterious Juliana who was never heard of again and apparently not even mentioned because her grandmother obviously didn't know about her mother's sister. Johanna wondered why her great-grandmother had never talked about the sister in the convent. Did it hurt too much? How could she find out the name of the convent? The letters only had a date, no address or indication where the convent was located. It could have been in another country for all she knew. Why had the notes stopped? Her mind was asking the same questions now as the ones her namesake had posed in the diary. Had Juliana cut herself off from her family completely? From what she read in the diary, the two sisters were very close. It was hard to imagine Juliana never writing to her sister again.

The girls followed her to the turret and she led them up the winding stairs. "This is where I think Juliana was held captive for a while. Look at the inkwell, the pen and the note she started. It's addressed the same as the other notes and in the same handwriting," Johanna said as she unlocked the door and opened it.

"Oh, cool. Wonder what happened to her?" Jen said.

"I guess that's the castle mystery my grandmother mentioned in her letter. I'd like to solve it, but don't know quite where to begin."

"We'll have to search everywhere. Have you gone through all the personal stuff?" Shawna asked.

"I think a lot of it was stashed in the attic. Look at the stain on the bed. Does that resemble blood?"

"Maybe she had a period," Paula said. "They didn't have tampons in those days you know, or even pads."

"True. But why would she be held prisoner in the turret? Obviously the convent was a lie. Maybe she was forced to write the letters."

"She had a lover. Could be her father locked her up to keep her away from the man," Jen said.

"That's a possibility. Then what happened to her after that? Did she escape and run away with him?"

"If that's true, there could be other heirs to the castle," Shawna said.

"I don't care. I want to solve this riddle. Maybe there are descendents in the village of people who used to work in the castle. We could question the villagers."

"What about Jakob? You told me his family always worked at the castle."

"There's a thought, except he can't speak English. One of the landscapers speaks English. Maybe I can get him to translate for me. He's quite good really. I'll go and give Paul some water first. Who wants to go with me?"

"I'll go," Shawna offered.

"Okay. We'll be back shortly," she told Jen and Paula. After filling a glass with water, she opened the door to the wine cellar and pulled the string to turn on the light. "Careful of these steps, Shawna. They're rather rickety."

"Shouldn't you take the rifle with you?"

"Why? He'll be still sitting there. Scared shitless, I hope." She followed the path where the dust was disturbed the most and when standing before the back wall ran her fingers along every edge she could find. "I hope I can find the mechanism to open the panel from this side," she muttered.

"Shit!" Shawna yelled and jumped aside, bumping into Johanna.

Johanna fell against the wall. Within seconds it opened to reveal the torture chamber. She shone the flashlight on him. As she had predicted Paul still sat in his chair. Sweat ran in rivulets from his forehead, his shirt soaked. He looked at her wildly. An unbearable stench of urine and feces greeted them and Shawna plugged her nose. Though they were nurses and used to a lot of smelly things, this was rather potent. Johanna's stomach lurched for a moment but she didn't show it bothered her.

"Bitch," Paul said through clenched teeth. "Get me out of this thing. Even jail would be better than this."

"Exactly. That's why I'm leaving you here so you can suffer. Drink!"

She held the glass to his lips but he refused to drink at first. Finally, he took a swallow and spat it at her. "Fine. Dehydrate then. I have witnesses to say I tried to give you fluids. If need be, I'll hook you up to an IV so you'd better drink from the glass."

"You wouldn't dare."

"Don't tempt me. Soon as I realized where you were hiding, I made my plans."

"Impossible. You didn't even know about the secret passages and this room."

"How do you think I found you, Paul? Drink!" she ordered again and almost poured the water down his throat. "If you're good, I'll bring you some soup later on. We can't have you dying on us now, can we? Come on, Shawna. Let's go."

"Let me out of here. I promise I'll confess everything to the police!"

"No! Pigs need to live like pigs!" Johanna said in an icy tone and left the chamber. Shawna was already waiting for her in the wine cellar. The panel closed and she let go of her nose.

Johanna leaned against the wall for a moment and took a deep breath. "Phew, that was awful. I can't leave him like that. I almost feel sorry for the guy," she said. "I don't think I can go through with it. I'm going to call the cops right now." Tears ran down her cheeks and dripped onto her clenched hands. No matter how much she wanted Paul to suffer, to do this to another human being was completely out of character for her and at one point she had cared for him.

"Johanna, how did you feel about him when you were in your zombie state?"

"I felt terrible. All I could think about was getting better and find the bastard."

"Then how can you feel sorry for the monster who did that to you?"

"I can't help it. But two wrongs don't make a right."

"Don't weaken now, Jojo. Let him suffer for a while. Remember what he did to you, what you think he did to Paula. After all, we're nurses. We can take care of his health. He needs to feel what you felt all those months."

"What's the use? He can still communicate, move his body. It's not the same."

"It's close enough." Shawna placed an arm around her friend's shoulders and hugged her briefly. "Come on now, where's the strong Jojo we all know?"

"I guess I can play with him for a bit before turning him over. He isn't really suffering yet, just uncomfortable," she gave in, unused to this show of affection from Shawna and feeling rather moved by it.

After locking the door to the cellar behind her, Johanna, still trying to quell her shakiness, said to the waiting girls, "Okay, that is done. Let's go talk to Jakob now."

Like the day before, they found Jakob supervising the landscaping. Johanna approached him. "Jakob, where is the translator? I want to ask you some questions."

Jakob called Klaus, who quickly joined them. The young man lifted his cap and Paula instantly batted her eyelashes. He looked to be in his early twenties, very fair, with eyes the deep blue of pansies. Open admiration shone in his eyes as he answered Johanna's questions, but kept his gaze riveted on vivacious Paula. She explained to him what she wanted to know. Klaus reluctantly averted his gaze from Paula and swiftly spoke to Jakob who nodded thoughtfully and answered him.

"He says he knows about the two sisters. His parents told him."

"What happened to Juliana Von Hertzenberg?"

"She went to a convent. No one ever saw her again."

"That doesn't help me much. Could anyone in the village answer my questions?"

Klaus repeated the question to Jakob, but the old man shook his head and told Klaus something.

Klaus looked at Johanna. "After Juliana left for the convent, a strange woman came to work at the castle as Johanna's governess. She was from the big city. Jakob doesn't remember her name."

"That's too bad. I don't know how I can find out," Johanna said.

"Jakob just told me you need to look in the attic. Maybe there are some records stored there."

"There is also a million years of dust and spiders up there," Johanna muttered. "Okay, I guess we'd better tackle the attic next. Neither have I examined all the cupboards in the study. There could be accounting books there. Thank you, Klaus, Jakob. You're doing a wonderful job with the gardens. Klaus, do you think you can repair the fountain? I'd really like to see it cleaned and the fountains going."

"Yes, I will try to fix it," Klaus promised and touched his cap in greeting.

"Come on, guys, let's go search the attic and the study."

"You know I'm starting to enjoy myself," Jen said. "Who knows what we'll find up there."

More cleaning people had arrived and the castle buzzed with the sound of polishing machines, vacuum cleaners and other cleaning equipment. All the rugs were gone from the floors and put outside where several young girls were beating them. Everything was starting to shine and sparkle and look the way it was supposed to.

As Johanna walked through one of the long hallways followed by her friends, she noted the mahogany sideboards, now polished to a high sheen, beautiful vases and ornaments on top of them. They had all been covered with dust covers so she had no idea they were even there. The lamps that graced the walls were made of brass, now also gleaming, the glass shades washed and allowing more light and gilded mirrors reflected their images as they passed them. "In a few weeks we won't recognize the castle," she said over her shoulder.

"It's magnificent," Paula breathed. "Oh, I wish..."

"So far, I don't think it's ever been a happy place. I hope to turn it into a happy place when the first needy children arrive. Remember, I need nurses on duty. So, if you want to live here..."

"I'm seriously considering it," Shawna said.

"So am I," echoed Paula.

"I'd give you each your own suite. Once the cleaning is done, I'll get the renovation people in and have bathrooms installed. I can turn two rooms into a suite. How about it?"

They climbed the stairs to the attic. Johanna had taken the flashlight along and after opening the heavy oak door, shone it into the dark space. "There is a light somewhere but there are so many cobwebs that you can hardly see."

After finding a stick she swiped at the cobwebs. Like the rest of the castle, everything was hidden beneath dust covers. Carefully, trying not to disturb the dust too much, they removed the covers to find large chests, old rocking horses, a cradle that Johanna drooled over, toys dating back a few hundred years, racks and racks of clothing. She opened one of the chests and gasped. Inside were stacks of velvet boxes resembling the one her grandmother had given her. She picked one up, opened it to gaze at what looked like an emerald necklace with matching earrings.

"I wonder if these are real," she said softly opening one box after another. "Why would they keep them up here if they are?"

"Probably paste. No one in their right mind would keep expensive jewelry in the attic."

"Well, it's an unlikely place for a thief to look, that's for sure."

"Look at this," Paula exclaimed. "It's filled with ledgers. Maybe you'll find what you're looking for in them, Jo."

"Okay, look for ledgers in the years nineteen hundred and five to nineteen hundred and eight."

"I did. There are several. Here they are." She handed the ledgers to Johanna who leafed through them quickly.

"I can't find anything except household expenses and wages. Maybe the governess is just a myth."

"You're chasing ghosts, Jo. I doubt you'll ever find out what really happened to Juliana."

They examined all the chests' contents, the rest of the attic until Shawna complained that she was hungry. Johanna looked at her watch. "You know, it's past seven. We've been up here for hours. Let's go and wash up and go to the village to eat."

"And leave Paul here by himself?"

"So? What's he going to do? Raid the castle?" Johanna said with a grin. "I'll feed him some soup before we go. I think there's some packages of instant soup."

"Man, you're cruel. I didn't think you had it in you," Jen said, "but you should consider cleaning him up at least. You can't leave him sitting in his own shit like that. He'll end up sick!"

"Doesn't he deserve the treatment he's getting?" Shawna said, her voice rising.

"Well, I still don't think it's right," Jen muttered. "You don't want him to become ill or you'll end up in jail too."

"As if I really care!" she grumbled while heating water for the soup. She knew Jen was right, but she didn't want to untie him. A thought occurred to her. "Shawna, there's a garden hose outside that the gardeners have been using. Can you go and fetch it for me? It's quite long. It may reach all the way to the dungeons."

"You're not serious! You wouldn't," Paula said.

"How else do I clean him up?"

"I agree with Jen. Never thought you could be this hard and callous."

"I had all those months to think about revenge. And now I'm getting it, thanks to the blueprint of the castle."

By the time Shawna came back with the hose, Johanna had finished making the instant soup. They trooped down to the dungeon, Shawna and Paula dragging the hose while Jen stayed upstairs to attach it to the kitchen tap.

"For God's sake, Johanna, you can't do this!" Paul yelled as he saw what she was planning to do.

"Paula, hold the flashlight will you? Jen, you can turn the tap on now!" she yelled loud as she could, hoping that Jen could hear her. She did, because in a few moments when she tried the nozzle, water sprayed out.

She aimed it at Paul and hosed him down. He squirmed, yelled and cursed. Each time he squirmed it gave her a chance to hose beneath him.

"Okay, that's enough. He should be fairly clean now."

"You've made a hell of a mess on the floor though."

"I'll just hose that down to the dungeons," she said and steered the mess far enough away that the worst of the smell was gone. "Okay, now to feed him. Pity, the soup's almost cold."

As she ladled the broth into Paul's mouth, he choked a few times but swallowed at least. When it was all gone, she was about to leave when he said, "And you can stop your haunting games, too. It doesn't scare me in the least."

"Haunting? We were up in the attic all afternoon."

"Bullshit. You were down here all dressed up in some old fashioned nightgown and your hair braided."

She fingered her ponytail. "I don't think so. You must have seen the real castle ghost."

"It was you."

"Sorry, can't claim that one. Maybe the castle ghost is helping me," she said with a giggle. "Did she tell you her name?"

"It was your voice but I couldn't understand the lingo."

"Since when can I speak another language? Think about it, Paul."

"There are mice and rats down here."

"So you have even more company."

"You're nothing but a low-down..."

She noticed his voice was hoarse from screaming and she sternly banished her feelings of pity. "That will do. I'll be back before I go to bed to bring you some more broth or water. Don't worry. I won't let you starve to death. That's too easy." The girls had already gone upstairs, Shawna taking the hose with her. For a few moments she studied the pitiful creature in the chair and almost felt sorry for him. He sure as hell didn't feel sorry for me, she thought, yet the feeling of remorse would not leave her. The temptation to call the police was great, but she wasn't a quitter, always finished what she set out to do, and as always was stubbornly determined to see this through to the end.

THEY RETURNED FROM THE village well satiated. After putting away the food they had bought for the next day, they relaxed in the parlor with a glass of wine.

"I'm exhausted," Jen said. "I hope your friendly ghost doesn't bother us."

"I don't think she will. Like I said, she seems to be interested only in me. Oh, I forgot to tell you. It's not only me, the ghost has been haunting Paul. He thinks it's me."

"If he thinks it's you, it has to be the first Johanna, your great-grandmother," Shawna said.

"Or maybe Juliana," Johanna said thoughtfully. "If only she would speak more than just a few words and in English. It's past midnight. I have to call Tristan. You guys coming to bed?"

"Even though Paul is downstairs and tied to that chair, I still feel uneasy. I wish Tristan would hurry up and get here."

"I hope he stays away a few days yet. Once he's here, he'll call the cops. Anyway, I'm going up. After I've talked to him I'm going to bed. Goodnight."

She climbed the stairs wearily, every bone in her body aching from the unusual activities of that day. After trying several times to call Tristan, she finally got through to him.

"Hi honey," he greeted sweetly. "What have you been up to today?"

"We spent almost the whole day going through stuff in the attic. I'm exhausted."

"I'll be there in two days to help you. Don't overdo it, okay? You're still recovering, remember?"

"I'm fine. Don't worry about me."

"But I do. By the way, I talked to Dick and the FBI has a new lead. They got a report that Paul has been spotted in France."

"Oh?" she said innocently. "You're not thinking of going there are you?"

"No. I've decided to let the FBI handle it. I went on a wild goose chase once. All I'm interested in now is being with you."

She said goodnight to him and plugged the cell phone in to charge it overnight. Two more days of punishment for Paul, she thought as she took off her clothes and climbed under the covers. She giggled. France indeed...

CHAPTER THIRTY-EIGHT

AFTER TWO DAYS OF SEARCHING FOR CLUES ABOUT THE MYSTERIOUS Juliana, Johanna decided to give up and concentrate on the renovations of the castle. She was also weary of her punishment of Paul and was awaiting Tristan's arrival eagerly. It was time to hand the man over to the authorities but she'd let Tristan handle that part of it. Several times she'd seen the ghost but never clearly and she couldn't understand the words. Always she heard her name and a few words following it. Fortunately, Jen, Shawna and Paula had not seen or heard the ghost. Except for the thought that Paul was down in the torture chamber, they were actually enjoying themselves, Paula was right into the new decorations and Shawna and Jen were supervising the renovations of the rooms and additions of bathrooms.

She herself had taken on the task of overseeing the kitchen renovations. It would take time, she knew, for everything to be ready before she could set her plans for the castle in action, but it was all coming together and the castle was slowly returning to its old glory. She had the workmen knock the walls from between several rooms in one wing, where it was possible, to form a large playroom for children. The East wing she was renovating for her own use and that of her friends and family. Obtaining renovation permits was no obstacle, as long as she didn't change the general look of the castle. The authorities were glad that Von Hertzenberg castle was being restored.

Herr Hague, a renowned architect, had gladly taken on the project. He was an elderly man, partially retired, with a great interest in the castle. His great-grandmother had been a maid there once and in his broken English he delighted the girls with his tales of woe and romance.

His great-grandmother had fallen in love with one of the groomsmen and though they were of lower class, the parents would not consent to the marriage. Gerda, his great-grandmother, became pregnant and it ended up being a shotgun wedding after all. Johanna really liked the humorous architect. Whenever he told his stories, he delighted them and made them forget the secret in the cellars. His blue eyes would twinkle merrily, he'd puff heavily on his pipe as he spun his tales and the girls were sorry when he had to leave at the end of the day.

The work continued steadily under the supervision of the girls, Herr Hague and Jakob. Old stuffed mattresses were all thrown out and burned and she'd ordered new ones and pillows that were delivered the same day. It was the first night since their arrival that they slept comfortably. She bought new furniture for the rooms she'd designated for the children. The antique furniture she placed in other rooms where adults would sleep. She also took much of the furniture from the attic and used it throughout the castle. Even though they had been in the castle less than a week, it was taking on a new face, much to Jakob's delight.

The castle grounds were taking shape, too, and a joy to behold. The fountain spurted continuously now that it was repaired, the scrubbed cherubs gazing happily down upon the mauve, white and red water lilies floating on the sparkling clean water. Everywhere she looked, flowerbeds appeared that she'd not noticed before. She could imagine the gardens next spring when every flowerbed was planted with new flowers. Behind the castle a crew was repairing and rebuilding the stables, above them quarters for stable hands.

Johanna sat on the scrubbed marble steps waiting for her friends to wake up. That evening Tristan would arrive and she looked eagerly forward to his arrival. When she'd talked to him the night before, she told him she had a scoop for him. He'd questioned her, but she had remained firm in her resolution not to tell him about Paul just yet. It was better to explain it all in person. Now, she regretted her actions and wished she had done everything differently. But it was too late for regrets.

She sighed as she stood up to go to the kitchen. It was time to feed Paul, which was becoming a tiresome task. The man was timid now, hardly said a word. Among his things she had found a vial containing some yellow powder. At times she was tempted to put it in his food, but had thought better of it. She'd be lowering herself completely to his standards and he was no better than the lowest scum crawling the earth. She had already done enough things that were out of character. She loved life, people, children, animals, and now she could hardly believe she had sunk so low to seek this kind of revenge. Each time her thoughts dwelled on Paul, she had to take a trip back into the past and remember the misery he put her through.

PAUL STRUGGLED WITH THE leather straps that held his wrists. The chafing hardly bothered him anymore. "Bloody bitch! I'll get her for this!" he muttered as he twisted his wrists to loosen the straps. "I'll kill her! Next time she comes down here, she'll get a hell of a surprise! Whore!"

Desperately he twisted, becoming frantic in his efforts to escape his bonds. Perspiration ran in rivulets down his face, onto his chest. His breath came in short gasps as he labored. Suddenly, he managed to pull one arm loose. For a moment he stopped his efforts to gather his wits. Then he quickly untied the other wrist and the headband. He loosely wound the straps around his wrists and laid the strap around his forehead. The only way he could hold it in place was to lean his head back.

He'd no sooner finished, or he heard the creaking of the panel.

THINKING ABOUT PAUL CAUSED her to remember that it was his feeding time. Without waiting for one of her friends to accompany her, she went down to the wine cellar and opened the panel. Paul seemed to be asleep, his eyes were closed and he did not even look up when she stepped into the torture chamber. For a moment she thought he was dead and experienced a pang of fear. But then she saw his chest move. He was breathing. She moved closer and shook his arm. "Wake up! Feeding time for the pigs!"

Suddenly, his hand shot out and grabbed her by the throat. Where he summoned the strength from, she didn't know. The bowl of soup crashed to the ground. Wildly she tugged at the arm while gasping for air. His fingers squeezed her throat so hard, she gasped for breath. She wasn't a weak woman, yet even by using all her strength she couldn't remove his hand. Not a sound came from her lips except some gurgling. Somehow he had loosened the strap on one wrist and undone the other and the one around his forehead.

She must have caught him in the act because his feet were still bound to the chair. They crashed to the ground, the chair prohibiting him from moving further. Her heels dug into the ground trying to find foothold to get away from him, but his hands pinned her. He breathed heavy into her face, his eyes resembling a rabid animal, foam bubbling from his lips. Her nails raked his neck, the side of his face. Droplets of blood dripped slowly onto her face. It all seemed to happen in slow motion and she couldn't scream, couldn't call for help as the breath was slowly squeezed out of her and she felt herself falling, her surroundings fading.

A dull thud and the sound of glass shattering brought her back to reality. The vice around her throat relaxed, Paul's hand slowly sliding down to her chest.

"My God, Jo. What were you thinking of coming down here by yourself? It's time to call the police. I'm going to do so right now!" Paula said while bending over her friend. "Are you okay?"

"Only just," Johanna answered in a hoarse voice. "How the hell did he get loose?"

"Wriggling desperately, I suspect. I hope I didn't kill him. What a waste of good wine!"

"Trust you to think about the wine!" Johanna scrambled up and looked down at the unconscious man. "Help me get him back into the chair."

Between the two of them they managed to drag Paul up and seated him on the chair. His head lolled to his chest, red rivulets dripping from his hair, the wine resembling streaks of blood.

"Tristan will be here by dinnertime. I hope we can keep him contained till then," Johanna said yanking Paul's head up and securing the strap around his forehead again and fastening it securely. With deft fingers she searched his skull for cuts, but she only felt a large bump and a small cut above his forehead. After feeling his neck for a pulse and finding one, she checked the wrist straps after Paula secured them to make sure they were tight. "He's just unconscious. You must have hit him pretty hard."

"Jo, call the police now! Good God, if I hadn't come along and looked for you down here—I don't even want to think about what might have happened."

Johanna hugged her friend briefly and headed for the wine cellar. "I need a bath after having that filthy pig's hands all over me. I'll let Tristan deal with him and the police."

"You're so bloody stubborn! Honestly!"

"So I've been told many times."

"Someone should stand guard."

"Are you offering?"

"I feel like puking. The man disgusts me."

"And that's the woman talking who drooled over Paul Blake when she first saw him in the hospital? Physically, he hasn't changed much." Johanna reached out and yanked her friend out of the chamber. The panel closed and she headed for the stairs to the kitchen.

"That's not fair, Jo. I was just talking about the way he looked. And you have to admit he was a charmer. You fell for him!"

"Unfortunately, yes. Although I wouldn't quite call it falling for him. I thought he was charming and would make a good husband."

"Hardly a basis for marriage. It was all too rushed anyway."

"Enough already! Let's make some brunch. Are Jen and Shawna up?"

"Yes, they're having a bath. Jen and Shawna will freak when they hear what happened. They should be down soon."

"Good. Maybe we'll drive to Zurich to buy more supplies. We're running low on groceries, too. By the time we're done, Tristan will be here."

"Someone should stay here to keep an eye on Paul."

"No. I doubt he can wriggle out of those bonds again. They're so tight now, he'll barely be able to move anything but his fingers."

JOHANNA WAS SHAKEN. HER neck hurt and so did her throat and her head throbbed. Soon as she got upstairs, she ran up to her room to get some aspirin. Standing before the mirror, she looked at her reflection. "This was too close. I'll be glad when Tristan is here," she muttered while examining the bruises on her neck. Her T-shirt was dirty. It was cooler outside anyway, so she hunted for a turtleneck and put it on instead. The collar nicely hid the bruises. Quickly she hurried downstairs to join her friends who were waiting for her in the kitchen.

She didn't say anything about the incident with Paul, but Paula, as always, couldn't keep her mouth shut.

"Guess what happened? Paul got loose somehow and almost killed Jojo."

"What? Jo, you've got to call the cops," Jen said and shivered. "I can't wait to get out of here for a while. This whole thing is getting to me."

It was getting to Johanna too, though she'd never admit to that. Her voice was croaky when she answered. "He's unconscious right now and tied up again. Tristan will be here tonight. I'll let him deal with it."

"What if he gets loose again while we're gone? What's wrong with your voice?"

"He won't get loose."

"I'm not so sure about that," Paula said. "He tried to strangle Johanna. That's why her voice sounds strange."

"It'll pass, Paula. I'm just thankful you showed up when you did. As for loosening the straps, it took him all this time to loosen the straps. A few hours won't do it and he'll be out in la la land for a while anyway.

How about we go for a drive today to look at the surrounding scenery and do some more shopping?" She needed to get out of the castle and away from Paul as much as the girls. Even more... Unconsciously her hand went to her neck. The aspirin had taken care of the throbbing headache, but nothing could take care of the remorse she felt and the guilt about taking the law into her own hands.

THEY RETURNED HOME JUST after dinnertime, the small trailer laden with parcels and the trunk filled. Johanna was having everything else delivered. The supervisor of the renovation crew had given her a list of supplies they needed so they had fun choosing bathtubs, shower stalls, and other bathroom equipment. She was also having a custom bathroom built for children who needed special equipment.

Eagerly, she looked for a rental car when they drove up to the castle but Tristan had not arrived yet. Disappointed, she dialed his cell phone number but there was no answer. She hoped he was on his way.

After they had unloaded the parcels and boxes, she suggested taking some food and water down to Paul. "Who's going with me?" she asked her friends.

"I'll go," Paula said, seemingly the bravest of the three.

"We'll all go," Jen and Shawna said at the same time.

Paul was conscious and sat dazed in the chair, his eyes rather glassy. When Johanna ladled the broth into his mouth, he'd no sooner swallowed it all when he puked. "I think you've given him a concussion," she said examining his pupils.

"I hit him pretty hard with that bottle," Paula said eyeing the broken glass on the ground and the dark wine stain.

Paul looked a sight, his hair now dried but sticking out from the sticky wine, his face stubbly with half an inch of growth and vomit dribbling down his chest. "Tristan should be here soon if there were no delays," Johanna said. "If not, I'll call the police."

"Let's hope they don't lay charges against you."

She hadn't considered that possibility. "Well, we don't have to tell them I've held him here for three days and nights."

"Look at the mess he's in. You think they're going to believe you?"

"He's unconscious. How about we go and get some warm water and soap and clean him up? I guess we'd better put his pants on, too."

"That means we have to untie him. What if he regains consciousness?"

"Well, how about we lay him on the cot and tie his hands to the sides. That way we can clean him up, put some clothes on him and maybe one of us can hose the place out."

"We just hosed it this morning. I'll go and get a mop and bucket," Shawna said.

"I'll go with you to get water, towels and soap. How about shaving him?" she asked Johanna.

"No, we won't bother with that. Let's hurry and get it done before Tristan gets here."

Shawna returned with a bucket and mop and quickly went to work. Jen fetched water, soap and towels. Between the four of them they dragged Paul to the cot and lay him down. Shawna resumed her mopping.

"You can wash his private parts, Jo. After all, you're his wife," Paula said.

"Was his wife."

"Sorry. I forgot for a minute about his bigamy. Looking at him lying there so innocently, one would never suspect him of all those horrible acts."

"Good grief, Paula, stop it. The man is a monster!"

"What are you going to tell the cops?"

"I'll deal with that when they get here."

They had barely returned Paul to the chair and tied him up when a voice sounded from the cellar.

"Johanna?"

She twirled and flew into his arms. "Tristan, I'm so glad you're here."

His arms tightened around her for a moment but then he held her at arm's length. "What's this? What have you been up to?"

"It's Paul. Don't you recognize him?"

"Hardly. He looks different. How did you..."

"It's a long story, but now that you're here we need to call the cops."

"Before we do, I think you'd better tell me how you caught the guy and why he's unconscious," Tristan said while frowning down at her and glancing at the basin of water.

"You're still angry," she said and pouted. "We had to clean him up. He puked. When I went to take him some food and water, he had loosened the straps somehow and attacked me. He tried to choke me, Tristan. Fortunately, Paula came down to look for me and hit him over the head with a bottle. That's why he's unconscious right now. I checked him out and he has a light concussion."

"Even more angry now," he said but pulled her into his arms and kissed her briefly on the lips. "Let's get out of here so you can tell me the whole story. He doesn't look like he's going anywhere," he whispered in her neck and pulled her into the wine cellar.

Paula grinned and motioning Shawna and Jen to do the same, headed for the stairs. They needed a few moments alone.

Tristan pushed the panel and watched it close. "Now, young lady, how did you manage to catch the bastard? You know, my hands were itching to give him the beating he deserves. I had to use all my willpower to stop myself when I saw him sitting there."

"I had a feeling he was still in Switzerland and hiding in the castle somewhere. Then I found the blueprints and that's when my plan formed."

"Blueprints?"

"Of the castle. Come upstairs, I'll show you," she said pulling his hand.

"Not until I do this." He drew her into his arms again, this time kissing her passionately. "I've missed you so," he whispered when he finally drew away from her lips. "I love you, you stubborn brat."

She giggled happily. "And I love you, Tristan MacDonald. I'm glad you're here. Paul's punishment was becoming a tiring task."

"How long have you had him here?"

"A few days. Jen, Paula and Shawna helped me. At first I didn't tell them anything, but Paul was haunting them and they were threatening to go to a hotel thinking it was a ghost. I had to tell them. Plus I was afraid he'd hurt them."

"How could he haunt them?"

"You wouldn't believe the secret passages in this place. You can go almost anywhere and spy on people."

"Really! I think those better be kept secret. I wouldn't dare make love to you thinking that someone could be watching us."

"Let's go upstairs. The girls are waiting," Johanna stood on her toes and kissed him fleetingly on the lips.

"Okay. I can see this will be a long night," he said with a grin, his love for her overpowering the anger he felt at the danger she'd put herself and her friends in and for not involving the police.

IT WAS WELL PAST midnight when they were finally alone and in her bedroom. "Come here," Tristan said, reaching out for her and pulling her into his arms.

She melded against his naked body feeling his arousal against her belly. "I can't believe you're not too tired," she whispered, and for the first time allowed her emotions to take over. Tears she'd held back finally escaped. "Tristan, I'm so sorry," she whispered between sobs. "I should have told you and never taken the matter into my own hands. It was a stupid thing to do."

"Seems you always have to learn lessons the hard way," he murmured while stroking her hair.

"Yes. I'm a stubborn, willful and I feel guilty as hell. All the time I had him down there I kept having to remind myself of what he did to me. But, as Jen told me once, two wrongs don't make a right."

"Honey, I wish I hadn't gone to Edmonton so soon after returning from Haiti. It was too soon to leave you. It was all too fresh. You needed someone close to you to help you overcome your anger."

"Can you forgive me?"

"Yes, of course I forgive you. Though from now on, please talk to me? Tell me about any anger or inner frustrations? I'll be your husband soon and that's the only way a relationship will succeed. We need to share everything with each other." He lifted her chin and kissed the tears off her cheeks.

"First thing in the morning I'll call the police. But for now, all I want to do is hold you and make love to you."

"Aren't you too tired?"

"For this? Never..." he said and silenced her answer with his lips.

Their lovemaking that night was a slow ballet, their senses heightened by the absence from each other, their bodies waltzing to imaginary music as they blended into one, their souls meeting, touching, yearning for more.

Satiated, they fell asleep in each other's arms but Johanna did not sleep for long. Her faithful ghost woke her, this time with an urgency that she didn't understand. She peered at the misty form and watched it slowly materialize into a more solid form. Untangling herself from Tristan's arm, she sat up and gazed at a replica of the photograph's she'd seen of Juliana. She understood now why Paul thought it was her. Juliana in her misty appearance resembled her a great deal. A long blond braid hung over one shoulder. She was dressed in a long white cotton nightgown similar to the ones she'd found in the chest of drawers.

Juliana's lips moved, she talked to Johanna but she couldn't understand what the girl was trying to tell her. "Is it Paul?" she asked. "Is he trying to get out of the chair again?"

Juliana shook her head wildly and rubbed her belly.

"Strange. You understand me, yet I can't understand you. I wish you could speak English. From what I've read and heard about ghosts, don't you have some kind of guide to translate for you?"

Tristan moved, his hand groping for her. He mumbled, "Sweetheart, you're talking in your sleep."

"Sorry," she said, and tried to project her thoughts. Surely ghosts could hear thought?

But slowly, the apparition faded and the room was once again hulled in darkness. Johanna lay down and curled against Tristan. Her task wasn't over. She had to yet uncover the castle's secret.

CHAPTER THIRTY-NINE

FIRST THING IN THE MORNING, EVEN BEFORE BREAKFAST, TRISTAN called the police in Zurich. He still had the card given to him by detective Bernard Goelitz when Johanna was in the hospital there.

"Tristan MacDonald," Bernard said, surprise in his voice. "I never expected to hear from you again. How is Ms Von Hertzenberg?"

"Thankfully, she recovered. We are here at the castle and I have something for you I'd like you to pick up."

"Really? And what might that be?"

"How about Paul Blake?"

There was silence on the line for a few moments.

"You are kidding me, right?"

"No. He has been hiding in the castle all this time."

"Impossible. We searched the castle from top to bottom."

"But what you didn't search were the secret rooms and passages."

"You know, we asked the old man about that but he said he never heard that the castle had any."

"Johanna found ancient blueprints of the castle. She came here a little more than a week ago and hunted Paul down. She's got him confined in the torture chamber. I just arrived yesterday."

"A suitable place for him," Bernard said with a sarcastic laugh. "We'll be there as soon as we can. Make sure he doesn't escape."

"I don't think he's in any state to escape, but I'll explain all that to you when you get here."

He hit the off button and turned to Johanna. "Okay, that's done. The police are on their way."

"Good. I'll be glad to get him out of the castle and safely locked up," she said. "Plus, he needs some medical attention, but I think he'll be okay. I already checked on him and cleaned him up. He's awake and asking for something to drink. I'll go down shortly and will give him some coffee."

"Not by yourself you won't. He'll be extradited to the States. You'll be required to witness against him."

"And I'll do that gladly!"

"Okay, let's have some breakfast then and you can show me what you've accomplished so far. From what I saw briefly last night, the castle is undergoing quite a transformation. At least, once Paul is under lock and key, we can get on with our lives."

"Not until I solve the castle's secret. Otherwise Juliana will never leave me alone."

"Your grandmother?" he asked, frowning.

"No. Seems my great-grandmother Johanna had a sister called Juliana. There's a mystery surrounding her. No one was even aware she existed. I found all that stuff in a diary and some letters in the jewelry box hidden behind the secret panel in the desk."

"Mm, another secret you kept from me. Seems your life, this castle, is laced with mysteries. It would be nice to just start a normal life," he said, though jokingly. "Juliana appears to you?"

"Yes, she is the castle ghost. I think I recall mentioning it to you when you were here before."

"I remember. What about you, Paula? Shawna? Jen? Have you seen the ghost?"

"Nope. Only ghost we heard was Paul," said Jen for all three of them. "Seems the ghost has singled out Jojo."

"Are you sure your imagination isn't working overtime, honey?" he said looking at Johanna with raised eyebrows.

"Don't be silly. I don't suffer from an overactive imagination and neither am I drugged this time around."

He patted her lovingly on the arm. "Sorry, I had to ask. So how do you propose to solve the mystery?"

"I don't know. I've run into nothing but dead ends so far. If only I could understand her. I saw her last night and asked if she couldn't bring along an interpreter."

"So that was your talking in your sleep."

"Yes. I didn't think it wise to tell you about her until you were wide awake."

The echoes of the knocker drifted into the kitchen. "Someone is here. Must be the police," Tristan said and got up to answer the door. Johanna and her friends followed him.

"Bernard, I'm glad you're here to relieve us of our cumbersome guest." He shook Bernard's hand and invited him into the parlor.

"I don't think so. We'd better fetch the prisoner first. Where is he?"

Tristan grimaced and motioned him to follow. "Come with me. Johanna, maybe you could make some fresh coffee meanwhile?"

Bernard called out to the officers waiting outside. Following Tristan, they trooped to the kitchen and down the stairs to the wine cellar. Tristan found the ridge on the stone wall and ran his fingers along it, just like Johanna showed him, then he pushed slightly against the wall and the panel opened.

"Well, well," said Bernard with a grim smile and holding his nose. "The rat is caught. Cuff him," he ordered the officers and repeated the order in his language.

The officers entered the chamber, their faces mirroring disgust at the stench that greeted them. Though they had hosed out the dungeon several times and Shawna had mopped the floor the day before, there was no ventilation down there and the stench of his excrements hung heavy in the air. They untied the straps. Paul didn't resist, didn't speak a word. His already pale face was a deathly white, his eyes glazed.

"What in the world did you do to him?" Bernard asked Tristan.

Tristan grinned. "Ask Johanna. She's the one who caught him."

"A woman? All by herself?"

"No, with the help of her three friends." He waited for the officers to lead Paul out of the chamber, through the wine cellar and up the stairs and closed the panel.

Bernard shouted some orders after the officers then followed them up the stairs into the kitchen where Johanna and her friends waited.

Paul resisted for a moment, his eyes momentarily returning to normal were now filled with intense hatred as he stared at her. "Bitch," he said in a hoarse voice. "I'm going to get you for this. Just wait. You'll never sleep easy again!"

"Not in this lifetime," Johanna said calmly, managing to mask the stab of intense fear his statement produced.

The officers yanked him forward and half carrying him, led him away. Bernard sat at the table and waited while Johanna poured him a cup of coffee. "The castle has undergone a remarkable change," he said. "It's beautiful."

"Thank you."

"Do you plan to live here?"

"No, not all the time. I am turning the castle into a holiday resort for needy children from all over the world. I plan to involve charity organizations to help fund the project because I have to hire a full staff suitable to deal with handicapped and sick children. The castle will be open all year round."

"You have big plans. I admire you," Bernard said openly appraising her.

"Thank you again."

"And now I must ask you the necessary questions and how Paul Blake came to be in incarcerated in the dungeons of the castle."

"I understand. I'll take any punishment you deem necessary," Johanna said.

"I don't know about punishment. I'm just interested to find out how you did it. What made you believe he was hiding in the castle?"

"While I was in my zombie state, I had a feeling he was still here or had returned here. What better place to hide than a place the police had already thoroughly searched? The castle has so many hiding spots besides the secret passages. When I discovered the blueprints of the castle and saw the secret passages and rooms, I knew for sure he was here. The plan unfolded spontaneously. Soon after we arrived I noticed missing food items from the fridge and the cupboards in the kitchen. I wanted to punish him, but I really didn't have a clue as to how I'd do it. I asked my three friends to accompany me to the castle and when I realized I couldn't tackle him on my own, I confided in them and they assisted me. We captured him, bound him to the chair and that's where he's been the last two days and three nights. He made one attempt to escape and I was foolish enough to go and see to his needs alone. He attacked me, tried to strangle me. Thankfully, Paula came looking for me and hit him over the head with a bottle. I suspect he has a mild concussion."

Bernard stared at her. Johanna didn't know what to think, his face was immobile, his eyes told her nothing. Then suddenly he burst out laughing.

"Now I've heard everything. Look at her! Just a slip of a woman and she captures a man who's eluded the police, the FBI, Interpol, everyone! Madame, you deserve a gold medal! Though why on earth you didn't call us right away is beyond me. You were playing a dangerous game."

"I know that now and regret not having called you right away. It was wrong to take the law in my own hands and mete out punishment."

"Let us be thankful that no harm has come to any of you."

Johanna felt her cheeks burn with embarrassment as he bent over her hand and kissed it. She didn't know whether to laugh with him or to be insulted at his laughter. Finally, the humor of it all tickled her and she joined in his laughter, soon joined by her friends and Tristan.

"I take it then there are no charges against Johanna?" Tristan asked in between bellows of laughter.

"The lady should work for the police. She can't help it if the guilty party is delusional and tells tall stories about a woman holding him captive for days in punishment for his crimes. Madame, my compliments and now I must leave. Soon as we arrive in Zurich and put Paul Blake where he belongs, behind strong bars, I'll contact the FBI."

"Thank you, Detective Goelitz," she said softly.

"We thank you, Ms Von Hertzenberg. You have rid the world of a dangerous criminal."

"He's not gone yet. I just hope, once the FBI takes over, they throw the key away of his jail cell."

"And I hope so with you."

"Would you like to attend the grand opening of Von Hertzenberg Resort for Needy Children?"

"I'll be waiting for the invitation." He smiled, touched his cap in greeting, and left the kitchen.

"Phew, that's a relief," Tristan said.

"What?"

"That they didn't put you in handcuffs, too."

"I expected some kind of punishment for what I did."

"You're a stubborn wench," he said sending her a wide grin and pulling her toward him. "Maybe that's why I love you so much. Once you set out to do something or make a commitment, you don't back out. Let's try and work that personality trait to the good in the future."

"Okay, that's enough of that," Paula said. "We've got work to do."

"When we open the castle for business, I think I'll invite the villagers to participate in the opening. After all, their ancestors all worked here at one time," Johanna said thoughtfully, already thinking ahead.

"Good idea. And I'll work on TV and news media promotion," Tristan said.

CHAPTER FORTY

TWO MONTHS PASSED AND JOHANNA WAS NO CLOSER TO SOLVING Juliana's mystery. Though she had concentrated mostly on the renovations, every now and then she still searched for clues and Juliana appeared to her at will now on a daily and nightly basis. She had become used to her appearances. No one else could hear or see her, though occasionally, Tristan felt a cool draft where there shouldn't have been one.

She noticed that Juliana's talking and appearances were becoming more agitated all the time and wondered about it. It was strange that she understood everything Johanna said to her or conveyed in her thoughts, but Juliana spoke no English herself.

The last of the renovations within the castle were in progress in the cellars. Though she wasn't really using the cellars for anything, she wanted the walls strengthened, repaired and the cellars cleaned up. Even the attic was cleaned, the items stored there either utilized somewhere in the castle or neatly put away. One day, when she had time, she'd go through all the trunks and boxes stored there. The landscaping was completed, the stables repaired and the living quarters above them finished. The swimming pool and spa were nearing completion, too. She'd ordered a bubble so it could be used in winter as well.

One of the last items to be installed in the castle was a special stair lift for people in wheelchairs.

Autumn was starting to show its nose and the mornings and evenings were quite nippy. The leaves on the trees were starting to change color and she knew winter would arrive before long. She had no idea when the first group of children would arrive. After having contacted various worldwide charities, she was still waiting to hear from them. The opening of the castle was scheduled for October.

Tristan had quit his job with the paper though he insisted on remaining a freelance reporter—his first project the story of Paul's capture.

The FBI had contacted her and his trial was set for March. She was glad. Some of the pain of his betrayal and attempt to kill her would have healed by then, though the scars would forever remain on her heart.

"Penny," Tristan said.

She startled out of her thoughts and jumped. "Oops, didn't hear you sneak up on me."

"Bad conscience?"

She grinned and stood on her toes to kiss him. "Hardly. I was just thinking that the work is almost done."

"Then what are we going to do?"

"Have the opening. I thought it would be nice to bring Mom and Dad over. They haven't been on a holiday for years. And maybe we could have the opening and our wedding together. If you approve of course."

"I'd like nothing better, but do you have enough time to arrange it all?"

"I'll have to bring Jen, Paula and Shawna back. I don't know if they can get more time off work."

"What about your offer? Have they reacted at all?"

"They're still thinking about it. Jen doesn't want to leave her boyfriend behind of course, but I offered him a job, too."

"Honey, I've never asked you, but is there enough money for your venture? What if the charities don't support it?"

"There's plenty. The interest alone will take care of the upkeep of the castle and the wages."

"But eventually it won't be enough. It takes a lot of money to do what you're planning. Look at the food alone you'll have to buy every month."

"I know. But I'm sure I'll get financial support from the charities. Anyway, what am I going to do with all those millions? That's not even counting the jewelry in the safety deposit box in the bank. That alone is worth a fortune."

"Well, I'll continue to support you, but I want to be my own man. I'll have no one say I married you for your money. I will continue my freelancing."

"Of course. I never expected anything different," she said with a smile and hugged him briefly.

"Let's go and see how the cellars are progressing," Tristan said. "Maybe eventually we can find some use for them."

"They have some historical significance so I thought I'd leave them the way they are. Look at all the torture equipment and the cells. Of course the skeletons I had buried in the graveyard. Pity we don't know who they were. Too late for DNA testing. Some of them powdered when they tried to move them."

They went down to the wine cellar, now brightly lit with the new lighting Johanna had installed. The cobwebs were gone, the bottles all cleaned of dust.

"We have a lifetime of wine stored here," Tristan muttered.

"We'll use quite a few bottles for the opening."

The torture chamber, too, was brightly lit as were the passages. She'd thought it an adventure for children who could walk to take them through the passages down to the torture chamber and the cells. But that would be up to the therapists she'd hired and companions. Already, she had letters from people volunteering to help. She felt sure her venture would be a great success.

Several men were at work in the cellars, one of them laying bricks, another chipping away at old cement. Suddenly, Juliana appeared beside her, the white nightgown a bright splash against the brick wall. She gestured wildly gazing at the man chipping at the cement between some bricks.

Johanna silently said, "What is it Juliana? You don't like that man?"

Juliana shook her head. She moved closer to the wall and started to claw at the bricks as if she wanted them removed.

The bricklayer stopped for a moment to wipe sweat off his brow and turned to his supervisor and said something. The supervisor frowned and told Johanna, "Wall not so old. Other bricks. Bad cement. Bricks will fall."

"Tear it down then and build a new one," she said. "That's if it's necessary."

The supervisor walked the length of the wall and felt the sides. "False wall. Very strange." He gave the bricklayer an order and continued with his own job.

The bricklayer picked up a jackhammer and put it to the wall at the top. Johanna and Tristan stood back and watched. Before long, part of the original wall appeared. Glancing beside her, Juliana stood quietly, watching, her gaze riveted to the bricklayer's actions.

"Mein himmel," the bricklayer cried and stepped back.

Johanna and Tristan approached the gaping hole and saw what had caused his consternation. A skeleton stood upright, a long blond braid still intact hanging over one shoulder blade, a tattered gown, that could have been the white nightgown was still intact though gray with dust and yellowed with age.

"It couldn't be," Johanna said softly as she touched the braid carefully.

"I think it is," Tristan said. "I think your mystery is solved."

"We'd better call the police. If we touch the skeleton, it will fall apart," she said looking at Juliana standing so close to her. "I wonder what happened to Juliana."

"I doubt if we'll ever know the complete truth. I suspect she died up in the turret and the parents thought it best to keep pretending she'd gone to a convent."

"But why? Unless she was murdered…"

"What makes you think that?"

"Remember the stain on the mattress?"

"I'll call Bernard. He'll know what to do," Tristan said while digging for his cell phone and the business card in his pocket.

"Bernard? This is Tristan. I have another mystery for you to solve."

"Paul is safely in the custody of the FBI. What mystery?"

"We found a skeleton. You'd better come and take a look and bring some people with you to remove the skeleton from the wall."

"That could be centuries old. Same as the other skeletons you found down there."

"No, this one dates back to just before nineteen hundred and eight. We think it's Juliana Von Hertzenberg's remains."

"Really? I know the legend well. She reportedly went to a cloister and no one ever heard from her again. Okay, I'll come this afternoon."

Johanna instructed the workman to leave the wall alone and continue his work elsewhere and they went back upstairs to wait for Bernard.

LATE THAT AFTERNOON BERNARD arrived. The men he brought with him removed the rest of the brick wall while Tristan and Johanna watched, Juliana never leaving their side.

"You know, this skeleton is remarkably preserved. Maybe because it was sealed off from oxygen," Bernard said.

When the last bricks were removed they made an amazing discovery. On the floor, by the skeleton's feet, lay the tiny skeleton of an infant.

Bernard pointed at the small skull. "Fractured. Taking a wild guess, the girl died in childbirth and they killed the infant."

"That's terrible," Johanna said as a cold chill ran down her spine.

"Little late to lay charges against anyone. The parents probably wanted to hide the shame she'd brought upon the family name. Again taking a wild guess, they must have held her captive in the turret until she gave birth. Then she would miraculously return from the cloister. I don't know why they killed the infant though. They could have adopted it out, which was often done in those days."

Tristan suddenly squatted and peered at the tiny skeleton. "Look at the infant's leg," he said.

Bernard looked closer at the tiny skeleton and nodded. "That explains it. The leg was malformed. They wouldn't have been able to place it with anyone if it was handicapped so they killed it instead. We'll have forensics determine the sex of the child. For now, we'll leave everything the way it is until you've made arrangements for proper burial. I suppose that's your plan?"

"Yes. We'll bury her with her relatives in the family crypt," Johanna said while listening to Juliana's soft sobs. Now she finally knew what Juliana had been trying to tell her all this time.

But it wasn't the last of the mystery. As the men continued to work in the cellars not far from where they'd found Juliana, they uncovered another skeleton. The ribs were shattered, a bullet lodged in the spine. They had no idea who it was except that it was the skeleton of a man.

"Maybe it's Juliana's lover," Johanna said.

"That could be. But what was his name?"

"I think it's mentioned in the diary. I'll have to read it thoroughly. Maybe Juliana's spirit will finally find peace and the ghost of Hertzenberg castle laid to rest."

"Mm, could have been an attraction," Tristan said.

"Or something to scare the poor children half to death," Johanna said with a grimace.

A WEEK LATER THEY held a small memorial service for Juliana, her baby boy that Johanna named Christian and Juliana's lover, Günter. They had no last name for Günter because it wasn't mentioned in the diary. Johanna had ordered coffins for both Juliana and Günter. The baby was laid to rest with his mother.

It was a small memorial service in the castle chapel only attended by Tristan, Johanna and Jakob. The minister was from the village. Knowing the circumstances he spoke of forgiveness, mercy for Juliana's parents' souls.

After the brief ceremony both coffins were taken to the graveyard, the head stones Johanna had made looked almost out of place against the old crooked stones. The large bouquets of roses she'd ordered were a splash of color in the somber graveyard, their red petals resembling drops of blood, the white baby breath a strong reminder of the infant that never had a chance. The beautiful red blooms a grim contrast to the young woman's life, snuffed out at such an early age.

After forensics finished their examination of the skeletons, they confirmed that the man was shot, the girl and infant murdered. Juliana by possible stab wounds as they found scratches on her pelvic bones to indicate this. Maybe Juliana threatened to expose them after her parents or midwife killed the infant and that's why she, too, had to die.

Tears trickled down Johanna's cheeks for Juliana, her baby and her lover. She thought about her own life that could have ended so fast if Paul had succeeded, before ever having had a chance to live life to its fullest and growing old gracefully.

Tristan put an arm around her shoulders as they walked back to the castle and pulled her tightly against him. "So sad," he said. "At least they're at peace now."

"I don't think completely because Juliana is still with us though she seems happier. It's upsetting to know that my great-great-grandparents were so cruel."

"Times were different then. If a girl had a secret lover, it would bring shame to the family name. And of course the fact that she was pregnant didn't help matters."

"It makes me feel ashamed of the Von Hertzenberg name. It will be in all the papers here that my great-great-grandfather murdered his daughter and grandchild."

"No need to feel shame. You can be proud of your parents, your grandparents and your great-grandparents. They made a new life for themselves in Canada and did well."

"And now it's time for us to start our lives together," she said softly. "How about we set the date for the opening and the wedding?"

"Good idea. Thanksgiving sounds good to me. I know they don't celebrate it here but we do and maybe we can start a new tradition. How about you call your parents and invite them?"

"I just hope they agree. They don't like leaving the nursery in strange hands, but Steven, the foreman, knows the business as well as my father and I'm sure he could run things for a while. Mom and Dad could do with some time off."

CHAPTER FORTY-ONE

IT TOOK SOME CONVINCING, BUT JOHN AND LESLIE DID COME AND her wedding day was perfect. The weather was frosty, the sky blue and sunshine bathed the castle and grounds turning it into a perfect autumn picture.

The castle was filled with guests as was the Inn in Hertzenberg. Its guests were mostly reporters from all over the world. Johanna was excited when several celebrities showed up. The news releases Tristan sent out to every newspaper he could think of had done its job well and most of the invitations to the opening were accepted. Dick and his wife and their children also came, Johanna footing the bill for their plane tickets. Dick was Tristan's best man and two of his coworkers at the Langley Advance were groomsmen.

She was even happier when Paula, Shawna and Jen announced that they'd decided to take Johanna up on her offer and would work at the castle for a while. Her life was almost perfect. Only one thing still marred her happiness—Juliana's constant appearances. She'd so hoped that she'd be at rest now, but she still appeared at random. At least she looked happier and she rarely spoke anymore except to say Johanna's name.

"What are you thinking about, Jojo?" Jen asked while placing the tiara on Johanna's hair and arranging the veil.

She'd picked out a very old wedding dress from the clothes in the attic. It fitted her perfectly and she wondered which bride had worn it before her. It felt appropriate to wear one of the Von Hertzenberg dresses. The lace and satin had yellowed with age making it a creamy color, as was the veil. She'd had it dry cleaned and checked for flaws but the dress was in perfect condition, as if it was never worn by anyone. After checking all the photographs in the attic she had not found one bride wearing that dress. Maybe it was meant for Juliana. In the diary it said that a husband was chosen for her.

"Just thinking about everything that's happened and how happy I am now."

"When will the first children arrive?"

"Soon. The heads of the charity organizations are attending the wedding and the opening, so I guess I'll find out some time today."

"You should see the ballroom. It's magnificent. They've been decorating all morning. Are you nervous?"

"No, not this time."

"And this time I don't have any feelings either, except good ones," Jen smiled.

"Do I really have to wear this, Jo?" Paula complained.

"Yes. It looks beautiful on you."

"I feel as if I've stepped a hundred years or more back in time."

"Stop your complaining, Paula. Won't hurt you to wear a high neck for a change instead of all that low-necked stuff showing off your boobs. The dress accentuates your waist. Look how tiny it looks now."

"No one will look at me," Paula said.

"Nonsense. You're beautiful and you know it," Johanna said admiring her bridesmaids and maid of honor. Like her, they wore dresses from the attic. She couldn't find matching gowns, but each had an elegance of its own. All three dresses were made from heavy velvet. Paula's was maroon with cream lace trimmings. Shawna's deep blue and Jen's emerald green. All three had their hair pinned up by the stylist from Zurich Johanna had hired.

She gazed at her reflection in the mirror and this time smiled happily at the bride. Once again she wore the jewelry her grandmother had given her. Leslie had brought it along at her request. The tiara she'd fetched from the safety deposit box at the bank. Its jewels matched the necklace and earrings.

Leslie entered and gasped. "Johanna, you look as if you've stepped straight from a movie screen. You look beautiful!"

"Thanks, Mom. Is everything ready?"

"Yes. Tristan is waiting impatiently. I'll go downstairs and will tell your father to come up and escort you."

AN ORCHESTRA PLAYED *Ave Maria.* It was their choice of music instead of the traditional wedding march. The ballroom was filled with guests and villagers, the villagers picked out easily because of their traditional costume. People uttered soft gasps as Johanna slowly walked across the dance floor to where a temporary altar was built. All she had eyes for was Tristan. He held her gaze as they approached. She hardly felt him taking her hand in his. All she could concentrate on was the love she felt for this man, how close they were already and the new life they were starting together.

The minister spoke most of the ceremony in his native language, but they didn't care. They had to learn to speak it themselves and right now, all they were engrossed in were each other, the words going by them in a haze.

As the minister pronounced them man and wife, a choir hummed softly to change into a jubilant chorus as they turned to face the guests.

Cameras clicked, TV cameras focused on them and everyone clapped and cheered as they walked to the bridal table.

Caterers, also dressed in traditional costume, brought in several tables and quickly covered them with white cloths. Silver trays laden with roasts, poultry and other foods in silver covered dishes were brought in and set on the tables. They had chosen smorgasbord because of the large amount of guests.

This time, Johanna thoroughly enjoyed her bridal dinner and she didn't resent the constant calls for a kiss. After everyone was finished, the caterers quickly cleared the tables away and it was time for speeches. Rather than have everyone sit through countless speeches, Johanna had chosen to speak to everyone herself.

With Tristan by her side, she walked to the front of the ballroom and stood before the microphone.

"Ladies and gentleman, members of the press, distinguished guests, I herewith declare Von Hertzenberg resort for needy children officially opened! I thank you all for being here on this joyous occasion. After almost one hundred years of closure, Von Hertzenberg castle will once again ring with happy voices, laughter and music. Thank you again, and please enjoy yourselves.

Her short speech was greeted with loud clapping and cheers. Her cheeks hot from embarrassment she waved at the orchestra to start playing and holding Tristan's hand walked to the dance floor with him.

Tristan looked down at his bride's flushed face as he swung her across the floor to the tune of a waltz. "Happy, sweetheart?"

"I couldn't be happier. I just wish Juliana would find peace," she said as she saw Juliana standing on the side of the floor watching the dancers. "Oh my God," she exclaimed and stopped dancing.

"What is it?" he asked following the direction of her gaze, but he saw nothing unusual.

"I'm sure I just saw my grandmother."

"It's probably someone resembling her," he said soothingly. "Let's go and greet the guests. They've been waiting for us."

"No, just wait. It is my grandmother. She's coming toward us, and she's with someone. My grandfather..."

"Are you sure?" he said still not seeing anything.

"Yes. I'm positive. They're smiling at us. And now they're changing suddenly and they're young again."

"If I didn't know you better I'd say you were hallucinating. Maybe you did drink too much champagne," he joked.

"Don't be silly. Oh, Tristan, look..."

"I'm looking but I don't see anything."

"It's a girl who could be my twin sister. I think it's Johanna, my great-grandmother. They've discovered each other. And Johanna is carrying a baby. Juliana is running toward Johanna and the baby now. They're embracing and Johanna is giving the baby to Juliana. Oh, Tristan, they're so happy. I wish you could see this."

"I wish I could, too. I feel rather left out."

"You do believe me, don't you?"

"Yes, I do. You must have been born with the gift of second sight."

"This is so wonderful. They're all looking at us now and smiling. Now my grandmother is coming toward us. She's holding out her hands."

Johanna let go of Tristan and held out her hands, too. As her grandmother touched her hands, she felt a brief tingling almost like an electric current run up her arms. And then it was gone and for a moment she felt just as lost as when her grandmother was buried. Except she knew now that death was not the end. Her grandmother joined the waiting group and Johanna watched as Johanna senior held out her hand. Juliana placed her hand in her sister's and slowly they faded.

For moments Johanna waited, but they were gone. She turned to Tristan, "You'd better dance with me. People are giving me strange looks."

"I noticed," he said with a grin as he swung her into his arms and continued to dance.

"And now Juliana is finally at peace and reunited with her family."

"And it took you to accomplish that."

"All because of Paul really. If it weren't for him, I might still be just living here, wouldn't have looked at the diary and maybe not even had had the initiative to try and unravel the mystery."

"Oh, I don't know about that. I think curiosity would have gotten the best of you."

"Maybe..."

The music stopped and the musicians took a break. Tristan didn't lead her back to their table. Instead, he took her arm and led her to the front steps of the castle. Darkness had settled and a full moon winked down at them. The sky was ablaze with thousands of stars. But the most beautiful of all were the decorations on the grounds. Thousands of twinkling lights graced the trees, the front of the castle and lanterns marked the driveway. The fountain had a multi colored spotlight directed at it, turning the water into a rainbow delight.

She didn't see Tristan's signal. Still gazing up at the stars, suddenly fireworks erupted. She gasped when two intertwined wedding rings formed in the sky, in their centers, their initials.

"Tristan, did you see that?" she said as the last of the fireworks winked out.

"Yes, my darling. That was my final vow to you, two links that will never be broken."

About the Author

Martine lives in scenic Canada on the West Coast. She is single. Her life revolves around her books and various hobbies. She is an avid reader of historical romance, and has at least thirty more novels she may get around to polishing one day to get them ready for publication. She has won awards, was published when very young, and has worked as an editor and artist for a magazine and wrote a children's column for that magazine.

4087299

Made in the USA
Charleston, SC
26 November 2009